Apart

from *Love*

Sᴛɪʟʟ Lɪꜰᴇ ᴡɪᴛʜ Mᴇᴍᴏʀɪᴇs
Bᴜɴᴅʟᴇ I:
My Own Voice, *"as told by Anita"*
Woven with
The White Piano, *"as told by Ben"*

USA Today
Bestselling Author

Uᴠɪ Pᴏᴢɴᴀɴsᴋʏ

Apart from Love©2012
Uvi Poznansky

This novel can be read as a standalone novel, as well as a part of *Still Life with Memories*, a series describing events in the life of a unique family from multiple points of view.

Published by Uviart
P.O. Box 3233 Santa Monica CA 90408
Blog: uviart.blogspot.com
Email: uvi.author@gmail.com

First Edition 2012
Printed in the United States of America
Book design, cover design and cover image by
Uvi Poznansky

Contents

The White Piano

Chapter 1

As Told by Ben

About a year ago I sifted through the contents of my suitcase, and was just about to discard a letter, which my father had written to me some time ago. Almost by accident my eye caught the line, I have no one to blame for all this but myself, which I had never noticed before, because it was written in an odd way, as if it were a secret code, almost: upside down, in the bottom margin of the page, with barely a space to allow any breathing.

The words left some impression in my memory. I almost wished he were next to me, so I could not only listen to him, but also record his voice saying that.

I imagined him back home, leaning over his desk, scrawling each letter with the finest of his pens with great care, as if focusing through a thick magnifying glass. The writing was truly minute, as if he had hated giving away even the slightest hint to a riddle I should have been able to solve on my own. I detested him for that. And so, thinking him unable to open his heart to me, I could never bring myself to write back. In hindsight, that may have been a mistake.

Even so, I am only too happy to agree with him: the blame for what happened in our family is his. Entirely his. If not for his actions ten years ago, I would never have run away to Firenze, to Rome, to Tel Aviv. And if not for his actions a couple of weeks ago, this frantic call for me to come back and see him would never have been made.

And so I find myself standing here, on the threshold of where I grew up, feeling utterly awkward. I knock, and a stranger opens the door. The first thing that comes to mind: what is she doing here? The second thing: she is young, much too young for him. The third: her hair. Red.

I try not to stare—but to my astonishment, this girl with the kittenish eyes seems to be my age, so much younger than I have previously expected. Her name is the one thing I know for sure: Anita. She moves fast, and with a slight sway of the hips, just like my mother, which makes me want to forget, for a moment, that she is not.

She lays a hand on my suitcase, and she drags the thing—as if it were a wounded hostage—into what used to be my room. I walk in behind her, captivated, at each step, by folds playing across her tight, short skirt.

"There," says Anita.

And she kicks the thing to the corner of the room, shoving it along the way from side to side to make it fit, somehow, under the shelf, where some of my old childhood knickknacks are still on display.

And there, half hidden behind my old baseball mitt, is a flimsy metal frame with a dusty glass, under which is a picture I have nearly forgotten: a picture of my family from ages ago.

Here is me, a ten year old boy smiling timidly, with a metal brace shining across the front teeth. Here is dad, hugging me with his right hand, and mom, hugging me with her left. The ring on her finger happens to catch the light. Their cheeks nearly touch, because they were such a perfect fit—or so I thought.

Meanwhile, Anita turns on her heels to ask me, "You tired?"

"No," I feel compelled to lie, because who is she to ask me anything.

"OK, fine," she says, shrugging. "Want some warm milk or something, before bed?"

To which I say, "What, you think I'm a baby?"

With one swift step Anita is right here beside me, which takes me entirely by surprise. With no shame whatsoever, she looks me up and down and bursts out laughing, a deep, throaty kind of a laugh.

"You? A baby? Oh, no," she says. "Definitely not that. What are you, twenty-five now?"

"Twenty-seven."

"Your father told me so much about you."

"Really? He did?"

"I feel like I know you already," she points playfully at the picture. "See there, how tight they used to hold you?"

I shrug, and she goes on, "I can almost hear them say, Don't touch this, Ben. Don't touch that. I can almost hear you, too, like, Don't touch me here. Don't touch me there. Just don't. Don't you dare."

And before I can say anything, she takes hold of my right hand, then my left, swings me playfully around the room, and pushes me directly to bed, with a twinkle in her eye. "So? Want a goodnight kiss?"

"No," I say, because who is she to play mother to me.

"You sure?" she says.

Which is when I sense for the first time that she may be lonely here, in our old apartment, surrounded by these yellowing pictures, besieged by forgotten history, which must seem so distant to her, because it belongs to others. She must be lonely as only a new bride can be, with my father out there in the hospital.

"Sure, I'm sure," I say, with an unsure voice.

"You look awful tired, lying there," she says. "Don't fall asleep with your clothes on."

"What do you care?" I say. "And oh, by the way, Mazel Tov... So sorry, I totally forgot, I ought to congratulate you."

But she does not seem to mind what I say, or for that matter, what I do not, and I know it, because a second later her lips are on me—on my forehead, really—moist and soft, and her hair brushes my face, it is fragrant, and this is like no goodnight kiss I have ever felt before. So I close my eyes and breathe her in, wishing, suddenly, for more.

Anita spreads the blanket over me and it comes down heavy, heavy enough not only to stop me from shivering—but also to fix me in place, straighten my limbs for me and then, iron out every fold on my skin. I am home, the same home I was in such a hurry to leave ten years ago, just before my parents divorced.

I turn over to the wall, and immediately turn back, trying to catch her scent, which Anita has left behind her, quite carelessly, before halting there, by the light switch. Which makes me wonder: will she stay—or will she go?

With a click she turns off the light, and then closes the door on her way out.

I find it hard, you see, to be hostile to her, or to blame her for the accident, because at first glance she looks innocent, almost, and because her fragrance is so potent, to the point of making it known that she is in heat, and because this place, where I grew up, seems to play tricks on my mind.

In my weakness I feel, all of a sudden, like a child, a man-child gazing at the light, the pencil of light rolling in right there, under the door.

So there I lie, staring at the ceiling, where shadows are flickering, as if they were trapped here from a time gone by. I remember the voices seeping through the wall from the direction of my parents' bedroom.

Mom said, "What's the matter, Lenny?"

And dad said, "Oh nothing, dear."

There was a long silence, after which mom said, "Are you having a *thing* again?"

And dad said, "What thing?"

And she says, "You know exactly what I am talking about."

In place of an answer he tries to hush her, saying, "The walls here, they are so thin, dear. The neighbors, they may hear you. And the boy, he's barely asleep—"

"Don't—don't you hush me now, Lenny! I want an answer from you. I want the truth."

"Please, Natasha, not that again."

"Yes or no, Lenny! Are you having an affair?"

"No, dear, but even if I did, you know well enough that it would mean nothing, just nothing to me."

"Who is she, this time?"

"You," he said, turning serious now. "You are the woman I adore."

That was no lie. He did adore her—but at the same time, dad seemed to believe that a man was entitled to have some fun on the side. After all it was mom who encouraged him to leave the apartment every evening when her students came in for piano lessons. Which was why he started idling around, and spending so much time at some ice cream shop, down at the pier, where that girl, who stood behind the counter with her two scoops on top, was only too happy to serve him.

So mom ended up throwing her ring at him. It rolled away—perhaps under the sofa, perhaps elsewhere—and never recovered, because it reminded each one of us of that time, and of being hurt.

Not long after that, they divorced. I dropped out of school and travelled away. And that girl, so I was told by my aunts, moved in with my father right away. Incredibly, they reported, she looked like a younger version of mom—in every respect but one:

Anita was a simple girl, even vulgar, and with no high school diploma. In short, she was what my father must have needed at the time: a real change. Someone who would look up to him.

Nearly ten years down the road, Anita told him she was pregnant, which brings us to the time of the disaster, which can also be described—if you care to celebrate it—as a wedding.

I check my watch. Ten minutes past midnight.

Tired as I am, the closest I can come to sleep is tossing until the sheet gets all coiled around me like a rope, which makes something rustle there, in the back pocket of my bluejeans. I draw out the envelope, which my aunt handed me only an hour ago, on the way from the airport.

"Here, Ben, this here, it's for you," said my aunt in a low, secretive voice, which I took to mean that we should avoid talking right now about what was inside.

I nodded back in vague gratitude, hoping, really hoping it was money, and why not? I was nearly broke, because of buying the flight ticket to LA on such short notice.

Meanwhile, aunt Hadassa pulled a small mirror from her purse and nudged her puffy, white hair. It was built up and tilted, somehow, over the eyebrows, which were painted in impossibly high arches.

The cab came to a stop. I got out.

"Oy, you look so much skinnier now," she sighed, her bulging eyes afloat, suddenly, in tears. "No one to take care of you, I'm sure. Quick, give an old woman a hug! My, my, look at your cheeks! I cannot even bring myself to give you a good pinch! You know, in 1939, when I lived in Paris there was such a shortage of food—"

It was the wrong moment to tell her that I had heard that story before, so I just wrapped my arms around her, taking in the smell of bad teeth, hair spray and chicken soup. It was mildly nauseous, so I straightened my back, stuck the envelope in my back pocket, yanked out my suitcase and waved goodbye.

The cab, with aunt Hadassa blowing a kiss in it, trailed away into the night.

Twenty-one minutes past midnight.

The pencil of light has just turned charcoal. I find myself troubled by the fact that the envelope, which I feel between my fingers, seems too thin to contain what I hoped it did.

For a second I prick up my ears, thinking I have just heard Anita's footfalls outside my door. She must be as restless here as I am. Then, all is quiet again, so I get up, fumble in the dark to turn the desk lamp on, then tear the thing open, only to find my hope dashed.

Inside, there is nothing but words.

Dear Ben,

I'm afraid you may see this letter as an exercise in spreading gossip, which I insist, is not my intent at all, but as rumors go, this woman, Anita, is known to be nothing but trouble, so I must warn you. Stay away from her. She's a slut! I told your father the same thing, and much good has it done me.

I am saying all this not only because she disinvited me from that wedding. In my time, women were decent enough to think twice before taking someone else's husband. Sex was far from being a necessity, and I can promise you one thing: becoming an old maid never killed anyone.

At any rate, you would be right to doubt some of what I am going to include here, because of course you cannot believe everything people tell you, but I suppose there is some truth in it anyway, which I strive to find as best I can.

My sources, whose names I am not going to divulge, were amazed at this woman right from the start, when they peeked through a half open door, expecting to find your mom there, even though it was a week after that ill-advised divorce. Instead, they took a glimpse of Anita. She was biting into an apple, and wearing not a stitch of clothing— with the possible exception of a little red bow in her piggy tail.

The same sources tell me now what an incredible amount of attention she gave, just a month ago, to shaping every detail of her crowning moment, when she, the new Mrs. Kaminsky, would make her grand entrance, appearing openly at long last—for all to see—with your father.

Mind you, there was to be no rabbi, no chuppah, no stomping of the glass, even. Instead, she came up with a what you might call a whimsical notion, the notion of flying with him in a hot air balloon, and then landing, somehow, in a clearing amidst the guests. Arrangements, I hear, were soon made—despite your father's fear of heights which, for some reason, he neglected to mention.

Oy, the poor dear! He was saved, that fateful day, from boarding the craft; saved, thank God, on account of a blunder, an honest mistake by the owner of the hot air balloon, who—according to hearsay, which I usually disregard—ended up losing his license, due to the fact he had overloaded the basket, a week earlier, with thirty kids, more or less.

Mind you, that man may have miscounted them. The balloon had come dangerously close to tipping over when the wind whipped up, sending it adrift: first south, heading to San diego, and then across the border, past Tijuana, and farther down, deep into the inner parts of Mexico.

It was at the last minute, then, that Anita had to come up with something new, something splendid and sophisticated and stylish, and above all, suitable for a grand entrance. Your father tried, in vain, to suggest this idea and that; in response to which she said, No, this is not classy enough, and No, that is not classy enough either—until her eyes fell, of all things, on the piano: your mom's piano!

It is at reading that last sentence that my chin drops in alarm. Mom's piano is dear to me. It is an exquisite grand piano, with ornately carved decorations, designed for some royal palace. My father bought it for her just after their honeymoon. That was the time she still entertained hope, a great hope to become a distinguished concert pianist, because after all, she came from a long line of musicians. Her great grandfather was the famous Abraham Horowitz, who graduated from the Kiev Conservatory at the turn of the century. He rose to stardom rapidly, and toured every large city in Russia, where he was often paid with bread, butter and chocolate, rather than money, because these were tough times.

Of his three sons, only one survived. Joseph Horowitz aspired to become a violin player, but his hand was damaged for life during the pogrom in Odessa. So instead he became a music teacher, and developed a method, a unique method to memorize long passages of music, by practicing it back to front.

His son Benjamin Horowitz, who became a conductor, took that method one step further. Instead of the traditional way of playing through the passage repeatedly, you would commit it to memory, or rather to your subconscious mind, by means of performing it every night before falling asleep—without holding the instrument in your hands. He was a notorious spendthrift, and the only inheritance he left his daughter Natasha was his impossible dream, the dream of rising to stardom.

So mom prepared herself for the promising career of a struggling musician. Dad supported her in every way. He had to attend recordings and rehearsal sessions and to watch her practice, plan programs, and cope with acoustics, conductors, and orchestras. For him this was no easy task, because mom had great ambitions, and being on the verge of success, they were matched by equally great disappointments.

And then, then I was born.

Mom gave up her recitals, and instead started giving piano lessons. Slowly, her dreams started to fade. The family moved to a small apartment, where the piano, as I remember it, occupied half the space of the living room.

The other half turned, eventually, into clutter. It housed my clunky baby stroller and my rusty tricycle—because who knows, maybe we would need it someday—as well as an out-of-date encyclopedia, which was incomplete because one of the volumes was missing, and disorderly stacks of notebooks and sheet music, which leaned against the walls.

The piano towered over everything. It seemed so massive, so out of place that you had to squeeze around it, or else crawl underneath the belly of the thing.

But when mom played it, all that did not matter. The walls vanished and so did the clutter, because it was so riveting to watch her. You could see her long, delicate fingers as they went flying over the keys, to the point of turning, magically, into a blur. Her hands became transparent, and her ring, I remember, turned into a glow. She was air, she was music! Even when she stopped playing, those strings inside were still reverberating.

Twenty-two minutes to one.

At this instant, standing here over the pages of the letter, I remember that sound, and it can—even now, so many years later—take my breath away: the sweet, intricate sound of harmony. It was with this sound playing softly in the back of my mind that I went back to reading:

> *As I told you, Ben, tongues are wagging all over town, saying that the last thing Anita was interested in was music, nor was it harmony. No, dear. What impressed her was the polished surface, the ebony color, the ivory white keys and the brushed black keys, all of which could serve her (or so she thought) as the classiest, most perfect backdrop for the grand entrance at her wedding.*

This was the most perfect instrument she could imagine, by which she could finally beat her enemy: your mother. By a strange reversal, your mom's own signature piece would now be used against her.

And so the piano was transported, at great pain and, so they tell me, at great expense. It was placed on a special platform, and the whole apparatus prepared to be wheeled, at exactly the right moment, from behind a curtain.

It would go right onto the center stage of the wedding hall. Everything was rehearsed that day, and carefully timed. Fog machines were placed discretely between the white, tapered legs, ready to emit clouds of dense vapors, so the scene could become mysterious.

The top was polished to perfection. And as the right moment approached, Anita mounted it, striking this pose, then that—until finally relaxing into one that she must have considered graceful, yet seductive.

To avoid distractions, this woman wore no ornament other than her cleavage. Leaning back on her elbow, she let the strap fall away to reveal the full curve of her shoulder. There she laid, one leg crossed over the other with the knee bent, right in front of the plump, rosy breast.

She examined the view in her hand mirror, from here, from there, and enhanced the pose even further, by scooping up her gown, draping the folds—just so—and then, pointing the high heel directly at the surface.

Your father who—as you know—had never played an instrument in his life, was made to sit on the bench next to the piano, facing her. I had warned him against playing the fool, but then who can blame him. My, my, the poor dear must have been in the stupor of love. Men are liable to make mistakes at such moments.

He was instructed to play—or at least, pretend to do so—by throwing his hands dramatically into the air, in accordance with a song, which would be played by a hired musician, somewhere in the back, behind the scenes. The song would open with the unforgettable words, "Look into my eyes," and would go on to promise, "You will see, what you mean to me..."

From what I hear, a hush fell among the guests when, emerging from a cloud of smoke, the piano became visible on stage. There was only a slight squeal, escaping from the wheels under the platform— but that was covered, tactfully, by the song. "Search your heart," it pleaded. "Search your soul. And when you find me there, you will search no more..."

Your father, as I said, had a fear of heights. I am told that he seemed a bit uneasy at the edge of the stage. Behind his back, down below, there were faint sounds of waiters moving swiftly around the tables, setting china plates around the flower arrangements. The place was buzzing with whispers, which may have distracted him.

At one point he rubbed his eyes, and seemed itchy, for some reason, to take off his glasses.

Most of the time, his hands flailed in the air, following the music dutifully, just as instructed. But then—when a puff of smoke suddenly burst under him—he stopped waving altogether and instead, started clearing his throat.

Accounts of what happened next seem to be conflicting. I am going to give you the best approximation of the dialogue. Make of it what you will.

Stop that, said Anita, and she said it, somehow, without moving her lips. To which he said, What? And she said, Not now! Don't cough! And from the corner of her mouth she hissed, Just smile, dear! Smile! Nu, he tried, as best he could, to do what she asked, and managed to cough up a smile, which is not an easy thing to do, especially when all those guests are staring at you.

She said, What kind of a smile was that? Stop it! Which slipped up, somehow, from the tight space between her teeth. And she went on to cry, Look at me! Look at me now! Straight into my eyes!

Which he did try, really. He tried it while rubbing his eyes and popping them and saying, Where? Where? I cannot see a thing.. Damn smoke!

A whisper of this entire exchange could be heard over the music—but luckily, only by the those closest to the stage. The rest of the guests were swept away by the song, which brought everyone to tears, most of all Anita, because you see, it was so very touching.

And they nearly missed the point, right there at the end, when your father pushed back his bench in a sharp, and some say rebellious motion. He wiped the fog, quite irritably, from his lenses, and stood there for a second, a breath away from the ledge. Oy. Perhaps he did not see it.

Then, to the sound of "Everything I do, I do it for you," he fell headlong into the crowd.

It is here that I turn the lamp off and step back from the desk, resisting an urge to crumple the letter.

Much of it, especially the sentences describing Anita, I cannot judge at all, because gossip can turn anyone, even the most innocent girl, into something she is not. As to the sentences describing my father, they seem so out of character with the way I know him.

The fact that he agreed—or at least, did not disagree—to play the fool in his own wedding seems strange to me. So is the fact that he fell off the stage. What was he trying to do, kill himself?

A few days after this ceremony I received an urgent call from someone in Santa Monica Hospital, who said I should come see him at once. Which is why I am standing here, in what used to be my room, counting and recounting the crooked blinds, the shadows twisting out of them, so slowly, and the hours remaining until the break of dawn.

Seven minutes to one.

And now, out of everything I have read, the only words I wish to retain come from an older letter. At the moment they go turning slowly in my mind, making no sense whatsoever. If this is a secret code, I cannot find a way to crack it.

I have no one to blame for all this but myself.

Father And Son

Chapter 2

As Told by Ben

Today at the hospital, Anita cannot get enough of being called Mrs. Kaminsky. Her eyes twinkle with joy. Intoxicated by her newly found power, the power of a married woman, she seems to have no idea what to do with it, yet. I notice that it is with great exuberance that she gets the pain drugs and the crutches for my father.

And so, around noon, once the release papers are signed, I lift my father from the wheelchair and help him into the car. We arrive home after a long drive, during which nothing is said. He barely looks at her, nor does he look at me. I suppose he is trying to arrange and rearrange in his head what led to the accident. Perhaps he can sense a certain tension between us—or else, he may be dazed. The morphine is about to wear off.

I do not mind the silence, honestly. After ten years of absence I have nothing to say to this man, whom I hardly recognize. He looks older. No, not older. Just old.

I wonder what happened to him. I do not mean the irritation of the mucous membranes, which might have happened because of the cloud of smoke onstage at their wedding. At least, that is what they said at the hospital. And I do not mean

1

the bruises on his face, or the cast on his leg, or the brace on his back, or the crutches. It is not just the injuries. I mean, really, how come he inhabits a different body now.

Then I wonder the same about me.

Where are we, father and son? Have we been erased, somehow, as if we were figures drawn in dust, where some grains here, some there have been blown away? Not much is left, barely a trace of how I admired him—and later, how I raged.

So I go through the motions of being a son.

I carry my father into the building, up a flight of stairs, then walk him into the apartment step by step, first to the bathroom, where very sternly, he refuses any help.

"I have had it," he mutters to himself, "up to here."

Well, you cannot win an argument against someone this stubborn, and so I stay outside, as if I were a guard.

Then, before I can breathe—bang!—there comes a loud sound, and I push the door open and see the floor, and him lying there in the puddle, with a look on his face that is so surprised, so deeply miserable, because of the shock, you see, and because of losing control, and having pissed, as he fell, all over himself.

Anita plays the devoted wife. She rushes into the bedroom to bring out a change of clothes. Meanwhile I push the wheelchair, folded, into the living room, over some clutter, which is scattered all around the dusty floor, and then around the piano.

It stands here majestically, blocking your view, as large and out of place as ever, as if it has never been moved away, or used, not too long ago, as a prop for a grand entrance in some wedding.

The air in this place smells of decay, and the silence between us is heavy. I reach the old sofa and push it back a bit, making space so I can unfold the wheelchair. The throne is ready, and it takes a few tries until my father is seated in it.

Now there he is, holding the crutch in his hand, as if it were a royal scepter, and his face is blank again. That moment of humility, when he was vulnerable, is now gone, and I cannot care less that he is back to himself, back to ignoring me. There is my father, and so far, he makes no move.

So in turn, I pace in and out of the corner of the living room, determined to avoid sitting next to him. On a whim, then, I decide to find me a place on the floor, and I throw myself into the shadow of the piano—right under its belly—which is now my cave, my little home, just the way it used to be when I was a six years old. Only now I have to slump, and even bend my head a little if I want, still, to fit inside.

From down here I can see Anita: her ankles, really, and bare feet as she comes, hips swaying, across the floor. And now there she stands, between me and my dad.

She spreads a kitchen towel across his lap, on top of which she places a large tray. Sliding across, from one edge to another is a cup, a porcelain tea cup in the act of finding its balance. It has a flowery design, which I dislike. I do not remember it, so it does not belong here. This woman must have brought it with her, when she moved in with my father. From this angle, I can see him between her legs.

There is a wisp of steam twisting there, in the cool air between them. I close my eyes and take in her fragrance and the aroma of the freshly brewed tea. I imagine the beginning of a hairline crack, right at the joint where the porcelain handle meets the shapely body.

I can hear my father sipping, and his spoon clinking, clanking against the lip of the cup. I can hear the rustling of her dress as she must be bending again, her chest over him, this time to pick the empty cup, which she slams—without hesitation—right on top of me. I mean, on top of the piano.

And somewhere in the background there is also a tick-tock sound. It is faint—but it makes me count, makes me mark time.

I imagine it is just his heart, or perhaps the distant beat of a metronome. Mom had one, I remember that. She used it to keep a constant tempo. I listen to the sound, but what I cannot hear—what is missing in this place—is her music. The sweet, intricate sound of harmony.

My father points his crutch at the piano.

"The cup," he tells her. "Take it, take that thing. Don't leave it there."

Anita picks it up on her way to the kitchen, where a tea kettle starts shrieking; which reminds her to turn back and ask cheerfully, "More tea, anyone?"

"No!" we cry, almost in unison. "Absolutely not! No more tea!"

Once she is gone he turns to me and, to my astonishment, he says, "I am so blessed." Which makes me suspect, right there and then, that something is not quite right, I mean, not only with his body but maybe with his head, too.

And so I cannot help asking, with a chill in my voice, "Blessed? You? In your condition?"

My father looks at me, for the first time he looks deep down into my eyes and then—not finding what he wanted to find—he pauses for a minute.

"You used to be such a sensitive kid," he says. "So fragile, so delicate. What happened, son? You have changed."

I look back at him, defiantly, and I say, "I sure hope so."

"You are still angry," he says. "Are you? After all these years, angry about mom?"

To which I say, "No, just about the piano."

And he is about to say something, but I do not let him, because something in me flares up and I cry, "What happened to *me*, you ask? How dare you? What about you, how could you?"

He hesitates to ask, What? And so I go on to say, "What, do I have to say it? It was mom's piano! She took such care of it... It was perfect, pristine! And now——"

A blush spreads across his face.

I curl myself even tighter in my cave, trying to hold myself, hold me from bursting in anger. And I scream, "I hate you! I know what you have done, what you've allowed her—this Anita of yours—to do. All that horrible, horrible damage!"

He glances in the direction of the kitchen door, wondering perhaps if Anita can hear me. And so I raise my voice even louder, "The ugly marks! The spills, I mean, from her tea cups! The scratches from her high heels! The dent, you know, from the weight of that woman."

And I cover my face, wailing, barely able to say, "Mom will never come back now. She will never, never play here, not ever... All because of you... You have spoiled it, damn you... Spoiled everything for us both."

It is then that he leans over, as much as his brace will let him, trying perhaps to reach out to me. There is, I notice, a strange glint in his eyes.

And he says, "I understand. I know how you miss her. But try not to blame everything on me. Besides, mom has no need for it. The piano," he says vaguely, "it doesn't matter, really."

I look at him, utterly in confusion, because this is different from what I wanted, which was some trace, some admission of guilt. It seems that—as usual—he has none.

"Mom can play," he insists, "even without the piano. Yesterday," he says, "in the hospital, I woke up. It must have been well after midnight, and for the first time in a long while my heart was pounding with such force! I was so alive and could hear everything with great clarity. Everything, son, was as clear as a dream! And then, then I could hear her. I am so blessed. She let me hear it."

And I say, "Mom let you hear *what*, exactly?"

"Music," he says dreamily. "Do you remember her fingers, when she played for us, how they looked?"

"I do," I whisper in return. "I remember. It was a total blur."

And he says, "Exactly. That's how it was, last night. I could feel her presence. She came close beside me, right there by the bedside, and held me, touching me softly, caressing my arm, stroking it slowly, all the way, right down to the wrist. And I turned the palm of my hand, and opened it to her, to receive her."

Which suddenly brings to mind a long forgotten moment, when they sat on this sofa, which was brand new back then, its pillows still puffed up and firm. I bounced on it for a while, then got off, leaving a space there between the two of them. And dad looked at her over the divide, and said, "Play for me, Natasha."

And she said, in a tired voice, "I can't. You know I haven't practiced. It's been such a long time. I think I'm losing my touch."

And he looked away, saying, "Just say it. You're blaming me for all this."

There was a long silence, which left both of them worn out—until she reached out. Mom passed a finger along the back of his hand, and his hand turned over, so that she could tickle him.

And to my great relief, their hands joined. If not for the glint of her ring, you could no longer tell which were his fingers—and which hers.

With a vague stare, my father mumbles, "And then, as she touched me, the air stirred... It was reverberating, vibrating with music. And I—I noticed the fingers, the blur—a total blur, just the way you said—which is how I knew it was her."

Uncertain what to make of this I ask him, "And her ring? Did you see it? Did it glow when she played?"

Which makes him, all of a sudden, come unglued from this memory of last night, and snap at me. "Ring," he says, grumbling. "What ring? It was lost! She threw it, threw the thing at me, the day she left. You know that very well, don't you."

He looks at me with outrage. Perhaps I remind him of something in her, and he rambles on, "What a difficult woman. Whatever I did for her, it was never enough. I mean, not ever! She always had to lean on me, and she leaned so hard."

But then, with some effort, he overcomes his anger and he says, "You may not trust me, or what I say, but all the same there she was, playing for me. Her fingers," he says, "they were flitting, all across my skin, and I closed my eyes, just to be focused, to feel her. With such speed she played, such fury, even."

"And you heard it?" I ask, not really wanting to believe him, but remembering suddenly how, every night before bed, mom would tell me to practice my fingering, to play notes in the air—without touching the keys at all—because that was the method passed in her family, from generation to generation: the method of committing a long piece of music to memory.

"What do you mean, did I hear it," says my father. He seems to dislike the question, because he never doubts himself. "I sure did. I sure as hell heard it."

"What was she playing, then?" I inquire.

"The left hand," he recalls, "it was playing broken chords. And it alternated, you know, between two scales, where the notes were sharp and rising. And the right hand, it was playing a melody, which hovered in the air, trembling up there, over the left hand chords. After a while the music became wild... It became agitated, and so did I; which made me see things—"

"What," I ask, "what was it you saw?"

And I note that he is listening—but not to me—trying, perhaps, to steady himself, to find, somewhere inside, at the core, a constant tempo. Perhaps, like me, he can hear a beat, the distant beat of a metronome. I wonder if he, too, is counting time.

Then, in an odd tone of voice he says, "I saw the top, the shiny top of her piano. It flashed as it opened. And there, in that surface, which looked almost glassy, as if it were a mirror, you could see her eyes."

At this point I am ready to berate him, because anyway, what is so special about the top of that piano, other than the dent, and those marks and scratches? And who, in his right mind, can see it appearing there, out of thin air, right next to a hospital bed?

And the eyes, where did they come from, the twilight zone? He must be insane, don't you think? Insane—or totally out of his mind!

So I say under my breath, "Fat idiot!"

And he snaps again, as if he could hear me, and he says, "Don't call me fat!"

Startled, I glance at him. "You never question yourself, dad, do you."

"I do not," he says. "I know that top was not there—but still there it was, and I saw it."

I wave my hand at him, which annoys him. He seems saddened by my disbelief.

"It was lifting," he insists, "just like that, lifting open before me. Like a wing, you see, with the edge sweeping up over you."

"Don't you tell me, I know how it looks," I tell him.

"Like a wing," he repeats. "A wing, held in place by a crutch. And *that*," he says to himself, with no further explanation, "*that* was the way we were, your mother and I. A wing and a crutch."

I wish to tell him No, I don't think so—even though this time, his words find an echo in me, and I can almost hear that wing, flapping in the air above us, and then coming down heavily, and leaning hard, right on top of its support, its crutch, with a jolt and a creak.

Then suddenly—in the shadow under his wheelchair, where the sofa used to be before I pushed it over—right there, I think I see something: a few traces... Can you see them? Shaped like little loops, pressed lightly one after the other, into the dust.

I crawl out from under the belly of the piano, and there I find it, after all these years, buried in layers of dirt: my mother's lost ring. Only now it is a bit stuck. It seems to be frozen in place, and it has no halo.

I dig it out and I shiver, because here, in my hand, is a token of my family, the way it used to be; the way it had better be. Whole. Perfect. Ideal. Worthy of all that pain, the anxiety, the longing. Now, if I open my hand—even a little—it may slip away.

Here is my past. I would like to think it was in harmony. I must keep hold of it, so I can keep my grip.

My father is watching me. His eye, the one I can see, is set in its socket, and from there it discloses a hint, just a hint of suspicion. I rise up over him and at once he clenches the armrests, and steers the wheelchair away, not knowing what I hold in my fist, not aware of the cold, metallic touch, or of how much it can make you hurt, in here—but noticing, perhaps, the tears streaming down my face.

Here is that thing that, once upon a time, would light up and zigzag in the air with such spark, such energy, when she played for us. And then—after mom threw it away—nothing was ever the same again. No one would believe me if I told them. And now that I found it, I am at the point where I begin to doubt it myself.

No Omelette For Me

Chapter 3

As Told by Ben

For the last hour, two things have been happening, each causing its own type of discomfort. I will them to go away, go away already. Still I can sense them, one becoming stronger, the other—more distinct, even as I try to recover the ghost of my dream, or at least find my sleep, which has receded, like floodwaters under a relentless, blazing sun.

I recognize then that my sleep has become as shallow as a plain puddle, and wish I could immerse myself back in it, calm myself down, and not pay attention to these things, one arousing unease, the other—hunger. At this point my eyelids are so heavy, and if I keep them shut I could still sink back, still lose myself. Yes, I would float, like a baby in the dark liquid of the womb, and it would feel so good, and as cool and shady as nighttime...

It must be late morning, because outside, in the garden below, the sprinkler has begun its singsong. Which confused me at first, because I thought I heard something else. Then by small, imperceptible degrees, it became nothing more than background noise, so that the thing, the voice I have been hearing, could become clearer, and claim my full attention.

So first: I can hear a tune.

How shall I describe it? It is a monotonous repetition, like that of someone who knows only one song, and is committed, for no good reason whatsoever, to go on singing it.

And so she goes on, and on she goes, never stopping, never growing tired—no matter how tiresome that tune may be, or how quickly it manages to drain the joy, or any remnant of anything close to pleasure, from the life of anyone around her.

So I cover my ears with the pillow, with the thought of how content I would be, at long last, to sink my head into the soft material, and stick my nose deep, deep into it, breathing nothing, and thereby ending this torture, ending it for good and forever.

Then Second: before I can move, I can sniff trouble. Here it is, the smell of bread baking.

Tinged with vanilla and honey, the scent has come in, perhaps sneaking around the door, finding its way through a crack, or puffing through the keyhole. It is forming, even now, into a channel, an invisible channel floating somehow in midair, right above me, swelling up there as if it were an extension of my nostrils.

By now, my stomach is growling, so I have no choice. Up, up and away flies the pillow, off come the blankets! I walk out of my room—hair uncombed, chin unshaven—and find myself waking up to hunger. Or at least, to an undeniable craving.

Framed by the kitchen door, standing there with her back to me, she cranks open the oven. Fume comes out of its gaping mouth, inside which lay two freshly baked loaves, shining with the gloss of egg wash, and sprinkled generously with crispy, toasted sesame seeds.

With a large oven mitt, this woman—my father's new wife— puts her hand inside, and takes hold of the baking pan. I can hear a slight sizzle. Now her thighs tighten. One foot is rising behind the other as she pivots, bringing the loaves right under my nose.

"Ben!" says Anita. "There you are. You hungry?"

And without waiting for an answer she lays the pan down, and lifts one of the loaves onto a wooden cutting board. Then Anita sets it down next to the egg salad, which is heaped on a large, oval china platter, which is entirely new to me. I suppose she has gotten it recently, perhaps as a wedding gift. The platter has ruffled edges and—quite ridiculously—it stands on one leg, as if it were a fossil of a stork.

It is part of a large assortment of china bowls, in which dips and spreads are artfully presented: garnished with chopped parsley, and decorated by thin cucumber slices and plump cherry tomatoes, they are displayed right here, on the tablecloth. And there, behind the table, slumped in his wheelchair, is my father.

With great exuberance, Anita sets down the salt and pepper shakers, fills a glass jug up to the brim with orange juice, and another with grapefruit juice. She keeps bringing more stuff, more food to the table. Why she does it I have no idea. It is fully loaded already.

Perhaps she is eager to impress him—and me as well—by putting her skills on display. Or else, she likes excess. This woman may be in the habit of overdoing things. There is a fever of excitement about her, which could easily be contagious.

Meanwhile she goes on humming, in a perfectly flat voice, with no pause and to no end. "Look! look! look," she hums tediously, never actually reaching the rest of the phrase, "Look at me."

Anita does it totally out of tune—to the point that the original song has gone missing, or else it is impossible to recognize—but in a cheerful manner all the same, which in a strange way, starts to make it endearing to my ears.

My father listens to that dull, repetitious noise until he can take it no longer. "Now, why on earth do you sing?" he interrupts her. "What is all this chirping about? No songs, for God's sake, and no more food. And that thing, that egg salad. You know how much I detest it, don't you."

"Fine," she says, shrugging. "How about an omelette, then?"

Before he can open his mouth I set my chair across from him, and flopping into it I say, "Sure!"

My father folds his arms and stares out, with deliberate focus, through the window. There is not a cloud in the sky, so who knows what it is that he sees out there. "No, nothing for me," he grumbles. "This breakfast would have been so much better, don't you think, Ben, it would have improved so much if there was nothing here at all, if instead of all this, there would be just a plain cup of coffee."

I cannot help noticing how Anita manages to ignore what he has just said. Incredibly, she does not take it as a slight. Her face shows no sign of feeling hurt. There is nothing there, nothing but freckles. By contrast, my mother would have pouted, because of all the careful planning and all the work, you know:

The shopping for ingredients, and kneading the dough, and letting it rise hours in advance of the meal, and braiding it, and rinsing and chopping and slicing the vegetables, and squeezing the juice—in short, all that went into preparing such an elaborate breakfast, which men, mom would say, never seem to note, let alone appreciate.

She was such a proud woman. I can just imagine her pursing her lips, until the line defining her mouth became rumpled, erasing itself by turning as pale as the skin around it.

Unlike my mom, Anita just laughs it off.

"Soon," she tells him, "you will get your wish: before you know it, there will be nothing left. Nothing to eat but crumbs. Don't you wait too long."

And she turns the bread knife around, so that now the blade is pointed at her, and the carved wooden handle at my father. This way, it would be safe for him to take hold of it.

"Here," she says. "Cut yourself a slice."

The wheelchair creaks, tilting away in a shaky manner. "I have no appetite for it," says my father, with a stubborn tone in his voice. "No appetite for anything, really."

She turns from him, impatiently this time. "Enough!" she says. "Snap out of it! You must get stronger. Someone needs to bring in the dough. Between the two of us, it's you who's the bread winner, no? Ain't you?"

Instead of an answer, his jaws tighten. He hangs his head with a sense of pain, even desperation, worried perhaps about his job, or his health, or both.

And at once, without missing a beat, she bends over and gives him a real reason to suffer, because she elbows him right there, between his ribs; which immediately sets him straight, and gets his full, undivided attention. I can sense, somehow, that she is about to play us one against the other.

"Seriously now," says Anita, pointing the bread knife at all the food, heaped so bountifully on the plates and the bowls. "What d'you think? This is all for you?"

"Who, then?"

"It's for the boy," she says, rising up from him and bumping her hip against me. "He's hungry, see? Look at his eyes."

I doubt either one of them can figure out what I am about to say, because my mouth is full—but all the same I venture to spit out, "I am not a boy."

To which she just smiles. Her eyes are cast down at me, cast in the shadow of her eyelashes, so I cannot really read her—but I can recall how they looked last night: bright, even luminous, they shone at me from the dark, that first moment I saw her, like the eyes of a cat.

"Not a boy," I swallow, and take another bite. "I am a grown man."

And she says, in a taunting tone of voice, "Now, who asked you."

"I want you," I start telling her, and find myself having to stop, and gulp down. Then I repeat, "Really, I want you to stop this! I mean it. Call me by my name. Now, why can't you do that."

"And I want my coffee," my father cuts in. "Now, when am I going to get it."

"You will get it," she says, turning on him, "when you give a little."

He says, "My God, you are in heat. Now how does that happen, in your condition? Cool off already, in front of the boy! What do you expect of me? You wanted to get married, so now we're married. Mazel Tov! What more do you want?"

"I want you to look at me," she says, thrusting her chest out in front of her. "You haven't been here for two weeks, since the wedding. And now that you're here, you ain't really here. Am I even wanted here? I'm a woman. I need to feel desired, and I need to be held by a man."

At this point I feel obliged to peep in, for the third time, "I am not a boy."

And she wipes her brow. "My God," says Anita, as she turns away from my father. "I'm so hot. Don't you wait too long." And with a harsh motion, she flings the knife on the cutting board, right there between us.

It gives a sharp sound, which startles my father. His mouth is mirrored in the surface of the blade, and suddenly it becomes clear to me that the oven is not the only one fuming—so is he.

He raises his eye to her, and jealousy escapes. He glares at me, and a warning shoots out. What does he want from me? There is nothing I can do. He hates me for staring at her and he hates me for trying not to stare.

Now there she stands, by the counter, measuring the coarsely ground coffee, one tablespoon then another, right into the basket of our coffee percolator. He groans, which sounds like a bubble over a flame.

I can tell they have a language between them, a language without words: Anita glances back at him, he gives her a nod with his head, and in turn she secures the top, as tightly as she can, on the percolator. Her feet tap around the linoleum floor. For whom is she performing this dance, I would like to know.

Anita is bare legged, buttoned up in an oversized, short sleeve cotton shirt, which probably belongs to him. It is crumpled, maybe from rolling around in her messy bed. Although, judging by my father's condition, as well as his mood, that may have been the only action she got last night.

I can easily see her the way he does: his shirt hangs loosely around her, refusing to disclose any hint of her curves. You can only guess her nipples, because even as you try to pin them down, they sway on her body, roll with every step, when she walks and when she stops, right there by the stove. And only when she turns the button, raising the heat to medium, do they mark their place, briefly, by pressing against the coarse fabric.

Then, rising to a tiptoe Anita takes a peak through the clear glass knob, right there on the top of the percolator, to check if the coffee is sufficiently brewed. Her hair is gathered loosely, and coiled into a French twist. Some strands have unravelled, and they are dangling around her face and over one shoulder, hemmed in by a soft, reddish fuzz. I try to imagine how it would feel to twirl that curl around my finger.

The same reddish fuzz flashes, for an instant, right there, from her armpit, as she lifts her arm to pour out his coffee. Anita hands him the cup and he sets it away from him, far in the middle of the table, saying, "Now go, go get dressed already. We will take care of things here."

"We?" I say. "Who's we?"

"You," he says. "And I."

I rise up against him.

"You?" I say. "You can barely move, and what kind of things are we talking about? I don't know much about taking care of anything here, especially when I am hungry, and right now I am hungry, very hungry, and what about my omelette?"

"And what about me? I'm hungry too," says Anita. "I've got such a huge appetite this morning. And you know," she hints at him, "there is a bun in the oven."

This is when he makes his move. My father leans forward in the wheelchair and to my surprise, he wraps his arms around her waist, gathering her to his breast. She lets out a cry and lays her hands over his shoulders. Her fingers flutter around his neck, and glide down to his back. And so she stands there, embracing him.

It is amazing to hear her now: by contrast to her singing, her giggling voice is full and rich. In no way can I explain it.

He rests his head gently against her belly, rubbing his forehead against it. I think I smell his scent on her, which makes me turn my eyes away, because I know I am the stranger here, and this moment is so private, so intimate between them. Touching her, and being touched in return, seems to bring out a change in him.

"Look at you," he says, and for the first time this morning, there is laughter bubbling up, deep down in his throat. "Now where is that bun? I cannot feel it. It is slightly flat, no? No wonder you have such a big appetite! Why, it is an appetite big enough for two."

She tickles his earlobes and he smiles. "So let me do this for you, he says. "Today I will make you an omelette, a big one, like you have never tasted before. Don't say No, Anita."

"Mrs. Kaminsky," she corrects him, playfully.

"Yes, indeed, sweetheart," he says, because it is so easy to please her. "Now go, go already, put some clothes on you, my dear, slightly pregnant Mrs. Kaminsky."

Up to this moment no one has told me anything, in a precise and direct manner, about her pregnancy. Maybe they decided to let me figure things for myself, if I can; which makes me feel a little indignation. The entire situation is new and baffling to me. Also scary, somehow. I am ashamed to admit that I have no clue, looking at this woman, how far along she might be.

She does not look pregnant, not in the slightest, does she.

My father is no longer grouchy—but now I am. I am mad, really: mad at him, mad at Anita. With burning eyes I try to pierce through her, even as she places herself, ever so slowly, deeper in his embrace. In this position I can spot, for the first time, the round line of her belly.

There: now she freezes. Anita stands still, and so does time. Then, by barely perceptible degrees, it is starting to happen: each of her limbs softens, and then changes position—at the slightest measurable angles—until she is about to release herself, perhaps with the thought of turning, little by little, towards the door.

She seems so vulnerable. With a penetrating gaze, I imagine laying my hands on that shirt, which hangs so loosely around her. I strip her of that thing, and cast it aside. In my mind she is bathed in morning light, and naked. I imagine seeing clear through the skin, that fair, translucent skin of her belly. I wonder then if it is as freckled as the tip of her nose. Then I lose control over my fantasy. Somehow, it takes an unexpected turn.

Eyes closed, I immerse in darkness, the deep, dense darkness of her flesh, which is moist and marbled, here and there, by blood vessels. I find myself floating inside. And the pulse, which at first was but a faint echo in my ears, is now becoming more pronounced, as if—even without knowing where I am headed—

I must be getting there. I lose myself, blindly and completely, in the beating of that sound. And it is then that finally, I arrive.

The void is here, encased by a slippery, glistening lining, which is streaked by tiny veins all around me. A swoosh can be heard, and I sink into the wave, sensing that something new, strange, even menacing is beginning to take shape here, in these lukewarm waters, something for which I am still struggling to find a name.

A cell? No, not as simple as that. A threat, I say to myself, a new threat for me.

I open my eyes and at once, fear awakens in me. No, not just fear—but something more severe, something like a rage, a murderous rage. Right now it is a vague emotion, still without form.

I do not even want to know at whom it is aimed—but I recognize that it is fueled, in part, by desire. It turns me white with anguish, as if I have just walked through glass, shattering it —or let my fingers spread open, dropping an egg to the floor, or a fossil, the fragile fossil of a fetus.

I move the knife away from me and—trying to avoid any rush moves—I turn to take a look at Anita: her outline is framed, for an instant, by the kitchen door. The next instant she is gone.

It is then that I ask myself, with great agitation, What is it? What has happened here, to grip me in such agony, such panic, even? And I hesitate to give myself an answer, because it makes no sense to come out and say it—but all the same, this I know: that cell floating inside, in the dark liquid of her womb, and constantly growing, constantly multiplying with such vigor, such aggressiveness, will soon become me. I mean, a copy of me:

Perhaps even better than me, because at this point I am already worn out. I am not a boy anymore, which is something that by now, I have learned to regret. At twenty-seven years old I am unsure, somehow, of my own direction, my own purpose in life. For fear of looking like a complete failure, I cannot tell anyone about this—least of all my father.

I have no one, really, no one to whom I can turn.

Trying to regain my calm I tell myself, Don't be stupid. You have nothing, absolutely not a thing to worry about. You sense danger where there is none. What is the threat in that cell, that minute, insignificant matter which, by now, is probably no bigger than a sesame seed, or a grain of salt?

And as soon as I hear me say, Don't be stupid, I remember being six years old. I remember having the same sense of panic, and trying to calm myself in the exact same way, when mom went to the hospital, saying, "Be a good boy for daddy, and how would you like me to bring you something, a little surprise?"

I remember then, that she came back empty-handed. I was careful—very careful—not to ask her where my surprise was, because I could tell that she had no answers. Mom laid in bed many days, with eyes red and swollen with tears.

And later—when she finally got up, and by accident she saw the baby carriage, my old, crooked baby carriage which dad had fixed up and cleaned and polished, and from which he had removed all the rusty spots—then a shudder passed through her. And she turned away and went back to her bedroom. It was there, through the keyhole that I saw her, folded up on the bed, as if there was a great pain in her.

I gaze at my father, trying not to think about his new wife, this woman, Anita, who managed to displace my mother; trying not to cringe with the expectation—no, the certainty—that so will this new, fresh copy of myself. My brother. My rival. Once born, he will displace me, in my dad's arms and in his heart.

"So, can you help me, Ben?"

I turn in the direction of the voice, surprised to see the wheelchair at the other end of the kitchen.

"So, can you get me a bowl?" asks my father.

And having asked it, and then having to repeat the question once or twice, he seems equally surprised, as he studies the blankness of my stare.

I do not lift a finger. In my mind I can already see him—or rather, the ghost of him—walking proudly down the street behind a baby carriage, so the whole town can see this newborn and adore him. And I ask myself, What is my place in that picture. Where the hell am I.

By now, my father has managed to maneuver around the counter, in the direction of the refrigerator. Out of its open door he takes out a carton of eggs, and turns his head over his shoulder, asking, "So, Ben, how many for you?"

"Never mind," I tell him. "I lost my appetite. No omelette for me."

Apart from Love

Chapter 4

As Told by Anita

L ater, when I wake up, it takes me a while to grasp where I am, and even longer to figure out that I've lost time, that time has passed. The last thing I remember is like, making breakfast for him—and now, somehow, it's late afternoon.

I'm lying here on my side, with the bedside lamp shedding a dim light behind me. I can tell that his side of the bed is empty. Why am I here? How did I get here? Why am I so dazed, so confused? And where's Lenny?

I gaze across the ceiling and along the walls, trying to pick out every shade, every hint. And there, opposite the bed I spot my wedding dress which—now I recall—I've hung on the coat rack, right there in the corner.

The corner of the bedroom is the only place here which I reckon is truly mine. Strange, no? I still feel that way, despite having slept here with him, on and off, for like, the past ten years. I keep telling myself that I must claim this space, claim it as mine, right away. And maybe I will one day, when the baby's born.

I try to picture a crib here, next to me, and at once everything looks so much brighter. I hope the baby can soon feel something of what's in my heart—but not the confusion.

Staring at that corner I know one thing, and I know it real clear, at once: this lovely dress, made of heavy satin and trimmed with lace and beading and what not, which I've dyed, the morning after the wedding, orange at the top and purple at the bottom, so it can still be used in the future—like, at dances and parties and stuff—this dress isn't gonna fit me no more.

Up to now I've pictured it in my head, shining awful brilliant, just like a rainbow, and swirling all around me; and with every step, billowing between my legs, and like, making me adorable, so adorable in Lenny's eyes—but now that I touch my belly and feel the beginning, the very beginning of change, right here around my waist, what's the point of all that.

On the floor, under the hem of the dress, I can see two pairs of shoes: one is my new, white satin shoes, which Lenny's bought for me, like, two weeks ago, just for the wedding.

When he wants to, he can be real kind. He knows so well how to spoil a woman. He gave me a ring with a pink sapphire. I bet you it's real! Also, a gold chain with a locket, which at the last minute—like, just before saying, *I do*—I decided not to wear. I wanted to look classy, and worried that it's gonna be a bit much.

And the other pair? Now, that's my very first pair of high heel shoes. They're worn out, but still kinda bright, and chipped only a little. To this day I'm totally crazy about the color: hot pink!

Ten years ago I spotted them up there, in a store window, and for a whole month I stared at them every day, on my way home from school, and my heart sank, knowing I didn't have no money to buy them. I liked how the side of the strap was like, spruced up with a plastic rose, which has since fallen off. Awful cute, it was!

Then I found a job at this ice cream place, down there at the Santa Monica pier. I got my first week's pay, and was so happy, so thrilled to rush in and buy them, because they wasn't only pink—but glossy too, and because now I was just like an adult. Ma took one look at them and slapped me, which made me figure that now, I was gonna have no choice but to apply plenty of makeup, so that this side of my face, which was flaming red, won't stand out all that much.

Then she slapped me again, this time on the other side, which turned out to be just as stinging—but at least, it solved the problem for me, 'cause now I found myself, like, pretty even; you know, balanced on both sides.

Ma said I looked like a bitch in them shoes—but I didn't care, really I didn't, because it was my sixteenth birthday and it was my own damn money, for me to do as I please, and because I had to fight her, like, tooth and nail to keep the little I had, so that she won't take it from me, for my sake of course; and because most of all, I thought them shoes made me look just fine.

Now I can see one pink shoe standing lopsided, held up somehow in-between them white shoes; and the other pink one lying there, turned over, like some open-mouthed baby whale, trying to rise for a breath from a sea of dust.

Me, I still remember the first time I wore them, which was also the first time I met Lenny.

He was standing out there, on the other side of the pier. The lights on the Ferris Wheel had just started to come on. They was gleaming there, directly behind him.

Somehow I could spot his outline in the distance, in-between the swirly letters, which I couldn't read, because from the inside, which was where I was standing, left was right, right was left, flipped into looking kinda foreign, which can really confuse you. But I knew them letters spelled the name of the place. They looked cool, too, like they're gonna drip and totally melt, floating up there on the pane of glass between us.

It was a hot summer evening, and the place was awful packed. I paced back and forth behind the counter, serving the customers, dishing out fresh smiles, scooping Dutch chocolate here and vanilla there, and trying to get a beat going, trying to sway my hips and at the same time, steady my step over my new, hot pink high heels, which isn't near as easy as you might think —at least, not on the first try.

After a while I noted that he started pacing just like me, back and forth, and with the same beat, too. I liked the bounce of his step. Right away I thought he was gonna make a fabulous dance partner. And I knew, really I did, it was gonna be a wild night.

You won't believe how wild it turned out to be—but in a different way than you might expect, like, an entirely different way. He was so handsome, too, with that slicked-back hair, just like them stars in the old movies!

And like, there was something about his walk, about the way he carried himself, that reminded me of Johnny, mom's previous boyfriend, the one who confessed to her that he couldn't get no respect from his wife.

Just like him, Lenny seemed to be in his early forties, and like, he was talking to himself from time to time. I bet he was rehearsing some excuse. Which made me bust out laughing, laughing so hard that my hat—that ice cream uniform hat, made of hard white paper folded in half—nearly flew off my pony tail. I mean, if you find yourself in such a bind, having to come up with one new story after another for the old wife, you might as well just get rid of her, and get yourself a new girl.

The minute our eyes met, I knew what to do: so I stopped in the middle of what I was doing, which was dusting off the glass shield over the ice cream buckets, and stacking up waffle cones here and sugar cones there. From the counter I grabbed a bunch of paper tissues, and bent all the way down, like, to pick something from the floor. Then with a swift, discrete shove, I stuffed the tissues into one side of my bra, then the other, 'cause I truly believe in having them two scoops—if you know what I mean—roundly and firmly in place.

Having a small chest is no good: men seem to like girls with boobs that bulge out. It seems to make an awful lot of difference, especially at first sight, which you can always tell by them customers, drooling.

I straightened up real fast, and it didn't take no time for him to come in. I was still serving another customer, some obnoxious woman with, like, three chins. She couldn't make up her mind if she wanted hot fudge on top or just candy sprinkles, and what kind, what flavor would you say goes well with pistachio nut, and how about them slivered almonds, because they do seem to be such a healthy choice, now really, don't they.

He came in and stood in line, real patient, right behind her. So now I noted his eyes, which was brown, and his high forehead and the crease, the faint crease right there, in the middle of it, which reminded me all of a sudden of my pa, who left us for good when I was only five, and I never saw him again —but still, from time to time, I think about him and I miss him so.

I could feel Lenny—whose name I didn't know yet—like, staring at me. It made me hot all over. For a minute there, I could swear he was gonna ask me how old I was—but he didn't.

And so, to avoid blushing, I turned to him and I said, boldly, "It's a crime?"

And he said, "What?"

And I said, "To be sixteen. It's a crime, you think?"

And he said, "Back in the days when I was young and handsome, that was no crime."

And I countered with, "Handsome you still are!"

He had no comeback for that, and me, I didn't have nothing with which I could follow it up. So I asked, "So? What kind of cone for you?" but that woman cut in, 'cause I was still holding her three-scoops tower of pistachio nut on a sugar cone. And she started to cry out, and like, demand some attention here, because hey, she was first in line and how about whipped cream? Or some of that shredded coconut?

So I smiled at her, in my most cool and polite manner, and squeezed out a big dollop of whipped cream, which was awesome, 'cause it calmed her down right away.

And I scattered some of them coconut flakes all over—quite a heap—and went even further, adding a cherry on top. At last, I raised the thing to my lips, because at this point, it was starting to drip already.

Then, winking at him, I passed my tongue over the top, and all around the ice cream at the rim of the cone, filling my whole mouth and, just to look sexy, also licking the tips of my fingers. Then I came around the counter, swaying my hips real pretty, and steadying myself over the wobbly high heels. I came right up to him, and before he could guess what kind of trouble I had cooked up in my head, I kissed him—so sweet and so long—on his lips, to the shouts and outcries of the offended customer.

The manager was like, outraged, not only because of this incident—but also because pink shoes wasn't allowed, no way no how, only black uniform shoes. She grabbed my ice cream hat, that thing made out of white paper, and pulled it right off my head, and threw it to the floor, smashing and crashing it. I was fired right there, on the spot.

He came out right away after me. I bet he figured it was his fault, 'cause it was over him that I've lost my job.

So he said, "Hi. My name is Lenny."

"Anita," I said, licking my lips, because they was still kinda sticky and tasted sweet, and because I think I look hot when my mouth has a shine.

It was getting awful dark already. And he said, like, "So, where do you live?"

And me, I figured that tonight, it would be good to hang out at home, 'cause ma was gonna be working late again.

We lived in the same one-bedroom place ever since I was five, when pa had paid the first month rent—but then he forgot, somehow, all about sending the second. Sometimes, things may fly right out of your mind. I totally get that.

Because of Santa Monica's rent control, the place was kinda cheap. Still, ma said that paying it was hard for her, 'cause without a high school diploma—which she never got, on account of never going to no high school—without that, no one wants you, and there is no way nowhere to get a decent, well-paying job.

For the last couple of years she worked as a cleaning lady by day and an unarmed security officer by night, both at the same place, a local clinic. Tonight, I figured, would be her night shift. So when Lenny asked, "Would you like me to take you home?" I said, "Yes, take me."

"But," he said, "no more kissing, I mean it now. I do not want any trouble, and you are too young, you know, much too young for a man my age."

He had a fine way of talking, like no one else I knew. He talked, like, with such a clear cut enunciation. I'm awful proud of this word. It was from Lenny that I learned it. *Enunciation*. For my part, I could teach him a thing or two about *trouble*.

So later, while sticking the key in the door, I turned to him and said, "Trouble, that's my middle name," which was a line I used sometimes, 'cause it sounded so clever.

"No, really?" he said.

To which I replied by asking, "What, you think it's a crime? Like, kissing me, I mean?" And he said, "It's just... I do not want to start something which can lead nowhere, really."

What could I say to that, except, "There's no one home. Stay a minute. Is that a crime, too?"

I handed him an old record, something slow from the sixties, which years ago used to bring tears to ma's eyes, because—in spite of looking so tough—she still had a soft spot somewhere in her, even if most of the time you can't find it. She used to play it often—but now not so much no more.

So I thought he might like it. Lenny put it on the record player, so in a second the mood was better, even though the thing squeaked from time to time.

He turned to me the minute I untied my pony tail, and told me I reminded him of a girl he used to know, and would I like to dance.

I stepped out of my shoes and into his arms, and before he could say anything I slipped out of my dress, too. I thought I looked, like, a little too slender in my panties, so I told him to close his eyes—but at this point, because of being so aroused, and trying so hard not to show it, I forgot all about them tissues at each side of my bra, which now and again, made a slight swoosh.

Later I wondered if he wondered about that.

I rose to the tips of my toes, feeling the touch of his shirt and the pleat of his pants, right against my bare skin. And I placed my hands on his shoulders, and felt his hands on my hips.

And so he held me there, a long, long time in the dark. And me, I got to touch his lips, and that crease up there, on his forehead, and we swayed back and forth: I clinging to him, he— to that one girl, the girl he used to know.

Then he moved away abruptly, saying that he was too old for me, and anyway, what was he doing, he had a child, a boy just a year older than me. So I took a step closer, like, to close the gap again. And feeling lost, like a stray kitten out in the cold, I said, "Just hold me, Lenny. Just hold me tight. I need you so bad."

And the minute I said it, I knew he needed to hear these words, needed to know that he was really needed.

After a while I whispered, like, "Just say something to me. Anything." And I thought, Any other word apart from *love*, 'cause that word is diluted, and no one knows what it really means, anyway. Then he kissed me—even without the ice cream —and said my name, like, he tasted it in his mouth, and rolled it on his tongue, which made me awful happy. And we started our dance again:

I came as he backed away, and then in reverse, I backed away as he came, and we came and went, went and came this way for a long while until, all of a sudden, the front door opened and there was ma, standing there with a new boyfriend this time, a guy whose name I didn't even know.

She opened her fist—I could hear the bong of the keychain as it dropped to the floor—and before she could slap me, I ran as fast and as far as my legs could take me, right out the door.

Then, yelling *Bitch* at the top of her voice, ma picked up my dress, which had been left there, in the middle of the floor, and threw it. She threw it flying down the staircase after me—but for some reason, them pink shoes stayed behind.

They stayed until the next day, when Lenny went there for me, to get some of my stuff. Perhaps he figured he was in charge of me now, and so he paid for a motel room, and went on paying it, 'cause it was on his account that I lost my job and the roof over my head, both on the same night.

Who's there? What was that, just now?

I can feel, like, a slight breath behind me. I can hear the click of the knob, on the bedside lamp up there, over my shoulder. It's made the light stronger, and the shadows—sharper. I need to know who it is—but at this point, I don't barely feel like turning around.

And I can't decide if this is so because I'm still pretty dazed, or because lying here on my side feels better, so much better for the cramps. I bet I can figure who it is simply by spotting the reflections, right there in the mirror.

It's a freestanding mirror, tilted over its feet, set in an ornate oval frame, which is so classy, and like, fit for a queen, and which used to be hers. I mean, his ex-wife. But then, just the thought of it—I mean, the thought of catching sight of myself in *her* mirror—is like, strange. It gives me goosebumps.

And it isn't just old wives' tales, or just my nerves. I've seen images of Natasha. Lenny keeps them old pictures stashed away in the drawer, next to his side of the bed, and—like, quite by chance—I found them one day. If not for the age spots spreading over the pictures, and if not for the yellowing, you could swear that face is mine.

So whenever I find myself passing there, by that mirror, I close my eyes, or turn my head away. And I ask myself then, What on earth did he find in me—a simple girl, with no high school diploma, who at times can't help but making him bored stiff?

What did he need me for—me and my lousy *enunciation*—when he had already married this woman who, by everything I've learned about her, was so fine and so talented, and came from an awful long line of musicians?

And why, why did he tell me, that first time we danced, that I reminded him of a girl he used to know?

Lying here, in what used to be *her* side of the bed—a side which isn't mine, at least not yet—I'm thinking about her, worrying, like, Is she gonna come back here, any time soon, to claim her place?

The other day, standing there behind the kitchen door, I could hear Lenny. He lowered his voice when he told his son that yes, she'd been there, in the hospital, visiting him. And I think he said that he'd shut his eyes, just to be focused, to feel her; which is a bad sign for me.

I'm wondering now how much time I've lost, and where Lenny might be, 'cause if not for his injuries, and being stuck now in a wheelchair, I can picture him in my head real easy, pacing back and forth somewhere else right now.

It Is Not Too Late

Chapter 5

As Told by Anita

I can hear a noise of some kind, clicking awful close to my ear, on the other side, I mean, Lenny's side of the bed. I try to stay still, because of this dull pain, and because of wondering if, somewhere deep inside, my baby can feel it, too.

Then I turn my head—just a little—and take a peak over my shoulder. I glance real quick at that standalone mirror, which is facing away from me. And what do I see reflected there, if not something that's, like, so strange to my eyes, so unusual, that it makes me want to blink, or wipe them in awe.

Three squares of fuzzy wool are being held there, suspended in midair. Directly behind them hang three shadows, under which you can see three chubby old women, crinkling their noses— long, longer, longest. They're straining their crossed, beady eyes with great focus, under three pairs of glasses, and clinking, clinking, clinking three pairs of knitting needles, like, all together now!

And there, on the floor, you can see three balls of thick yarn chasing each other, and from time to time, getting tied in knots, every which way across them fat ankles.

Anyway, at first glance them old women look kinda similar, like a rough, wrinkled copy of each other, what with those high arched, strange eyebrows. I pinch myself, but they're still there—in the mirror as well as outside of it—no matter how long I try blinking and wiping my eyes. It takes me a while to tell them apart:

The one sitting to the left, she's toothless. The one in the middle has a pimple on her veined temple. And the one to the right, well, her nose isn't only the longest, but also the knobbiest of all three.

Wrapped around her neck is a long tape measure, the edges of which roll all the way down and curl there, in her lap, next to a pair of scissors.

All of a sudden, like something has clicked in my head, I know who she is: this is Hadassa Rosenblatt, known to all as aunt Hadassa—though nobody can tell me exactly whose aunt she is anyway—she was the one spreading nasty, awful rumors about me, saying I was dating some other boyfriend, like, behind Lenny's back.

At the time, I decided to make things real easy for her, and told her there's no need for her to come to my wedding, and in fact it would be so much better if she'd stay as far as she could from me; which made her sisters, Frida and Fruma, stay home, too. Since then, my mind is kinda at ease—except for wondering, Why the gossip? Why did she try meddling in my affairs? And now, ain't them three sisters gonna curse me, like witches do, in old children stories?

And what on earth have they been doing here, in my bedroom, sitting behind me, watching me so quiet—so mute like, even—that for the last hour I didn't hear no squeak out of them? Or else was it me, was I too sleepy, too dazed to notice them?

In a blink of an eye I can tell that aunt Hadassa can tell, somehow, that I'm awake, and that I've been watching her for the last few minutes.

So at once, she straightens her back and elbows aunt Frida, who in turn elbows aunt Fruma. And they all nod a slight nod to each other, and each sister in her turn pulls some yarn from her ball and then kicks it, so it goes into a whirl and then settles there, at their feet. All of which seems so smooth, so precise, so much like a chorus line; which reminds me what Lenny told me about their past.

I remember, he said that one of these days, he'd like to finish his story about them, which goes something like this:

Having fled from Poland during World War II, the three Rosenblatt sisters arrived in Paris, where they discovered glamor, or at least the chance for it.

They bleached their hair super blond, so as to put the shtetl, and the horrors they must have suffered, right out of their mind, along with the old way of life.

Around the same time, they changed their names to Brigitte, Monique, and Veronique. Along with their names, they threw out a few other things which had failed to serve them: their long, dark skirts, and their modesty.

Wearing frilly underwear and black stockings, they auditioned for a show at a nightclub, a highly acclaimed nightclub called the Folies Bergère—only to be rejected, because sadly, their dance routine was too nice and conservative; which made them furious, and even more driven to make it.

So with clenched teeth, they learned how to lift their skirts, and flap them about in a highly erotic, flirtatious manner. After several months of hard, painstaking work, the three sisters finally became an overnight sensation.

They ended up joining a cheaply produced show in the nightclub district of Montmartre. Their fame spread. They became known for their fancy cancan costumes, which left them practically naked.

Their earlier, orthodox upbringing didn't seem to inhibit them in the least. Behind the curtains, they went from one scandal to the next, and had countless affairs.

They never married, or had children. Later, in secret, they told Natasha that at one time Brigitte—also known as Hadassa—had gone through a difficult abortion. She couldn't afford a real doctor, so who knows what instrument was used there.

Soon after, she'd been kicked out from the show, because sadly, she couldn't perform the required cartwheel any more, or even the high kicks.

All this is, like, awesome! But me, I find it hard to believe that there was a time when aunt Hadassa could do any of that. To this day, she still wears the black stockings, as do her sisters, and she can keep a beat, an incredibly fast beat, which you can hear by the clicking of her needles. Anyway, she's declined with age. Her flesh looks doughy, and she's kinda heavy.

Looking at her makes me decide one thing right away: I'm never gonna grow old! I simply refuse to do that.

Lenny tells me that later, when they moved to the States and settled in Los Angeles, the Rosenblatt sisters became very close to his wife. They adore Natasha, perhaps because of having no kids of their own; which in the end, comes down to hating me.

Of one thing I'm sure: if they could wave a magic wand, or a needle or something, to undo whatever binds us, Lenny and me, to each other—this marriage and above all, this pregnancy—they would do so without thinking twice.

What's more, they seem to keep a secret among them, when it comes to this question: where's Natasha? She hasn't shown up here for the last, say, five years; which is cool with me—but still, strange.

If I ask them about it, which I did at one time, the sisters would find a way to skirt the question. And if I ask Lenny, he would hide the truth, somehow, with a kiss, and anyway, he won't give me no real answer, either.

All of a sudden aunt Hadassa clears her throat and says, "Nu? Why are you staring at my eyebrows?"

To which I say, "Who, me?"

"Oy, dear! When you're older, you'll understand," she says; which serves only one purpose: to inflame me.

And so I ask, "Understand what?"

Aunt Hadassa wraps the yarn onto the left needle, and loops it around. "Understand this, Anita," she says. "The thing about eyebrows: it is the first thing to go, when you get older."

Me, I don't have nothing to add to this piece of wisdom, to which she adds, "They hang down, I mean, heavily, over your eyes, and show your age, being so droopy and white, and so slick, to the point of resisting any fix, any type of makeup."

"I'm never gonna grow old," I state.

Which makes her curl her lips, like she knows something I don't. "Give it time, dear, give it time! My, my, Anita, you'll end up just like me, having to pluck them! Pluck-pluck-pluck! And then, just so you can look halfway presentable, paint them right back in, dear—as best you can."

"Really," I insist. "It isn't your eyebrows. It's that nose on you. That's the thing that fascinates me."

Naturally she seems surprised to hear that; which forces me to clarify, "I really, really hate it."

"So do I," she admits, for no other reason than to try to appease me.

Now aunt Hadassa slides the knot onto the other needle, and so does aunt Frida, and aunt Fruma too, in her turn. Their arms seem pretty wrinkled, like yesterday's newspaper.

I lift my pinkie finger and tilt it ever so slightly, as if holding a teacup.

"Hey, aunt Hadassa," I call. "See here, my hand?"

"What about it?" says she.

Now waving my fist in the air, I say, "I just want you to know that if you ever stick your nose, like, anywhere close to me, or to any of my private affairs, you're gonna leave me no choice, see, but to punch it. Seriously, that's one thing I learned from my ma, and I warn you now: I learned it real good."

"Ha," she puffs. "Your affairs, they seem to stick out like a sore thumb, and right in our noses, too. It is you who, by fainting at the most ill-advised time, forced this stink on us, on our delicate sensibilities."

"Why, how d'you mean?" I ask, totally confused.

"Who do you think has been taking care of you all day," she says, "Ha, princess?" And aunt Frida joins in, "Who has been wiping the dribble from the corner of your mouth?" This, while aunt Fruma chimes in, "And who, do you suppose, has been changing that pad, down in your cute little panties?"

"What?" I ask, in great outrage.

"Yes, dear," says aunt Hadassa. "Lenny, he found you right there, right outside the kitchen door. He said he'd called you, and called you again, then again, because the omelette, it was almost ready, and you never answered. So he figured you must have left."

"And the omelette," she continues, before I have time to catch my breath. "Oy, it was getting cold, and of course it is no good cold, so finally he figured, of course, that he was hungry, because all he had for breakfast was coffee. You know he is sick of your egg salad, right? He never eats it, dear, now does he. Why you keep making it is beyond me!"

By now I've opened my mouth to answer, which at once makes her raise her voice. "So," she says, "he transferred the omelette to a plate, and added some butter on top, and waited a bit, just to let it melt, and to make sure you, dear, were not coming back. Nu, then he just ate it, after which he came out and realized, all of a sudden, that quite sadly, he had been mistaken; that in fact, you were there all along, in the corridor, lying flat on your back, and barely breathing, too. Which is when he picked up the phone and, finally, called us for help."

In disbelief I say, "Help? I don't need none of your help! And where, where is he now?"

To which she says, "My, my! He is so exhausted now, after all that excitement, I mean the wedding first of all, and then his stay at the hospital. Too weak, I am afraid, to be of any use! And his son, Ben, nu! What can I say? Men! They managed to lift you, somehow, and carry you to bed. So now, consider yourself lucky, dear, to be in one piece. As soon as we came, they went out."

"Out? Out where?" I ask.

But in place of an answer she just waves her hand, saying, "I do not wish to lump them all in one heap, but somehow, you see, men can never take care of themselves, let alone take care of us women. They are never there for us when we need them—now are they!"

For a minute I hesitate to ask, "What did you say, just now, about changing my pad? What pad?"

Which makes her lay down her square of wool and say, this time real slow and careful, "You know you are bleeding, right?"

It is then that I try to jump from the bed, because not only do I feel ashamed, even violated, which of course isn't the first time in my life—but all of a sudden I sense a cramp, just like a stab, down in my stomach, in the same place where so far, the pain's been dull.

So she hurries over, and places the palm of her hand, like, real heavy, on top of my shoulder. "You can't do that, dear," she says, pushing me back, and propping up my pillow—even as I rise up to ask, "Why? Why the hell not?"

"Nu," she says. "Just be a good girl for me and lie down, nice and easy now, and for God's sake, be still. Take up knitting if you like. I can bring you instructions," she adds, "for anything. Baby blanket? Baby socks? Just tell me, dear, tell me what you like."

Despite her offer, I'm sick of the way she keeps saying *dear*.

There's no way for me to know what she means by that, because her tone is like, bitter, and it don't hardly agree with the sweet taste of this word, and because she keeps repeating it all too often; all of which tells me one thing: aunt Hadassa is torn. She can't decide between wishing me ill—and helping me back to my feet.

"I won't lie down," I say, defiantly. "And I really, really don't like knitting."

Her painted eyebrows arch even higher, and I begin to get an uneasy feeling, because at this point, she's much too close to me, and the light bounces off her needle much too sharply, and now the tip is right here, against my skin, and it scratches.

I point a finger at her, like, right in her face, to make her take note of my nails. "Shove off! Away from me," I tell her. "I mean it, don't you dare come any closer to me with them fine needles."

"I see," says aunt Hadassa.

She wraps the yarn around her index finger and plucks it, as if to transmit a message by wire. "A feisty little kitten," she says, "are you now!" At which time aunt Frida asks, "She's a kitten?" and aunt Fruma confirms, "Yes: a feisty little one!"

By now Aunt Hadassa has stepped back, and with a tight-lipped expression she sits there and starts sewing the three squares of wool together, using some fancy sort of a stitch, and clicking her tongue, and sighing, like, "My, my."

After doing this for a while, she pushes them glasses up her nose, and raises her eyes to me and says, "I'm trying to talk to you, dear, like I was your ma, you know."

To which I say, "And what makes you think I need another ma? One's more than enough! And you, you don't know nothing about my ma."

"I guess I don't," she has to admit. "But being pregnant is not for sissies, dear. You must make sure you are strong, like me."

At hearing this, I can't hide my disgust. "If this is what strength looks like, I swear, I'm gonna take disease."

"I see," says she. "In that case, it's not too late, you know."

And before I can ask, "What is?" she goes on to drive the point home.

"I have done it before, and it can make things so much easier for you, because really, you like to run around and have your fun, don't you. And here you are, poor dear, lying in bed, confined, probably, for weeks, if not months. Now with all this bleeding going on, my, my, who knows what has happened there."

She points her needle at me, stressing, "Maybe it's no good anyway, I mean, not viable, if you know what I am saying—"

"Don't—don't you dare say it," I flash a warning at her. "For God's sake, bite your tongue!"

At that minute, aunt Hadassa picks up the scissors; which is when I suddenly remember that piece of music which I heard with Lenny.

He took me to some opera, Wagner I think, which was long and kinda difficult to get, but he told me to listen, and he explained it all to me, and from there I remember them, the three Norns: They spun the thread of fate, and they sang, like, the song of the future.

Beware, they sang.

Beware, I tell myself now, as aunt Hadassa holds up the yarn, and snips it.

And with a sigh she leans into her feet and gets up. So do her sisters, and all their images in that oval, standalone mirror, right there in the opposite corner.

"Nu, we are going to leave now," she says. "We are going to hurry out, dear, because we do not want you to tell us we should go. Just think about it, will you? I was just saying... It is not too late, really... You are in pain, dear, I can see it quite plainly. And there is still time to end this."

The three sisters file out with a quick, matching step, and go out to the corridor, followed closely by a whirl in the air, in which you can spot three bounces—high, higher, highest—of three balls of yarn.

And as they make their final exit, I shout at them as loud as I can, despite that sharp pain right here, in my guts, "Aunt Hadassa!"

I hear them stopping in their tracks out there, behind that door.

"What is it," whispers one. "What does she want," whispers another. And the last one answers, probably with a wave of a hand, "Who knows... Maybe, just to meow a little."

Which in turn, makes me roar, "Who needs you! You, who think you can tell me what to do, and what not to do, and whether or not my pregnancy is like, viable, and should it come to full term, or not! I just wish that you leave me alone! Get the hell out! Get out of my womb, where it is not your business to be! And if I don't see none of you never again, it's gonna be too soon!"

A Promise, Aborted

Chapter 6

As Told by Anita

For a while I leaf through this book, which Lenny's bought me. I bet he's real excited. He so looks forward to becoming a father, the second time around. I can just see him in my head, like, holding the baby's hand, guiding him already in his first steps. Then, letting go, he's gonna take a step or two back, and hold his breath, waiting there for the little one to walk into his open arms.

Lenny's gonna buy him a brand new tricycle, and teach him how to set his little feet on top of them pedals, and push, push harder, even harder—yeah! Just so! And again: Go on, push, until—oh boy! With great joy, he's gonna clap his hands, because here—for the first time—you could detect a move, a slight move ahead.

And then, a few years down the road, he's gonna surprise our child with a large, shining bicycle, and adjust the training wheels as time goes by, until they wasn't needed no more; at which point, Lenny would remove them, and hold them in his hands, like, to weigh them for a moment, and try to wipe the rust, and wish that time would like, slow down, just a little, because it's hard, so hard for the old heart to let go.

Yes, Lenny needs a son: someone to need him, trust him, and make him trust himself again.

I turn the page over, only to find some of them words much too long—but I read them anyway and like, I *enunciate* them, as slowly and as clearly as I can, 'cause it's gonna make him proud of me, and make me worthy of him.

The book says that just four weeks after *conception*, basic facial features will begin to appear, including *passageways*, I repeat, passageways that will make up the inner ear, and arches that will *contribute*, contribute, I say aloud, to the jaw. And it says that the baby may now be a quarter of an inch long, which sounds like they're talking about some lizard, or maybe a fish.

But the book don't say nothing about what I'm really worried about, which is: how to become a ma—and at the same time, how to be totally different from my ma.

Me, I often wonder about that, 'cause it's kinda hard to know the right thing to do, even with the best of intentions, when all you have before you is nothing, nothing but a life cursed by violence, and by misery, and by a long list of mistakes.

Like the time when I was fourteen, and ma called me *Bitch*, for no better reason than me telling her that, like, I'd missed my period. I wasn't sure if she called me that because I was pregnant—or because she didn't want to hear it.

At any rate, ma pondered the *situation*. This was what she called it back then, a situation. And she gave me a smack across my face when she figured it was Johnny's baby, which was real bad, not only because he was already married—but because he was also dating her at the time. And if there was one thing she hated, it was the idea of sharing.

After the blow I could taste blood in my mouth. And when I touched it with my tongue, one of my teeth felt kinda loose, and after a while it started to rock back and forth.

Once she simmered down, ma said, "There's still time. It's not too late."

And she took me to that clinic, where she'd just joined the cleaning staff. And they did her a personal favor, so that instead of paying a full charge, she could put in some extra hours, like, for a few months. And there, they took care of the *situation*, but not of the tooth.

And so, I ended up losing it.

Me, I'm awful lucky, 'cause you can't tell it's missing—unless I'm having real good fun and busting out laughing, which sometimes makes me forget to keep my mouth shut.

But right now I have to bite my lips.

Either that, or dig my nails, like, deep into the flesh of my hand, so that them cramps, they're gonna stop, or at least fade away. So I close the book, reach over to the bedside lamp, and click its knob.

And at once, the place has changed. All these fancy pieces of furniture, and this entire bedroom, in which I don't really belong, with its walls—those here around me and those over there, beyond the threshold, out in a corridor—all of these things ain't solid no more. In a blink, they've lost their bright, yellow sides as well as their opposite, dark sides.

There ain't no contrasts anymore, so that now, you can't define no objects as, say, a four poster bed, or a coat hanger in a corner, or a wooden headboard, part of which is reflected there, in that mirror.

And instead, the whole space has become kinda fluid, like a gray, smoky swamp, given to the wild storm in my head, in which a shard here, a shard there start floating, in a total muddle.

And I ain't even sure if them shards are, like, in the shape of things that have already taken place, or the shape of things yet to come—but somehow I know that from now on, no matter what happens, I ain't alone: There's new life in me.

I touch myself under the blanket, brushing my fingers real slow, from the navel up to the crease right here, under my chest, which is where I can feel the change: My breasts, they've grown so much firmer than before, and my nipples, they've gotten so much larger, like a drop turning into a ripple.

I let my hand hover over the place where I imagine my baby, and picture in my head how them things, them passageways start to form, connecting like, by magic, from here to there, forging little nerves in all the right places inside this tiny creature, all quarter inch of him.

The two of us feel this bond, this warmth right here, coming across the thin gap between the skin of my belly and the skin of the palm of my hand. And so, we're happy. And then, then I stop to breathe—I gasp—I breathe deeper, deeper, so I can take it, take the pain.

Which in a flash, brings back to me that which I want to forget. It's the memory of that clinic, where they took care of the *situation*, and of how I came to, in that horrible place, and found myself lying there, flat on my back, feeling wounded.

Immobile, I stared for a long while at some blurry sort of a border, which gave a cold, metallic shine, not getting at first that it came from the rail, the side rail of the bed, which was raised, like, well above the level of my head.

So even without thinking—or knowing where I was—I felt like an animal, trapped.

Trying to come out of this state of paralysis, I started to notice a slight noise, 'cause them coil springs, they was creaking under me, which sounded almost like a sigh. There was mist in my head, and I tried to clear it, tried to focus.

The bed was awful high, so even if I could somehow gather my strength and take hold of the rail, even if I could lower the thing and then, swing my legs right there, over the edge—still, I wasn't sure if my feet could reach down, all the way to the floor.

All the while, there was a sound, a sharp sound breaking through to me. Someone out there, someone I couldn't even see was screaming, screaming real wild, like a kid scared out of her wits, crying for help with no clear words, and without ever stopping.

The ceiling loomed over my head, and the floor was white and shiny, and a smell rose from it, a pungent smell of some cleaning detergent. Me, I looked around me, and now I could see that the room had several other hospital beds, all of which seemed as shaky, and as high as the one in which I was trapped, on account of being set, somehow, on wheels.

I could make out some outlines, white outlines of bodies on white sheets. A few stretched flat on their backs; others, like, curled in the shape of a question mark.

Them women, I gathered, they was just like me: having a situation, and letting someone take care of it for them, and trying to forget, and heal from that which, like ma said, had to be done.

All of them seemed to be caged, much like me. Their faces was washed out, their expressions—numb. They was just knocked, like, out of their senses.

Looking at them I became kinda curious. I asked myself, who was the one screaming, 'cause they all seemed to be so sleepy, so eerily quiet, even though from time to time you could see a head turning, or a hand lifting or falling.

And me, I even became angry, madly angry at that unseen woman, whose voice pierced me. She roared, arousing something in my heart which was so annoying, so alarming, so crazed even—until at last I thought, Enough! Just shut the hell up! Why isn't nothing being done here, I mean like, anything to silence her! Slap the madwoman! Restrain her! Strap her in a straightjacket! This is a clinic, after all! Tie her up, so she can't stir up trouble no more!

And on that note, all of a sudden it came to me: somehow I knew, right then, that she was no other—no one else but me.

And still unable to stop myself from wailing, I began to listen, I mean, really listen to my own voice. I tried to take apart the different notes flying—with such force, such anguish—out of my throat.

I could hear different breaths, different speech sounds. Some was like, open, some—blocked. Finally I made a complete sense of it all. It was then that at last, I got it.

"Ma," I heard me raving, on and on and on, "Ma, take me, take me from here, take me, ma, please! Take me before it is too late!"

Little by little I regained control over myself. And the voice—my voice—which by now was like, hoarse from shouting, became softer and softer still, until, at last, it faded away.

I laid there exhausted, trying to catch my breath, asking myself, When would she come? When would she take me back, take me home?

And I knew right then that I won't never be quite the same. This was the day that changed me. From now on, my life would be measured not by a stretch of years, my fourteen years—but by the depth of this pain, this sorrow.

So I asked myself, What could I bring back, what would I remember out of it?

With some effort I recalled being led into the operation room, trembling a little in that skimpy paper gown, being told to mount the bed, and like, feeling them fingers—so cold on my outstretched arm—as the nurse had tried, several times, to find my vein.

But then, after that I couldn't recall nothing, nothing but that screaming, that goddam earsplitting screaming in my head. Thank God that was over.

I went back in my head, searching for an earlier moment, the moment I'd stopped in front of the entrance door, shedding tears, even kicking the stairs and pounding the wall with my fist, refusing to go into that clinic. I recalled arguing with ma, pleading with her to let me go, let me turn back, 'cause it was a school day, and I shouldn't miss it, really.

But she insisted that what I shouldn't miss was my future, because it was no good for me to repeat her mistakes, and if I did better in school, and scored better grades, especially in math, and learned, at long last, how to subtract my age from hers, I would know just exactly what she meant.

At any rate, keeping the baby was out of the question, 'cause it would, like, screw up my entire life. After all, she said, I was still a little girl myself, and despite thinking myself a woman I knew nothing, really, absolutely not a thing about parenting. And what's more, I didn't have no partner, no man with whom I could share the burden.

And by *burden* she meant, raising a child; which made me feel awkward, and like a burden myself.

At last I found myself having to obey her, because like, part of me reckoned she meant well, and she was right, too. And anyway, as everyone says, ma knows best—even though she went on dating Johnny for a whole month after that.

But the other part of me recoiled in fear at the thought, the mere thought of entering that door. I didn't want no procedure, 'cause I wanted so bad to hold on to the baby. In spite of everything ma had just said, I believed I was, like, destined to have him. Me, I could see, yes, I could just picture what lied ahead.

My little one would gurgle and coo right here, in my arms. I would be brushing my lips over his scalp—ever so gentle— careful not to touch nowhere close to the tender spot, right there at the top. I could almost feel the fine fuzz of his hair, real soft, tickling my cheek.

In my head I could kiss, I could almost swallow his tiny fingers. They would wrap around my finger, their nails so pink, so incredibly clear. And the little hands, they would stroke my hair or like, search for my breast.

Then I would touch the nipple to my baby's lips, and watch him latch on and like, suck, suck, swallow, breathe; suck, suck, swallow, breathe.

All the while his eyes would be fixed on me, curious to see, to separate my face out of that blurry chaos, that first, misty sight of lights and of shadows. And so I promised myself: I would give him that which I never got. I would become such a good mama, like no mama ever was! I would keep him safe right here, close to my heart.

The loss of this hope, that was the thing that was so painful. I couldn't hold it back, my grief. It came like, rushing, bursting out of me as I was lying there—even before I awoke, before I took full control of my body, or regained my spirit. It came out with every breath, every roar as it blasted off, soaring into the air above me. The roar of a wounded tigress.

This was the Anita whose voice I heard, for the first time in my life, that day twelve years ago.

Because who the hell cares? Who cares, really, if *there's still time*, and who cares if *it's not too late*, when your arms is empty. Who cares about the future, when your destiny is lost, and your promise—aborted, and by God, there's no way, no way no more to undo the damage.

A girl, a wild girl with green, kittenish eyes, that's how most people see me in their head, how they choose to fancy me. But then, who're they to decide? Can they hear what's inside, in my head? Me, I know different. There's a voice, there's a roar of a tigress in me, like, a fierce mama tigress, ready to leap into action and do anything, anything to protect her cub.

Beware, because this, you see, is the Anita I am today.

N Over L

Chapter 7

As Told by Ben

Already she has a blue mark on her arm, and another one on her thigh, maybe more. And it is unclear at this point if these have happened earlier, when she collapsed, or in the last five minutes since my father found her, during which he has been trying, in vain, to lift her by himself. When the fact finally occurred to him that in his condition, he was too clumsy for the task, he made up his mind to call for help and so, here I am.

Anita is lying there, legs folded, in the worst possible corner in this corridor, which is poorly lit and even worse, poorly ventilated. I slip one hand under her back, and another one under her knees, and pick her up. I find myself surprised not only that she has fainted all of a sudden, not only that she is now in my arms, her head bobbing up and down over my shoulder with each step I take—but more than anything, surprised at how light her body is.

How can she be pregnant, I ask myself, and immediately answer by asking, What do I know. Her heart must be working harder now, working for two, really. No wonder she is lightheaded. Anita, I guess, is off-balance because for her, this must be a time of change.

Once inside their bedroom I lay her down, roll her knees over to the center of the bed, turning her away from the edge, and place a pillow under her head. Then I rise away from her, to throw the windows open.

Hearing the squeak of his wheelchair behind me, I turn to my father. I look at him as if to say, Well, what now? And he returns a look with an equal measure of confusion, as if to ask, Look, Ben, can you tell, is she breathing?

I snatch a small, hand-held mirror from the dresser by her side and feeling important—at least as important as a TV brain surgeon—I hold it to her mouth. "Yes," I report, because in no time, the glass has become clouded. "So? Now what? Shouldn't you call someone, or take her to an obstetrician? I mean, just to make sure—"

"I'll call aunt Hadassa," he says. "For sure, she will know what to do."

I can hear the wheels turning on his way back to the hall, then, a dial tone, and his voice. "Listen, there's a problem," he says, in an urgent tone. "Yes. No, this time it's not me. It's Anita."

There is a brief pause, after which he goes on to say, "Well... I wish I knew. No. I have no idea what happened, exactly. She was making breakfast, fussing over it in her own, excessive way. And she was just fine. I mean, she was fine one moment and then, the next moment she is lying there, flat on the floor. Just like that. So, can you come? I need you here. Who said you are not welcome? Why, now what gave you that idea?"

He pauses to listen and then, in a reassuring tone of voice, he promises, "Really, you are. Yes, you are welcome here. Always. And Frida. Yes, of course. And Fruma too," he says, sounding as if all three of these women have just descended, with a heavy thud, right on top of his shoulders. "Absolutely. Listen, this is no time for games. Well, seriously now, when will you be here?"

The conversation drags on in the background. Meanwhile, I bend over Anita to check her pulse. I place a wet towel over her feverish forehead, and unbutton her shirt, to make sure she can breathe with no obstructions.

I try to avoid looking at her body—but still, I can see the ticklish point under her chin, and the long line of her neck, which is plunging into the collar, and the jugular vein fluttering there, and the nipple, half of which is peeking out from the shadow, down there under the opening of the shirt.

Her ribcage starts flaring up now with rapid, disorderly breathing, as if to escape a nightmare. This, I figure, is something she must face alone. And so I turn away from her and take a searching look around the room.

For the most part, it looks familiar: the same freestanding, oval mirror, tilted there, in the corner. The same four poster bed, which as I recall, was delivered in boxes from a manufacturer in North Carolina, and which took my parents two days to assemble, because the instructions were, unfortunately, less than clear, and so they nearly gave up.

Still, there are a number of changes here. First, I miss seeing their wedding portrait which, years ago, used to be displayed quite prominently, in a thick, richly decorated frame, suspended from a nail right there, above the headboard. All that remains of it now is some plaster, smeared in a rough, hasty manner, in a sloppy attempt to fill in the hole of the nail; also, a rectangular outline up on the wall, where the frame used to hang, and where the paint still retains its dark, nearly original tone; while around the edges, the paint has faded a long time ago.

And second, I miss seeing the pure white silk sheets, which used to wrap so neatly, so tightly over this bed. They were embroidered in the corner with an elegant monogram, designed, of course, by my mother. It was an overlay, I think, interlacing two glyphs: a slanted, longhand N, combining some of its decorative strokes with an L: Natasha over Leonard.

These sheets have been replaced, recently, with a royal blue bedspread. Pretentiously royal, I should say. It reminds me of a storm at sea, because of the color, I guess, and because of the folds rising and sinking here every which way, as if a gust of wind has blown across the surface, creating friction between that which is air and that which is fluid, and drawing ripples all around.

And there, lying on top of them is Anita, the woman who displaced my mother. Her rest, if you can call it that, is agitated —but then, at the sound of my father's voice, coming faintly from the other end of the apartment, she spreads open her hands and her face brightens. She seems to relax, even smile.

From here, it sounds as if there is some distress in his voice. "This is Lenny," he says, starting a different conversation now.

I can see how her eyelashes start flickering, ever so lightly, over the freckles.

"It's me," he repeats, to someone out there. "Me, Len."

My father talks now with an unusually slow manner, and with clear intervals, stressing every word; which makes me curious. I wonder who is it now, who is at the other end of the line.

He lowers his voice, but I can still hear him saying, "Just listen, dear. It's me. It's Lenny."

By now Anita is trying to open her eyes, if only by a crack. I have no idea if she could hear anything, or if she has caught sight of me. I wonder, can she see my outline, can she make it out against the bright sunlight in the window, and does she recognize, through the narrow interval between her eyelids, who I am.

So I whisper to her, "Anita..." which makes her nod her head.

"I carried you here," I say, "because you were dizzy. I mean, you fell."

She mumbles a long sentence, most of which I can barely understand.

"So, how are you feeling?" I ask. "Any better, now?"

Anita opens her mouth and out comes a big yawn.

I wait for an answer and before long, I can hear her purring softly, and from time to time, shivering slightly in her sleep. The rhythm of her breathing is regular now. So I unfurl the blanket over her, and cover her up to her ears.

I imagine my father standing right here, in my place at the foot of the bed. I step back and in my mind, picture him taking a step forward, lifting the edge of the blanket, which is still settling over her.

His hands go in, searching playfully for her feet, touching the creamy skin, fondling her toes, rolling each one of them ever so slightly between his fingers; which makes her arch her back, stretch out her arms, and twist her body around until she is turned over, on her back. She points her toes towards him with a cry of pleasure.

Anita utters a groan as he applies gentle pressure to the soles of her feet, caresses the arches, the heels, the ankles. Her knees spread open and fall apart, until she takes control of herself and brings them together—only to have them spread open again.

I close my eyes because this way, I can see with greater clarity. The entire blanket is coming alive, folding and unfolding, stirring with their passionate tangle. From time to time the ripples rise to mark the line of his back, or the curve of her embrace.

Waves come and go, crests roll in, followed by deep troughs, all giving a hint here, a hint there of the ways of their bodies, aching for each other, desperate to cling, to hold, to be taken.

Then, in my mind I conjure up the missing presence. The presence of the forgotten woman.

I gasp, for there she is: mom steps in from the shadow behind the mirror. Even if I try, I cannot grasp her. She advances slowly until she is standing right here, a few steps removed from the bed, tired, covered with a fine layer of dust, the dust of a long travel. By now it has caked on her face, because of the sweat that has already dried up. And in that crust, a crack here, a crack there bring out the crow feet by the corners of her eyes.

There is a stack of sheet music in her hands, which mom lets scatter in her path across the floor. Perhaps by now she has grown weary of her journey. I imagine it has been a while since she heard an ovation, since she took her bow in front of a crowd. And now, somewhere out there, a kid must be playing, practicing notes which are drifting in through the open window, out of sequence, confused.

She is wavering in her mind whether she should stay here, in this bedroom—which is hers after all—or walk out the door.

Finally, her exhaustion weighs in. Mom looks around her for a quiet place, and as if she were a stranger, she tiptoes—so as not to disturb—to the corner of this bed, where she turns her back to the two of them.

Her weight makes barely a dent on the mattress. She curls herself, tightening her arms over her knees and interlacing her fingers, which helps her keep loneliness away. Then she starts falling asleep, in the same place where the monogram—Natasha over Leonard—used to be.

It is then that I open my eyes and walk out of the room, closing the door behind me as softly and as gently as I can.

A Woman, Forgotten

Chapter 8:

As Told by Ben

From here I see the wheelchair, deserted. My father has managed to rise from it and now I can hear him down the hall, cackling in victory over this thing, this contraption, this symbol of his handicap, which is despicable to him. He is trying to walk. More precisely, he is swinging his crutches, a bit precariously I think—and in return, he is being swung by them, back and forth and over and again, making a small advance, a minute one really, with each attempted step. For him, this must be a dance of triumph.

Stopping for a moment by the console table he dials, listens, and redials. His ear is pressed to the handset, which is connected by a long, spiral cord to the phone, which is nearly buried by various papers, and hidden behind an old alarm clock. The cord is stretching tensely in midair, or slithering behind his back as he goes back to hobbling to and fro across the floor.

There he goes, reaching the wall, banging it accidentally with the bottom of the crutch and then, somehow, turning around, aiming to reach the opposite wall and bang, turning around again, while listening intently to the earphone. With each footfall, my father attempts to cut through some stutter. He tries, it seems, to restart a conversation.

He pays no attention to me. Still, his voice is deliberately lowered, which tells me this is private. I should turn away, really, and keep myself far out of earshot—but for some reason I make no move, and no sound either. Why is the connection so bad, I wonder, and who is it, who could it be at the other end of the line?

My father swallows his breath several times, his face turning pale, his eyes—miserable, until finally he bursts out shouting, "Listen, it's Lenny! Can you hear me, dear? In God's name, Natasha, it's me—"

Which makes me take a step forward, fumbling to find the right tone, the right words but at the same time, crying, "What? You're talking to mom? Where—where is she? Give me, let me talk to her—"

For a moment, his eyes seem to pop right out of their sockets, and his face reddens in embarrassment, as if he has just been caught in a covert little hideaway, committing some shocking, scandalous sin. He freezes, with the handset suspended in midair. Then slowly, and with full intention, he sets it down in its cradle, and stays there guarding the thing, which is still clasped firmly in his hand.

"What is that? What are you doing?" I plead. "Mom is back! It has been a long time, five years I think, since I heard her voice —"

"Yes," he says. "It has been that: five years. But first, we need to talk—"

"We," I insist, "have nothing to talk about. All I know is, mom is back from her tour." And with that I leap forward and try to snatch the thing, I yank it right out of his hold; which is when he pounces on me, and his knuckles turn bone-white around my arm, and I feel him gripping me tightly, until it hurts. I have forgotten how strong he is.

"Listen," says my father, between clenched teeth. "Listen to me! It is about her."

By now I am yowling in distress, "What? What the hell do you mean? What is it, about mom?"

And so he releases me. "You better sit down," he says. "It is something you need to hear."

For a moment I consider the pleasure I could get out of arguing with him over whether or not I should sit, and what does he know about me, about what I need, or about anything else, for that matter—but then I take control of myself and, noting that there is no chair here, in the hall, I just clear some papers off the console table, and stand there, with my back to it, leaning against its edge.

All the while I consider what to say, and how to stay on the attack, before he can come out—as I know he will—and give me some bad news.

And so, I charge him, "It is always secrets with you. I hate you for that."

Which, to my surprise, he accepts. "I hate it too," he admits. "Having to have secrets."

"With mom," I say, "things are simpler. You know, from time to time she would tell me something about herself. She would write to me, even."

"Oh yeah?" he says. "And how long ago was that?"

I figure that the last note I received from mom was—let's see —at least two years ago, maybe three. It amazes me now that all this time, I have given little thought, if any, to the silence between us.

I suppose I did not feel like telling her about myself, because around that time I quit everything. I left my studies at the Facoltà di Medicina e Chirurgia in the university of Firenze, after only a couple of years. And so, I figured, the less letters from my parents—the better.

I isolated myself, and attributed the sporadic nature of our correspondence to the frequent changes of my address, as I moved often, from one place to another across Italy.

"And her handwriting," says my father, pressing steadily ahead. "To you, son, was it clear?"

Her beautiful handwriting. It is engraved in my memory. As a child, I used to study it and copy it repeatedly, beginning at age five, when she wrapped her hand over mine, and taught me how to hold a pen. Between the first and middle fingers, she said, and hold it in place like this, by the thumb.

Mom used to draw text with the nib of a calligraphy pen. She would produce a smooth, fluent line, changing it—as if by a magic wand—from thick to thin, connecting the end of one glyph to the beginning of another, with a stroke that was so fine, truly, fine to the point of becoming invisible, almost. It had such a consistent slant, just like that monogram, embroidered on her silk sheets.

But then, this note—the last note she sent me—which I can see before my eyes as if it were right here, rustling in my hands, this one, I must admit, was different. It had none of these delicate pen strokes.

On the contrary, here was an ugly mess. The words were scattered. Some of them were scratched over, as if some frenzied chickens got loose on the page. What happened? What could possibly explain this unusual sloppiness?

Back then I decided to gloss over it, thinking that on her tour, mom must have scribbled this note hastily, while rocking, perhaps, in a car of some clunky old train, or taking off in a small airplane, fighting stormy weather on the way to her next performance.

"Well, son?" he says. "Have you ever wondered about that note?"

I glare at him without saying a word.

So he takes a step closer, which makes me lean back.

"You know," he says, "she wasted ten sheets of paper, maybe more, to write this thing to you. She labored so hard and so long over it, until finally it was written, and then she threw the pen away, to the other side of the room, saying she was too tired to try this again."

"Now how do you know all that?" I challenge him.

"Because," he says, "I was there."

Which catches me off-balance, and I cry, "No! You are lying to me! You and mom, you had already separated by then. And she, she was traveling! It was you who told me so! And you knew, didn't you, that I would believe you, because... Because for her sake, I wanted it to be true! You said she was touring, taking her performance all over the world, and appearing in glitz and glory, in the best concert halls, and to rave reviews, too! New York, Moscow, Tokyo... How, then, could you possibly be there, in the same place with her—"

"No," he says darkly. "You are not listening to me. Now, it is hard enough to tell the truth—and even harder to tell it when you have already decided to block it out."

"Here I am, listening," I say, waving both hands in the air, and bowing to him, mockingly. "See, here? I am listening now."

"I was there, Ben, sitting by her bedside, even as she was writing to you. That's how I know. And," he adds, "I came prepared. I brought a stack of papers with me, and an envelope, you see, with your address already typed in, so I would not have to bring a stack of envelopes as well; which saved her the trouble, so she would not have to copy that, too."

He tries to read gratitude in my eyes—but I know that he cannot find it, because there is nothing there but a burning accusation.

"Then you lied to me, both of you!" I cry. "You made an idiot, a complete fool out of me! There was no tour? No travel around the world, no concerts, even? And what about the reviews?"

My father bites his lip, and with each one of the questions I shoot at him, his teeth leave deeper marks; which brings out the rage in me, and I point a finger at him, and pass my judgement. "You!" I bellow. "You always hide things from me."

"Well, no. Not always," he corrects me. "Did I not tell you, just last night in fact, that she was brought to the hospital, to visit me? That she sat there, beside me? That she touched my arm—"

"Aw, I thought you were just seeing things."

"No, son. No. Now, we are talking reality."

"Reality?" I laugh, with an acid tone. "What is that, really?"

"Your mom," says my father, "never left town. Now, that is reality. And," he adds, "she never bothered to take her grand piano out of here. Have you never asked yourself, Why is it still here?"

After a moment of confusion, I demand, "So then, where is she?"

And glancing at me cautiously, without committing to specifics, he offers, "It is a nice place, Ben, a pleasant one, really."

"What is the name of it?"

"Sunrise Assisted Living."

"What? Assisted Living?" I scream. "You fucking bastard! How dare you put mom in a place like that?"

All of a sudden—even as I curse him—I remember how mom contemplated such a place for uncle Shmeel who, at the ripe age of ninety, was still living by himself. She felt a bit uneasy about the whole thing, I mean, having to decide the fate of the old man, who in the end would blame her, with great bitterness, for the loss of what he cherished most: his independence.

She sifted through a list of these so-called homes, muttering that they were designed for people in the last stretch of life; which is why the name *Infinity Home* was so insidious, and the name *Our Sweet Home* was, at best, misleading—as was the name *Sunrise*.

"Sunrise?" I say deridingly. "That place is for old people. Not for Mom!"

"Indeed," says my father. "She was only thirty-nine when I noticed it for the first time. I remember: she gave me a look as though she did not understand what I had just said. Then I noticed that from time to time, she had trouble saying the names of her students. She seemed unsure about names. A year later, she could not remember the word Piano. Can you imagine that, Ben?"

I shrug, "Anyone can forget a word here and there."

But he would not let me deny it.

"No," he insists. "Not a woman with her musical gifts! The way she used to play, Natasha could have become world famous, one of the greatest concert pianists! How, how could that happen? Ben, how could your mom forget *Piano*?"

At a loss for a better answer, I suggest, "Maybe she was under stress?"

"She was terrified," he says. "At first, they prescribed antidepressants. Then she took antibiotics for six months, to treat what doctors thought might be Lyme disease. The neurologist suggested an MRI scan, a scan of the brain. But then, when the results came in, they said that at this point, there was no way to tell whether there was anything wrong, or whether Natasha's brain had always looked that way."

Now I feel I cannot absorb, cannot take much more of this—but there is no stopping him. The sentences keep pouring out, as if a dam has broken in him.

"The most difficult aspect," says my father, "was that we used to be a team—but now I had to start making the decisions on my own. All except one: she was determined to divorce me, which was my fault—but her mistake, because unfortunately, she deteriorated so much faster after that."

"Stop right there," I tell him. "It makes no sense to me! Why would she want to leave you right then, at the turning point of her life, when you could be there, by her side, fighting to hold her back, away from the brink?"

"This," says my father, "is something I, too, do not understand. Up to that point Natasha has changed, quietly, and grown so much stronger than me, to the point that, no matter how hard I tried, there was no pleasing her. Then she got word, somehow, about my moment of weakness: my fling, this little, one-night thing—that was all it was, back then—with Anita."

I look at him as if to say, Who cares about your moment of weakness? So far it has lasted ten years.

He looks away, saying, "Your mom, she was mad at me. She flared up in anger. It was painful. More painful than I had expected. Was she too proud to forgive me? Did she expect me to fight harder for her, so that she may take me back someday? There was no way to know. My God, she let me feel I was done, I was no longer needed."

"But, dad," I say, "did she believe she could face it alone, whatever *it* was? Was she willing to risk everything, and for what? For no better reason than pride?"

"God," he says. "I wish I knew."

"Enough," I say. "I don't want to hear it."

"That's just the thing, Ben. Natasha kept quiet, all these years, and so did I, for her sake. Gradually, her memory problems got worse and yet, no one knew: not our friends, not even her students, because she was so afraid, afraid to lose them. Teaching, for her, became more than a livelihood: it was the last token of her independence."

"You should have told me, dad."

"Well, how could I? There was no one here to whom I could talk."

"So, since then, has mom been diagnosed?"

"Well, son, it took a long time," he says, in a tired tone of voice, "Four years after she had left me, that was when they found out, at long last. And you, Ben, you were in Europe then, off to your medical studies, or something, with a light suitcase, and a heart heavy with anger, who knows why."

I want to say, Because I had to go, to be some place else. Because I had no family, with you cheating and mom throwing her wedding ring away. That's why. But without waiting for an explanation, my father moves on to say, "I just could not do it, could not bring myself to open up, to tell you about it."

Suddenly his voice trembles, and he wraps his arms around me, which makes me unsure if this is to lean on me—or perhaps, to protect me.

"Ben," he says, "this disease, unfortunately, it can strike in the prime of life. Natasha was forty-six when, after years of knowing that something was going terribly wrong, and not being able to put a finger on it, they finally diagnosed her."

"And," I hesitate to ask, "does it have a name?"

There is a sound by the entrance door, then a knock, once, twice, three times—but neither one of us moves. There is a somber expression on his face. His gaze is locked into mine, and something passes between us which I cannot express in words.

Meanwhile, between one knock and another there is a smaller sound: the click of the clock. Under the glass crystal, the black hand moves around the dial, from one minute mark to the next. It advances with a measured beat, the beat of loss, life, fear —until at long last, my father takes a long breath, and allows himself to say, "The doctors, they call it Early onset Familial Alzheimer's disease."

Then he passes by me on his way to open the door; which gives me a moment to think of mom.

I picture her staring at the black-and-white image of her brain, not quite understanding what they are telling her.

The doctors, they point out the overall loss of brain tissue, the enlargement of the ventricles, the abnormal clusters between nerve cells, some of which are already dying, shrouded eerily by a net of frayed, twisted strands. They tell her about the shriveling of the cortex, which controls brain functions such as remembering and planning.

And that is the moment when in a flash, mom can see clearly, in all shades of gray blooming there, on that image, how it happens, how her past and her future are slowly, irreversibly being wiped away—until she is a woman, forgotten.

So when aunt Hadassa pops her head through the door, and marches in followed by her sisters, and each one in turn brushes a finger across the console table to check for dust, I push by them with barely a nod. And before my father can say a word I bolt out, and hurl myself down the stairs.

I can hear him behind me, calling, "Ben! Ben!" And I know he is doing his best to limp, somehow, down the stairs, to try to catch up to me, because in his mind, this is an unfinished conversation. But by then, I am already running at full speed down the street, running away, far away from it all.

Where Was There

Chapter 9

As Told by Ben

I t is evening already, and a light breeze starts coming up from the Pacific Ocean, where the faraway, ruffled surface can be seen, mirrored—by some trick of twilight—in row after row of splashy store windows. And one intersection after another, a gust of wind blows, ever so gently, across my path. I wish it would lash its tail. I wish it would turn vicious. A storm would have been perfect, really.

Since noon—more precisely, since that conversation with my father, from which I was fortunate enough to break away—I have spent hours running in circles, trying not to think about what I have learned from him, and about having to face her, because maybe it is not mom I would be facing, but her illness.

I have been bouncing back and forth between Abbot Kinney and Wilshire, losing myself in a web of streets. Some places, especially those close to Santa Monica bay, seem vaguely familiar. I figure I must have visited them a long time ago, as a child. My hands still keep the memory, the touch of wet sand, and the sequence of scooping it, packing it tightly into a bucket, turning it upside down, away from the wave rolling in, then lifting the bucket away to see a castle take shape. But on the whole, gazing at this town now from a higher elevation, I feel detached.

A foreigner, that's me: unwanted and unwelcome in a strange, foreign place.

Car horns can be heard honking as I dart across the street. From time to time a police car cruises by my side and I can sense a quick, curious glance, which I ignore. I have no idea where the hell I am going; which makes attacking the streets with such anger, such blind, aimless haste a bit confusing, because of being unable to tell whether I have arrived—or whether I am still at the outset of a new ramble.

Between one footfall and another I am not here, I am not there: neither at the end of a journey, nor at the beginning.

Forced to slow down I push my way through the thick of a crowd, some of which are walking about without a care in the world other than nibbling on candy bars, sipping expensive coffee out of paper cups, chatting loudly about nothing in particular, and checking out the jewelry stores, boutiques, nail salons and massage parlors, all of which abound here, in this affluent neighborhood near Montana; while others, the outcasts among us, are beginning to shrink away, fading stealthily into dark corners, to prepare themselves for the coming of the night.

These *others* are lonesome, faceless figures. Right there, where the shadows of one streetlamp crisscross the shadows of another, a panhandler is unfolding his torn piece of cardboard on the pavement, stiffly laying his limbs on it. In the alley, some distance away, another layabout is arranging a foul-smelling, brown blanket on some rotting sofa, with the stuffing ripped out of it, which someone has discarded next to the trash cans. In a minute he will be not just covered—but entirely erased from view.

My pace has picked up again. I am running furiously, as if chased by ghosts. By now I find myself not only drifting, not only lost, and not only short of cash, which I have left back there, in my bedroom—but above all, short of breath; all of which are better, in my opinion, than turning around to find my way back home. I am utterly driven to go astray.

So I push myself farther and farther away, sickened at the mere thought of that place, where the whitewashed facade of the two-story apartment building, built in the 50's, seems to conceal some secrets; where—behind this or that window—you can spot an eye taking a peek, following you through a crack between the blinds; and where inside, the air is stale.

Home. That is the place where, ten years ago, the gossip surrounding my family, together with the silence, that sudden muteness between my parents, drove me to despair. So I tried to distance myself from both of them. At the age of seventeen I thought I would go crazy—or else, to escape madness, take my own life.

The walls had been closing in on me, and even more so—on my mom. I remember the last time we talked, which was also the last time I was given the chance to hug her—and missed it.

It was well after midnight and my homework was still far from complete, when suddenly, inspiration struck: I came to the realization that come what may, trigonometry was not a subject in which I would ever excel. I might as well drop out of school. No one would miss me there.

So for a while I sat idly in my bedroom, scribbling and looking blankly out the window, after which I closed my notebooks with a slap. And then, on my way to the bathroom I noticed her door, which was slightly ajar, and through which I could hear some noise. Mom was packing a suitcase.

"Ben?" she said. "As long as you are still up, can you do me a favor? Bring me that thing from there—"

"What?" I asked, reluctantly; which made her turn her back to me and say, "Oh, never mind. I will do it myself."

I repeated, this time more willingly, "What, mom?" And a minute later, "I am already here, so let me help," followed with, "please, mom," but to no avail. "That's all right," she stated. "Never mind. I'll do it myself. It would be easier than having to explain."

I resented the way she said it, which allowed me to go back to my room—but at the same time, placed a weight on my shoulders, saddling me with the burden of guilt. Back then, nothing was more annoying than, "Never mind. I will do it myself." I wondered, why would she ask for my help—only to reverse herself immediately, and refuse it? Was it her way to needle me? To show the extent of my weakness, laziness, dependence? To match it with an equal measure, the measure of her sacrifice?

Quite often mom would frustrate me by insisting on doing it herself—whatever *it* was—and each time, for a slightly different variant of the same basic reasoning: because she wanted the thing to be done right, or because she was afraid it would be too heavy for me, or too hot to handle, or something.

Play. Rewind. All these years I have been playing her voice over and over in my head, rewinding this last conversation, and tormenting myself by focusing on the wrong phrase: the one at the end.

"Never mind. I'll do it myself."

Now—only now, at nightfall—do I realize my mistake. Suddenly, as if discovering a new twist in an old piece of music, I can detect a certain note of stress, right there, from the beginning, the moment she opened with the phrase, "Bring me that thing from there."

So I slow down the replay, and listen carefully to each one of these words—only to wonder about the other words, the unspoken ones, those that were missing, strangely, from the conversation. What *thing*? Where was *there*? Why would doing it be easier than having to explain? And how could I be so dumb as to miss the early, telltale signs, back then when she started forgetting things?

Simple things, such as the names of her students, and how to teach music, or play Beethoven's fifth. And later, how to put words on paper, and mail me a letter, and why not call me, why not tell me the truth; and how to talk to him, to my father; and most of all, how to forgive betrayal.

So for me, home is where her illness has been buried, up to now, under a thin, undisturbed layer of memories.

Or should I call them lies.

I think that in the future, I should refrain from talking to my father, and especially, from asking him any more questions about her. Let him not upset that image, which I have been striving so hard to construct, the image of mom, framed by their life together, because if this image collapses, so will I.

Still, I am unsure if her forgetfulness should be called an illness. Those doctors, they could have made a mistake. Two years in medical school taught me one thing, which is how terribly easy it can be to make an incorrect diagnosis. I recall a study of brain autopsies, in which roughly half of those diagnosed with Alzheimer's before death did not, in fact, show any evidence, I mean, evidence of the right degree of brain lesions to support the diagnosis.

If there is one illness which—in this case—seems too far-fetched, it would be Alzheimer's. My mother is now in her early fifties: much too young, I think, for anything like that.

Yesterday, arriving at LAX, I hoped this could be a short visit, short enough just to take my father out of the hospital and make sure he is all right. I planned to spend no more than a week—but now, now that I know more about mom, and about where she is, I may have to stay longer and think about my next steps.

At this point, the crowd has thinned out to the point of disappearing altogether, somewhere there, in the distance behind me. Looking straight ahead I can see the outlines of two or three runners, jogging along the wide grass median, which is splitting the traffic. And in a few minutes they, too, have receded from view.

I look around me and suddenly, I know where I am.

This is San Vicente Boulevard, where homes are known to be among the most expensive in Los Angeles County, and the people living in them are so fantastically rich and so content and successful that you, a mere mortal, can never catch even a glimpse of them, because of the barriers of carefully trimmed vegetation, and the towering trees, and the fancy fences, and the locks behind locks, gates within gates.

You can only imagine the picturesque views spreading before them out of their back yards, views of the Pacific Ocean or the Santa Monica Canyon, which must give them great joy, and persuade them to stay there, nestled in their safe, secluded existence.

The reason I know this place, the reason it ignites such emotion, such passion in me, is not the sight of these homes—but the majestic trees, whispering in the night air. Planted at regular intervals along the median, as long as the eye can see, they are named *Naked Coral Trees*. *Naked* because—according to my father—they shed their leaves annually.

I know this because at the age of fifteen I used to come here with him, every Saturday for an entire spring. During that period he worked for the Landmark Division of the City of Santa Monica, reviewing applications for the Landmark Designation of trees. To this day I have no idea what that means.

Dad talked little about his job, and cared for it even less. He was a writer at heart, and during spells of unemployment he would do two things: at night, scribble furiously in his notebook, and during the day, acquire new skills—which he did with great ease—and change his line of work, trying to make do until someday, some fine day when he would strike gold with his yet unfinished book.

During our walks that spring, dad would point out the tree: Its fiery red flowers, that looked like fat pinecones at the tips of irregular, twisting branches, and the seeds, which in certain species were used for medicinal purposes by indigenous peoples. The seeds were toxic, he warned, and could cause fatal poisoning. I learned that mature Coral trees should be watered frequently—but not during the summer months. In fact, he said, the less water in summer, the more flowers you can expect the following spring.

I cross two lanes of traffic, come closer to one of those Naked Coral Trees, and with great awe, brush my fingers across the trunk. It is a contorted, elephantine thing, with a roughly textured bark, and thick roots clinging fiercely to the earth. This being early October there are no flowers, no leaves, even. The tree seems to take on a humanoid appearance, as if it were the body of a character, or even several characters, mangled beyond recognition.

It is a stunning sight, which has fascinated me since childhood. Above me, the bare limbs—some of which have been pruned recently—are branching apart, and looking at them you can imagine a knee here, an elbow there, someone wrestling, someone in embrace.

As you walk past them, the trees seem to tell you a story line by line, scene by scene. In one tree I could see a man and a woman, kissing; in another, a father and son.

I remember one time, during our Saturday stroll, I asked my father for some details about his family. At first he seemed relaxed enough to tell me—at more length than usual—about my grandfather, whom I never met, because he had died long before I was born. I got a distinct sense that dad was, somehow, still afraid of the old man, who had pressed him hard to achieve that which he himself had failed to become: a lawyer.

"So," I asked, "what did you do?"

A brief laughter erupted on his lips. "I told him that I had registered at the university, and would be majoring in Law, just as he had always wished—but somehow I neglected to mention that the closest I ever came to registering was flipping through an outdated course catalog, while sitting on the toilet, and dreaming about something else."

"And," I hesitated to ask, "did he ever find out?"

"Well," said my father, and in a flash, his face turned red, "if it occurred to the old man that this might have been a nasty lie, he admirably concealed it."

I listen to his voice, which is still here, echoing in my head, and all of a sudden I grasp that he grew embarrassed not only because of his obligation to his father—but to me as well. Perhaps a sudden sense of shame caught up to him, shame for falling short of becoming an acceptable role model. Or else he had a premonition—a fear, even—of how I would treat him, not too far in what was then the future.

Which makes me realize one thing: up to a certain point, I wanted to become a man just like my father. And from then on, I wanted to be anything but. Which made me spend a whole decade in diametrical opposition to him, so that I wound up living a life based directly on his, as though I had never left home.

At daybreak I wake up, snuggled there between the roots at the foot of the tree, to a sharp pang of hunger; which drives me back home.

After a brisk walk I turn into 10th street, and the moment I spot the apartment building, the sprinklers in the garden come alive: first with an intermittent stutter, and then with a full-throated singsong; which makes me take a step back, and notice a rainbow hovering, trembling there, in the spray of water.

It brings back a moment, an unforgettable moment of that morning, ten years ago, when my mother walked out slowly—with her head held high—as if she was blind to the splash.

Now I wonder if mom knew where she was going. What was her goal, her direction? Where, in God's name, was her *there*?

I remember how her wet dress clung to her body, and how she receded into the distance with her packed suitcase, which seemed to become soggy after a few steps, never once stopping to wipe it, or to turn her head back.

Her tears are still here, in the rainbow. I wait for the nozzle to go through its circular motion, and then slip past it, sensing the last of the mist, right here on my skin. At that moment I imagine myself crossing right through her ghost. Perhaps there is a touch, a light touch between us.

I feel a breath of air as she fades away and I come in.

Without asking a single question, my father opens the door and to my surprise, he wraps his arms around my shoulders. The old clock starts ringing its alarm. It startles him, brings him to a halt for a minute—but then, with great relief, he kisses me; which makes me mumble, "Were you waiting up for me? Really? Oh. Sorry, dad. I guess I was lost."

"Lost?" he says. "Here, in Santa Monica? How do you manage to do that? This city is no bigger than two miles in any direction—"

"It takes time," I have to admit. "It takes concentration. And above all, it takes some kind of effort."

Keeper of Secrets

Chapter 10

As Told by Anita

T he bleeding was real bad last night, and there wasn't no one there I could call for help—or so I thought. I've managed to slip off the bed, and go wandering around the apartment, supporting myself, somehow, along the walls.

I get myself a drink of water. At first, all's black around me—except for the two luminous tips, which mark the hands of the alarm clock down there, in the hall.

Me, I can't hear no breathing and no snoring nowhere in this place, which makes me shudder, shudder at the thought that what I've feared all along is happening, perhaps, right at this moment: I'm trouble, I mean, too much trouble for him, so Lenny must have gone. He's left me here, so now I'm all alone in this place. Abandoned.

Them blinds, they're flapping, beating against each other in the breeze, down there across the sliding glass door, which is slightly open, and lets some cold air into the living room. And sneaking in, between one blind and another, come thin streaks of moonlight, which fill me with fear.

They look just like swords, advancing stealthily across the floor, giving a sudden, silvery flash when you least expect it, and like, aiming their blades at that hateful, monstrous thing, which seems so much bigger in the dark: her piano.

I drag myself away from the light of the moon. Exhausted, I flop onto the bench. I stare at the polished top of the piano, which seems to radiate from the shadows, and where, I know, there's a long, twisty scratch. For sure Lenny blames me for it. He's cross with me, most of the time. And I bet he won't never forgive me, on account of that mistake, which I made nearly three weeks ago, at the wedding:

I should've kicked off my high heels, or at least, pointed them away, so they would hover, like, just above the surface, when—in front of everyone—I laid myself down on top of the damn thing.

And maybe it wasn't a mistake exactly, 'cause for Lenny, the piano is so much more than a musical instrument, which makes me hate it. I really do. Me, I can't exactly explain it—but like, I wish it would disappear, or break down, or something.

I remember the first morning I spent here, in this apartment, a month after his wife had left him. I sat down right here, on this bench in front of her piano, which looked whiter than white, because it was displayed against the background of a silvery blue wallpaper, which buckled at the seams, here and there.

With great caution I brushed my fingers lightly across them keys. And from the belly of the beast a sound came, shaking the air, a soft, low grumble ending with a hum; which startled me.

Facing me was her notebook, with a beautiful signature, which had plenty of twists and turns across the cover, and which was kinda hard to read—but at last I could make it out as *Natasha*. Next to the notebook was an old picture of her. I could see right away that she could easily be mistaken for my sister: her face was just like mine, and so was the red hair.

A majestic bust—the bust of Beethoven—perched above me. At the time I didn't hardly know who or what Beethoven was. Anyhow, I was so scared that it made my hair curl. The bust seemed to gaze fiercely at the air with them marble eyes, eyes as intense as they was vacant. I turned around and could see Lenny, right there on the sofa, looking at me strange like, as if he was seeing some ghost.

He came over and sat down on the bench right here, beside me, and turned the photograph over, to hide his wife from me and perhaps, from himself. I thought he would put his arm around me, so we could start kissing—but instead, he took a long time to explain about them keys, and studied my fingers carefully, which made me feel awkward, and sorry, too. Sorry that my fingers wasn't longer, and sorry that I couldn't spread them apart no wider, the way Natasha could, being a pianist.

I was real sorry that my thumb looked kinda thick, which meant I was a simple, earthy girl. This, according to my ma. She ought to know: years ago—before being hired as a cleaning lady —ma had worked in Venice Beach, down at the boardwalk, as a fortune teller.

I remember her eyes. They looked downright stunning under the false eyelashes. As part of her gig, she would read the palm of my hand and like, shake her head with great concern for my future, so the hoop earrings would tinkle, as would the beaded necklaces and the jangle bracelets. Then her fake crystal ball would light up, at which time she would take firm hold of my hand and like, raise it up inside her fist, to show the crowd gathering around us how my thumb looked, how stubby it was, and how my lifeline, there on the palm of my hand, had an unusual, split end.

This scared me, really—because me, I was only seven years old back then—and it made some of the onlookers drop their jaws, like, in great awe.

They would come even closer, and press around us, eager to gain some insight into their own fate, and into each line on their palms and each little mark, and what all of them things could possibly mean. For a good price, ma would give out advice—mixed in with some warnings—which she crafted, like, in vague, immensely puzzling phrases.

But then, she didn't explain what the trouble was, exactly, with the split end of my lifeline; which left me kinda wondering. For sure ma couldn't tell, back then, that I would hook up with someone like Lenny: a married man who had a son a year older than me.

Now, in spite of sitting right next to me, Lenny didn't notice no problem with the shape of my thumbs; which was lucky, 'cause he raised his eyes for a second to the bust of Beethoven, and then, with a sudden spunk, like he was about to take a long, difficult leap, asked me if I wanted to learn how to play music.

And I said yes, 'cause I was sixteen, going on seventeen, and so I hoped that my hands could still grow a little, and maybe with some practice, my fingers could kinda stretch out, and become as long and as nimble as Natasha's. And then, perhaps, he would stop comparing us to each other all the time in his head, and—to my relief—he would give up trying to mold me, like, in her shape.

Let me be me, Lenny. Just let me be who I am.

During the next few days, I toyed with the idea of enrolling in a Beginning Piano class in Santa Monica College. Lenny was real eager about it, and he even paid the tuition fee for me, and promised it was gonna open me up to a world of wonder, and inspire me, and teach me about them notes, and about rhythm, chords, and pedaling, and how to apply them basics to classical music.

But then, a few weeks later, when I came back from the first class session, he changed his tune, perhaps because I made the mistake of testing my power over him:

I told him that I'd met two young students in class, one of whom had said, "So what d'you say, let's have some beer after class?" and the other had offered to carry my books, which immediately sparked a big fight between them.

And the music professor, he tried to pull them apart, and by accident, he got in-between them—in the line of fire, so to speak —which left him with a big bruise right there, under his eye. And sadly, he couldn't explain things as clearly as I'd hoped, on account of having to press a big icepack to his face.

Lenny tightened his lips, and when I saw his face my heart fell inside me.

I told him, real honest, that I'd ended up carrying my own books, and never had no beer with anyone but him, and that I didn't need no handsome boys when I already had him, that he was a grown-up, a smart, accomplished man, and that—no matter what happened—I would be his, only his, if only he would have me.

And while saying that, I opened my arms to him—but still, Lenny remained kinda distant, and he had an unfamiliar look on his face, which I couldn't figure out, like he didn't want nothing to do with me. The pleat in his forehead deepened and then, all of a sudden, he burst out with, "It is over, Anita."

Me, I didn't cry, didn't beg, didn't ask for no explanations, or hit him on the chest, even. Instead, I just froze there for a moment, with my arms still hanging, like, wide open in the air, and something went—boom!—exploding in my heart; after which I finally stirred, and went to the bedroom to collect my things, and looked for my hot pink high heels, which had rolled there, deep under the bed.

I stuffed them shoes into my backpack, along with my low-cut blouse and a pair of jeans and the course catalog, without wasting no time—not even once—to wipe my tears with my sleeve.

Lenny came right after me and leaned on the bedroom door, to stop me from bolting out. And he said, now in a changed voice, "Wait, Anita. It is not what you think."

So I slapped the backpack over my shoulders, and got up and rose to the tips of my toes to kiss him—long and hard—on his mouth, so he would have something to remember me by. And then I stormed past him, pushing my way out.

He rushed to the balcony, and from there, leaning over his desk, he cried after me, "Anita, stop! Just stop, will you? Let me explain..."

And running to the street I cried back, for the whole neighborhood to hear, 'cause I wasn't the one who had something to hide, "Forget it, Lenny! I don't want no explanation from you—not now, not ever!"

Which was the moment he said, and his voice sounded pretty painful, even from the distance, "She is back. That is why it is over. It just has to be over, now."

This marked the beginning of turmoil, of several years full of doubts and suspicions, with more ups-and-downs than the Ferris Wheel, down there on the Pier, and the Roller Coaster, combined. His wife, Natasha, came back, and she stayed for a while. Then she went away, finding a place to live here and there, perhaps with one of her girlfriends or with aunt Hadassa, or elsewhere.

And each time I moved back in with Lenny, she managed, somehow, to return. And me, I had to leave, 'cause like, I didn't want to have to face her. So I went back home to ma's place, swearing I won't want to see him no more. Finally, about five years ago, she left, this time for good, but like, who knows. And since then I haven't heard nothing about her—not from Lenny, not from anyone else.

Meanwhile, I've gone ahead with the Piano course, even though I've given up any hope on extending my stubby thumb, or growing my fingers any longer. And from time to time I would buy some piano sheet music for beginners, like *Caprice* by Paganini, and practice it—but only in school, and never when he's around, 'cause them keys, they may stick under my fingers, which would make my song stutter—and Lenny expects me to be perfect. He expects me to be her.

Which is why—in spite of me working so hard to try, to become better—he still complains.

Like, I've learned more ways to say things, and improved my vocabulary. I'm awful proud of saying *vocabulary*; which in plain talk means I have a lot of new words up here, in my head, which can confuse me sometimes, and even leave me speechless— unless I sound them out loudly, right away. Even so, Lenny says that my grammar is atrocious. I am, in his words, a *work in progress.* I wonder if she ever felt as choked by him—I mean, by what he expects—as I do.

And so I'm sitting here in the dark, in front of her piano, folded over my stomach because of this sharp pain, which makes me scared silly. I wish ma was here, 'cause like, even if she would give me a good slap, still, at least I could feel a touch, which would be better than this sorry state of being here, in the back of beyond.

Me, I'm so lonely I want to wail, to cry, to wash away the hurt— but my eyes, they're burning. They're dry, like, completely. I guess that being depressed is so much better when you can't shed a tear.

So instead I raise my head and with wild, vicious force, I bang my forehead, then bang it again against the keyboard. I'm free now, so free to attack it. The beast wakes up, and from its belly springs a sharp, fierce cry, which makes the air tremble in bursts, short bursts coming at me, doubled by echoes from every wall, every corner.

Meanwhile, in the background, I can hear them blinds, like, smacking each other, and giving way, suddenly, to a gust of wind. And there, in the opening of the glass door, which leads to the balcony, I spot his outline, standing behind the tape recorder.

The moonlight shines briefly on his shoulders as Lenny crosses the threshold. With a slight limp he makes his way in, and leans over my shoulders. And I can feel his strong arms wrapping around mine, arresting me, blocking my attempt to bang, bang, bang the keys. He turns me around—but me, I try to refuse him, and I fight like a savage, like a cat, and something surges in me, so in my fury I push him, I shove him away real hard, till he falls to his knees before me.

It's then that he locks his hands around me, and all of a sudden he lays his head, so tender like, in my lap. And there, in the dark, I touch his forehead, surprised to find not only the usual pleat—the one that brings back to me a memory of my pa—but a few more wrinkles, screwed up over his eyes. Which makes me figure out his expression: tormented.

So I hold myself back from saying, Where was you, I was awful lost here, all by myself for so many hours, and I thought that for sure, you've gone away. And instead I caress him, and take his face between my hands, and smooth his forehead with a kiss, asking, "What is it, what happened? Lenny, you crying?"

In place of an answer he fumbles in his shirt pocket, and from there gets his bifocals—even though the only thing to see here, in the darkness, is a patch of moonlight, which is blurry anyway, even with perfect vision; and the only thing to read is my face.

He puts the glasses on, like, to hide behind them; which makes me wonder. During the last ten years I've learned there's something about his wife, Natasha, something he conceals not only from me, but from his son, even. So I reckon it must be laying heavily on his mind.

"Oh, Lenny," I say, "just tell me what it is, will you? How hard can it be, to stop being the keeper of secrets?"

"I am worse than that," he says. "I am the inventor of lies."

"You're a writer," I shrug. "So, you make things up. What's so wrong with that?"

He turns away from me to wipe something in his eye, which makes me figure that he's shutting himself off.

So I try again. This time I say, "Let me read your stories."

"No," he says. "My writing is not the place where the fiction is."

"But Lenny," I plead, "don't you think you could make things so much easier, for you and me and everyone else, if only you said something real, like, if you told me the truth?"

He shakes his head, refusing me, trying to pull himself out of my hold, which makes me lose my balance and fall to my knees opposite him, right there on the floor, between the claws of the piano, so that now we're face to face.

There's more light now, which brings out more of him. And so, seeing him in such an agony I say, "You've taught me so much, Lenny. I note every one of your words, especially the ones I don't hardly get. I repeat them in my head, so that later I can figure out what they mean, and even use them, instead of just saying *things*."

"All I know," he blurts out, "is this: the words you learn—she forgets."

He don't really name her—but we both recognize who it is he's talking about. By now I know that Lenny knows that I don't want no explanations from him, no matter how hard he gets, or how closed his face becomes. I'm not one to pry—but then again, maybe the time's come for him to try, like, try to confide in me. Maybe prying things open isn't such a bad idea.

And so I suggest, "Why not tell me something about her?"

"No," he says, biting his lips. "I have said too much already."

Me, I watch him in silence, and before I can say nothing he adds, "No. There is no way for you to understand, to take in what she is going though."

"Maybe not," I say. "But just, try me."

"No," he repeats, a third time. "Yesterday, I tried to tell Ben, which was a mistake, a big mistake. Oh hell... What kind of a father am I? I should have kept my mouth shut, because since then he has left, and stayed out all night, who knows where. And with these legs under me, I can do no better than sit there, on the balcony with the tape recorder, and just, let my mind wander... *Rewind, Play, Rewind, Play*... I will never forgive myself if —"

"*Stop*, just stop it! Stop torturing yourself," I cut in. "Maybe he just needs some time alone."

He turns his head away, over his shoulder, and glances at the thin, vertical intervals, right there between them blinds. By now you can start to detect, as if by reflection, a balcony. It's kinda identical to ours, and cast back from the other building, the building directly there, opposite us.

It seems like Lenny's trying to guess—by the graying of the dark—how much time until daybreak. He presses the sides of his head, till a vein flares up on his temple, pulsing there between the nails of his fingers.

"If anything happens to Ben it would be on me. It would be entirely my fault. My God," he says. "I should have buried the whole thing, and kept it there, in the grave."

He don't speak no more after that.

By now, the night is almost gone. It's peeling away, like an old, silvery blue wallpaper, rolling in from the corners. There, in the balcony facing us, an old woman comes out in a loosely tied bathrobe, rubbing her eyes, kinda sleepy. She waters her plants, floods her dry geranium, then goes back inside, pulling the sliding glass door shut behind her, with a long, deafening screech.

Lenny winces. I can tell: this isn't what he's listening for.

Now, more familiar sounds: a car is being started in the parking area, making a knocking noise, 'cause it's an old clunker and the engine is still cold. Finally it lurches, somehow, into the street and you can hear it like, turning away, even as the brakes of another car is being stepped on, followed by a sudden, rubbery squeal.

This isn't what he's listening for.

It's Morning. You can hear water gushing through the pipes inside the walls, because there, in the apartment next door, someone has just started taking a shower. Meanwhile, in the garden below, the sprinklers come on, spluttering water one spit after another.

This isn't what he's listening for.

For him, all them sounds are being drowned out by the tick, the incessant tick, tick, tick of the old alarm clock. The little hammer on top of it is idle, and so is the twin bells. They're just hanging there, left and right of the hammer, reflecting this whole room, and the piano, and us, too. We seem so unlike ourselves, bent out of shape in their brass finish.

So tense, so distorted, so small.

It's almost six. The hour hand's dropped down, as if defeated, at last, by the force of gravity, a force which the minute hand is still trying to fight. Now it seems to have come to a stop. It's stuck there, just short of its mark.

I stare at it thinking, I should get up from the floor already. I should take hold of the clock, ignoring its curvy surface, which shows a mirror image of my hand, and of my split lifeline. I should wind up the key, right there in the back of it, so that time's gonna move forward, and the little hammer at the top's gonna hurry up and at last, strike them bells.

Just then, quick footsteps can be heard, climbing the stairs. And by the rhythm I know who it is—and so does Lenny.

So we hold each other and struggle, somehow, to our feet, and I hand him his crutch so he can reach the entrance door, in a big hurry, and like, greet his son.

And watching him as he turns away from me, I think to myself, He's afraid, he don't want to tell me nothing—but still, I'm glad he's started to open the door for Ben.

Things could be so much simpler. If only...

How sad it is that at this moment, when Lenny is injured and here, behind him, I'm holding my belly because of this dull pain, this is the time we keep ourselves apart, in an effort, a lame effort to play our game, play it now in front of the boy, as if, I swear, as if all is well.

Oh, at last—the alarm! The ringing of them bells! The sound of laughter... How lonely it must be, to be the keeper of secrets, the inventor of lies.

In My Defense

Chapter 11

As Told By Anita

In my defense I have this to say: When men notice me, when the lusty glint appears in their eyes, which betrays how, in their heads, they're stripping me naked—it's me they accuse of being indecent.

Problem is, men notice me all the time.

How can a girl like me ever claim to be innocent? Even if I haven't done nothing wrong, I'm already soiled, simply because of their dirty thoughts.

And sometimes, it's because of their actions. Like the time I was twelve, and Johnny shoved me into the bathroom and pinned me to the floor. And afterwards, he pointed his finger at me, saying *I made him do it*, 'cause to him, I looked sexy, more sexy even than my ma, whom he was gonna take on a date, just as soon as she would come back from her evening shift and like, freshen up. But I, he said, was fresh anyhow.

So I try to forget the yellow stain at the foot of the toilet, and the hard, sticky floor, both of which took care of the freshness all right—but still, to this day I go on learning how to live with the blame.

And it don't matter, really, if I try to keep my eyes lowered, and stay out of the way, and wrap myself in something modest, like this old, rumpled blanket which I've just fetched from the sofa, 'cause any second now, they may be coming in here.

So I bundle myself, bringing the corners of the blanket under my arms, and tying them tightly over my breast, so the edge winds up gathering the flesh, a bit like the pleats of a curtain. Oh shoot, I don't hardly care! I've come to dislike the way I look, and dread that thing in me, which they see as a *power*—but I know as a curse.

The more bewitched they claim to be by the way I look—the more I reckon I'm in danger. I swear, I've had it up to here with men who say they was ruined by a woman.

In the end, they tend to recover, and one way or another build themselves back up. And they do it, without fail, by destroying her. So, like ma says: to keep myself out of trouble, and my name clean, it's *strength* that I need—not power.

Which is why I've turned away, the moment Ben came in and was kissed by his pa. I knew right away that I must put as much distance as I can between us. Even there, from across the room, I could feel, like, something which couldn't be denied, passing between his eyes and mine, behind Lenny's back.

Right now, Ben's trying to shrink away. His back's kinda bent, his shoulders—angled forward, like, to defend himself, in his own timid way, from his father, and from any further contact, any further show of love. And his gaze, hanging heavy under those long, dark lashes, seems so sad, so full of regret, because of a moment, a brief moment of joy being held in that embrace.

The features of his face, they're so fine. They seem to be penciled in. By some mother-like instinct—which is totally new to me—I can tell Ben's kinda lost. He's like a boy, longing to feel the worn-out, familiar feel of his mama's apron, and breathe her good smell, and just stand there, giving himself up, and crying, and waiting for her to wipe his wet face, and take away the hurt.

In my head I can only imagine how shocked he must feel—despite knowing about Lenny and me—to find me in this place, instead of his ma. You can tell he's swamped, totally swamped by this new reality, as well as by his memories, and like, hopelessly sunk in his daydreams. Somewhere deep inside, he wants me to be her.

I bet he has an old, vague image of his ma, from a long time ago. By the way he looks at me, I reckon he can find her, somehow, in my face. For him, I ain't here at all. I'm see-through.

When Ben realizes his mistake, he seems to become annoyed. I bet he's worried, worried about his ma, and about the past that keeps haunting him, keeps coming up to the surface. Me, I can't even define how he relates to me, exactly, 'cause it keeps changing. In the last two days, ever since I met Ben, I've found him confused—and confusing:

I pity him, seeing how consumed he is by desire. His entire body is like, burning up. And his eyes, they're fluttering around me until—like a moth heading, in a roundabout way, into a light source—they connect with mine. I can sense his hate sometimes, and at once pull back from him, 'cause I spot how hard his jaw is set, and even, how murderous the spark right there, in that shadow under his lashes, which reminds me of some animal, getting pretty tense, like, getting ready for the kill.

And so, while Lenny and his son huddle together by the door, exchanging words, I sneak out of the living room. First, I tighten the blanket again across my chest. Then I rush past them, across the hall and the corridor, and into the bedroom. From the closet

I pull out an ice-blue, long sleeve dress. It's hers—but all the same, I put it on. It fits. I'm safe. I'm shielded.

After a while I notice that their voices, which have been flaring out in heated talk, have given way to silence. So I crack my door open, and listen, and I can't hear nothing at all, so I tiptoe down the corridor.

And from here I catch sight of Lenny, lying there across the sofa. After a night with no sleep, fatigue must have caught up to him. His glasses, they're askew: one lens magnifies the high forehead, the other—his thinning, sleeked-back hair.

My heart aches, it goes out to him: his lips, they're tight even now, guarding the gate, like, the gate between being awake and dreaming. He don't talk in his sleep, not even a word—but right now a snore escapes, quite by surprise, from the corner of his mouth. His arms, they're folded across his chest, like he's holding himself prisoner.

And around the corner, there's a sound of steps, so I know Ben's there. He's pacing back and forth, this way and that around the walls, like, to measure his cage, same as his father.

I turn back and the minute I mount the bed, I hear someone rapping softly on the closed door, saying, "Anita?"

"What is it, Ben," I ask, bluntly. "What d'you want?"

His voice is muffled. "Nothing," he says. "I—I hope you are feeling better this morning," he says. "I think I am going out, in just a few minutes, to see my mother. I mean, to visit—"

Which takes me completely by surprise, 'cause since she disappeared, I've been waiting to hear word about Natasha. From time to time I would ask Lenny—only to get a kiss and nothing, nothing else in return. So, for the last five years I reckoned she don't want him to speak. I reckoned it's for her sake he's silent.

So now I fling the door open, and as I face Ben I let slip, "You gonna visit her? Like, where? I mean, she's back?"

"He did not tell you anything about her, did he," he says, stating rather than asking. I don't even have to say it, Ben knows. I can tell he's been through secrets. Like me, he's been fooled. He totally gets how it feels.

And so I have to lie, "Tonight, for sure, Lenny's gonna reveal everything. Really, I swear."

Ben tries to say something, which curls his lips in a strange way. If not for the bitter look, you could call it laughter. "Would you like to know? Would you? Would you want me to tell you," he advances, "right here, right now?"

"No," I insist, hoping he can't see through me. "I'd rather *he* did."

"I see," he shrugs.

And so I counter, "Do you," and then we're just waiting there, on each side of the threshold, not knowing what to say and where to go from here.

Finally Ben comes up with, "So here, here is something I wanted to ask you. Forgive me, I know nothing, really, about you —but please, try to put yourself in my place. Suppose you were going to visit your mother, and wanted to remind her, I mean, about the past. About your childhood, perhaps—"

"The past? My ma isn't too fond of that. I won't bring it up with her, if I was you—but of course, if you was to pay her, that's totally different: she used to be a fortune teller, for real. I bet she could tell you a thing or two about the future."

With a confused look, he passes a hand through his tousled hair, trying to smooth it the same way as his father—only in his case, it resists and falls right back, over his brow. "Please," says Ben. "Help me... There is no one else. I mean, no one I can trust. And it is not easy for me to try, to beg you for an answer. I find it nearly impossible, to seek advice like this, without giving up something, some information about my mother; which apparently, you do not even want to hear."

"So," I say, "just don't," which makes him angry.

"You," he snaps, "you must find all of this strange, and much too ambiguous."

"Ambigu-what?" I say. "Just tell me plainly, Ben: what is it you want?"

He stands there, kneading his hands, looking kinda torn. "Mom and I, we have not talked for a long while," he admits. "I want her to be able to look back, somehow... I mean, I want her not to forget. Now, how would you go about it?"

In spite of the pity I feel for him, I don't really want to help him. It's gonna go against me, 'cause Natasha is my enemy even when she isn't here. If she wanted to, I reckon she could take my power away.

Go, go away already, I tell him in my mind—but aloud I say, "Just talk to her. She's gonna get it."

"No, I am afraid she won't," he says, grimly.

Against my interest I pity him again, this time for being so full of doubts, and so sad, and most of all, isolated.

"Just tell her a story," I suggest. "Bring up something, anything from the heart."

"I cannot. I do not know how," he mumbles, painfully.

Me, I must be out of my mind to try to take him out of a tight spot; which in spite of myself, I'm getting closer to doing. "Think of something you share, both of you. You're gonna be surprised, she's gonna listen. She's gonna tell you stories about you, which you don't even know about yourself."

"No," he says, with a grave tone in his voice. "I doubt she can."

And I say, "Wait—wait here, don't move. I have an idea."

Which is the moment when, because of that stupid sense of pity, I ignore this feeling, down in my guts, that tells me to shut the door in his face. Instead, I make a bad mistake: leaving the it open I take a step back, and roll myself over the bed, all the way across, to Lenny's side. And from his drawer I pull out an album, a thick album with a metal clasp, which locks over the gilded edge of its pages, about which I know: I'm not supposed to know nothing.

Still, I can tell you that there's one picture, one special picture missing there, in the middle of the second page.

The reason I'm so sure about it, if you must know, is that it took me a few tries—first by trying to pick the corner, then by heating the glue with my hairdryer, which kinda damaged the surface, and later, by threading a floss under it—to remove the picture and finally, stash it away.

"Here," I say coming back, carrying the album to him. "You must know this album, right? Just look at it together, you and your ma. The rest's gonna come easy, I promise."

He smiles, like he's overcome by a thrill. As if being greeted by an old friend, he passes a hand, so tender like, over the cover, feeling the fine cracks in the leather, the raised spine.

Meanwhile, he lets me go on holding the thing. So by now I have to support it with both hands, it's awful heavy. At last I give up. I take a step back and sit there, on the edge of the bed. Ben draws closer. He unlocks the clasp. Now he's spreading the pages wide open, right here in my lap, over my wrists.

And together we look at the pages: how they're turning yellow along the edges, how brown spots are like, blossoming all over them, and how them photos look faded, even though they're protected, under the seal of clear plastic sheets. On each page there's glue, lined in strips. It holds the photos in place— but also, because of the acid in it, destroys them.

"God," he lets out. "It takes so much guessing to study these images. Just like a memory: you are left clinging to something which now, is no longer a record. Instead, it is just... Nothing. I mean, nothing more than a hint, a suggestion."

With a clap Ben shuts the album, and takes it off my hands, and slips it under his jacket. So now it's held in place by the close-fitting waistband, and pressed to his chest by both arms. Already I see him standing kinda taller, more erect than earlier this morning. I bet it's because of the weight, the extra weight he's carrying now, next to his heart.

Like ma says: the heavier the load—the more you straighten yourself. For me this is something new, something that only now that I'm pregnant, I begin to understand.

My hands, they're empty now, and like, I can't give him no help no more. Which wakes me up to a change: from the corner of his eye, he's looking down at me, and a glint flashes there, under his lashes, a glint which I've come to know all too well. It exposes his desire, his craving to touch me. To him, who cares what I have to lose. Like, who cares that I'm carrying a baby inside. Who cares whose wife I am, or whose son he is. Who cares how we got to this place.

Suddenly here we are: a man and a woman and nothing in between—other than a tremble in the air, and a thrill, the sharp thrill of danger.

In a blink of an eye I can see the trap, and I hate him for setting it up—even if he did so without intent. And I hate, hate, hate myself for being caught in it. Sooner or later, my innocence is gonna be called into question, and who's gonna believe a girl like me?

This brings back a memory of ma calling me *Bitch*, because of what happened back then, when I was twelve, between Johnny and me. Me, I argued with her, insisting that no, don't call me that, I get to decide who I am and what I am, and what I would be, I—and nobody else but me. And she countered that if he'd touched me, we already knew—beyond any doubt—what I'd become.

At this point the only thing, the only barrier that seems to make Ben stumble, and holds him back from taking me, is the sight of the dress—which Natasha used to wear—hanging stiffly, kinda like ice, over my body. I find myself grateful, awful grateful to her, 'cause in a way, she's shielding me.

This way, he can't strip me naked—not even in his mind.

So I gather my strength, and before he can pour out his feelings, and confess to have fallen, like, under my power, and tell me he's ruined, all because of me, I wave my hand and tell him to go, go away already.

Ben seems unhappy to be dismissed so casually. I bet he's thinking me cruel to him. He's asking himself, like, Why is the bitch playing so hard to get? She's drawn me here, to her bed— hasn't she? He seems so unsure about himself, about what, if anything, he is supposed to do now. But if he's feeling ashamed, it's not for wanting his old man's woman—but sadly, for what he considers his own flow, his show of impotence.

He hesitates, then turns slowly, to walk out of the bedroom; at which time I can swear I see an outline there, over his shoulder, far in the depth of the corridor. Maybe I'm seeing things, but—for just a second—I detect a flash, reflected like, in someone's glasses.

Down there in the shadow, someone's recording every detail, listening to every damn whisper of this scene.

Record. Play: a man and a woman, and nothing in between.

I want to ask, Is it you? Is it you, Lenny? Why ain't you coming to my help? But instead, I just slam the door shut. All I want to be is alone. Why do I feel guilty when I haven't done nothing wrong.

Then I raise the corner of the mattress, which is where I've stashed away that old picture, the one that was glued in the middle of the second page of the album. The sight of it calms me down, at first.

I pick it up and study every detail—like I've done so many times before—because like, the image may go on fading, until in the end, nothing's gonna be left. I'm so charmed by it. This moment delights me as if I had lived it, even though—or maybe because—it's stolen.

In it, a baby is about to be lifted from a cradle by his mama. His face, it's awful close to the surface—but barely visible. You can only guess it, 'cause the paper is a bit damaged, and most of the lines is like, out of focus—except for a dark contour, which is still intact, marking the shadow of his long, curved lashes.

I put a hand to my belly, and touch my lips to the image, right there, over that shadow. I wonder if this is how my baby's gonna look, and marvel at the thought of how his eyes would change when he wakes, or falls asleep, or rolls them, like, in the sphere of his dreams, and then later, when he grows up to become a man, 'cause it's so easy to fill in the details on a page that's like, almost blank.

On the other side, right there behind the cradle, the mother —whose lips, and cheeks, and freckled nose, they're all just like mine—she's leaning over him, with open arms.

Her face is serious, without the slightest smile. She's looking directly at the camera, at the one taking the picture, whom I've previously imagined to be Lenny—but today, I find a change in her. This time, it's me she is facing.

The way she looks at me is severe, critical, even disapproving. I bet it's because the laugh lines have dimmed with time. But then, her eyes! Oh God, they're so clear, so full of pure, glorious light; which, for a moment, brings me close to despair. I'm in awe. Look, I have goosebumps! The two of us look the same, just like sisters—but oh, how I wish I could be more like her!

Me, I don't have nothing more I want to say in my defense— except to ask you again: put yourself in my place. How can a girl like me ever claim to be innocent?

A Place Called Sunrise

Chapter 12

As Told by Ben

T his is no nightmare—but it sure feels like one. I am gritting my teeth, determined to find my mother among the inhabitants of this place. If not for having a purpose here I would pinch myself, even though I know: Here, there is no waking up.

I am so astonished, coming in, by the attention my arrival seems to stir in these listless figures—some sitting, some standing here and there, scattered around the large dining hall—all of whom look more dead than alive.

One of them, a figure with lean, spindly hands drags herself towards me, knuckling down on the handles of her walking frame. With each shuffle, each jerk forward, her veined, confused eyes keep widening, as if by some hope, some wishful recognition. And then she thrusts her hands to grab me, and in a hollow voice, "*Mine kind!*" she shrieks, "*mine kind!*" which as I recall, is Yiddish for *my child*.

The words reverberate across the space, and they seem to agitate everyone around me. Moaning there in the background, a bent figure stands up and then, like a bat out of hell, echoes that earlier shriek, "*Mine! Mine kind...*"

Another one, a seated figure hunching her shoulders over her empty hands, which are nestled in her lap, lifts her head for a moment to gape at me, and her mouth is black and utterly toothless. So now I begin to make sense of that which I thought I heard, even before the door opened: The trembling of her thin, strained voice.

It takes me a bit to take in the speech sounds, which are changed, because of the lack of teeth, and disjointed, because of an occasional catch, deep down in her throat. I am listening carefully—until at last I figure out that this, incredibly, is an old lullaby.

Twinkle... Twinkle... Little star... Her black mouth breathes slowly into the air, into the gathering of these bent, misshapen shadows, in whom life seems to be no more than a dim residue. *How... I wonder... What you are...*

What is this, I ask myself, what sort of a home have I entered? What is this place?

Meanwhile, standing there near the vase, by the long dining table, her busy hands covered with disposable plastic gloves, is a young staff member, dressed in a neat, light-blue nurse uniform. I should really say a *Care Giver*, which is what they prefer to be called around here, at Sunrise Assisted Living.

With swift, efficient movements, she is stretching open the mouth of a large garbage bag, replacing the flowers in the vase, wiping some spills off the Formica surface, and picking up spongy leftovers of white bread. I watch her for a while and finally make up my mind to approach her, and I ask— in a voice choked, suddenly, with excitement—about Mrs. Kaminsky.

"Who?" she says.

"Mrs. Kaminsky," I repeat. "Natasha? Natasha Kaminsky?"

"Oh," she says, and in place of an answer lifts her gloved hand and points over there, to a narrow window in the far corner of the room; where, slumped passively in a chair next to the bent figure, is my mother.

For a moment I cannot move, cannot even raise a hand to my heart, where it starts racing wildly, because I have to keep my grip, and clutch the photo album, which is hidden under my jacket, and which is quite heavy. It was Anita, my father's new wife, who suggested I bring it along, just in case we may stumble, my mother and I, into a moment of embarrassment, or run out of things to talk about.

That woman, how can she offer advice when she knows nothing, really.

I dash towards mom, wondering how I failed to notice her just a minute ago, because clearly, she looks younger, I mean, younger than the rest of them, by two or three decades, at least. Mom is in her early fifties and so, she seems out of place here. Perhaps I should take her back home.

She must have been hidden from view, perhaps by that bent figure, whose skeletal arms hang there, shivering over her shoulders. So going around him I come closer to my mother, and now I can see her profile, which is lined so delicately with light, the late morning light streaming in through the glass.

Her eyelashes, which used to have a red tinge, are nearly transparent now. Except for an occasional blink, she sits there motionless, letting those cold, crinkly hands part her curls and comb them, as if she were someone's broken doll.

Her lids fall shut over the hazel mist of her eyes, every time those fingers drift forward, brushing the hair, and casting a shadow over her head, which makes me uneasy. What is it with her?

Does she feel the quiver, the cold touch of these hands? Is it possible for her to ignore it? Has she grown used to it—or has she trained herself, somehow, to shut herself out, as if she were asleep, so she can no longer sense these figures around her, and this horrible place, which to me, seems like hell on earth?

And if so, how can I wake her up? Can I reach her at all? And how am I supposed to start over, I mean, to renew the conversation with my mother—in the presence of strangers?

Just looking at her stuns me, not only the light crowning her hair, a pale light which casts silver twists into that which used to be such a brilliant, fiery rust; nor the uneven gloss of her lips, which conveys a few touches, here and there, of discoloration; or the dry texture of her skin, which is gathered, in fine stitches, around the corner of her eye.

These things I have imagined a thousand times before. I have braced myself for any surprises, painting mom in my mind with one aspect of aging after another, because I knew—and said it repeatedly to myself, so as to fix it in my mind, and not to forget —that ten years, ten years have elapsed since the last time I saw her.

No. It is her distant, absent-minded stare which astounds me most of all, and not because it is new to me—but somehow, just the opposite: Her expression—or more precisely, lack of one— seems so incredible to me exactly because in a flash, I recall that which I have hidden so well and so long from myself: The fact that I saw my mother that way, at least one time back then, in the past.

In spite of the marks of time, and the change of place, she seems to have gone back, and frozen, somehow, in that moment.

I remember: I had just come back from school, and pulled my bike up the stairs, and flicked the kickstand, which made the chain rattle. And my algebra book landed, suddenly, with a smack on the floor, but I left it there, because I was eager to tell mom about scoring an A—and in biology, no less—and to ask her about her upcoming performance, because it was to be Beethoven's fifth, which to this day, I find deeply moving.

I found her sitting in her usual place, the bench down there, in the living room—but this time, she was turned with her back to the bust of Beethoven, and to the white piano.

My father who, for some reason, must have come early from work, and was watching her from some distance away, sitting by his tape recorder on the balcony, turned to me and—before I could utter a single word—made a subtle signal, putting his finger to his lips, indicating silence.

And without a sound, his lips formed the words, Careful, Ben, slow down. You can see she is tired, very tired today.

So I started backing away, and very quietly, picked up my book from the floor. And after a while my mother, still looking outside as if in thought, said in a flat voice, "Did you finish your thing, your homework? Did you practice already? Don't cut it short, or your playing will suffer. Mark my words—or for sure, you will come to regret it."

I remember. Then—as now—she might as well have been staring at a brick wall, rather than out of a pane of glass.

So now I force myself to forget the bent figure hanging over her, and I kneel down before my mother and breathe deeply and say, "Mom?"

And I wait there on my knees for a long while, and change my position to a squat, hoping that eventually, she will come up with something to say, because she did so that last time.

And I wish that in her heart, she is as exhilarated as I am at this moment, because that can easily explain why she is sitting there, speechless.

"Mom?" I whisper. "It's me, Ben."

I never prayed before, so now—while trying to balance the combined weight of my body and of the album—I am looking for words, the right words to call on Luck, or Fate, whatever: Please, give me a sign. If my mother can catch sight of me, if only she can laugh, I think all will be well.

"Here I am, mom," I press on.

What was I thinking, I ask myself. Of course it will take some time before she turns to look at me, before she smiles, even, and takes me into her arms, to make me feel warm again. Years, years have passed since mom heard my voice. To her this moment feels, perhaps, as if it came from another lifetime. Still, I must trust that she will, somehow, find a way to forgive me, forgive my long absence; which is not an easy thing to do, for a woman as proud as she is—I mean, as she used to be.

"I am back," I tell her. "Mom, look at me."

The young staff member cuts in, calling me from across the room. "You better sit," she says. "You better get comfortable."

"Thank you, I will," I say, and adjust the album, which is covered right here, under my waterproof jacket, and secured in place by both arms.

"And" she adds, "if you need anything, my name is Martha." Then her eyes turn away as if to say, Whatever it is, I have seen it all.

I watch her picking up some wet tissues from the floor, and stuffing them into the bulging garbage bag. Only now does it hit me: The smell, the pungent smell of chlorine bleach from the nearby toilet, and of stale water from the vase, and of withered flowers from the belly of the bag, and most of all, of soiled diapers.

"Here," says Martha, dragging a chair towards me, "grab this one."

So I make an effort, an uneasy effort to get comfortable, by flopping myself into the seat, and unzipping my jacket, and taking out the photo album, and then putting it in my lap, closed.

I bend over to my mother, saying, "Look here, I brought you something."

There is no way to tell if she has heard me. Her gaze is fixed, as steadily as before, on the same small pane of glass, through which the sun is blazing; which makes it hard to figure out what she sees out there.

I push forward, aiming to view it, somehow, from her angle, which at first, is too hard to imagine:

In my mind I try, I see a map, the entire map of her travels around the world. A whole history. It has been folded over and again, collapsed like a thin tissue, into a square; which is suspended there—right in front of her—a tiny, obscure dot on that window.

And inside that dot, the path of her journey crisscrosses itself in intricate patterns, stacked in so many papery layers. And the names of the places, in which she performed back then, in the past—London, Paris, Jerusalem, San Petersburg, New York, Tokyo—have become scrambled, illegible even, because by now, she can no longer look past that thing, that dot. She cannot see out of herself.

She is, I suppose, confined.

I take my eyes off the flash in the glass and then, pointing at the photo album, I beg my mother.

"Look," I say, "can you remember—"

Which is when, in the blink of an eye, I notice that those fingers, above her head—the bony fingers that keep playing with her curls—have halted for a second, midway through the hair.

And there, leaning towards me over mom's shoulder is a lifeless face, in which the cheeks are sunken, the eyes are ringed by shadows, and the spirit—starved, desperately starved, perhaps for some regard, some human exchange, some token of attention—even if it is intended for somebody else.

"*Mine kind*," he pleads, with bewildered passion, seemingly convinced that he knows me, because—wherever he is—this soul, I guess, is already lost.

It is sad to say, but he is no longer hampered by a sense of reality, nor by memory; both of which must have dimmed in him, a long time ago. I have no idea how best to react, because how can you push someone back who is barely standing on his feet, and how can you tell him to go away, when he is far from being altogether there.

"Give me," the jaws open in his skull-like face, and the arms come for me.

And I hesitate, unsure if he wants to give me a hug, or to get the thing out of my hold.

To my relief, Martha rushes over and—gently but firmly—wraps an arm around the old man's waist, where the edge of the diaper peeks out from the loose pants. And she leads him away, leaving me in the corner to face my mother, alone.

Then, to the sound of the thin, painful voice in the distance, breathing the words, *Though I know not... What you are... Twinkle, twinkle... Little star*, I glance at my mother.

I wonder if what I am going to say about this or that photograph will make any difference, because now I am starting to lose heart. I doubt we can ever find a way—be it a way back, or a way forward—to connect to each other.

The time I remember is no more than a wrinkle for her.

And so, vacillating madly between hope and despair, I sit there for a bit, utterly still. Then I make up my mind. I clench a hand over the cover, the antiqued leather cover of the album, and feel the intricate detailing, the raised spine, and the spot of rust right here, on the metal clasp holding it all together. I unlock it, and lift the cover. And when I look down I realize that it has fallen open to the very last page.

This, now, is where I have to begin.

She Is Looking Out The Window

Chapter 13

As Told by Ben

These photographs take me by surprise, because only now, in this cold, high noon light, I can see how badly they have deteriorated, and because in each one of them a teenage boy, whom for a second I cannot recognize, looks back at me. He is standing a bit awkwardly, pressed there in between him and her, those out-of-focus figures, which look so much like my parents—only younger.

The boy is tense. There is a crop of fresh zits on his brow, and his hand is held, for some reason, to his chin. The page sways in my hand. Its gilded edge turns, catching the sunlight. The photographs bend softly with it and give a sharp glint, which is when something leaps back to mind and I know who he is, and why he is doing it.

Holding it open I raise the album from my lap, and peel away the clear plastic sheet to expose the page. I tilt it to my mother, saying, "Remember? You warned me, weeks before my Bar-Mitzvah, that pictures will be taken, no ifs and buts, that's the way it is, and to make sure I have a nice complexion when the moment comes, so that one day, when I grow up and stop misbehaving, and stop being so immature, we can all look back on the good times; which scared me, mom."

She is looking out the window.

And so, I continue.

"So then," I say, "in the synagogue—utterly mortified in front of the crowd—I had the presence of mind to hold my chin. I held it there for dear life, held it all through the ceremony, because of this pimple, you see, which began to bud right there, on my skin, and because I had been stricken that morning, in the most vigorous manner, by a fear of looking at myself."

I listen to my voice and suddenly hesitate, wondering if I should describe these pictures to her. Why should I talk? Why should I play what I remember, when mom might have recorded the same scenes herself—but in an entirely different way? I mean, she sensed them from a different angle. Indeed, she must have a different story to tell, a different story about which to be silent.

I know that what I am about to say should be about her—not me. I strive to make it so. But I doubt I can.

"Look here" I urge her, thinking I have just caught her blinking. But when I raise my eyes to her, she is looking out the window.

"Look," I implore, "this is you, mom, sitting there, in the front row, during the service. On one side of you is dad, looking away, maybe at me or, more likely, at the Rebbitzin; and on the other—an empty seat, in memory of grandma, who had passed away less than a year before."

"Your hair was pinched up, see? Just perfect, mom—not even a loose strand. And you wore that ice-blue, long sleeve dress, which was simple, deceptively so, because it made you look so elegant."

"And here," I point out, "is your pearl necklace. A minute later—I mean, right after they snapped this picture—you rose to your feet, because up there at the podium I had just finished reading my Haftora. And the pearls, they scattered to the floor, and were dinging all over the place, because the clip had snapped. Or maybe because you had forgotten to fasten it properly, again."

"And so aunt Hadassa, who was sitting there, in the next row, directly behind you—see there? You can tell, this knobby thing can be nothing else but her nose—she clapped her hands and jumped up and made everyone laugh nervously, by yelling, Mazel Tov! But at that moment, it was unclear to me if she said it because of the pearls, or because after all, it was my Bar-Mitzvah."

"Look! This is a closeup," I press on. "A closeup of your hands, almost touching the challah cover, which was white velvet, I think—but in the picture, it looks beige, almost. Maybe because of the blemishes here, all over the surface."

"And dad was right here, by your side, the moment you lifted the cover away—even though his face is cropped out somehow. Now, if you focus—right here, next to the edge—you can get a glimpse of him. Can you tell? This is the fabric of his sleeve, right here, around your shoulders."

"And his eyes, they were shining—remember?—because he stood there, admiring the braiding of the challah, and explaining in great detail, to everyone around us, how cleverly you had measured out the dough and baked it, so that its weight would be just right. I mean, it would be exactly the same as my weight at birth, which was somehow symbolic, I suppose—but in my anxiety that day, I could make no sense of it at all. It only made me realize that I was no longer hungry."

By now I have run out of things to say about this page, so I turn it, flipping back to an earlier place in the album. There I can see a freshly dug grave, with a pot of flowers—but decide to skip it, because this is about grandma, I mean, about her passing away. I have nothing to say about that.

So I glance sideways at my mother. A beam of light draws her profile, sketching the line of her nose, barely touching the curve of her cheek. If I wanted to, I could just extend my arms and hug her, because there she is, opposite me, and the distance... The distance, you see, is so close—but I hold myself back.

She is looking out the window.

Perhaps she is immersing herself in the grays and purples quivering there, on the other side of the glass, reaching a blur in the cold October sunlight. Perhaps, with great patience she is waiting there, waiting for the night, for the darkest hour, which is when her image may finally appear. It will come to the surface in front of her as if it were a sunken spirit, rising from the deep. Out of nowhere.

For now she seems lost, searching for something—perhaps her reflection—in vain.

I worry about mom, about the little things, which to someone else—someone who does not know her as I do—may seem trivial, insignificant. I worry she is missing her pearl earrings. I must find them for her. The little hole in her earlobe has shrunk away, turning somehow to flesh.

In a whisper I say, "Mommy?" and wonder how the air vibrates over the tender membrane of her eardrum, how it changes into noise, how she gets it when pitch rises, when it falls.

Can she sense the change?

At what point does it translate, somehow, into meaning? By what path does it penetrate, going deeper? Does it excite the nerves, fire signals up there, between regions of her brain? Does it make *some* sense, at least at times? Is there any point in talking to her? Is she listening? Can she detect the thin sound—scratched like an old, overused vinyl record—which is coming faintly from behind, from the far end of this space? Can she understand the words? Is there sorrow in her? Is there hope?

Then the traveller in the dark... Thanks you for your tiny spark...
He could not see... Which way to go... If you did not twinkle so...

And before the last sounds tremble away, I turn to look at the direction of that voice, and see an old, seated figure, stooping there over her hands, which are nestled in her lap. She stares at them as if to ask, Why are they empty? What was I holding? When did I lose it? Then her eyes break off. They are rambling now, wandering about, as if to call for help. Why am I here? Who is there? Who are you? And a minute later: tell me, where is home? Would you take me there, take me back, to the place where I belong?

Meanwhile I sense a crisp sound, the sound of fabric rustling here, in my ear, and the staff member, Martha, is leaning over my shoulder.

She takes a glimpse of the album and says, "This you?"

And I say, "Yes."

And she points, "And this, your mom?"

And I say, "Yes."

And Martha says nothing at first. She rolls up her sleeves, the light blue sleeves of her nurse uniform, and comes over, driving a large mop across the floor, which she ends up pointing at my shoes. So I get the hint, somehow, and lift them in the air, so she can wipe the floor under my chair, after which I can relax. Now Martha rests the mop in the corner, against the frame of that window, and comes back to stand here, in the patch of sunshine in front of me. And with her plastic glove she rubs out the sweat, because it seems to tickle her forehead, and run down the side of her nose.

She studies the photographs for a bit, at the end of which she says, "You want her," meaning, my mother, "to take a look?"

And I say, "Yes."

"Let her hold it," she suggests.

And I say, "What?"

And without bothering to explain, Martha pulls the disposable gloves off her plump fingers, and grabs the heavy album from my hold, which makes it close suddenly, with a loud slap. Then she brings it across the divide, so now it rests in my mother's lap.

"Now, let *her* open it," she says.

And I say, "What? How—"

"Like this," she says, and wraps her chubby hand around my mother's fingers, which are laying there limply, so fragile, so delicate. Martha presses them somehow into the photo album, letting it flip open where it may, which happens to be somewhere there, in the middle. She winks at me and then, turns away. This, now, is where I have to go on.

My mother is still. She is looking out the window.

For all I know, by now she might have found an outline, a faint trace in that square of glass, running though it in zigzag, this way and that, like a fine, hairline crack. Perhaps she is dreaming of her double, her other self floating there, pale, nearly transparent, over the fuzzy colors of fall: on the outside, looking in.

For a second I wonder if I, too, can spot that mirror image. I search for an eye—but even without detecting it I reflect on what it may see, watching us from a detached, neutral position, out there. It may look carefully into us—or rather, into *them*: a withdrawn, aging woman; a young fool. One has been forgotten, the other—deceived.

Something, perhaps a ray of sun, flickers across the floor between them. There they are, hanging at the edge of that pool of light in the corner. Careful not to touch, not to step, not to drown in it.

This scene, I figure, can be altered not only by the point of view—but also by the medium, the clarity of the lens. And so I imagine that eye, observing us through the imperfections, through the thick and thin of the glass, trying to account for the distortions, judging what is true and what is false in us: us, who are distorted.

The eye is studying, perhaps, the way we—no, *they*—are slumped: two strangers in two chairs across from each other, hesitant, unable to grasp for the real version of themselves, unsure of the bond between them: a mother and a boy.

I think I can see that eye. It looks in, unblinking. It can read the signs of our silence. I want to speak—but find myself unable.

And she, she is looking out the window. May God help us both.

I bend over to point at a picture, there on the open page, which brushes against her bosom.

"Look, mom," I say, and my voice is choked. "Here," I try again, "this is my first piano recital. Remember? You had all your students practice so hard, especially me. I was seven years old, and was assigned to play a lovely, cheerful piece: *The Entertainer.*"

"Right there, there I was, coming forward when my turn came up, and bowing to the audience, just the way you had taught me. I had no stage fear back then, because I had never stumbled in public before. And here, see? I adjusted the distance between the piano and the bench before taking my seat, just the way you had instructed, so I may reach the keys. And there, by these pleats in the background you can tell: someone was standing there, unseen, ready to whisper to me, to guide me from behind the curtain, if necessary. This was you, mom."

"And for a second there, I closed my eyes—see?—thinking about what you had told me: to draw a difference, a sharp difference, between my version of this piece, and the cheap version which could be heard, from time to time, in our neighborhood: it was meant not to delight in the music for its beauty—but to announce, with a chirpy, irritating repetition, the arrival of some ice cream truck."

"And so, I began. I touched the keys and incredibly, from the first note I felt my hands flying, in full control, over the keyboard. On the repeat, I played the melody an octave higher; after which I glanced at the audience and could spot grandma, looking up at me. Here," I point her out. "You can tell how my music delighted her, and set her feet in action, because look: they went tapping under her, all over the floor."

"And mom, my heart was so light! I felt happy and at the same time—reckless! There was no need, really, for you to be there, to watch over me. I hope that did not disappoint you, somehow."

"For the first time in my life, the piano came alive under my fingers. I was Wild! Strong! Invincible! Which reminded me how, around my third birthday, I had assembled a drum set of sorts, with trash cans and lids and pots and pans. I had rung and slammed and beaten them with all my might, and with full abandon—until, mom, you stopped me."

"Now I took my bow, and to the sound of cheers, my heart swelled big inside of me. I thought: I had brought them joy and in return, they were giving me a long, loud round of applause. My God, I could reach out to them! I could touch them, which was an entirely new revelation to me."

"But I was worried, mom, because you would not say a word, let alone pay me a compliment. Perhaps you were afraid of what it might do to me. 'Let it not go to his head,' I heard you tell dad that night, after you had tucked me in. 'Anything,' you said, 'would be better than an inflated ego.'"

"So out of respect to you, dad, too, refrained from giving me a pat on the back. Next morning, Grandma said nothing, not a single comment—but she gave me a piece of chocolate under the table. I gave it back. A good word, a little encouragement, that was all I wanted. It would have made all the difference."

"And yet—under your guidance—I would react with polite humility, denying myself any sense of pleasure, when someone praised me. I was trained so well, mom, to keep running on empty. Even so, despite my humble mumble, I was dying to get more.

After a few more years of this, I knew that by now, no word would ever be good enough. If someone said, Good work, Ben! I wished they would fall to their knees and touch their head to the floor, and give praise to the Lord for having looked upon my face, and listened to my music, because after all, I was The Entertainer! I was an Idol, no less!"

She is looking out the window.

I lean back, no longer referring to the photographs, talking now out of blind pain. I talk freely, as if in front of a stranger I have just met in a foreign place, perhaps in some airport; a stranger whom—beyond any doubt—I shall never see again.

"Mom," I say, hoping she cannot hear me. "Mom, I became so greedy, so eager for admiration that for me, the only escape was to quit playing altogether; which I did, mom, just before turning thirteen. Still, I admired you, and looked up to you, praying that you would give me more things against which to rebel. I remember that. You called it *misbehaving*. Stop it, you said then. Stop being so immature."

This is when I hear the clap, and when I sit up I can see that the album has been pushed shut, perhaps by accident, between her hands. My mother has closed it. This is a simple fact—but to me, it is startling. I consider it, wondering: does this mean what I think it means?

Has she been listening all along, taking in my long-winded whining? Has she grown tired of it? Would she want me to describe something else—something about her, for a change?

So I lift the front cover, even though her hand is still there, on top of it, close to the metal clasp. This time the album falls open to the beginning, or rather, to the second page, where something is amiss. Something is not right, not quite right—but at first, I cannot put my finger on it.

At the top of the page, there is a picture of mom smiling at the camera, which means she was smiling at my father. She is young—perhaps in her early twenties—and you can tell she is pregnant.

At the bottom, there is a picture of a little boy with long lashes. You can tell how excited he was, how fascinated by that single, twisted candle in front of him, on his birthday cake. And if you look closely in his eyes you can see a twinkle, and that flame right there, reflected twice.

She is looking out the window.

And it is not until she lays her hand flat right here—between the two pictures, in the middle of the page—that in a flash I realize: there is a picture missing.

There is a picture missing.

It is a simple fact, which makes me uneasy, anxious even, as if my heart has just skipped a beat. It feels as if the story of my life depends, for its completeness, on having a record for that moment—a moment back then, at the beginning—when my father snapped this picture.

The only record left to me, relating—in some way—to my birth, is an image of a loaf of bread: a braided challah, weighing exactly as I did as a newborn baby, which leaves me now with a lump in my throat. Where is my first baby picture? Was it taken? By whom, and why?

Did my mother take it with her, in her suitcase, when she left home? Or did my father tuck it in his purse, so he could take a peek from time to time and see me, and remember that moment, even when I traveled far, far away from him? What has been lost here, lost to memory—and what has been gained?

Then, to the thin sound of, *As your bright and tiny spark... Lights the traveller in the dark... Though I know not what you are... Twinkle, twinkle, little star*, I get to my feet.

This, now, is where I must close.

I bend over as if to bow before my mother, the way she herself taught me to do, at the end of my little performance, so many years ago—but then, just before I can lift the album from her lap I sense a change: a slight movement.

She has lowered her head. And now, her long fingers start gliding over the clear plastic seal, feeling through it, perhaps finding the subtle impression of an edge, I mean, the edge of the first picture. It is raised—by the thinnest measure—from the surface of the page. Her hand slides over, now feeling the edge of the second picture. Her gaze seems to be focused straight down, at the void right there between them, in the middle of this page.

In awe, I stand back. She is looking now, looking directly at the missing picture.

The Family We Are

Chapter 14

As Told By Anita

The moment I come out of the bedroom—trying to forget what's just happened between Ben and me—that's the moment I see Lenny standing there, next to the entrance door. He takes a step forward to reach me, which alerts me at once to a threat, 'cause I've seen him jealous before.

Me, I can tell how he must be feeling right now, 'cause I've been there myself. From time to time, I would drive myself crazy thinking about him and Natasha, about her coming back here, or him going away with her. Then like, I would fly at him, with fire in my heart, crying that I hate, hate, hate him, and that I couldn't take his secrets no more, and whatever! And no matter what Lenny would say, I would end up going into a jealous rage.

Rage, it can like, scorch everything around you, and make it all rise up in smoke, till you don't hardly know who's your friend and who—your enemy, so you can't really trust no one. And most of all, you can't trust the one you hold dear.

At such moments I find that I miss being with my ma, who threw me out of her place long ago. I miss her, because inside—where no one else can see—I'm still a child, and because with her I'm at ease, and I don't have to torture myself, and I don't have doubts about nothing, 'cause she makes things cut and dried, even if she has to slap me for it.

So even though we're married now, I don't really feel I belong here, in this place. An outcast: that's me.

So I storm past him—but Lenny lays his hand on me. Grabbing me by the shoulder, he brings me to a standstill.

"*Stop*! Stop, Anita," he says. "We have to talk."

"Whatever," I say, "I'm done talking," even though we both reckon that like, the only thing I've swapped with him since this morning was my silence for his.

And he goes, "Maybe *you* are—but I am not."

And I don't say nothing, 'cause like, what's the point? Between his son and me, I bet I know whose story he's gonna believe.

And so he presses on, "There is something, Anita, something I must tell you."

"What," I say. "You leaving me again, Lenny?"

"Going back to work," he says, which takes the wind right out of me.

"Really?" I gape at him, and notice that his briefcase is right there on the floor, at his feet. "So soon? You sure you're up to it? Like, with the limping and all?"

"Yes," he says, and lets go of me. "It is time. I cannot afford staying home any longer."

And, seeing that I stare at him as if to ask, Now, what does that mean, he goes on to say, "It means, jobs are hard to come by, Anita. Especially," he adds, "at my age."

"Fine, then," I say, and lift his briefcase from the floor, to save him the trouble, and I hand the thing to him. But instead of taking it, he grips me again, this time by my waist, and turns me to the light, like, to read me.

"It is not Ben I want to talk to you about," he says.

I wonder if he can tell what's in the back of my mind, which is the place I keep words, words too long to make any sense, and other things I'm trying to forget.

"Really?" I say, hearing sudden relief in my voice. "It isn't?"

And I press my head to his chin till I feel him wiggling his upper lip, 'cause my hair is frizzy, and so it must be tickling his nose. And through the fabric, the thin cotton of this dress, I feel his hands on my body, his flesh against mine, and it's coming forward, so I reckon he wants me, like, awful hard.

"Take it off," says Lenny.

So I slip the dress off, 'cause it don't belong to me, but to Natasha. Wearing it must have been a mistake, 'cause this thing brings her back to him, and for some reason, it brings out other feelings, which I'm not sure I get, exactly. So I step out of it, and see it puddling there, on the floor, like a piece of blue ice, melting.

Then, on the whim of a moment, I rise to the tips of my toes and stretch for a kiss; which he denies me. And instead, Lenny looks straight into my eyes, saying, "In a word: I want you to know that maybe, I have lied to you."

Now, that's just like him: lying to me; which he then doubts; which he wants me to know, so he's protected from guilt.

And before I can point it out, or ask him why anyone would say, *In a word*, only to follow it with a full sentence—and a long one at that—Lenny goes on to say, "I have told you, just a minute ago, that I do not wish to talk about my son. But now that I think about it, maybe I have lied."

I can see my image flashing across one lens, then the other, right there in his glasses. And it looks kinda small, and odd, too, 'cause each one of them surfaces is like, a bit curved. There... Now my image has met the frame. It's gone, vanished into thin air.

Me, I'm feeling, like, a tinge of shame—even though I didn't do nothing wrong. So I'm waiting on edge, right there in front of him, now with my eyes lowered, holding my breath to hear him, 'cause who knows what he thinks he's seen.

To me, he's the witness, and he's the judge, a judge with a bias in favor of the other side. And here's the accused, ready for the verdict. Here I am.

Lenny starts talking to me, and what he says isn't nothing like what I've expected, and it takes my breath away.

"You may be looking at my son," he says, "and at me. You may be watching us, thinking, These are strange people. This is not a family I would want to live next door to, let alone in the same home—but this, Anita, is the family we *are*."

And in a whisper I repeat, "Yes, we are."

And something makes me warm all over at the mere sound of what he's just said, 'cause like, if even he, Lenny, don't barely know what's strange and what's not, then who knows? Is there anyone normal, out there? What is it exactly, *normal?*

And I don't mind me being odd, when so are they, when so are all of us.

And I can see how, in the days to come, I'm gonna have to find my way, somehow, between them two men, 'cause I get it: Lenny needs his son, and he can't risk another split, another tear between the two of them. We must all try, as best we can, to forgive each other, and to accept us, accept the way we are.

I find myself awful glad to be near him, 'cause at this moment I ain't an outcast no more: he's made me a part of something which—even if it's damaged—still, all the same, it's as close as you can get to being whole.

"We," I echo, "are a family."

"A family," he admits, "with a load of secrets."

Lenny raises his eyes to the ceiling as if to find the right words, which must be kinda hard for him, 'cause now he takes his briefcase from me and like, tries to take cover behind it. At last he lets out a sigh.

"What I have to say," he tells me, "is about her."

In return to which I let slip, "It always is."

He backs away, so I tell him, "Lenny—don't you stop! I'm here, listening."

And he says, "You may remember that time, five years ago, when Natasha came back, and you left, swearing it was all over between us."

And me, I nod, "I do."

And Lenny says, "I tried very hard to mend things with her. If we could start over, if life could go back to the way things used to play out, it would have meant so much! Not only for us —but for Ben, too."

"Natasha," he says, "had stopped giving piano lessons by then, and from time to time she would seem—how shall I describe it?—withdrawn. In spite of this, she acted as if all was fine, and so did I. For the most part, we were getting closer again, so who could ask for more? She and I managed, somehow, to settle into a daily routine—until one evening, just before going to bed, the phone rang. I picked it up on my side of the bed; she—on hers."

His lips tighten, and for a long while he don't say much; which forces me to ask, "So, who was it?"

And he says, "It was her doctor."

And me, I ask, "What, was she sick?"

And Lenny says, "Yes," which seems to take a lot out of him, 'cause now he's turning pale. "She was," he reveals. "And still is."

And so I run to the kitchen and bring him a chair and have him sit there and try, and catch his breath. Then I bring him a glass of water, which at first he tries to refuse.

So I give him a look. "In a word," I tell him, "drink!"

So, he drinks; after which I ask, with caution, "So—what did the doctor tell you?"

He's raising his eyes again, but the right words can't be found nowhere close to him—not on the ceiling, or on the wall, or the floor, in this corner, or that. So instead, Lenny shuts his eyes and, like, stumbles into saying, "The doctor, he said: Mr. Kaminsky, the tests came back."

"At this point," he recalls, "I took a hard swallow. The doctor paused briefly—perhaps taking another look at the test results—and then went on to say, I have some difficult news for you. Your wife, I believe, has a form of Alzheimer's."

I take the briefcase away from him, 'cause it's just about to fall, anyway.

And so Lenny can't brace himself no more, 'cause at this point, he don't have nothing to hold on to, and nowhere to hide. Instead he just sits there, with the empty glass, saying, "Alzheimer's," and then again, in a voice that is nearly gagged, "Alzheimer's."

And after a long pause he adds, "At the sound of this word, Natasha was confused and I—I dropped to my knees. I remember, she could not get it, could not understand what was going on and told the doctor, Wait, hold on, I cannot talk to you now. Call back later, something is wrong here. No, not with me —with my husband."

Lenny takes off his glasses and like, wipes something from the corner of his eye, and my heart goes out to him. And then, then the strangest thing starts happening to me. For the first time in ten years I feel not only for him—but for her, too.

I pity her, which surprises me, and allows me to watch the whole scene in my head, as if—by some magic—a curtain's risen, and I find myself right there to watch, or like, to snap a picture of the past, of that moment between them:

I see him crouched there, on the floor at the foot of the bed; and her plopping the phone in its cradle, to stop it already, stop that voice, that muffled voice that keeps coming back, saying, Hello? Hello? Is anyone there?

I hear her coming over, wrapping her arms around his, and asking, like, What's wrong, what's wrong, Lenny; and him saying, No, dear, it's nothing, I promise, nothing at all, really, and sobbing, sobbing with no tears and no sound.

I bet he knows that from that moment on, he would be alone, really alone, and that he must go on, and keep this thing under wraps, so that no one who's known her before would ever think to put her name and that word—that horrific word—in the same sentence, or anywhere close to each other.

And before I can snap another picture of her, and place it there, in the back of my mind, I see her walking away. Her robe's like, flapping behind her, letting the light shine through, and then—poof!—she's gone, perhaps to turn off the bedside lamp. Still, I can't get rid of the ghost of her image. It still kinda hangs there, like the end of a shadow, a long shadow left there, in the center of a picture, even after the body itself has crossed out of the frame, and has long vanished.

This, now, is the way I draw her in my head: coming back, like, to touch him softly, to ask what's the matter, what has happened here. At times she's like, clinging, at times hovering there, over his shoulders, a faint trace of a thing, turning fainter with time; one that can't remind him no more of her, her whom he knew: The mother, the wife she was. The girl she used to be.

So I take a step closer to Lenny, and this time I don't allow myself to be stopped—not by him, not by that shadow, and not by nothing else I've seen in my head, just now. And I brush my lips over his hair, and spread my arms real wide, hugging her hugging him.

I can't see his face, 'cause it's hanging down, like it's buried between his shoulders. "I must be going," he mumbles from deep down. "I must be going. I cannot be late for work."

And standing here, by his side, I let him lean on me, so he can rise, somehow, to his feet. Lenny turns his back on me and a minute later, the sound of his footfalls can be heard, one thump after another, shaking the stairs.

And after a while, it kinda blends away into the other noises, till you can't tell it from the hum of traffic down there, in the street.

Now I close the door. At long last, this I know: I don't need an answer no more for that question, the one that confused me so, the one I've been asking myself, with such pain, such agony, for the last ten years. And I won't need to guess, not anymore, why he told me—that first time, when we danced—that I, I reminded him of a girl he used to know.

Go Back To Your Mama

Chapter 15

As Told By Anita

L enny's gone, but still, I'm thinking about him, about how he's touched on that time, the lost time nearly five years ago, when I went out the door, swearing I ain't gonna come back to him, not ever. What he hasn't said—and what left such a bitter taste in my mouth—is how he told me, back then, "You are a nice kid, Anita. Go, go back to where you came from. Go back to your mama."

And what he don't know is that ma wasn't all too happy to see me, "Because," she said, "I told you so, didn't I? Didn't I say, he's gonna grow tired of you, and dump you before you know it? He's gonna go back to his wife, 'cause it's her that he wants— not you! And if not her, then—then, it must be something else with him, always something else, like, looking for other women. Maybe they remind him, somehow, of that thing, who knows what it is, which he found in her. Maybe what he's really looking for is just, like, the *idea* of her."

And when I mumbled, "Whatever," ma said, "I knew it! She can twist him around her little finger, if she wants to."

She didn't tell me nothing else about this thing, this *idea of her*, which ma thought was fixed, somehow, in Lenny's head, like

1

some piece of music; and I, I didn't ask. Instead, I bought a six-pack for her and a six-pack for me, and we sat down on her pillows, on the narrow iron bed, drinking beer; she talking, me weeping all night, after which ma wiped my face, and grabbed the palm of my hand—like she used to do in the old days—to read it.

And she told me to stay put, to wait for her, 'cause she had something crucial, something real big to tell me, like, about the future. I reckon she saw *some* clue of what was coming—but didn't quite grasp it, not in full, anyway, 'cause the next thing you know, ma went out, came back a second later, picked the empty beer bottles, and took them with her. Along the way she gave me a peck, smack in the middle of my forehead, which surprised me.

Then, having kissed me goodbye, she went out again, and then... Then, on her way to work, right there on the corner of Euclid Street—Bang! I could hear the sound, out there—she was killed in a car accident.

I stayed in her place till the end of the month—but couldn't stay longer, 'cause me, I didn't have no money to pay for the rent, on account of not having a job. So I started moving from one place to another, trying to hide behind someone's garage, or in a little cove on the beach. Sometimes I shared a room with this friend, or the other. After a while, I lost count of all the places where I'd lived. Which is why I don't want to ever think about finding a new place again.

A few months later—I can't even say how many—I was walking, like, in a daze down the street, and raised my eyes from the ground. I found myself on the Pier, staring at the swirly, painted letters of the ice cream place. And then, in a flash, it hit me: this,

this was the place, the very same place where we had met, Lenny and me, that first time.

I backed away, all shook up. Words started drifting in my head. I thought about him, and about how far away, even absurd the whole thing was, I mean, like, the idea of us together.

And I thought about the hunger, and them buckets inside, full of chopped nuts and cherries and coconut flakes. The air trembled, and in it I caught a sniff of cream, and a whiff of waffle cones, which at once awakened the pain, right here in my stomach. How strange it was to be back here again—only this time, on the outside, 'cause that's, like, a totally different place— even if most people don't really care to know it.

My feet carried me, somehow, till I stopped right there, under the *Santa Monica* signboard, which arched over the entrance to the pier. And no way, I swear, there's no way you could even begin to guess my surprise when all of a sudden, I spotted Lenny up there, behind the large window of *The Lobster*. Sitting inside, there he was, holding a margarita glass, laughing his head off, and like, having a real good time.

I could see the slice of lime on the lip of his glass, and closed my eyes—but still, was blocked from smelling it.

I tried, in vain, to bring back the touch of salt around the rim, and the scent of butter on mashed potatoes, and the meaty flavor of wild mushrooms, and the pleasure you get with every gulp of hot, thick clam chowder. I could almost lick the spoon, and pinch the bread, and wipe the bowl with it, 'cause I had known all that. Me, I had been there with him, like, a lifetime ago.

I leaned over the railing of the pier, and for a second hoped he would see me. How could he not, with my hair flaming red, and blowing, long and wild, in the winter wind, which swept across the divide?

Now I could see the girl sitting there, opposite him. She raised her glass and clinked it against his, then cuddled up to him, like, to whisper something up close, in his ear.

I don't hardly know if there was something odd with the air, which stirred past me with cloud after cloud of salty mist; or the sheet of glass over there, which must have had some flaws all over it; or the mirror image of sunset, which buckled out of shape, in and out of the flaws; or else, was it the film of tears, which formed in my eyes; or the sorrow, which came in like a tide, to wash over me—but in a blink, everything blurred.

Everything started swimming in front of me: like, the shadow of her little black dress, the flash of her gold earring, even the blond streaks in her hair. All of them things, which lived on the other side of the layers—the layer of mist, and of glass, and flaws, tears, wash—they all rippled a bit and then, settled into a haze.

I blinked again and at once, things went back to the way things should be—except that the girl was still there, by his side, where I should have been, had I not left him.

I had never met his wife before, but of one thing I was sure: this girl wasn't her.

She was no Natasha. I don't know how I could tell. Maybe it was the way she laughed, flinging her hair back, and batting her painted lashes, and opening her mouth real wide—but this I knew: this girl, she didn't have no class—but then, unlike me, she was bending over backwards, just to fake it.

When they came out of the restaurant, I couldn't help but follow them from a distance, like a stray kitten, holding back a purr, ready to roll over for the rub of a hand.

He hailed a cab and leaned into it, talking to the driver. For a minute I thought I caught Lenny glancing at me, over his shoulder, but no—maybe I only wished it. Then she kissed him. He opened the door for her. She climbed in, closed the door. He kinda waved, once. The cab merged into traffic, and away it went.

Meanwhile, I lost him in the crowd. A minute later I spotted him again. He was turning on his heels and oh, shoot! I couldn't believe it: he started weaving his way between this shoulder and that, walking back closer and closer, directly here, to me.

And my heart pounded—oh God! How it pounded!—so, so hard inside me; after which I hung down my head, hoping he didn't see me—or else, if he did, I was hoping that out of pity, he would turn away, 'cause I was too thin and too dirty, and didn't have nothing pretty to wear, all of which made people around me look away, or look right through me, like I wasn't there, even.

Me, I made a quick move, trying to slip away—but already, it was too late.

"My God," said Lenny, now facing me. "You look horrible."

What he said next blew me away. I felt like, this moment wasn't real, because in a softer voice he told me, "How I missed you."

For a second I wanted to say, Really? It don't look at all like you missed me, isn't it so, Lenny? And don't even think you can use me, and then like, walk all over me. I may look like shit right now. I reckon I do—but no, you ain't gonna dump me, never, never again! And anyway, where is she, where is the dear wife, Natasha?

But instead, in a meek tone, I said, "How can you even say you missed me. You, you told me to go away."

At that moment Lenny was lost for words, because he knew me, knew me well enough to get what I hadn't said, too. So he took off his winter coat and hung it around my shoulders, very gently, like he was afraid I would break, somehow. And suddenly, it felt kinda good.

"You are shivering," he said then.

"Me," I denied, "shivering?"

And he offered, "Let me take you home."

So I hid my face behind the collar of his coat, knowing it's gonna smell awful bad by the time I'm gonna have to give it back. "Home?" I said, and now my voice was muffled. "Me, I don't have a home."

"I meant," he corrected, "let us go home, together."

Which brought up the anger in me. "You," I raged, "I don't need you! And don't you think that I do—'cause I swear, I don't! You told me to go back, back where I came from. So here I am, Lenny. I'm down in the muck, deeper than deep."

He stretched out his hands to me, like he wanted to pull me in, to save me. And in spite of myself I flung the coat off, and shoved it, right there, into his open arms. "Take the stupid thing, and your pity, too! Stop acting so grand, and feeling so, so sorry for me! And you," I pointed, "*you* go back! Go the hell back where you came from!"

People started looking at me now. They whispered to one another and pointed at me, like I was naked or something, which made me hot, crazed even. I blushed. It felt kinda strange, being visible again. The anger surged in me, it threatened to burst out, like, any moment now. And Lenny tried to say something—but me, I won't let him.

I raged on, "Don't you dare say nothing to me now!"

And he said, like he didn't even hear me, "How I missed your voice."

And I said, "So listen to me, and listen good: I can get food, and I can get a place to sleep, and on a good day I can get a job, even! One day, Lenny, one day I'm gonna get back on my feet, I swear I will—and for sure, I'm gonna do it without you."

And he said, "I know it. I have no doubt about it." And then he added, "But Anita, I need you—"

"For that," I countered, "you can get that girl. I bet she's gonna come back to you, like, in the flick of a finger, and be fucking nice, Lenny, and spend the night."

"No," he said. "Now, you listen: it is *you* I need. I miss you."

"Don't," I said.

To which he said nothing, but his eyes did his pleading for him.

And I said, "You can't beg a beggar."

And he said, "You may not believe it. I do not believe it myself, when I hear myself saying it—but really, I even miss the way you speak."

And I said, "I ain't gonna talk fancy no more, Lenny."

And he said, "Not to worry: you never did."

So I had to make it extra clear to him, "I ain't gonna *enunciate* them words, like you told me to, Lenny."

"I understand," he said. "This is so incredible. I can listen to you all night long."

And I said, "You can?"

He took a step closer. "I should learn it from you, Anita."

"Learn what?"

And he wrapped his coat around me, even gentler than before. "Like, your way to say it."

"Say what?"

"Them words," he said, winking.

"You making fun of me?"

"No," he said, serious now. "It is so cold. Let us go now, Anita. Let us go home already."

In the five years since then, I've noticed a change in him. There wasn't that feeling no more, like he was waiting for something to happen, or for his wife to knock on the door, any moment now. Somehow, she wasn't there, which made me grow edgy. I couldn't fight her, 'cause how d'you fight air? How d'you crush it? How d'you know when to duck, or even, when you're open to attack?

In my mind, she's become a threat, an unseen presence, about which he refused to say a word.

And the heat between us has cooled off. I would dab some perfume on my wrist, and light a candle next to the bed—but instead of coming in, Lenny would stay out there, on the balcony, perhaps to write, or to press them keys on his tape recorder. Some evenings he would call me to join him, and we would just stand there, watching the sky getting dark as the sun went down behind the opposite building.

At times, Lenny would bring out his typewriter and let me play with it. I would set my fingers in place, and spread them on the keys, like I could type. He would ask me to talk about my ma, like, what she had told me before the accident, or what had happened to me during the lost time, out there on the street. He wanted me to tell all this, not to him—but to his tape recorder.

And once I started, I could say anything—any damn thing—without him cutting in, or getting angry, or making a sound, even.

I would be in a different place then, so far away, as to forget he was there, listening. *Record.* I would talk and talk. And if it was too much for him, Lenny would surprise me by taking himself elsewhere: he would go inside, and sit on the bench, and wait till I was too tired to go on. *Stop.*

After such a night, it would be hard for me to fall asleep. And if I did, I would soon open my eyes with a feeling of dread in my heart, and like, trying to break out of a bad dream. It's always the same dream, too, and it's been coming back, over and again, to haunt me.

Just yesterday—when I laid there in bed, bleeding all day, not even knowing where I was—that was when at last, the dream found me.

In it, I find myself in a public place, which is strange to me—even though I know, somehow, that I've already been here. I've visited this place, perhaps the night before.

It's raised like a stage, and flooded with light: a harsh glare, which blinds me. For a minute I can't see nothing in the dark, beyond that ledge—but I know that them faces are out there, blank and blurry. They're all there, hushing each other, gazing at me.

I see myself standing there in front of them, naked.

Red-faced, I hunch up as tight as I can. I fold over my thighs, trying to hide, to cover my body, my shame—but my hands, they're way too small, so my nipple slips out of my fingers. And there it is, circled by light, for all to see, and to jeer at me, and to lick their lips, which is like, glistening out there, tiny sparks hissing in the distance.

For a little while, my sleep is light. And so—even as I'm looking straight into that spotlight, or like, reaching down to touch the ledge of that stage—I can tell that all this is false, it's nothing more than a dream. But then I fall deeper, even deeper into it, and now I really believe what I see:

Some thread is crawling on my skin. Laying across my knees is a strap of fabric, which is frayed and stained, here and there, with my blood. When I pull it in, trying to drape it around me, or use it for a blanket, it resists. It don't hardly give in, 'cause it's tied to something—no, somebody—standing right here, directly over my bare back.

Me, I don't want to turn, but I take a peek over my shoulder. Wrapped in layers of rags and straps and loose ends, all of which is tattered and like, drenched in reds and browns, the figure seemed shaky. He lifts one leg, and tries to balance himself, teetering—this way and that—on one foot. His hand tries to touch the back of my neck—and misses it, grabbing a handful of air, instead.

And his blood-red lips, they're curled up, in something that looks an awful lot like a smile. A mocking smile, one that don't change.

In my dream, my feet must have frozen. I can't move, can't run away from him, or even climb off the stage, because at that point I'm weak, and too scared to even breathe, and because of that thread, which binds us. And so, rooted to that spot, I look up at him. At this close range, our eyes meet, and my heart skips a beat, 'cause at that second, his are empty.

Suddenly I catch sight of someone else, someone standing way over there, in the distance, behind him; behind the curtains, even. Except for her hand, which is caught in the light, it's hard to even notice her, 'cause at first she's like, real shy, even modest, and keeps herself in the shadows, out of the spotlight.

But then, she changes. Her long fingers, they're gathered, one by one, into a fist. And twisted around her little finger, you can find—if you focus—the ends of the rags, and the straps, and the thread, all of which extend from there to here, where he stands; all the way, to the joints of his wrists and his elbows, tying them like, real tight.

And from backstage, she's pulling him—raising, dropping, tightening, loosening—making the puppet move, shake, jiggle, even dance on the tip of his toe, and like, bringing him, somehow, to life. I gasp, thinking: she can twist him around her little finger, if she wants to.

Me, I cringe as he puffs, breathing something in my ear. "Go, go back home, go," says the puppet, in a voice that is not really his. "Go to the place, the place where you came from, you came from. Go back to your ma, ma, your mama."

And to the sound of teeth gnashing, I force my eyes open, and in one rip I tear the thread and break out, out of this dream, and find myself back here, like, in a safe place again.

And the last thing—just before the stage falls away, and things seem to blur out, and other things become solid, like the ceiling above my bed, which is finally all clear—the last thing I do is wonder, is she playing us all? Am I being twisted here, twisted around her finger, like he is? Am I a puppet, too?

Like, how can I be sure that I'm not?

I wake up. The first thing I do is move, 'cause I ain't frozen no more. I move them joints—the joints of my own wrists and elbows—every which way, to make sure I can do it at will. I look at them from this side and that, to check that they ain't tied, or pulled by something, like some blood stained thread.

And the second thing I do is say aloud to myself, "I told you so. I told you so, didn't I?"

My Own Voice

Chapter 16

As Told By Anita

I'm here, and this is amazing. Crumpled in front of me is his first attempt at telling my story.

Last night was real special for me. He came back from work, and after his son had moped about the place and finally, gone out for a drink or something, which was right after dinner, Lenny stepped out to the balcony, and instead of pressing them keys on the tape recorder, he opened his notebook—the thick one, with the worn cover, which must have seen better days—and said, "Come over here, Anita. Let me read you a little something."

I did. I plopped down and made myself comfortable on his knees.

The page rustled in his hand and he said, "This here, it is one of my early stories," and out of his notebook he started reading, like, *Leonard was first introduced to Lana at his boss's house...*

At once I thought, *Leonard?* Why *Leonard?* The name sounded too important, to formal to my ears. Plain *Lenny* would have been so much better, because after all it was his voice, and the story was clearly about him.

Them writers, sometimes they play these kinds of games, and use code names, I reckon, to distance themselves from themselves.

Anyway, I didn't hardly say anything, 'cause me, I was glad, so glad that this time, he let me in, and here I was, awful close to him. I'd known him, on and off—more off than on—for ten years, and in all that time I'd never, ever heard him read from his notebook for me. Strange: since the beginning he'd been a bit vague about his writing, slippery even. And I didn't mind. No really, I didn't, because... Well, because I accept Lenny. He is what he is: the keeper of secrets.

As it happened, I didn't hear his story last night either. This time, it was my fault. Right after the first few words I relaxed, and felt so at ease, and so warm inside, that I caught myself yawning.

My head lolled to one side, then another, and I think I dozed off—but anyway, Lenny didn't mind this time, not at all, "Because," he said, "it must be because you are pregnant. And the bleeding, too, must take a lot out of you."

He let me slip off his knees, and then moved aside so I could share the seat with him. "Your eyes," he said, "they are glazing over. Lean on me, right here. My God, Anita, you look so pale, so tired. Well, who can blame you?"

Which was kinda good, 'cause he didn't have a clue that it wasn't just me being pregnant, and tired, and what not—but on top of everything else, it was his writing, and all them words, the fine words he used, which confused me and made me drowsy.

Lenny was like, delighted by his own writing, and by me being there, silent, without butting in, because according to him

Natasha, his ex-wife, had laughed at him more than once, in the early years, the years of her success, during which he was out of a job. He hadn't forgotten the insult, but managed to swallow it, somehow—only to spit it out now, so many years later. She would say, like, Who does he think he is, Dostoyevsky?

Unlike her I just clung to him, and took in the moment, and tried to listen, as best I could, first hearing the sound of his voice and then, deep inside, the throbbing of my heart.

And then... Then I closed my eyes.

When I woke up—it must have been long after midnight—he was still reading, jotting down notes, erasing, and from time to time, pressing this or that key on the tape recorder. And he was talking, talking to me or, perhaps, to himself. *Rewind, Play. Play, Rewind.*

I propped my head up on his shoulder and looked up at his mouth, and the little muscles at play all around it, which didn't look near as tight as they've been, say, in the past few days. I could see that something had come over him: something even stronger than his passion to write. A great relief, that's what it was. Like, a load had been taken off his heart.

I bet it happened when he gave up his secret to me, the one secret he guarded most of all, which was funny, 'cause it wasn't even his—but Natasha's.

Now that I knew about her illness I felt kinda dizzy in my head. Like, I was playing with danger, soaring, even hovering in midair, over the high side of a teeter-totter, and spotting Natasha over there, on the opposite side. By some twist, our fate was like, linked. This time around, her luck was down, mine—up. I could sense the shock, the deep fall she'd taken, and the hard hit against the ground.

And I figured that now, she didn't barely have a way to come back. She wasn't a threat no more.

Meanwhile, Lenny went on scribbling. His right arm was holding the pen, his left—hugging me, which was cool. The night air was swirling around us. I watched the setting of the moon as it flowed down, so slow—so magical, even—till it fell away behind the outline of the next building. A star here, a star there gave a faint glint. Time slowed down, like, by some spell. I had goosebumps, 'cause I couldn't remember no moment but now, and no place but here, when I felt peace, complete peace between us.

And after a long while I caught the hint, the first hint of dawn, and I touched him, with nothing, nothing at all coming between us—not even that thing, whatever it was, Dostoyevsky.

I can't remember how he took me to bed. By the time I got up this morning, Lenny was already gone.

So now, it's a new day.

I go out to the balcony, listening for echoes from last night, like, echoes of me and Lenny. First I try to *Rewind, Play*. Then I *Stop*, and try instead to bring them voices out of memory. I prick up my ears for anything, any little thing that's still here, still left from that charm, that moment of pure calm—but no: all's quiet, quiet in the most regular, humdrum way, with a distant buzz of street noises.

It's late in the morning, which you can tell, 'cause the dew on the railing has dried up by now. His desk is bare, not even a pen left here, on the glass surface. And on the floor, a film of dust has already covered our footprints, so it's awful hard to believe that last night really happened, that it wasn't just another dream.

His notebook is nowhere in sight—but then, under his desk, right there in the trashcan, I can see a bunch of papers peeking out over the edge. I take them out, and smooth the edges, and try to flatten the creases, and blot out the ink stains.

According to him, only one of his stories was published, like, ages ago. The rest of them wasn't, on account of the fact that Lenny don't send them to no magazine editors, because, he says, he isn't quite finished improving a phrase here and there, and besides, most of them stories, they're just too private. So the more he tells you, the more he seems to leave something out.

Here, look: the first page is kinda messy. It's that story, the one he managed to publish, the one he read for me last night. Me, I can barely recall what it is I've heard. I think it's about a girl, a girl with blond streaks in her hair. Lana.

To win her over, a man can be seduced to do just about anything, and like, give up the one thing about himself which he values the most. Now as far as Lenny goes, I'm way too easy, which means, this girl isn't me. And for sure, she isn't Natasha.

Not long ago Lenny told me, "My writing is not the place where the fiction is," which I find strange, 'cause if not in his stories—then, where else can his fiction be? Is he writing the truth—and living a falsehood? If this is so, then the girl from his story must be real. More real than me, anyway.

Whoever she is, she must be someone he'd known way back in the past. I don't think he's seeing her now. I really don't.

Then again, I may be totally wrong: perhaps the only place where she exists is like, on paper, which explains why he didn't barely give her a strong, clear voice. To me, she seems a bit sketchy. In six pages of dense scribbles, the only line he let her say is like, *What is it with you tonight?*

With him, every little thing is huge—or else he's gonna make it so. And every gesture—even as trivial as a wink—can be a trigger, like, for a whole big drama, which may be the case here, in this story. I'm gonna read it later. I have time. At least, I think I do.

Here's another crumpled page, which is nearly empty—except for a single sentence, parts of which is crossed out. Between the scratches, it reads:

He's gone, but still, I'm thinking about him, about how he has touched on that time, the lost time nearly five years ago, when I went out the door, swearing I won't come back to him, not ever. What he hasn't said—and what left such a bitter taste in my mouth—is how he told me, back then, You are a nice kid. Go, go back to where you came from. Go back to your mama.

These are my words—not his.

I'm so surprised to find them here, suddenly on paper. I bet he hit *Rewind, Rewind, Rewind* and ended up going back more than he'd intended, which is how he found what I'd said on tape that night, when I couldn't fall asleep, on account of that nightmare.

I reckon he listened. Yes. He did.

Now I ain't sure how I feel about that. Part of me is glad; the other, not so much. I take the page with me, 'cause like, even if it's in his hand—or maybe because of it—this a part of me, of who I am.

And I go inside, into the living room, and sit there, on the piano bench, and lay my head on the surface, which covers the keyboard of the piano, which is kinda cool to the touch. And then I dream.

I dream about Lenny: How he's gonna come home this evening, and ask me to tell him something again, about myself, and about things I remember, things I'm painting in my head. After a while he's gonna go away, leaving me alone with the tape recorder.

Record. Stop.

Once my story is done, he's gonna come back to take some notes, and edit them over and again, scratching and erasing all night long, and like, going into the trouble of finding a way— just the right way—to carry my voice in letters, and in marks.

I reckon it won't easy for him to fix the way I talk—and at the same time, remain true to how I tell it, and to the feel, the real feel of how it happened.

I can just see Lenny in my head: He's gonna torture himself trying, somehow, to do it, so that tomorrow morning, at exactly the same time, when I'm gonna be sitting here again, on this very bench, I'm gonna be startled to find—out there on his desk —a gift.

A little something from him to me: A little piece of paper, scribbled side to side, top to bottom, with dense writing, and barely a space between the words.

As usual, it would seem as if he's sucked up all them spaces, because—even when he gives—Lenny don't really want you to get it. Or else, he wants you to work hard at getting it.

And even then, he wants you to figure out only small parts, some here, some there. Any which way, it won't help him. I'm gonna get it, 'cause them spaces, and the lack of them, may be his—but the words are mine.

I'm gonna snatch the paper, and find myself blown away, 'cause right there—in his hand, black on white—I'm gonna read the scrawl, the words of my voice, my own voice:

I'm here, and this is amazing.

And then:

Crumpled in front of me is his first attempt at telling my story.

Leonard And Lana

Chapter 17

As Written By Lenny

L eonard was first introduced to Lana at his boss's house, where he and a few other guests had to stand around waiting for dinner, with nothing but some dry nibbles to help pass the time, and nothing but the weather to keep the conversation afloat—until a full hour later, when she finally arrived.

He was seated at the table next to her, and noticed her long, wavy hair. It had blond streaks, and smelled good. The perfume was very subtle—just enough to put him under a spell. Naturally, he found himself tongue tied. He felt as if his boss expected him to be sociable and charming—which made him, without fail, even more rigid than usual.

He ate in silence, swallowing his pride along with a mouthful of chicken soup, and listened to the symphony of sounds around him: Le'Chaim! Le'Chaim! To Life, said the guests, wine cups clinking against each other, chuckles spreading, chewed-up words garbling into slurps and gulps, punctuated here and there by soup sipping intervals.

Lana was chatting across the table with his boss. Despite her bubbly laughter—or maybe because of it—Leonard thought he could detect a certain strain, a certain tension in her voice. She seemed a bit uptight, even nervous at times, which brought up in her a heavy Russian accent. It was especially pronounced during the first few sentences. Then it softened a bit, or maybe he learned to like the way it played out. Normally that accent would be jarring to his ears—but now, to his surprise, he found it musical, endearing even.

He noticed the various rhythms of her breathing—at times excited, at times relaxed.

Her wrist was so close to his that he could sense her warmth through the fabric of her blouse, and it set him afire. By the end of the main course he managed to ask her, with a sudden catch in his voice, to pass the butter. The effort left him speechless, and so he thanked her in his own manner, with a slight nod but without meeting her eyes.

What color were they? He had absolutely no idea. Her whole figure was, to him, a blur.

At this point it became clear to him that the entire evening was simply a disaster, and that the earlier he would leave, the better he could preserve some semblance of having enjoyed it. He was gone, quite abruptly, halfway through dessert.

A week later his boss, who could be overbearing at times, invited him to dinner once again. Caught off guard, Leonard heard himself being agreeable.

"Seven o'clock?" he said, "Sure. I'll be there."

This time he gave some attention to his appearance. Standing in front of the mirror, hands stuck in the sleeves, he pulled a sweater over his head. He flailed a bit until he managed, somehow, to find the opening; at which time Leonard saw his father's eyes rising up over the neckband. They looked squarely at him from the glass, tired and brown. The eyes were followed by a nose and finally—a mustache. That was the moment Leonard decided to shave it.

As the hour struck seven, he rang the doorbell. His boss was happy to see him, as were the other guests. Leonard was astonished to see Lana, even more beautiful than he remembered. This time, the conversation flowed with perfect fluency, which seemed incredibly lucky to him. They were seated side by side in the same places as last time. The challah bread was beautifully braided and so was her hair. The food was great, the company—divine!

He discovered that—just like him—she loved Opera. With a sudden blush, Lana told him that she could appreciate the purity of vocal tone. She said she adored Puccini and could even describe, in heavy Russian accent, several passages from the greatest Italian operas written by him. Her cheeks were so red, so rosy! She talked about *Tosca*, about *La Boheme*, and by the time she recited a few notes from *Madama Butterfly*, Leonard knew he had to have this woman, even though the color of her eyes was still a mystery to him.

She scribbled something for him inside his paper napkin and, taking a quick peek, he found her name, her phone number and a little doodle of a heart. Both Leonard and Lana got up to leave at the same time: halfway through dessert.

Little did he know that a week from now they would be sitting at the front row of the music center hall, holding hands and absorbing a heavenly soprano voice that filled the air with *Summertime*. She would know to tell him that George Gershwin found the inspiration to write this aria in a simple Ukrainian lullaby, and Leonard would believe her. A month from now he would rent an apartment, and they would be moving in together.

But at this moment—on his way out, just about to open the door for Lana—he knew one thing, and one thing only: he was walking on air. So elated was his state of mind, so grand was his happiness, his heart swelled in him with such a powerful pulse, that nothing else mattered.

Catching sight of the host winking an eye at the other guests, and hearing some muted giggles behind his back, all that left absolutely no impression in him—none whatsoever. He ignored that wink and those giggles, and closed the door.

The whole thing flew right out of his mind until a full year later.

One Year Later.

Leonard ate his breakfast glancing, from time to time, at that note that Lana had left for him. He was torn between a need to unfold the paper and an urge to crumple it. Either way, he found himself suddenly with the realization that now was the first time in a long while—a full year, in fact—that he was alone. Completely alone. A certain feeling was throbbing in his heart—something between relief, anger, sadness and above all, amazement that she was gone and he was free.

Leonard turned on the record player and sank into the sofa, determined to spin away the hours to the tune of cheerful melodies. He kicked off his slippers, stretched his legs across the top of the coffee table and closed his eyes, so that the sight of things would not distract him from listening.

The room disappeared. It was *Summertime.*

His ears started moving at the sides of his head like agitated seismographs, registering every minute reverberation, every note. On the inside of his eyelids, space started to sway around him, gently at first. It was marked by intervals, time intervals that flowed from the lyrics and swept over him, opening and closing in an increasingly complex sequence.

Summertime. It reminded him of their first date, and of the time that passed since then. True, Lana was a good companion. He loved her. He could find nothing to complain about.

And the livin' was easy...

For a whole year, she accompanied him dutifully to the Opera. And yet, time laid bare the fact that she was bored to tears sitting there, trying to entertain herself somehow by studying the costumes, the lighting, and the scenery—everything that for him was secondary. Only now did he realize that her proclaimed love of music was as real as the blond streaks in her hair.

For him the affair had started in glory, in an illusion of a joy they could share together, and then, for some reason, gone downhill—until hitting the low point yesterday, when his boss, who was by now about to retire, came into his office.

"Leonard old boy! What a lucky man you are!" said the old man. "Well, let me tell you this: all good things come to an end. My last day here, you know."

"I know," said Leonard, not sure what should be said in such circumstance.

"And how is Lana? What a woman, let me tell you, what a woman! I taught her everything she knows—"

"You did, did you?"

"About the Opera, that is! Those were the days, I tell you! What a woman, what a fine woman! What a lucky, lucky man you are! As soon as she met you, that first time—remember? The very next day, she borrowed all those books from me—the

Harvard Dictionary of Music, the *Cambridge Companion to Twentieth-Century Opera*, a fine book I must say, just too many words, too many words! And that's not all, she took *A Critical Biography of Puccini*, and another book, I think, *The Memory of All That: The Life of Gershwin*—you name it, she took it! All my CDs too—*Tosca, Madama Butterfly*—"

"For the love of music," said Leonard, with an acid undertone in his voice.

"Hell no!"

"How do you mean, No?"

"It was for you," said the old man, and then he did a strange thing. He winked.

With that one wink, something became clear in his memory, as if a cell cracked open. He saw himself standing there on the threshold—on his way out, just about to open the door for Lana—listening, attentively this time, to those muted giggles behind his back. He stood there, at that second, for what seemed like an eternity. He hated those other guests, he hated his host. They had all been laughing at him!

They knew, did they not, that Lana was putting on an illusion, a fine illusion just for him. There was no shyness in her blush. They knew she liked him, liked him well enough to lie to his face. That was some performance! He hated himself for being so stupid as to fall for it. He should not have shaved his mustache.

That evening, when he came home from work, she asked him about his day. He gave no answer. Later in bed, just before rolling over and facing the wall, he blurted out suddenly, "You don't understand me. You don't know a thing."

"What?" said Lana.

"Nothing," he said. "Not a thing."

"What is it with you tonight?"

He gave her a long silence as an answer. After a while he thought he felt the stroke of her fingers on his back, and suddenly could no longer take it.

"Why the devil did you do it?" he said. "Lying to me, everything—every little thing you said, from Puccini to Gershwin. You know nothing about all that, do you. Not a thing. You and your Ukranian lullaby!"

After that, he found himself unable to sleep, and was forced to listen for hours on end to the singsong of crickets filling the night air, and to the faraway noise of traffic. At sunrise, just as he started to dose off, an ambulance could be heard speeding across the street, its alarm rising sharply to a pitch, then falling away into the distance. Here and there someone banged the lid of a garbage can. Bang-bang. Then bang.

One thing missing from all of this was the regular rhythm of her breathing. In twelve months of living together, that rhythm for him was softer, sweeter, and more necessary than any lullaby. He turned over to find out that which he already knew: Lana was not in bed.

Her folded note had been left for him on the breakfast table. Now it waited there, crisp and white. He could see it even from afar, even as he sank deeper into the back cushion of the sofa. Oh, he would read that note, Leonard promised himself, he would, as soon as *Summertime* died down. No, maybe later, at noon—or even later still. Perhaps when darkness came and the crickets picked up where the music left off.

"For the love of music," he said to himself as loudly as he could, for there was no one else there with whom he could talk. "What does she know. Nothing, I swear, not a thing."

For some reason, his voice sounded hollow and unconvincing to his ears. *Don't you cry*, cried someone inside him. He wanted to close his eyes and drift away, anywhere but here—but his curiosity would not let him do it.

He found the sight of that note so peculiar, so distracting that he could no longer concentrate on the lyrics. Maybe it was not her fault. Not entirely, at least. Maybe it was him. It was the music, too. Listening demanded his full attention. It carried him away, to a different place.

Yes, his eyes were closed for too long. Maybe he never really looked at Lana. Leonard uttered her name once or twice and suddenly remembered that to this day, if someone would ask him about the color of her eyes, he would not know what to say.

In spite of himself, Leonard knew he missed the rhythm of her breathing. He missed it terribly. He needed to hear the swish of her hair, the soft whoosh of her footfalls, and above all, the way she talked.

He wondered what Lana knew about him, having studied him so diligently from the beginning. Then he wondered if he, in turn, knew anything about her. Who she was, the inner language of her thoughts. For the first time in twelve months, he wondered if her dreams played out in heavy Russian accent.

It was then that Leonard got up to his feet. Perhaps that note was nothing more than a to-do list. It could happen that way, could it not? Maybe she simply scribbled something for him, a doodle or a heart, inside that paper. A great urge swelled in his heart.

He went over to the table, picked up the note and very carefully, unfolded it—

The Entertainer

Chapter 18

As Told By Ben

I know this melody, know it quite well, and in spite of myself, it is pulling me in. I should have turned away when I had the chance, and run down the stairs. I should have left the door locked. I should have resisted the urge to cross the threshold— but now it is already too late.

I am startled to hear it, thrumming faintly inside, because for years I have imagined the piano crouching there, in heavy slumber, with no one there to touch it, no one to awaken its sound. In awe I take off my shoes, and now I can feel the hum, not only in my ears—but in my entire body, reverberating full and deep.

The notes are soft, hesitant, and the interval between one press of the key and another is too long here, too short there, a bit confused and inconsistent, as of someone whose mind is drifting away—or else, a beginner.

I have never seen a player sit by the instrument the way she does. Instead of sitting upright—like my mother—Anita is slouched. Her head is tilted to the left, close to the keys, as if she is longing to lay there, over the ivory surface, which is so cool, so calming. She lets her hair cascade, and flow down as it may, like a stream of molten lava spreading over ice. For all I know, she lets her mind be carried away, far away in a dream, to a place way down, way beyond.

Her eyes are closed, as if she is in a trance. The right arm drifts to the far right, and the fingers, they stroke the keys right there, in that position, in a playful sequence, one that is distinctly familiar to my ears. Her fingers fly closer, and repeat it, an octave lower this time. And again, they fly even closer, an octave even lower—and with a gentle stroke, repeat the same sequence, now for the third time.

Now the sound is slow, to the point of being utterly sluggish. Even so, it brings back a good vibe.

This is the intro, the opening for a piece of music I played a long time ago, in my very first concert, when I was seven years old: it was *The Entertainer.*

I think that somehow—without even knowing that I am standing there, looking at her—Anita can sense the draft, the rush of air from the open door. Her eyes flutter and at once, I can feel the beat of her heart, pounding there under the hum of the piano. I can see the sudden awakening, the scare, even; which is how I know, without a shadow of a doubt, that she has never practiced in this place.

To her, it must feel hostile. In spite of having taken some lessons—who knows where—she has never played our white piano. She cannot do it here, in my presence, or in the presence of my father. I suppose I know why.

With one step I close in on her, and hang over her shoulders; which brings a shudder over her. In an instant, Anita pulls her hand away from the keys, as if she has been caught—by a bad stroke of luck—in something worse than theft.

"Don't," I say. "Please, don't stop."

"No," she denies. "I didn't even start."

"Please, let me hear you," I plead, taking a step back, to give her some space.

Anita takes a deep breath. For the first time I realize how afraid she is, afraid of anyone listening to her music, especially my father. I suppose he expects her to be perfect; which must be an impossible burden. I understand it, because I have been there: growing up with a mother who had no tolerance for errors, and no forgiveness either, I have carried that burden before.

Even so, I have no idea what to say, how to calm her down, and make it clear to Anita that I get it, I do. To me, this is a moment of revelation: I can imagine not only how she feels—but also, how my father looks at her, how he thinks of the forgotten woman then, and something shifts in his mind, so that all of a sudden he sees in her that which, for a long time, he must have been yearning for: mom coming back—back from that place, a place called Sunrise—perhaps to forgive him, at long last. Let bygones be bygones.

In Anita, he may catch a glimpse of mom, reborn.

Mirrored in the open wing of the piano, her face is so young, so alive with the red glow of her hair. Her green eyes shine back from the polished surface. This, I suppose, is why my father is so drawn to Anita. Apparently, he wants her to learn to play the piano, but then—even though she is just a beginner—he expects her to reach a level which no one can sustain. Not even mom.

In our family, forgiveness is something you pray for, something you yearn to receive—but so seldom do you give it to others.

And so, Anita may never stumble, never make any mistakes, because he wants her to be exactly, just exactly like mom, who in her good years—before losing her balance—could produce such a heavenly sound, and vary it over an incredible range, from a murmur to a powerful burst, until her music would swell in you, and bring tears to your eyes.

"Go away, Ben," says Anita, without even turning around. "I don't want to play. And you, you can't make me! Hell," she says sharply, "I'll do as I please."

She pauses, waiting for an answer, and when I hesitate to give it, she glances back at me, over her shoulder. "What," she says, this time in a low, seductive voice, "you think I don't feel the way you're looking at me?"

I can find no words, and no way to come back at her. So before she can stir, and get up from the bench, I raise my right hand. Then I stroke the keys, using the same fingering, playing the same sequence I have heard her play, just a minute ago, with the same sort of dreamy sluggishness, so that the same phrase springs up from the deep, from the belly of the piano, and winds up trembling softly, quivering in the air, just like an echo, delayed.

I must have caught her at a weak moment, because now I detect a sparkle of tears. A shadow has just passed over her eyes, darkening them. Perhaps a memory of that moment—that ugly, embarrassing moment that happened between us, back there in her bedroom—has just crossed her mind.

I cringe every time I think about it: I found myself in her presence, burning with desire. There was no way I could hope to arouse her—but oh, how miserably I failed!

The demon in me struggled to break free, and I, in turn, strove to hold it back—but somehow, my efforts came to nothing, even worse than nothing, because now I have no doubt, no doubt whatsoever: she must hate me.

Watching me raise my hand, Anita may think it is meant to subdue her, rather than simply to reach for the keys. She may wonder why I am parroting her phrases, mimicking her flawed way of playing, because after all, on my mother's side I come from a long line of musicians, whose performance was legendary for being nothing less than perfect. She may believe I am doing it for no better reason than to mock her mistakes.

Now she darts a glance at me as if to ask, What, you laughing at me?

No, I wish to say. What I want is... Well, I am not really sure: perhaps, just to lay my head here, on your shoulder. Perhaps, to lean my brow against your lips. Perhaps, to touch the tiny freckles on your cheek. Above all else, I want—but cannot bring myself to tell you—I really want to hear you laugh.

Just like here, this note. Listen, can you hear it? This soft sound, rolling, rising, ringing up here?

Anita shakes her head, as if she could detect the whisper, the quiet whisper of my thoughts. To me, her pose is so alluring when she bends down to the floor, in the shadow of the piano, to pick up some crumpled piece of paper. Then she starts twisting away under me. For all I know, she is aiming to get up, to leave me here, alone.

Is this a game she is playing with me? I do not have the faintest idea. But if it is, perhaps I can beat her in it.

So then, bang! I pound the keys, this time fortissimo—with full strength!—as if to cry, Stop! No more darkness, no more gloom! There's a thud, there's a boom! Hear this, right here? Hear my voice? Tell me, Yes—you have no choice!

And before this phrase fades out Anita straightens her back, and places her hand on the keys. Then, to my astonishment, she plays the next phrase of music, this time with raw, intense force, which I never knew existed in her, bringing it to the verge of destruction, making it explode all around me. And I, in turn, explode with the following one, because how can I let her outdo me? I am, after all, *The Entertainer...*

Here I come! Here I drum! No more woes. Let me close! Let me in, hold me tight! Don't resist me, do not fight—

At this point Anita kicks the bench back, and I tip it over behind us. She sways her hips to the beat, and I tap the floor. And we find ourselves bouncing there, almost dancing in place, playing the piano side by side: she on the high notes, I—on the low.

Her intervals are somewhat uneven, her melody is off, here and there. But these things do not matter—not to me, anyway— because just like Anita, or even more than her, I happen to be out of control, maybe because it has been a long while since the last time I practiced. I have not touched the keys for so many years, out of nothing else but rebellion, a silent rebellion against my mother. So my fingers feel a bit rusty—and yet I respond, quite swiftly, to the way Anita plays. I do it in an instant, harmonizing the sound, filling in some of the awkward intervals with a flurry of chords.

Sometimes I find myself having to take my hand away, so she can play the same key immediately after me. On some notes, my right hand crosses her left hand, in an exchange that is wild and fiery—like no duet I have ever seen, or listened to! One way or another it blends, it mixes into a sound, which you might call a crude, unruly, unrestrained racket. But to the ears of a madman, it can be called music.

If my mother could see me now... If, out of nowhere, she would appear—which would make me jump to attention—I can only imagine how she would draw back, how she would wince at having to listen to this thing, this terrific uproar, which for some reason, makes it all the more delightful to my ears.

My mother is elsewhere, and I must admit: at this moment I find myself thankful that she cannot be here—but then, listen! In her place, someone else knocks, quite loudly, on the open door.

And without bothering to wait for an answer, our guest marches right in.

At the thump of her footsteps, my hand draws, abruptly, to a halt. Anita, too, stops playing, and she turns around, speechless for a moment. Meanwhile, the echoes of our cacophony can be heard throughout the small space.

You can imagine them bouncing off the walls, flipping over backwards, coming down again—until, at long last, they land flat, barely stirring, down there on the floor.

"My, my," says the old woman. "Am I late for something?"

"Aunt Hadassa!" I cry in surprise, and hurry to pull the cover over the keys.

If not for the rosy blush over her cheek, Anita appears to be cool and collected, much more so than me. The smile on her face is irresistible, and there is no way for me to tell if she is friendly, or just pretending to be so.

"Oh, come right in!" she says. "You're just in time!"

At this point I cannot help but ask, "In time for *what*?"

My question hangs there, unheeded. Anita leaps over the fallen bench and rushes into the hall, where she glances at the old alarm clock. "Gimme just a minute," she tells aunt Hadassa. "Lemme get my shoes on—"

"What—what is this?" I ask. "What's the sudden rush? Where—"

"Hello, Ben," says my aunt.

She pushes her glasses up her long, bulbous nose. The yellowing lenses are quite thick. They look like a pair of magnifying glasses, through which round, enormous eyes are looking at me, inspecting me carefully up and down. At last she concludes, "How you have changed!"

"Indeed I have," I must admit. "I am ten years older."

"Are you?" she asks. "And was it you just now, playing like a lunatic?"

I shrug, and my aunt goes on to say, "Why, you used to play better at the age of five! In those days, you were under a *good* influence, which is something I cannot say about present company."

"Sorry, aunt Hadassa," I mumble. "I am too rusty. I can no longer be *The Entertainer*."

"You sure it was you—not *her*?" she whispers, hinting at Anita. "To judge by the level of that noise, I was sure a stray cat must have slipped in, pussyfooting around, scratching its nails back and forth and all the way across, before starting to chew the furniture, or something."

So I lower my voice, imitating hers.

"Who knows?" I say, as if in strict confidence. "You may be right. The door was open."

For a minute, aunt Hadassa frowns. "Next time, dear, just be sure to bolt it shut," she says finally. "You do not want to deal with strange creatures, making their way in."

And looking straight at her I say, "Most definitely, I do not."

My aunt checks her watch, and rocks herself impatiently to and fro. Then she takes a step closer to me, and at once I step back, thinking that in a second, she would spring forth and pinch my cheek, the way she used to do in the old days, when I was a child—but as luck would have it, I have grown too tall for her reach. Or else, she has shrunk a little.

"My, my, how time flies!" she complains.

I have no idea if she is talking about the years that have passed—or the seconds ticking away, which you can hear from the direction of the alarm clock.

Then, with a deep sigh, aunt Hadassa turns away from me, brushing a gnarled finger across the cover of the keys, to check for dust. And when her finger comes out clean, she seems deeply disappointed.

"Anita!" she calls, checking her watch again. "Nu? The appointment is in half an hour!" And with acid sweetness, she asks, "You ready, dear?"

To which Anita answers, "Sure! Lets go!"

My aunt purses her lips with a firm pout, and before I can cut in, or ask anything, she plods heavily out the door. Her shoes are what you would call sensible. The wedge-like soles give a hard clonk and clunk, left and right, against the floor.

Meanwhile, Anita wraps herself with her winter coat, and buckles a pink belt around it. She gives me an alluring look, then scurries to get out, turning back only once, to close the door behind both of them. Now you can hear the light touch of her footfalls, following at the heels of the old woman. They are going down one flight of stairs, then another.

I draw closer to the door. And the minute I crack it open, I catch a glimpse of Anita, far below.

I hear her saying, "Oh—I forgot!" and the old woman groaning, and again Anita's voice, saying, "Lemme go back, like, just a sec. Wait, wait for me!"

And there she is, running back up, skipping two stairs at a time. Now she stops at the landing just a flight below, and raises her face to me.

So I ask, "You forgot something?"

"Yes," she nods, holding her belly, trying to catch her breath.

"What, shall I throw it down to you?"

"No."

"What is it, then?"

"Oh, Ben. I forgot," her breast heaves as she takes a deep breath, "I forgot to tell you something."

I wait. I take a step out, across the doorsill, and stand there, close to the railing. From here I can spot a change in her eyes. The shade has vanished and now, they are so bright, gleaming in green, and there is a childlike joy in them.

"It was a blast," says Anita, and her voice is so relaxed, on the verge of laughter. "I mean, that thing we did! I swear, I didn't dream it could be so much fun!"

What she says next takes me by surprise.

"Ben," she wonders aloud, "what was it? Was that music?"

I cannot tell her that it is, because in truth, I doubt it myself. So I shake my head, "No," wishing I could dare say, That was something else: something intense—but not as complicated as I would have thought, earlier. Perhaps, it was simply a clash, the clash of wills between us—or else, you could call it *Love*.

The instant this word crosses my mind, a look passes between us, and I am being held there in place, as if by a spell. Oh, let her not remove her gaze.

Let it pierce me, let it go deep. It is hilt of the sword that holds the wound from bleeding.

Let her search my heart, because what can she find there, but the cry, Come! Come to me, Anita! I am yours... If you refuse me—if you turn your eyes away—I fear that at this point, I shall fall. You have the power to bring me down—or else, you can make me fly.

The stairs have dropped from view. The railing is but a fuzzy, peripheral impression. I pay little attention to her arms, her legs, her body—only her eyes are in sharp focus.

In them I can see a bright flash—perhaps the flash of insight —over the darkness of the pupil, and flecks of golden light, sprinkled in a fine, intricate pattern all around the iris.

I cannot begin to guess how long we have been standing there, how much time has elapsed. Perhaps it has been as short as a second—or else, as long as forever; after which she lowers her eyes, and starts turning away from me.

"I see," she says at last. "That was your piece. You think this is just a wisecrack. You think you're *The Entertainer*."

Anita goes down a step, and for a minute, does not stir. Perhaps she is waiting, giving me an opportunity to speak, which for some reason, I just miss. Then she sways her hips, a bit seductively I think, and all I can do is stand there helplessly and listen to her footfalls, slowly descending the flight of stairs.

By now she is under the landing. I can barely see her, but I think she is whispering, perhaps only to herself, "Why, why can't you say nothing? Say any word—but that one, 'cause you don't really mean it. Nobody does. Say anything, apart from *Love*."

Nothing Surrendered

Chapter 19

As Told By Ben

N ow that her footfalls have died away I linger around, feeling awkward. I look down the stairs, and out at the garden below, and my nostrils flare out, drawing a long breath, detecting something different in the air: Some trace, perhaps, of perfume.

I cannot make up my mind whether it has been a mistake, I mean, just standing there in confusion, facing her, saying nothing—when in fact, in spite of what she may think, I had it: really, I had the words right there, at the tip of my tongue, to tell Anita how desperately I want her.

There is no need, no need, no need to torture myself. This woman is not for me. No, I repeat, not for me. I am lucky, so lucky I have managed to restrain myself, somehow, and bite my lips.

Nothing has been said, nothing surrendered.

Still, even now, I am choking back tears, determined to deny the pain. I know all the reasons in the world to keep silent. The least of them is gossip.

I can just imagine my aunt, who was waiting for Anita down there, at street level, keeping herself under the landing, well out of my sight. She must have been stretching her winkled neck, tilting her head in my direction as far as it would go, with the ears perked up, already guessing the whisper of a forbidden affair, and her nose raised, sniffing a scandal in the making, eager to share her suspicions with anyone who would listen.

How, then, could I speak, with the old woman there, ready to capture that which I was about to say, and then spin it on, and spread vicious rumors?

Still, gossip is definitely the least of my worries. No matter who was lurking there, trying to listen in, I would have dared not only speak to Anita, but even cry out—as if it could bring her back—Stop! Don't go like that. Don't you leave me!

Yes, I want to believe that I would have done it—if not for that other thing. What else can I call it but treachery?

Indeed, I feel like a traitor. Anita is married to my father. What's more, she carries his child. I should look away when she is around me. I should guard myself against her. I should guard my sanity. What it is that she does to charm me so, I do not really know. But the more I ache for her—the heavier my sense of guilt. I wonder, can he sense something of what I am going through?

Last night I thought I caught him, glancing at me with a strange look, with something close to pity playing there, in his eyes. I could have attacked him right then, at that very moment. Oh, if only he knew!

Perhaps then he would cast me aside and curse, even disown me. He would tell me I am no longer a son to him; not his flesh and blood anymore. Believe me, I do not wish to betray my dad.

I keep telling myself that I cannot prove my virility by robbing him of his.

Still, I am afraid of the demon in me, afraid of what it may do if I lose control, if I find myself overcome, suddenly, by a wild impulse. I pray I shall never reach this point, because then I may be tempted to take her, even by force—or else, kill him, so he cannot have her, no one can. And then... I do not even know. I may kill myself, out of shock and failure and despair, and most of all, out of remorse.

For now, I am glad I still have a grip over myself. Nothing has been said, nothing surrendered. So I try to tolerate the pangs of conscience, and at the same time, try to blame my father for everything. Oh yes, I argue with him constantly in my mind, because really, what was he thinking? How could he replace my mom, by bringing a girl in here, a girl who is a year younger than me?

Seriously now, how could it be my fault, when I was not the one creating an impossible situation—perhaps even a dangerous one—but instead, found myself stumbling, somehow, into it? Hell, how difficult was it for the old man to see that his actions would complicate things, wreck them beyond repair, not only for himself—but for all of us?

I mean, how dare he take a sexy redhead to his bed, in our home, and then call me to come back, to live here with both of them, in a cramped space, together, like three monkeys rattling a cage? Why, anyone would tell you: this is a zoo, really! I must find an escape—or else, very soon, I shall go crazy, utterly, hopelessly crazy. You do not need a fortune teller to figure this thing out, do you?

The nip in the air, and the sound of rustling must have conspired together to rouse a feeling of anxiety in me. I pass my gaze across the landing, where she has stood just a minute ago. Here, a bleak wind is playing with a few leaves, tossing them idly side to side, and then with one gust, hurling then over the chipped edge.

And under the landing, a narrow asphalt walkway lays aslant between the weeds. It is veined with cracks, and bordered by a hedge that in springtime, would be flowering. This being early November, it looks rather bare.

I go inside, where the air is stagnant, and pass by the white piano, where Anita and I have played together, only an hour ago. I push the cover away from the keys, and in one bang I come down on them, making them clang—but somehow, the music has gone out of me.

Nothing has been said, nothing surrendered. Still, I should have been more careful with her. Silent I was—but not careful. So now she has taken with her that word, the word she found on my lips, unspoken. I wish she would let it go, and let the pain in my heart remain speechless.

For my own sake I should have been much more careful. Now —even in her absence—I find myself in her hands, which feels strange to me. I am surrounded—and at the same time, isolated. I am alone. I am apart from Love.

I wish she could forget that word. Maybe she has forgotten it already. Now, instead of a sense of relief, this thought stirs something else in me: perhaps, rage.

She may be laughing at me, at this very moment, together with my aunt. Anita may be trying to coax the old woman to be on her side, and planning to charm her sisters, too, to win all of them over. She may be hatching a scheme to take my mother's place, to be recognized by all—even by her enemies—as the new

Mrs. Kaminsky, because now, with that baby in her womb, she is starting to grow into her new position, as the matron of our family.

At this moment Anita may be getting ready for that appointment, about which she refused to talk to me—but I could tell she was eager for it, which for some reason, infuriates me. What could be more urgent, more important to her than what I wanted to tell her? And how can she act as if nothing at all has happened here, between us? How can she do it? How, how dare she ignore me?

Heartless woman! I hate Love. I do.

I rub my hands against my temples, trying to soothe myself, thinking that Perhaps, this anguish is entirely unnecessary. There is no need to torture myself. No need whatsoever. After all, nothing has been said, nothing surrendered.

I pace around the walls, in and out of one room, then another. In my bedroom I spot the aquarium—the one grandma gave me, a long time ago—with its faint trace close to the rim, marking the level of water that used to fill it at one time. I remember the colorful fish, which dad bought for me then. In their place, the thing now houses a pile of my old T-shirts. I try one of them on, only to find that it is too tight on me, and that it smells of dust.

In the bathroom, the air is damp, even stale. Anita's comb lays next to the sink, with strands of red hair caught in its teeth.

On the shelf, just above it, is my father's tin of pomade, which he uses to make his hair slick and shiny. To the side of that are his shaving tools. Here is his badger brush, which is spotless. Wiped dry with great care, its bristles are tipped with silver. Resting against it is an elegant leather case, which holds his cut throat razor.

It brings back a memory. As a ten year old boy I used to stand right here, leaning against this very door, just as I am now. Wide-eyed I would stare in awe at my dad, watching him go through his morning ritual, which never varied. I can see him so vividly in my mind.

First, dad would soak a small towel in steaming hot water, and hold it firmly against his face, his eyes winking at me from the fogged up mirror. Then his eyes would turn serious, as he would go back to the business at hand.

He would lift the wet brush, using it to apply shaving cream to his chin, swirling the thing around and around, until the lather had formed into stiff peaks. At this point, he would put the brush down—but not before painting the tip of my nose with a dollop of white, fluffy cream.

Then he would stretch his skin between his fingers, until it was as tight as a drum, and angle the blade to it, and go through his first pass, traveling along the grain, shaving the hair with short, rhythmic strokes, and finishing it off with long ones. At this point he would bend down and let me help, let me lather his face for him, before straightening his back, and coming back up to the mirror, to study his jawline as if exploring some exotic, heavily wooded landscape. Then with a sure hand, dad would go through his final pass—the more dangerous one, when most accidents occur—this time, traveling against the grain.

It must be late afternoon, maybe five o'clock by now. My father, I figure, is about to come back. And here I am: his flesh, his blood. I am looking directly at the mirror, wondering, Where is that boy? Is he lost? Can I still find him, hiding here, inside these eyes? And who are you, I ask myself, a traitor?

In this spot, I am nowhere. And nowhere is a hard place to escape. So after a while I start wondering, What now? What shall I do? Now that I am home, where can I go?

I have no will. I have no curiosity. Of its own, my finger is passing with barely a touch along the blade until suddenly, catching on a spot, it halts. Rust, perhaps. I raise my hand over to the light, careful not to tighten my hold over the thing. A cold shine can be seen in intervals, shooting up and down between my fingers along the metallic handle. I can sense the edge.

I can see my wrist, a vein twisting through it with a hard pulse. I can see the delicate lines, guessing their way across the skin. How frail is life. Better close your eyes. Close your eyes, I say. Do it.

I close my eyes and with a light, effortless relief, my thoughts are lifted, flying away from the moment. They are lifted, turning over the edge, cutting up and away, heading for a far, far time in the past.

I have no will. I have no curiosity.

What now, I ask. What if I have no blood. What if I am no longer here?

All of a sudden I imagine I hear voices on the other side, which makes me hurry up and with a shaky hand, lock the bathroom door. I glance at the mirror, seeing nothing. Nothing but murky glass.

And it is at that moment that someone gives a knock, and a strong jerk to the handle, and cries my name, "Ben? Open up! Please, Ben, open up!"

I freeze, feeling too numb, too indifferent to even think of an answer, because I may have spent hours here, in this stuffy place, and who the hell cares? I, for one, do not care about anything and anybody. Really, I do not. Damn it all! I am free of emotion, and so should everyone be, in a perfect life. I have no pity, I tell myself, no pity for anyone—least of all for me.

For a while, the noise! It agitates me. Then—silence.

So I hang my head, and I am not really listening, not hearing a thing, not giving a damn. Then in a blink, tears well in my eyes, which is when the door bursts open, and dad is there, throwing his arms around me. And despite my resistance, he hugs me, and without saying a single word, he pulls me out of there—not before taking a moment to do something which to you, may seem dull—but to me, it is truly special:

Loosening his embrace, dad stretches out his right hand, and lathers his brush. Then, with a quick touch, he paints the tip of my nose—the way he used to do back then, in the old times— with a dollop of soft, fluffy cream; which turns me for an instant, as if by magic, into that long lost boy of years ago.

Above All, Survival

Chapter 20

As Told by Anita

I don't know how we got to this place, Lenny and me, and I don't really care to know. Let's just say that what's happening between us isn't exactly clear. Yes, let's leave it at that. At first I tried to tell myself he won't touch me because of the pregnancy. I refused to admit that the heat between us had been cooling off even before that—but now, like, there's no warmth left here no more.

Like ma used to say, when she called her customers to offer her usual special—I mean, the three dollar palm reading special —she said, "No, really? No warmth left? Trust me, it just looks that way—till you touch them embers. Red hot passion like that, it can't never die out. But see, it can change its color and blacken him inside, and like, turn to hate, or contempt, or jealousy."

"You better be careful," she said, "'cause when you least expect it, it's gonna flare out again."

Which forces me to take a hard look at where I stand, and like, avoid wasting time dreaming, or wondering about matters of the heart, fluid matters which may take me nowhere in a hurry, and which no one—not even ma—can't never predict. I have a hunch that I must be real careful now, and stop acting on a hunch.

From now on I'm gonna knock myself out doing something totally different, like planning every one of my next moves.

At this point there's one worry which is, like, blocking everything else in my head, and this is it: I've fainted once, I may faint again. So I can't go on alone. And even if I could, I shouldn't, really.

I must find someone here I can trust, someone willing to hold my hand and steady me, in case I'm too weak to stand straight. I don't give a damn what this someone thinks of me. I swear I can take it, 'cause now that I'm pregnant, it's more than just me. My little one is curled here inside me. I must take care of him. That's all that matters. I so wish ma was here. Without her, the place I'm gonna hear the sound—the sweet sound of my baby's heartbeat—is gonna be among strangers.

With her gone, where can I go? To whom shall I turn? Don't laugh, even if—on the surface—my solution may seem absurd, totally absurd to you. I reckon I must win the trust of the women in this family, which is to say them Rosenblatt sisters, armed with their knitting needles, and spearheaded by dear old aunt Hadassa.

At the time I told her not to trouble herself with coming to my wedding, and to stay as far as she could from me, which may have been the wrong thing to say to the old witch—but boy did it feel right!

You may think me crazy, totally crazy to even consider her. And maybe I am, 'cause how can I forget: it was aunt Hadassa who came up with that bright idea, the idea of abortion. With the sweetest fake smile you could imagine, she told me that for sure, there was still time, it wasn't too late to have it, and like, it could make things so, so much easier for me, because the way she sees it, I like to run around, and have my fun and stuff.

So right there and then I had the best fun I'd had in a long while: it was like, such a pleasure for me to let her have it! I swear, I was rude as hell! I shouted at her with such goddam delight, so she would know who's who in this place, 'cause guess what: the future of this family is right here, in my womb. Now don't you forget it!

But from now on I must swallow my pride—even if it chokes me to death. I must hold my tongue with them sisters, and like, be nice, and show respect, which isn't gonna be easy for me, 'cause you can look far and wide—but for sure, you can't find no witches more uglier than them.

I remind myself: above all, survival. So I must do something to turn them around, somehow, from hating me. I must, like, charm them into thinking of my baby as one of their own—even if to them, I'm always gonna remain the stranger.

Me, I'm used to being the enemy, but if they know what's good for them, they're gonna come around real soon and make peace.

It's in my power to bring them out of that slow death—that endless, idle boredom of old age, and make them come alive again, the way it must have been for them back then, twenty-seven years ago, when Ben was a newborn baby.

I can just picture them spinsters, crowding around the crib, fat bellies hanging over the little wool blanket, trying to walk on tiptoe, stepping over each other's warts, and carrying a bucketload of free advice, for which they wasn't even asked, let alone thanked, 'cause you see, there he was, so, so frail, and always crying it seemed.

So they must have wondered, like, was the little bundle of joy hungry or wet or sleepy, or was he just too cold or warm or sick or something. I can just see it in my head. They would tell his mama to burp him, and to clean his little tush and powder it— even though the three of them hadn't taken care of one, I mean, not even once in their life.

And Natasha, she must have been close to tears, 'cause like, being new to being a new mama, I bet she wasn't sure if she'd done things right, and she couldn't tell if there was enough milk in her breasts, 'cause like, the baby won't stop wailing. And them nipples, I'm sure they was hurting like hell.

It would be just like aunt Hadassa to say that if she was in Natasha's place—which thank God, she wasn't—she would ignore the pain. My, my, she would say, never mind a little discomfort, because you know, breast feeding is not for sissies, dear.

And she won't back down, I'm sure—even though the three of them hadn't done nothing even slightly close to anything of the sort.

And when all that advice won't do much in the way of calming the baby down, they would tell Natasha that it was fine, just ignore the crying, because anyway, it was meant to make his lungs strong and healthy—even though aunt Hadassa had to stuff her big ears with a couple of cotton wads, 'cause in spite of her own advice, I bet she couldn't stand hearing it no more.

Now I could make her feel needed again. I could even stun her, by inviting her right in, to meddle in my affairs in full view; which is what I did last night, when I couldn't take that noise in my head no more, I mean the old alarm clock, out there in the hall, which had become awful pesky with that loud tick-tock, tick-tock.

First I switched the light off, and held my hand just under the bulb to feel the air cooling off, and sat there in the darkening kitchen for a quite a long while, trying to amuse myself by touching my belly, and thinking about my baby, and about his future, about the long years ahead, which helped me tune out the minutes, ticking away.

Then I stood back up, trying to find my reflection, which looked real small and buckled right there, on the round surface of that black bulb. I wiped my tears—even though I didn't have no sleeves on me—after which I went to the hall and piled some papers and stuff, right on top of the alarm clock, to muffle that sound.

Then I called her up, and said, like, "Aunt Hadassa, I need you—"

"What for?" she said, real cautious.

And I said, "I have an appointment, like, tomorrow at ten—"

And she said, "You do, dear? Nu, what for?"

And by the acid tone in her voice I figured she was thinking that by now, it was too late anyway, and that I should've listened to her when there was still time, time for a proper abortion, because my, my, now it was week number twelve already.

So I said, "It's a real surprise, aunt Hadassa. You'll see. Anyway, let me ask you this: can you come here, like, early tomorrow morning, and help me get ready?"

And she answered by asking, "You not feeling well?"

And I had to say, "No, not that well, Aunt Hadassa."

"My, my," she clicked her tongue. "I'll be there, dear. We all will."

"I'm awful glad," I said, and meant it. "Don't know what I would do without you."

And I thought, In a few months from now, I'm gonna steal her heart. Aunt Hadassa is gonna feel, like, the grip of a little hand around her wrinkled finger. She's gonna pinch a chubby little cheek, and listen for a thin, ringing voice calling her name. And me, I'm gonna smile at her, and place my baby right there, in her lap, and watch her droopy eyes light up. She's gonna know that I know that she knows that from now on she owes me, 'cause like, I can make her feel wanted again, which is a mighty strong thing to feel.

It's in my power. Without having to say any of it, it's gonna be awful clear to both of us.

Up to now she hasn't give it much thought—but with a little help from me, she will. And then, then she'll change. She'll be *my* aunt—the stolen aunt Hadassa—whether she knows it at this point, or not.

I can't wait till tomorrow. I bet I ain't gonna forget the place where—for the first time—I'll hear the sound, the sweet sound of my baby's heartbeat. Only I wonder now, like, Will it be among strangers.

The Heartbeat

Chapter 21

As Told by Anita

In spite of the light spotting I refused to admit to myself, even for one moment, how terribly worried I really was. Lenny didn't come back, so all alone in the big bed I felt lost, like I was drowning, and had to hold my breath, somehow, till dawn, and then even longer, till the light of day, till my ten o'clock appointment, because I was so afraid I was gonna get some bad news, I mean, about my little one.

So now I pinch myself, 'cause at long last it's ten already, and here I am, in a half-darkened office, lying on my back, waiting, like, for a miracle, straining to hear a sound—which isn't here, isn't here yet—the sound of my baby's heartbeat. If something's wrong then it's time, time to find out.

With a heavy sigh, a woman in her mid-thirties takes a seat right here facing me. She types my name, so that now, '*Anita Kaminsky*' shines above me in large letters on a screen.

If not for her red eyes, and them sharply pointed ears, she would seem the perfect clinical type. Her thin mouth is pursed pretty tight, except to let out, kinda under her breath, that she's sick of all this, and who cares, nobody gives a damn, and really why should they, it's her life, and her problem is no one else's business, and to call her Debbie, she's a *sonographer*, and this plastic thing, this gismo she's gripping in her hand, that's called a probe. With that she begins sliding it around the bottom of my belly.

I hold very still. I don't barely move under that crisp, starched sheet. It has ironed pleats that stay there, like, straight as an arrow, even when it's spread open, right here over my legs.

Her movement is measured, precise—but all the same, I reckon my baby's squirming inside, because of all that prodding. It tickles me, too. I'm afraid I'm gonna pee in my panties, because that probe thing which is resting here, on my skin, feels kinda wet, kinda cool to the touch. For her, I bet all this is just routine. Me, I have to hold a full bladder, which isn't easy—but then, then the beat starts!

It sounds faint at first, just like nothing, and then all of a sudden it grows awful strong. Now that she's found it, and it blips loud and clear, the smile can't hardly be wiped off my face. If not for them red eyes, I would've asked her, like, if I was to come back the next day, would she let me listen again.

If not for them three witches standing there in the corner squinting at me—perhaps even wishing me ill—I would've lost all sense of shame: I would've cried and cried, and then cried some more. It's the most sweet, beautiful sound I've ever heard in my entire life!

But never mind me, or how I feel. You can see straight away that the most amazing change is beginning to take place right over there, out of that corner, when all three of them—aunt Hadassa, aunt Frida and aunt Fruma—come forward, like, in one heavy step, which makes the floor bounce right under me.

I've taken a risk asking them to come here with me, and I hope, I so hope it won't prove to be no mistake.

I reckon they hate me, 'cause from the beginning, from the time I fainted they've been hinting that this here pregnancy, it don't seem to be viable, and it should be aborted, and there's still time, like, to do it. Still, there's no one else to offer a helping hand, no one else to lean on, in case I'm gonna feel dizzy again. From now on, hate don't really matter no more, 'cause I need them.

Blip, blip, blip goes the sound, and them three aunts, they pop their round, bulging eyes and lean right over my belly, which is glistening in the dark with that clear gel smear, in which the probe thing is like, splashing around. And aunt Hadassa, she raises her painted eyebrows, and screws up her nose till it's glued to the screen, like she hasn't seen nothing like that in her entire life, which I bet, she hasn't.

Me, I thought I knew what to expect. From the book Lenny gave me I've learned that at week twelve, the baby's fingers would soon begin to open and close. His toes would curl, his eye muscles would clench, and his mouth would make sucking movements.

By now his eyes have already moved from the sides of his head to the front, and his ears is like, right there where they should be. I thought I could see all that in my head—but for sure, it isn't hardly the same as watching the real thing, 'cause the real thing is like, much more confusing.

"See, right here?" says the sonographer.

And I say, "No, what?"

And she points out, "The heartbeat, see? Down here, across the monitor?"

So I turn to the screen, which is as black as night, and fix my eyes on that white worm, which is radiating there, all the way across, with them shining spikes pulsing through it, one blip after another, running off at the right edge and then, coming right back in at the left one.

"Sure," I say, real bold, like I know what I'm talking about. "The heartbeat."

"Yes," she says, like we have a clear meeting of the minds between us. "This here, that's what you call a Doppler waveform, see? And it shows the systoles and diastoles in the blood flow velocity."

"Looks good," I say.

"For you," she says, "the important thing is this: Even in the presence of vaginal bleeding, which is what you have, we can depict a visible heartbeat. So obviously, the fetus is viable."

Here she lets me take a deep breath, and then goes on to say, "It means that the probability of a continued pregnancy is better than 95 percent."

"Looks good, awful good," I say again.

And from behind, them three witches mumble, "Nu? Looks good, doesn't it."

And they turn back to retreat into that corner, from where I can still hear them, whispering, "My, my," and clicking their tongue from time to time.

Meanwhile she freezes the image and prints a little picture for me, so that later I can show the little worm to my husband. Right this minute I ain't all that sure I want to do that.

She turns a few knobs, and pushes a few sliders and stuff on her keyboard, so a pale search light appears in the image. It's scanning around some dusky nooks and crannies, where silvery, flat layers—some thin, some thick—have sunk down into the dark, just like wet mud. It isn't barely clear to me that what I see up there is for real. Perhaps the light just flashes there, off the sludge, and what it mirrors back to me is like, false. Something just dreamed up.

The ray flutters about, slicing, somehow, across them layers of dense, grainy clay of what's inside me. At first I don't much mind all that slicing, 'cause it don't hurt me, and it don't feel like nothing, really.

With a soft, squelching sound, little specs glitter in the dark fluid. And there—just behind them specs—something moves! Something catches the light and like, wow! For a second there I can swear I see a hand: My baby's hand waving, then turning to float away.

This isn't exactly what I've expected, 'cause like, not only is that fluid kinda see-through—but to my surprise, so is the little hand. Like, you can spot not only the faint outline of flesh on them, but the shine of the bones coming at you, too.

Me, I'm here to protect my baby, to keep him safe from harm, even from the shadow of harm. So I tell her, "Now, stop that!"

And she points her ears even sharper, saying, "Excuse me?"

So I go, real slow, I say, "You heard me. Turn the damn thing off."

And them three aunts, they stop whispering amongst themselves. Right away they click their heels, like, awful hard against the floor to rise up, and aunt Hadassa says Oy, which is quickly echoed, like, Oy Oy, by aunt Fruma and aunt Frida. Anyhow, they seem eager to find out what it is I'm fussing about.

So I insist, this time much louder, "Stop, stop already! You slicing my baby!"

And the sonographer, she freezes the image, and tries to hold me off, saying, like, "Ultrasound scan only looks like a slice through the flesh, but trust me, it isn't."

And in turn I ask, "Is it fake, then?"

"Listen," she tells me, with a tone that is half-polite, half-tired, half-annoyed, "it's considered to be a safe, non invasive, accurate and cost-effective investigation in the fetus, and not to worry."

Here she glances, with some caution, at them aunts, 'cause by now they've come awful close to the screen, which is where she, the sonographer, stands, if you can call that standing, 'cause really she's leaning back ever so slightly, like, away from them.

"None of you fine women should worry in the least," she says. "As you may already know, ultrasound has become an indispensable obstetric tool, which plays an important role in the care of every pregnant woman. My job here is to take some measurements, which reflect the gestational age of the fetus, to arrive at the correct dating of birth—"

"All right," I cut in, 'cause by now I've figured that despite all this rattling, she means well.

Still, I'm glaring at her, like, to stop her from chattering, 'cause anyway she don't barely make any sense. "Go on, then," I tell her, "go on with them measurements, but from now on, you better be real careful."

In reply she mumbles something, making the mistake of thinking that from where I lie, I can't see her rolling her eyeballs, which seem, somehow, even redder than before. So just to make myself clear I spell things out for her, like, "We don't want to see no more slicing, you hear?"

She blinks, giving a slight nod to me, which means that at last, we have a clear understanding between us fine women.

The image comes alive, and there is that black bubble again, swimming in in its gravy. She marks an outer edge around it, which at once, brings it so close to you that like, it could almost swallow you.

And in it you can spot, yes, you can suddenly find—gleaming there, in and out from them fuzzy, gnarly shadows—the most beautiful side view of a baby:

My little one curled there on his back, like he's just about to start bouncing around. There, there's his face! He's bathed in light, with a round forehead and plump cheek and the cutest little nose you've ever seen. And there's his lips, which is like, gulping for air, the mouth opening, closing on his own little thumb and then, sucking it.

Aunt Hadassa drops her chin in surprise, and in spite of trying her best to contain herself, she gives a shrill little yelp, after which the sonographer tells her, like, Enough! And to leave the office at once, because she's had it already, up to here!

And with a sigh, she warns us that she may quit her job right now, right in the middle of this here session, because God knows how she's even managed to make it to work this morning. She's so broken-hearted after last night, which was when—without no warning—her husband got up and left her, because she'd tried and tried but no matter how hard she kept on trying, she couldn't get pregnant.

By now she's like, on a roll: She can't stop herself from talking to me, even though she don't pay no attention to how I'm twisting here, on them fresh sheets, and how I'm biting my lips, which I have to do, 'cause I need to pee so bad, I really need to go, like, right now.

But what can I do? She isn't a sonographer no more, just plain Debbie, who talks and blinks, blinks and talks to no end, telling me how he turned, for just a second, and looked back at her over his shoulder, perhaps waiting for her to beg him to stay —but in sheer despair she cried out, Well? Don't just stand there —go! Go already! And so, finally, he did.

I can see she's in pain, and she don't need no advice from me, 'cause my man isn't no better anyhow, and who knows what to expect of him now. So I raise myself on my elbow and lean closer and touch her arm to say, like, I'm so, so sorry for you, Debbie. So now she starts sobbing, she's in tears, which at least stops her from blinking all the time. She says she can't take it no more, like, looking at them fetuses sucking their stubby little thumbs all day long.

And her parents, she says, they come from the old country, where a divorced woman's no better than damaged goods, so of course she isn't gonna tell them nothing about all this, because like, what will they say? She would much rather talk to a stranger—someone she won't see no time soon—or just bury it all inside.

Then Debbie wipes her swollen eyes to stare at aunt Hadassa, and to say that this screaming, right in her ears, makes her nervous, because she's in a delicate state, which you can tell by the sound of her hiccups and from time to time, her sniveling.

Her hand, she says, may turn shaky, which is a sign of bad luck, because that would prevent her from taking them measurements, such as the Crown Rump Length around the head, right here on screen, and the Femur Length, and the Abdominal Circumference, all of which requires great focus and like, complete silence around her.

So without a word aunt Hadassa hangs her head, and beats a path of retreat across the floor, like a wise, old general knowing when to admit defeat on the battlefield. Her two sisters march out the door closely behind her, and together they all wait for me outside. I can hear them whispering excitedly to each other.

When Debbie is finally done getting herself together and taking all them measurements, she tells me to go empty my bladder, which is a lucky thing, 'cause at this point I'm ready to burst, like, before you can even finish saying *sonographer*.

Then I get out to the waiting room, eager to get out as quick as I can, to find out if Lenny's come back home. Along the way I'm trying to put my hands in the sleeves of my winter coat and buckle my pink belt around me—only to discover that it don't fit me no more, 'cause my body, it isn't barely as slim as I thought it was.

Looking down on it, a view comes to me in a flash, which makes me brace myself, like, for danger: Down there on the floor, aiming at me from left, right and center, is the sharp, pointed tips, the tips of three pairs of shoes.

Me, I look up, and can't barely believe what I see: Aunt Hadassa gives me a smile, as do her sisters. "Wait, don't just go," she says, in the most disarming manner. "Stand there!"

Gone is the acid tone in her voice. Gone is that squint of suspicion. Them witches, they look awful friendly this time around. At first I figure that having seen my baby, they simply have no choice but to glow, just because of adoring him—but like, it's a bit more than that.

"My God, you are fearless!" says aunt Hadassa. "I dare say, you are just like me."

"No," I tell her, "I'm tougher."

"A fighter, is what you are! I mean, you would kill to keep your baby safe."

To which I say, "You bet I would."

Then, seeing me feel around my belt, like, to find the next hole in it, Aunt Hadassa offers, "Here, let me help you with that, dear."

And she draws even closer, and wraps herself around me—mushy, droopy flesh flapping like wings under her arms—and clicks my belt into place, so now it hangs nice and loose around my waist.

Then she takes a step back, letting me lead the way out, which is when I know that she knows that there's no way I'm gonna let no one stop me.

No one—I swear—no one can draw this story to a close, by telling me there's still time, like, to end it.

This is week twelve. My pregnancy's viable, and it's not to be aborted. So now, as we walk out, we fine women peer straight into each other's eyes, knowing that at long last, we have a clear meeting of the minds between us.

Dead Man's Fingers

Chapter 22

As Told By Ben

A minute ago I would have cut my wrists, hoping, that way, to win his tears—but already, my attitude has changed. Now, it is one of defiance: I throw his arms off my back, and in one big step I break his embrace, getting myself out of it, now getting entirely out of his reach.

In a quick reversal of mood, I feel completely swamped by his attention. At the same time, I am dying of thirst. I mean, really: a thirst so burning that I start wondering if it can ever be quenched.

My father just smiles, pouring me one cup of milk after another. "Well, now," he says, once I have gulped down the last one. "Lets get some fresh air."

And so, an hour or so later, the old man and I are down at Venice Beach, which is nearly deserted, barely a soul around.

There in front of us, closing in on an unclear horizon, is an autumn sun, reddening every ripple out there in the ocean, every little wrinkle here on the shore, and casting endless shadows, shadows made of vapor and dust, which seem to be flowing along, right over the surface.

We stand side by side. We smell the salt in the air. We step off the paved boardwalk and into the soft sand. All the while, I am listening to myself thinking. Slapped by a sudden backwash of emotion, I realize that just now, for the first time in years, something has changed in me: I have said something quite unusual, which came about without planning—but also, without regret. Three times I have named him and me, bringing the two together into a single word: becoming one, as in We.

For just a minute I lean on my father, to fold up my pant legs, take off my shoes and roll my socks in them. Then he leans on me, to do the same.

We cross the border between the wind-blown mounds of dry sand, and the saturated, nearly flat seaboard, trounced by the tide. The waves roll in, threatening to swallow us whole. With a roar in their widening mouth, they are leaping ahead, then lapping the sand angrily, foam on their lip.

And scattered here all around us—going away this way and that, across moist and dry land—are traces: footprints of things big and small. You can figure out what they might have been, by that which they have taken away, by what has gone missing, and how.

Here, these must have been flip flops, and those over there, tennis shoes. They have come and gone, leaving behind them dents in the sand, clear, neatly arranged dents, pressed in by some rubbery bumps, within the perimeter of each sole.

There, a barefoot child must have passed; farther out, an adult. Five toes and the ball of the foot, then again, five toes and the ball of the foot, boring round, shallow hollows, little basins, where water starts welling up now, in the wet sand.

And here, tiny webbed feet must have hopped and landed, hopped and landed, opening sharp, three-pronged holes in the sand, where a gull has sunk in its claws. Each set of footprints is distinct. Each is stamped, you see, with its own design, each with its own sole.

And all of them seem to be traveling with a certain purpose, which is unknown to me, criss crossing each other, forging ahead towards some unclear target, pressing on steadily—but in a zigzag fashion, left, right, left, right, as far as the eye can see, until all of a sudden, a high crested wave breaks ashore, rubbing out part of their path; and thus, erasing from the surface—and soon from memory, too—that which only a minute ago was still here, could still offer some clues, and let you jot down some notes of the journey.

"I wish," says the old man, "we would never forget this hour."

And I think, Why, what a grand sentiment! I wish you could just be quiet.

And he says, to himself this time, "Winter is coming. The day is shorter, it seems. And the shorter it is—the more precious each minute."

And I think, No. Not for me.

My father says, as if he could hear me, "Maybe not."

He stumbles over some piece of trash, and, having to steady him, I think, Too bad. He is too heavy for me. So is his talk.

He says, "You think I do not understand how hard, how painful it must be for you, coming here to a new reality: a home without your mom. I wish you would talk, Ben. Talk to me about it."

And I think, Who the hell wants to do that.

He waits for an answer, but after a while he seems to give up. "My God!" he says then, gazing straight ahead. "This place! This place, it is almost too beautiful for words."

Indeed, it is. I fill my lungs with air, and my spirit swings so high at the thought of wetting my toes, that I laugh out loud at what he is saying, whatever it is. Let him talk all evening if it makes him happy.

He says, "I wish I could write it, Ben."

In place of an answer I run along the beach, the old man trailing farther and farther behind me. For a minute I stop, and stoop down to pick what at first I thought was a dead butterfly—but no, this is just an empty shell, the two halves of which are hinged together, bringing to mind a hardened pair of wings.

I touch it: dark-blue and rough on the outside, slick and pearly inside, it housed a mussel once. Now there it lays, far from the sea, no longer able to keep itself closed—nor can it attach itself to others out there, on the distant wave-washed rocks, from where it came.

I feel a strange affinity with this thing. It has been left here, to fill with dry, barren grains, now that life has left it. How did it arrive here? By what thrust, what rush of wave? Maybe, it loosened its shell—just a crack—waiting, waiting for high tide, for seawater to come through, to revive it. I imagine its flesh quivering there, inside its broken enclosure: so soft, so vulnerable. So much like me.

Perhaps, it tried to roll its way back, to cross the border between that which is bone dry, and that which can still nourish it. Snatched and quickly consumed, its shell has been picked clean by a bird of prey, or—when the waves finally came—by a starfish.

Then its armor was carelessly spat out by the water, having failed to serve its purpose. So much like me.

I throw it back, in the direction of the old man. I think I can hear him, calling me from afar, "Wait..."

A sudden gust has shaken my father and he falls, abruptly, out of sight. A second later, the top of his head reappears behind a mound of sand.

"Ben," he cries, "wait for me!"

So I am standing there a long while, long enough for my father to have overtaken me already—but then, nothing. Finally I rush back, and there he is, in shallow water, wrapped in his black wool coat against the wind, collar flapping, hem dripping. He takes it off, and thrusts it into my hands.

Then, precariously, he takes a step deeper, and points, "Look, over there!"

Which is when I spot a beam of sunlight caught, somehow, by a grain of sand. It is shining there, as if through a diamond. Under that sparkle, protected from the surge by a jagged wall of rocks, is the pool: the tide pool, in which I used to splash my feet a long time ago, when I visited here as a child, with him. Dazed by the sight, and by the visions it brings out, in layer after layer of memories, I open my mouth and close it again, like a fish out of water.

Meanwhile, my father wades out to the rocks, leans over the edge, and waves his hand to me with something cupped in it, part of which is dangling down. I am reluctant to ask, Well, what is it? So I glance at this thing, this seaweed which is dark green and somewhat fuzzy, because of the hair on its swollen fingers. One finger wraps around a second one, which twists around, coiling over itself, creating a loop through which a third one feels its way, nicking here, pricking there, trying to penetrate.

"See?" he indicates. "Dead Man's Fingers! Remember?"

"No, I do not," I say.

He can tell I am lying, because really, how can I forget? It was he who, years ago, during our frequent strolls here, along the beach, taught me about algae and stuff.

"You forgot," says my father, "about that summer? About us?"

"There is nothing I care to remember," I say. "Not a thing."

Now he avoids looking into my eyes. My father squints, facing the glowing horizon, where the sun is bleeding, so slowly, into its own reflections in the water.

I was nine, back then. Dad was employed—for nearly a year—by some organization, some nonprofit environmental thing. It set out to produce a report card of sorts, grading the coastal waters at various locations along the California coast, to indicate some risks, I mean, risks of adverse health effects to beach goers.

As a child, a sentence like that would seem like a mouthful to me, so I never asked what actual work he did there—but somehow, his knowledge about aquatic plants and creatures showed through; as did his enthusiasm, which swept me along.

And so, it was from him that I learned about this seaweed, called Dead Man's Fingers. It can spread far and wide—which ignited my imagination—simply by attaching itself to ship hulls, oyster shells, and drag nets, or by floating along with ocean currents. Or, it can stay put. Dad showed me how it anchors to the surface of the rocks, upon which it lives.

Now the old man is spreading the fingers of this thing over his own hand, letting it rise and fall, rise and fall with the flow and the ebb; plunging it even deeper, as if trying to fish something out of the water; something that escapes him, comes back for just a second, and escapes him again.

"I so wish," he says, "I could find the words. You know, I hoped to become a writer, when I was your age. I used to think I had it in me."

To which I say, "It should come easy for you. You are so good with words."

His smile is rather brief.

"No, not really," he says. "Ask Anita. For the life of her, she cannot string together more than two syllables in a word—but if she could, she would tell you how devastating, even excruciatingly painful it is to read, or even just listen to my book."

"Book? You're writing a book now?"

"Yes; didn't I mention it?"

"No, you did not," I say indignantly. "Not to me, anyway."

Which he tries to shrug off. "Anita cannot bear listening to it. She has a reluctant admiration, I think, for the fact that I keep at it with such patience, such dedication, even, keep crafting something which is so incredibly protracted, and in her mind, pointless. Somehow, I have managed to bore her to tears. Too fragmented. Too many words."

"I guess you do not care to entertain her," I taunt him.

"Exactly," he says. "I do not aim to bring her to a quick climax, or to satisfy her with a happy end, either, because for me, the end—the end is rarely happy, and at this point, it is still obscure."

"Then," I glance at him slyly, "no wonder she is bored—"

He cuts in, "You must think me an old man. A man easily deceived."

"No," I say hastily. "You are reading me all wrong. She is not what I am interested in. It's your writing. Tell me more about that."

"For a time," he says, "I tried to write in ways that would give her pleasure, but now, something must have changed in me. No longer do I wish to sweep her off her feet, so to speak. Instead, I wish to open myself—"

"Open yourself?" I cannot help but laugh out loud.

And taken aback, he asks, "Why, you find that funny?"

"Bullshit!" I cry. "This is nothing but crap! Mental masturbation, is what this is! A more secretive man than you is hard for me to imagine!"

So he corrects himself. "What I wish to open up is not me, but my characters—all of whom are parts of who I am—giving her the opportunity to know them, to come live in their skin, to see, hear, touch everything they do. Just, be there, inside my head for a while, which I admit, may be rather uneasy at times. If—if she cared to listen, which I doubt, she would allow me to pull her inside—so deep, so close to the core, that it would be hard to escape, hard to wake up."

"And what if she wouldn't?"

"Then, who cares? She might as well drift off, which is what she does, lately. If the story were written about her—which maybe it is!—she would not even be present to realize it! But you—you, I hope, would be interested in it. You would not close the book on me. My writing, you see, is no longer an attempt at fiction. It has changed. It has become more akin to collecting."

"Collecting what?"

"That which is here, in front of us. That which will not remain. You. Me. That which is said between us. Our voices. This moment."

He pauses for a minute. "Other things, too," he adds. "Things other people may think mundane. The crash of waves. The shells of those mussels, out there. To me, son, they have a meaning, just as if they were some precious, historical artifacts."

He waits for me to ask, What kind of meaning; but I keep silent. Finally he says, "Your mother, she used to string them together, to make a long necklace. She would stare at the inner layer of each shell, and tip it over this way and that to capture the light, saying it reminded her, somehow, of a rainbow. Remember?"

I cannot help but look away, as a sudden shiver goes through my spine. My father draws closer to me, and without taking no for an answer, he tightens my jacket around me and zips it up, to ward off the cold.

"There," he says. "The sun is gone. Time to go home."

On the way back he is quiet; reflecting, perhaps, on one more thing he wants to say. Then, opening the door, he comes up with, "Remember, Ben, how I taught you to use the tape recorder? I mean, to record your voice?"

And I say, "When was that?"

And he says, "Why, when you broke your foot."

And I cry, "What? When did I ever break my foot?"

"You forgot," he says, glancing at me, now with a hint of worry in his eyes. "Memory is such a fragile thing. I learned that when your mother—"

His voice trails off; then he finds it again. "You had just turned twelve," he says, "which is when you broke your foot, climbing that branch; the one that used to lean there," he points, "right over the balcony. It was a bit flimsy—remember?"

The image in my mind is a bit hazy at first; but then it starts clearing, and I can see, I can just see three eggs in a nest, just a little bit out of my reach.

"I had to saw the thing off," he says, "so it would not be so tempting to climb it again."

"Oh," I say then. "I think I remember. Yes, I do."

"You used to stand by the railing, looking bored, sad even, staring out there at the tree, gauging the distance to that nest over there; a distance which could no longer be bridged, with the branch cut off. My heart ached for you. So I had to do something, to take your mind off the sight of that broken limb."

"Yes," I say. "I remember. This was when you taught me to record my voice."

He points at the tape recorder, which is wrapped in plastic on top of his desk. "You know," says the old man, "the thing still works. If you ever get the urge, I mean, if you need to talk—"

"No," I say hastily. "I do not think so, dad."

"You used to think it was fun, Ben."

"What I think, what I say to myself is private, you know—"

"I know, son: it is just like a diary. So do it for yourself, then; not for me. Keep the tape in your room; lock it in your suitcase, or something. One never knows," he says. "You may want to listen to yourself one day, years later—"

"You still have my old tapes, dad?"

"I do," he confirms. "A whole collection of them, in fact. Old ones, with your voice, and recent ones—with Anita's."

The mere mention of her name alarms me. From that woman, from what she might say on tape, he might get the wrong impression, I mean, about her and me. And then, I am afraid, then he may want to kill me.

I feel bound hand and foot by the intensity of the look in his eyes—but then I figure, it is something else that burns in them; something completely different from temper. Of all things, compassion?

"And what about mom?" I ask. "What about her voice? Did you tape it, did you? Maybe, if—if you had her tell her own story, I mean, in her own words, you could use it, then, to reach her, to remind her of things; which could, perhaps, slow down the disease—"

"Sorry, Ben," he says, and I detect the choked tone. "I wish I thought about it years ago. At this point all I have is her music, the last performance, Beethoven's fifth—but unfortunately, not her voice."

"You," I say, with contempt. "You should be so angry with yourself. How, how could you lose the one chance—"

"By now," he cuts in, "it is already too late."

"No," I say, "it cannot be."

With great exhaustion, the old man takes off his glasses, and rubs his eyes with both hands. "Natasha, she no longer seems to recognize me," he says. "I think that by now, she has forgotten who I am, what we used to be to each other. She has forgotten that she threw her ring at me. She has forgotten all the reasons why, why this anger in her, why the fury, which seems so, so futile in the end... And soon, when your mom loses the last trace of rage, when finally it goes away... I am afraid she would stop being herself, then."

"You," I charge, "you failed to keep her here, at home. Even worse, you lost who she was. You lost her voice!"

He slumps in his chair. "Back then," he says, "it never occurred to me how much I would miss it. I thought she was invincible. I thought things would always remain as they are. Time was something I had. Time did not matter."

"What is the point, then," I glare at him. "What the hell is the point in that precious tape collection of yours."

"Memory, son, is a fragile thing," he says, shrinking back from me. "One never knows."

"Oh, forget it," I turn away, looking blankly into the dark outline of the balcony right there, opposite ours, trying not to think, not to taste the salt of my tears.

And then, out of nowhere, the shoreline comes to mind.

Perhaps out there, somewhere along the beach—buried under some decay, under the Dead Man's Fingers, deep down under layers and layers of sand—are those long lost traces: the footprints of a father and a son, pressing on together, side by side in a zigzag fashion, left left, right right, as far as you can imagine.

If you could somehow uncover them, and dig them—ever so carefully—out of the dirt, and dust them off, and preserve them, as if they were some cherished, calcified relics of an ancient tribe, then... Who knows. Perhaps then, you could bring back that which has passed, and name these two strangers; name them as *We*, once more.

Until then, there is only this moment. I can tell he wants to write, so nothing, nothing is being said right now between the two of us.

A Wall. A Space. A Wall

Chapter 23

As Told by Ben

That night I lay there, wide awake, annoyed by my misfortune, having to listen to the creaking of their bed. I cannot help thinking, Oh no, not again; not like last night!

Well, what do you expect? The walls are so thin here, in this apartment building, that you can easily hear snores and sighs—not only of the old man, but also of the next door neighbors. The pipes are gurgling inside the walls. And if not for the wind outside my window, which is sucking the blinds in, sucking them out, you could probably hear what some kid—out there, in the next building down the street—mumbles in his dream.

Unable to fall asleep I clap my hands over my ears, trying to ignore these sounds; trying to stop thinking. *Stop*, I say. Stop thinking about that woman, Anita, separated from you by a wall, a space, a wall.

She is lying there, next to my father, in that large, creaking four poster bed, which used to belong to my mom. Maybe—like me—Anita is tossing off her blankets right this minute, and shivering there, in the dark. I rise up. I lie down. I imagine stepping in, looking into her eyes. Does she close them, so as not to take in the faint, colorless moonlight, which is thrown back from the walls? I imagine touching her curls. In what shade are they glinting there, on the blue pillow?

And through the wall, the space, the wall, can Anita hear the pounding, the loud pounding of my heart? Can she feel me, breathing her name? Does she whisper back to me, Stop it, stop it right now?

Does Anita, then, turn away from me, to his side of the bed? Is she staring at the dark outline, the outline of his heavy back, his shoulder, set against the crushed sheets?

Does she move over, and try to cuddle him? And then— having done so—does she feel lost, even more than before, in that place? If not for the roof overhead, for which only he can provide, would she, perhaps, prefer me to him?

I wonder if at this point, Anita is removing her arms and legs from around the old man, thinking, perhaps, that to cling to him is like clinging to a fish, because really, he is much too slick for her. Now that they are married, he may take his affairs elsewhere; which is exactly what he did when mom was here.

My father may never give up his secrets; never be fully open with a girl like her. Perhaps he thinks her too vivacious, too young, or too simple. Perhaps there is *no* woman to whom he can truly connect. Here is one thing I hope she knows: she deserves better.

There it is, that sound again. It starts by squeaking and ends by creaking. My father must have rolled over, out of her reach. Is she closing her eyes, so as not to see, not to take in the light?

At last I can no longer take it, and get the hell up. I walk in the middle of the shadows, step out of the corridor, into the hall, the living room, around the white piano, heading in the direction of the balcony. I slide open the glass door, cross the threshold. I lean over the railing, breathing, breathing the night air, and no: not really thinking about her. Not at all.

His desk, taking nearly the entire space of the balcony, is a massive old piece of furniture, which has been beaten by use, and by the weather. My father refuses to bring it in—not only because of the lack of room, but because here, only here in the open, his mind is at peace. It can roam free, he claims, without interruptions, and without clutter.

A thick glass has been floated on top of his desk, to protect it from the elements. In the center of the surface is a small desk lamp, turned off. The tape recorder is here, on the left side. It is shrouded with a plastic cover, which is reflected, rather faintly, in the glass below. I remove the shroud, and find a tape already loaded. Then, out of an old habit, I press *Rewind. Record.*

One day you will hear my voice. You will know me. What can I say, but this—

Reflected on the right side of the desk is a cloud, moving slowly, veiling and unveiling the moon. Under it—I mean, under the shine of the mirrored cloud—I notice something else, lying flat: a bunch of lined, yellow papers stapled together, written in his hand. For a minute I hesitate, because what my father has written, what he has protected here, under the glass, with such care, must be private—but then, I find myself so curious, and the hell with privacy! I am his son, after all...

So I lift the edge of the glass—just a bit—and take hold of the stapled corner, and slide the papers out. They swish in my hand.

Which is when I hear a soft voice out of the darkness behind me, asking, "Who's there?"

To which I whisper, "It's me: Ben."

"You shouldn't do that," she says.

So I ask, "Do what?"

And Anita says, "You know: read his stuff."

"Oh, that," I say. "I was just bored."

"Bored?" she says, yawning, "I ain't surprised. His writing will get you that way in a big hurry."

Anyhow, she can see for herself that the papers are nearly unreadable, because his letters are small, and drawn in blue ink, which seems blurry in the starlight. Leaning closer, she turns the lamp on for me. And as soon as the first sentence becomes clear, I curse him, curse, curse, curse him, because how dare he.

"Damn it!" I cry. "These words, they—they are not his—but mine! My words—stolen!"

"You sure? This here, it's his handwriting."

"It is," I say, "but this, this is my story, which I recorded long ago, when I was twelve years old, maybe."

"Then," she says, "from now on, be careful. Like, think twice about what you say."

Somehow, what she means is clear to me, and there is no need to ask for an explanation. I better be careful about the words uttered—or else, they will be spun.

She presses *Stop* on the tape recorder, and whispers in my ear —what, I am not going to tell you.

And I am not going to tell you the smell of her hair, either.

But then, a moment later I forget all about being on guard. I find myself angry, so angry at my father—but even more than that, surprised. I have told him a thousand times already: my thoughts are mine, and mine alone! How dare he pretend to agree with what I say—and later, ignore it, and invade my privacy, exposing, in the process, some of my most painful, most intimate moments? This is a line he has never crossed before.

Anita gives me a look, which I take to be a warning. Then she places the shroud back in place, over the tape recorder.

"The way I picture it is like, this is his desk. He's always here," she says, "even when he isn't. So just, don't say nothing you don't want him to hear. You must be careful, Ben. The words you leave behind you, they ain't yours no more."

And with that, she turns away.

I shut the glass door behind her. I murmur, "Good night," knowing that no one can hear me inside. If she blows me a kiss, I cannot detect it—and so, neither can you. I do not even wish to look at her, because I aim not to see, and not to tell you even a hint of what I see. As I told you before, go! Go away! Or else, if this is where you must stay, just *Stop*! Stop listening. My thoughts are mine!

The rage swells in my chest. I want to burst into his bedroom, even before she gets there, and—slap!—punch the unsuspecting, heavy-eyed old man in the face. Instead, I just crumple the papers, and throw them to the floor and stamp, stamp, stamp my feet on them.

Which is when the glass door reopens, just a crack, and she says, "Ben—"

"What? What now?"

"If I was you, I would burn that tape."

"I cannot," I say, utterly frustrated. "It has my voice on it."

And she comes back with, "Unless—"

"Unless what?"

"Unless," she says,"like, you want him to know what you really think. Yes, I bet that's it! You want to draw blood."

And with that, she slides the glass shut, so instead of her face, all I see is a reflection of mine.

I look down at the mess I have made, thinking that perhaps, this is all a mistake. I may be wrong about him. Indeed, I am. He is no worse than me. He may have found himself curious, and the hell with privacy! He is my father, after all...

He used to be my hero. How could I forget: when grandma collapsed, it was dad who saved her. He breathed life into her; and it lasted in her for two whole weeks. Now, I suppose, he wants to save me. From what, I have no idea. Recently I noted the look in his eyes; they are so full of pity, as I have rarely seen in them before. He seems worried, unusually worried about me. At this point I no longer resent it—but still, it makes me uneasy.

At first I figured, maybe he is worried about my future: I mean, about my drifting aimlessly, and dropping out of medical school, and failing to get a job, and being unable to support myself—but no: never once since my return has he even come close to touching any of these subjects. I must admit: he is rather careful with me. If I am silent—so is he.

And yet, even when we do talk, there is a distance between us: a separation, which he seems to respect. A wall, a space, a wall.

And so, I am left to wonder. Why is he worried? What can it be? Perhaps, because of mom? According to him, she was diagnosed with Early Onset Familial Alzheimer Disease. At first I thought, it could be worse, and thank goodness it isn't a brain tumor—only to realize that during my studies in medical school, I heard of some people with brain tumor who got better—but never once did I hear of anyone who got better from Alzheimer's.

Now for the first time I consider the full meaning of that word: no, not Alzheimer's, but the one immediately before it, which up to now I have ignored, perhaps deliberately so: *Familial.* Which means, Hereditary. It is a tough verdict for mom, and the threat of one for me, as well—but far as I know, the only way for me to be sure of not receiving it is to die young.

Stop, I tell myself. Stop thinking now.

I remember: when I was six, we strolled together one morning along the beach. The tide was low, and dad picked up a shell, an empty, twisted shell of a sea snail, that had washed up on shore.

He handed it to me, saying, "Here, Ben. Keep it. It is a gift."

My father taught me then how to hold it to my ear and listen, listen with all my being; because, he said, the sound of the waves had been caught, somehow, inside it, which is a secret only few people know, because it only becomes clear if you stay there, very still, and forget everything else for a while. The sound, dad promised, would always remain—even if you took the shell far, far away from here, say, to the city, or to Santa Monica Mountains, out there. Even so, you would still hear it.

I remember doubting him. I thought, Oh well. High tide, low tide. Nothing stays. Nothing is forever.

I admit, in the past few days I have judged him harshly. Now I know, I can tell where I might have gone wrong. When the old man says, "The day is shorter, it seems. And the shorter it is— the more precious each minute," it is not *his* life he is thinking about. Perhaps, it is mine.

My father is doing his best to hold things together. Memory is a fragile thing. So he is trying to capture the moment, perhaps for my sake. At least, the sound of it. One day, if—if like my mother, I shall start losing it, my memory, I mean—I want to believe that dad will be there, as close to me as once he was, holding it to my ear.

Time in a fold of brain. The ocean in a shell.

I pick the papers from the floor, which is where they have been trampled on, and I flatten them under the golden lamplight, which warms the tips of my fingers. This is my story, I tell myself. This is me, fifteen years ago. Here is my voice. Here is his gift to me.

And so, I begin reading.

There it is, that sound again. And again—just like last night—it is only a whisper...

Only An Empty Dress

Chapter 24

As Told by Ben, Fifteen Years Back

T here it is, that sound again. And again—just like last night
—it is only a whisper. No, not now, mom... Just a little bit
longer. If I open my eyes, if I open them now, for sure I will fall
—

Lighter and faster than anything here I come, traveling
through the air, hovering as if there is no gravity. The toy-sized
houses below me are floating away; so are the trees. Here and
there they catch a ray of light, then dim away. After a while they
fall back into the stream of things.

From time to time I can see my shadow: there, there it is,
fluttering dreamily over the land, like a fish wiggling across a
vast, sandy bottom. The shadow is spreading as I leap over the
valleys, shrinking as I drift down toward the hilltops. From here I
can almost see, see over the summit, even over the highest,
sharpest rocks. They reach up to me, lick my toes and then, in a
flash I kick, I rise over them until—

I sit up in my bed with a start. The blanket has fallen off and
there is my foot, bandaged. Some boys are clumsy. Some boys
fall from trees, they get all bruised up and never learn a lesson, is
what grandma says. Everyone knows who she is talking about.

She is right, too. I hate learning lessons. I hope I never will.

I try to pull back the blanket and suddenly, here is that sound again—only clearer this time. How can I describe it? It is faint, like a moan, going up, down and then up again. Just listening to it sets my nerves on edge. Can you make any sense of it?

I remember asking mom about it. I said, "You feeling all right?" And she said, "Yes dear, why?" And I said, "I heard you at night." And she paused for just a second, but then went on, combing her hair. And I said, "So? What happened, mom? Were you hurt?"

And she waved her hand, the way she does to dismiss what I say, because to her it seems to make no sense. Then she smiled at me from the mirror.

But I pressed on saying, "Well?" And immediately noticed a change in her: the forehead was stitched with worry, and a little pleat was forming there, between her eyebrows, which meant she was doing the grown-up thing, trying to think of something to say in order not to say a thing, after which she said, "Oh that! I guess I was having a nightmare. Sometimes," she added, "I talk in my sleep."

And I came close, right behind her, and gave her a hug, and said, "So, if it happens again—then what?" To which she shrugged. I looked up at her, at her reflection really, because that was where I could find her eyes, and I said, "Should I come in, then? Should I wake you up?"

"Oh no," she answered, blushing a little. "Dad can do that."

So now, shivering a bit, I find myself cuddling the pillow, swaying back and forth, hypnotized by that moan and becoming angry, very angry with dad. How can he go on sleeping? It should not be that difficult to touch her, to have her snap out of that Oh, Oh, Oh mumble—I mean, really! If he did what he is supposed to do, I would not have to pop open my eyes, smack in the middle of my dream, right at the moment when I am at the top of the world, and wonder how to take care of things.

There is nothing I wouldn't do for mom, I mean it! Waking her from a nightmare is the least I can do. I will wake her—and no one else but her. So I slip off my bed. The floor is bare. It has a cold, stony touch. What you call darkness is really not all that dark. Faint moonlight seeps through the blinds, puddles over the sheets, spills all over the folds, and then crawls, with some hesitation perhaps, across the room.

I find the door handle and lean into it. I know exactly how much pressure to apply, especially around the rusty spot, so that —without a screech—it swings open.

Once outside my bedroom I make an effort to avoid limping, for fear of making a sound. So I slide across the hall, past the empty aquarium, which grandma bought me after my injury.

Coming dimly into view, as I enter the corridor, are the closed doors ahead of me.

I remind myself to sidestep the two squeaky floor tiles: one lies in wait right there, next to the toilet, the other—next to grandma's room. I don't want to wake her. She always has some boring old lesson to teach me.

So I move slowly, carefully, around those floor tiles, halting to listen after each step, one foot on tiptoe, the other—dragging along. You think this is easy for a boy, a tense, jumpy twelve-years old boy? It's not—but I cannot go back.

At last I am closing in on my target: the door at the end of the corridor. The handle is within my reach when, once again—

Oh, says my mom from within. Her voice rings so sweet, so melodious—each Oh coming to a higher peak than the last one—that all of a sudden, I am in awe. I step back, trying to make up my mind: is this a nightmare she is having—or perhaps something different? Should I rush in to save her—or perhaps not?

And as I stand there, utterly in confusion, I hear, as clear as can be, a little, distinct note, a squeak really: the squeak of a floor tile being stepped on, coming from the shadowy corridor, directly behind me.

I glance over my shoulder: outlined against her door, which is now flung wide open, there she stands: a small, hunched figure, raising a wrinkled finger at me. Grandma is short, but formidable: she is the real power in our family. No one is allowed to forget the fact that every month, the rent is paid for with her savings.

Which is why dad keeps telling me we should be grateful, very grateful. His face droops every time he says that, and his voice becomes strained. Really strained. So there it is. We have her to thank for the roof over our heads. In addition I have her to thank for the empty aquarium.

Somehow Grandma looks even smaller than usual, so I have to remind myself that in this family, she is the giant. She opens her mouth; but without her teeth—which are probably swimming in that glass of water, right next to her bed—you know it would be next to impossible to figure out what she is trying to say.

An intense look passes between us, without a single word.

I cannot imagine why she is still holding her breath. For some reason I get a funny feeling, a feeling that she is about to crumble, that she is trying, somehow, to call my name.

Her finger trembles in the air and then, I cannot believe my eyes, it is such a shock: like an old, broken doll, she comes crashing to the floor.

Mom cracks open the bedroom door and takes a peek from behind. I'm afraid that perhaps, she is wearing nothing but perfume; and so I avoid looking at her. "Oh my," she cries out, "oh my God!" Out comes dad and upon seeing me there, crouching down beside grandma and holding her white head, he goes back in and calls 911. Why I keep holding up her head I have no idea.

Because of the hunch on her back, the head is hanging in midair even as she lies there. Dad brings out a pillow and sticks it there, under her neck. Then he takes a deep breath, puts his lips on hers, and—to my amazement—he blows, which is the first time I see anyone doing something like that.

With each puff—I get it now—he tries to give her some air, so she may breathe again. Between one try and another you can take a look at her. She still seems to be looking at me, ghastly pale, and her finger is still quivering.

Mom visits her in the hospital every day for the next two weeks, then decides to bring me along. So I see grandma again, one last time; that is, if you don't count seeing her later, in the casket, when she looks even less like herself.

In the hospital, mom tells me she will go in first, and so I am left waiting outside the half-open door. From that distance, through the crack, I can see grandma. She is wearing a crumpled gown, which looks too big for her and too awkward, perhaps because they did not bother to alter it, the way all her dresses are altered, to account for the hunch. She looks white, like porcelain—but then, gripping the iron bar of the bed, gripping it with all her might she manages, somehow, by the power of pride, to wait there standing, so that mom can come up to her, and bend before her to give her a kiss.

Grandma notices me; for an instant we stare at each other, and I can see her papery lips move as she says to mom, irritably, "What on earth possessed you to do that?" And mom says, "What?" And incredibly, grandma answers by asking, "What did you bring *him* for?"

And mom looks dumbfounded, so grandma turns her back on her—but from where I stand I can still see her forming the words, "You think the boy should see me like this? In this state? That is how you want him to remember me?"

And at last mom understands her, and she goes back and gives a slight push to the door until it clicks shut, cutting me off.

And when mom comes out and we leave the hospital, she can see how angry I am, because I start kicking things all along the path, I mean stones, and cracks in the asphalt, and tires of cars, kicking them hard with my injured foot. If you would ask me, right there and then, why I keep doing it, I would not know what to say.

Who cares about pain! I kick, kick, kick everything in sight, and it is not until later that day—when dad says, "Want to come with me?" and I say, "No, no way!" and then ask, "Where?" and he mentions the Aquarium Supply Store, where we can get a bag of sand, and even a few rocks, fancy rocks from a real coral reef—that I kick myself for being so silly, which is when, finally, I stop kicking.

The store owner, a stout man with bulgy eyes, shows me the most beautiful fish I have ever seen. Some are transparent, some —colorful. He points out the Lemon Tetras, with a shimmering stripe all the way to the fin; the Black Neons, with a red band over a yellow band over their eyes; and the Kuhli Loaches, with muddy, vertical marks over their backs.

I glance at dad and somehow, he understands the question before it is asked; he smiles at me saying, Tomorrow, son. I will get them tomorrow. It is no good adding fish to the tank the same day you fill it with water. And I look away thinking, How did he do that? How did he get me? Did it happen because I let him?

And in a snap, my mind goes back to that night, the night which I am trying to stop remembering, when grandma lost her balance. And I wonder: when dad found me there, holding up her head, was he surprised? Was he curious to know how I appeared, at that very instant, by her side, just as she tumbled over?

Since then, he has never asked me about it, not even once.

Did he figure it out? Does he know I was waiting there, listening, just about to rush in and save mom, save her from something, perhaps even from him? Does he know that I know that he knows?

I wonder: can I make myself transparent, like those fish? And on the flip side, can I make myself obscure, so that no one—not even dad—can see through me?

That evening he helps me layer the sand, set the rocks and fill the tank with water. I turn on the fluorescent fixture at the top of the aquarium, and leave it turned on, so it glows through the night; and I imagine live plants rising from the gravel, and lots of fish, fish flicking their tail, shooting in and out of their hiding places between the silvery corals.

The call from the hospital comes in after midnight, and I know that the next day I will see grandma again, this time for the last, really last time. A time comes when even a giant crumbles.

I lay there in bed feeling cheated, somehow; cheated by myself, mostly, because I never gave her a chance to hug me, never took the risk to come in, come closer and say, Goodbye, grandma. And now all I can remember about her is that moment, from a distance, just before the door clicked shut. I go back to that place and I see her papery lips, and I know she is asking, That is how you want him to remember me?

Back home after the funeral I cannot find a moment alone. The place is buzzing with neighbors and distant relatives, including my three aunts, each of whom has eyebrows painted in, in place of the real ones. At first they talk in low voices, afraid, perhaps, that grandma might hear what they say, or come out to scold them for their manners. They bend over me and pinch my cheeks so hard that instantly, I forget all about the pain in my foot inside the bandages.

So I am forced to hide from attention. I stand there, very quietly, in the corner behind the tank, and feed the new fish, which dad got for me earlier that morning; just a smidgen between the fingers, like he told me... And then maybe one more smidgen, or two, because I hate learning lessons, and because I am bored and lonely here, in this crowd, and also because of the fish, because they look so hungry for these little specks. You can see them flocking up in a big haste, competing to reach the surface.

Then I go into grandma's room. It does not smell like her anymore. The bedspread is fresh, and tightly stretched. There is not a dent in the pillow.

The cup is still there—but her teeth have vanished; they are nowhere in sight. I try to imagine that I can hear them clattering. Then I peek into the closet.

It is tightly packed with her dresses, all of which been altered around the shoulders and back, to fit grandma. Most of them are brown. One dress has muddy, vertical patterns, just like the fish, the Kuhli Loaches. By the end of the evening all the dresses would be whisked away, right off the hangers; and my aunts— arms heavily loaded—would find it cumbersome to reach my cheeks again.

I am not stupid; I know that grandma would not need her dresses, ever again. She is not coming back, and so, there is no reason to keep them. Still, I feel that her things are hers—at least for a little while longer—and what do my aunts need with her stuff? Can't they wait? She was buried only a few hours ago, and her dresses are not going anywhere; they are not even the right size for them, and besides, it would be impossible to undo what was done, I mean, that alteration for the hump in the back.

That night, all is still. There is no crying, no moaning anywhere.

I get up and pace back and forth, hobbling between my room and the hall, which is lit by the reflections from the aquarium. I draw closer. A Black Neon comes toward me, turns tail, comes back aiming, it seems, directly at me. I focus at it. Magnified by the water, it is tapping, tapping into the glass until my eyes cross over.

Meanwhile in the back, suspended under the surface like a ghost, is another fish. I forget what it is called. It is white. It has red eyes. And right now, you can tell it is not moving.

I watch it for a while, and the longer I watch it, the more I realize that—quite strangely—the body is starting to tilt. By now it is nearly on its side; and the tail, which is so fine, so tender that it looks like it is made out of pure light, responds to little ripples coming from the other fish—but makes no motions of its own.

Before I know it my hand cuts into the water; it comes out dripping, with the fish lying there, helpless, between my fingers.

It seems to be gulping for air. Maybe it forgot how to breathe. I know I can fix it. First I rub the mouth, delicately, with my finger. Then I try to massage the entire body. I am doing my best, my very best to be gentle—but in the end, some scales tear off the body, and a tiny fin flakes away.

At this point, I must do something, and fast. Just like dad: he did what he could for grandma, and blew his breath into her; and his breath was magical, because it lasted in her, somehow, for the next two weeks. I can do better than that for this little body, even with a few scales or a fin missing. So, I take a deep breath, put my lips to the fish—but then the smell, the touch... It makes me pause for a minute.

Still, I cannot give up: I must be brave, just like dad—or else, the spell may be broken. So again I gasp, and with frantic hope, I give a full-blown puff. The red eyes seem to be looking at me, and the tail is hanging over my finger, and it looks limp, and a bit crumpled.

I cannot allow myself to weep. No, not now. So I wipe the corner of my eye. Now if you watch closely, right here, you can see that the tail is still crinkling. I gasp, and blow again. I blow and blow, and with a last-gasp effort I go on blowing until all is lost, until I don't care anymore, I mean it, I don't care but the tears, the tears come, they are starting to flow, and there is nothing, nothing more I can do—

Then I feel mom, the smell of her skin. Here she is, wrapping her arms around mine. Softly, gently, she releases the fish, and takes me to their bed, and dad says nothing but makes room for me, and I curl myself in the dent between them, and it feels so warm here and so sweet that at last, I can lose myself, and I cry myself to sleep.

Lighter and faster than anything here I come, soaring again through the air as if there is no gravity. From time to time you can see a school of fish flying dreamily overhead, rising to reach the little specks up there at the surface. Something with muddy, vertical marks comes ruffling towards me in the stream of things. At first I cannot tell what it is.

It scrambles over my foot, spreading fine, transparent ripples all around me. And it is at the very last moment—a heartbeat before it flutters away—that I can see it was nothing, only an empty dress.

The Naked Bulb

Chapter 25

As Told by Anita

S ince the bleeding began, I've been missing my ma more and more. If she was here I could ask her, like, How come I feel so alone. How come I can see, all of a sudden I can now see how my youth is wasting away in this place. Like, I have no air, I'm wilting here. And Lenny, he don't even pay no attention, 'cause he's back to his usual thing, which is: comb his thinning, gray hair—sleek it back, real slow and careful—and then work all day, write all night, either out or away.

Me, I thought getting married was meant to change things— but then, if things are changing it's not for the better.

It's funny how now—when she's out of my reach forever—I feel so close, so terribly close to her. At least now, ma don't push me back no more. She can't say, like, Enough, girl! Snap out of it! And she don't get in the way, I mean, in the way of me doing what I've been wishing for so long I could do, which is just cling, cling real close to her. I so miss the smell of her face: a mix of sweat, cheap eau de cologne and cigarette smoke. I try to dream up that smell, which gags me, and stings my eyes, and brings me close to tears.

If she was here I could ask her, like, when did she have the hunch, the first clear hunch that pa was gonna leave us, and how long after that did it happen.

At this point I don't know how much longer I can go on relying on Lenny, 'cause even when he's here, even when he fixes his eyes on me, there's something in them lately, something hard, even furious, which I swear, I don't really get.

Last night I was so worried—worried to the point of getting mad—because for some reason, Lenny didn't come home at all, even though I got all ready for him, all prettied up with my little black dress, which for the first time I had trouble zipping up, 'cause my belly had just started to grow, and to get rounder than it used to be.

He wasn't there—but to me, it felt like he could watch me through them walls. I felt choked. I even cussed him in my heart. I told myself it was just a dumb, crazy feeling, and to stop fighting for a breath. Still, it felt like Lenny could spot, somehow, the sudden blush that—in spite of myself—started flaming on my skin, the moment I passed by kitchen and laid eyes on his son.

In a blink, the air felt steaming hot all around me.

This was something new to me, 'cause up to this moment I didn't exactly care for Ben—even though from this angle, the slant of his shoulders looked just the same as his pa's. Suddenly my heart went pit-a-pat, which—I swear—didn't happen never before. If my husband was here tonight, if he hadn't left me, it won't have happened now. No matter how much I tried to cool it, here I was, blushing, on account of the fact that I've just blushed.

And Ben, he was leaning back, lost in his dreams in the corner. His pale face and his mussed up hair fell just outside the light, the dim, fuzzy light which had no border, no clear border anywhere on the kitchen table, 'cause there wasn't no lampshade over the bulb, on account of the fact it had been broken and removed, like, ages ago, and never replaced.

I bet you would have me turn away, which was the right thing to do—but it was already too late, so I didn't. Anyway, I could already tell that Ben could tell, by the swish of my hair, that there I was, just about to cross the threshold. His nostrils flared up, like, to breathe in the scent, the faint scent of my shampoo, mingled with a dab of perfume.

I could've walked past that door—but then, this I knew: whatever happened, in your eyes it would always be my fault. The boy wants me. He wants me real bad, and for that, I pity him. He would soon kill himself if he can't have me—but any which way, you would blame it on me. In your eyes, the boy can't be nothing else than naive. So of course, it must've been me, me who seduced him.

You would call me a bad girl—so then, why shouldn't I be?

For ten years I tried, as best I could, to be squeaky clean. It's too damn hard, and you don't never trust me anyway. So instead I could really go wild, and take my revenge on my husband, by giving him a reason—a *real* reason this time—to be jealous, so he don't need to go searching for one.

I beg you, Lenny, I whispered. Come back to me, or else... From this point on, things won't be the same, never again. I swear, I'm gonna do something bad, gonna hurt you, dear, so you won't never leave me like this, without even saying one word.

After a while I dried my eyes. Hell, what's the point praying, or hoping, or threatening, when anyhow, you ain't even here to listen.

So I came in, hips swaying, and looked down at the boy, saying, "Help me, Ben."

Which startled him. The features of his face contorted, like he couldn't make up his mind whether to be troubled by me surprising him, or not.

Either way, he sprang to his feet and with a shaky voice, said, "Sure, what—"

And I turned my back on him, and tugged at the zipper of my black dress, pulled it as high as it would go, so now it reached the level of my waist, and then I just stood there, waiting for him to make his move. And with trembling fingers Ben brought the two edges of fabric together—barely touching the back of my neck—and managed, somehow, to pull the thing all the way up.

"There," he said, with a catch in his voice. "It is done."

And then he stepped back, away from me. I reckon he was thinking about the late hour, and about his pa, who should've been here already, and about not being able to face him, 'cause like, how can you try to rob the old man of his woman, and how can you win any fight—let alone dare to stay in it—while having to carry, somehow, the terrible handicap of being young.

I licked my lips, so they would be real red and shiny, and smiled at him. Inside I was praying that the light in the bulb would blaze so bright, so fiery it would burst. And them walls, pressing awful tight all around us, would just melt away. And the pane of glass would sizzle, and the window frame, it would turn to ashes—poof!—like dust into thin air, so anyone out there in the street could watch us, as if there wasn't no walls, and we didn't have no shelter. Then there would be no secrets no more. Nothing left to hide.

Here, Lenny, I cried inside, take a good look! Here I am—not only for your eyes, but for all eyes to see!

And for the first time in our ten years together I thought, he's old. He's the old man passing out there, somewhere in the dark, limping stiffly on his way to some other woman, some fake blond, I bet. At the sound of my voice he would shiver, and look up. He would be unable to take his eyes off the boy. And the boy, he would just freeze there, in his seat, unable to take his eyes off me.

I hoped, with every bit of bitterness, that Lenny won't miss the look, the shy look his son flashed at me, when I slid into my chair and—real slow and naughty—began crossing my legs.

Which at once, made Ben tense up. I met his eyes, and could feel my look shooting through him, like it was a poisoned arrow. Now my legs was crossed knee on knee, and my lips was wet and parted, ever so slightly, and I began lowering my eyelids. Slowly his face dimmed, like, it fell into a black nothing, and then, I went back to thinking about Lenny:

As a husband, he may lose his temper with me, from time to time—but as a writer, he totally gets what I need. He lets me talk, talk, talk for hours on end, keeping himself out of the way, like, real nice and discreet, so as not to stop me from pouring my heart out in front of his tape recorder.

Me, I put my faith in him, knowing that Lenny would keep his word, he won't listen to nothing I say, 'cause some words, they rattle in your head, and their sound, it can be jolting to anyone, I mean, anyone but you, because they're yours. So you should hide them real good, keep them hushed up, like, under a blanket. Them words, they shouldn't be heard by no one—especially not those you hold dear.

Which makes me trust the distance between us. It keeps me safe—but at the same time, it holds us apart.

So at this moment—when I started punishing him by raising my eyes, and giving Ben that which he craved, a cruel little smile—the best thing that could happen would be this: Lenny would come bursting in.

I can just see it in my head. He would be breathing hot fume straight into my eyes, making me step back and blink. His forehead would be, like, swollen with rage. And that pleat in its middle, which used to remind me of my pa, would grow deeper than ever. And the vein by the side of his neck would seem to be knotted. With an awful screech Lenny would shove the table off to the side, and flick the naked bulb hanging over its place, till it swung violently to and fro, to and fro.

To his son I bet he would say nothing, 'cause if he did—if he said, like, *Stop*! Stop staring at her, she's fucking mine!—things could soon come to blows. Instead, he would just fix his eyes on Ben, scaring him right out of the kitchen. Then, not being able to hold himself back no longer, Lenny would like, explode. He would rip my dress in two and shout at me, and I would shout back, even cry. And then, then it would be all over.

The air would be cleared between us, and we could start fresh, almost.

I should be so lucky—but no; sadly, that didn't happen. Instead I raised my hand—like I was him—and pushed the table, and flicked the naked bulb. Under it—right there between the boy and me—stood Lenny's chair. It looked so empty, so bare that it glowed, like, real bright against the shadows.

There was a splotch of light that danced over the seat, like a dance of triumph, almost. It darted wildly from one edge of the seat to the other, and after a while it started slowing down, swinging only a bit, then only a tiny bit, till at last it stopped right there, right in the center. At which time I felt a little something, a little pang in my heart. Perhaps, remorse.

All the while, Ben went on sitting there, in his chair, pretty stiff and silent. He lowered his head, like, to study his own hands, so as not to stare at me. Nothing else stirred. Me, I glanced out the window: nothing stirred out there, either. You couldn't spot no one in the twilight—but in my head I pictured the old man turning away from me, and in that second I sensed his heart turning, turning against me.

Which is when I snapped my fingers, right there in front of my face, and told myself in a sharp voice, a voice that wasn't even mine, Enough already! Snap out of it, girl!

What's the matter with you, anyway? So, your man hasn't come home? Too bad, really! Who knows where the hell he is. Who cares with whom he's sleeping tonight. Jealousy is a tough thing, Anita. It's taken a bite out of you. It hurts. Yes, I can see the pain. So now, he hasn't come home—and the thing you worry about is *what*, exactly? Crossing your legs? Really? You out of your mind?

I slapped my own cheek thinking, I so wish ma was here.

She Deserves Better

Chapter 26

As Told by Anita

It's awful nippy here, inside and out, even though this is only mid-fall. Shut tight in front of me is the glass door, which I can't hardly open, on account of being tired, and a bit wobbly on my feet. Even so I can hear a sound, a muffled sound from the other side, out there on the balcony. From this angle I can spot him, kinda: at least his outline, bent over the desk, and the slant of the shoulders.

And I can't barely see a face, but somehow I can tell it's a familiar voice out there, saying, like, *Here is one thing I hope she knows: she deserves better.*

Which makes me shiver, even in my coat. The man, he's tapping his fingers tensely on the edge of the record player, pressing one key, then another, which brings up the voice saying, louder now, *She deserves better*, and again, *deserves better*, then, *better*.

That voice, it's Ben's voice—but them fingers, they're the old man's fingers. The instant he hits *Pause* is when my doubts go away, and like, I know who it is.

So I don't even need him to turn around, and I don't even want to ask him, like, Where was you, 'cause I don't want to hear no lies, and no long stories either, and above all, I tell him in my heart, I don't want to admit how lonely I am here, in this place, which isn't my home, Lenny, without you.

Still absorbed in his work with his back to me, he tries to slide open a drawer, a drawer which I haven't noticed in his desk before—not even the other day, when I went through the jumble of his papers, looking for clues, any clues of where Lenny had gone, or with whom he might be staying, or how he expected me to pay all them bills, because, like ma used to say, money don't come cheap.

I hope he finds things in place now, still in the right state of disorder. I hope I didn't mess up no pages of his writing—or else, his stories will make even less sense than they already do.

The drawer is damn clunky. It rattles a bit under his hand, like, the slides under it must have gotten rusty. Then it comes to a full stop, hanging in midair. He leans in to put his hand right there, inside the mouth of it, and his fingers are swallowed up by a deep shadow, which kinda scares me, like I've seen all this before, in a dream or a movie or something.

So in distress I gulp for air, just about to cry out to him, Stop! Pull out, Lenny! Your hand—no, don't talk, don't even breathe a word—it's about to be bitten off, like, if you don't hold your tongue, right now, hold it from telling me a lie.

Which is the moment he freezes, like he's just caught a sound, the light sound of my footfall. There's a chill in the air, which I can see right here, in front of my nose, 'cause like, the vapor of my breath starts rising, curling in the air and clouding the partition between us.

Lenny turns over his shoulder, and even before he can sense who's standing here, watching him, you can tell he's jolted, real shaken even, on account of not expecting no one here, at this time. He screws up his eyes, so I bet he's looking for his own self, mirrored back to him—only to catch sight of me.

In a flash he spots my outline, like, through them spots on the murky glass.

Lenny gets up from the chair, awful stiff, and in one limp he comes to a stand right there, opposite me. My God, he looks strange today, and not only because he looks kinda naked, I mean, without them glasses. His gray hair isn't even combed, like he's awakened right this minute, after a fierce fight with a pillow or something—or else, he hasn't slept a wink last night, just like me.

Only in his case it happened who knows where.

Me, I look straight at him. His eyes, they have something wild in them: tender one second, mad the next, with wrinkled skin under them, sagging like squashed, hollow bags. He leans into the glass, laying his hands left and right of me, but I can't be sure what's in his head, like, if he wishes to plead with me, knowing I'm soon gonna forgive him—or else, he wishes to wring the life out of my throat.

But he don't try to do neither one nor the other. Instead he says, "Anita," kinda gruff, "where is my son? You must know where he is, don't you?"

And me, I shrug, 'cause like, what am I, his keeper?

So again Lenny comes, "Look, I've checked his bed. I know he did not sleep in it."

And I say, "So? Neither did you!"

His eyes flutter for a second, like he tries to ignore what I've just said, and how bitter it must feel to be dumped, even if it's only for a night.

So I say, "Ben isn't a baby, anyhow. And he didn't sleep in *my* bed, if that's what you're saying—even if you ain't saying it, exactly."

And he says, "Listen, dear—"

And I say, "Stop calling me that! This word, it sure as hell don't have no meaning to you."

He steps back, all the way back to his desk, as if slapped all of a sudden by a gust of cold wind. So at once—in spite of my anger—my heart goes out to him.

"I am dead serious," he says. "For the life of me I cannot find certain papers. The boy cannot have them, Anita. Not yet. Not while I am still alive. Where is he?"

And I say, "Last thing I know, me and him, we was like, playing the piano."

"From what I am told," says Lenny, "the two of you were banging like a pair of lunatics."

And me, I shrug, which in a flash, ignites the fury in him. I know Lenny: he can be terribly jealous. He claims that jealousy is like a compliment, almost; the most honest compliment a man can give. In his mind I should be happy, awful happy that he loves me so crazy, so deep.

But never did I see him like that: torn.

When it comes to his boy, Lenny is usually so steady. He's been longing for him for so many years. I wish I had a pa like that. And even if my husband has some secrets, and things he don't share, still, I'm sure that as a father, he has an awful big heart—but now that Ben is back home, a change has come over the old man. He can't make up his mind between trusting his son—or suspecting him for a rival.

Lenny comes forward—nearly going into a skid—and with full force he bangs the glass door, like he wants it to crack, to fall down in pieces, and to scatter all over the floor, with sharp shards ringing, pinging around me, 'cause like, he can see something in me, something invisible, that no one else can see: a mark, a see-through mark on my neck, like, from the touch of his son, zipping up my little black dress, a stain left there by accident, almost.

So he demands, "I need to talk to him. Now you tell me, where the hell is he?"

Which brings a little voice into my head, whispering something ma used to say, which is, "Charm the snake and then, real slow, back away."

So I say, real soft and gentle, "You know, Lenny, you have two sons—not one. Right now, I know where one of them is."

And I unbuckle my pink belt, and open my winter coat—just enough to let him see how my dress clings to my belly, which looks kinda puffy, 'cause it isn't exactly flat no more.

And from the inner pocket of my coat I bring out a picture, which I must admit is kinda confusing, 'cause at first glance it's like, nothing more than a mishmash of gray, so you can't exactly get it—not all at once, anyhow.

So you must learn to be awful patient, and take your time to study them lights and shadows here, in the picture, like, real slow and careful—or else, have someone else come to your help, and point out that, like, this is the inside of me, and this here, see, is a nose, and this, the lips of my sweet baby boy.

I bring the picture up and hold it for Lenny, pressing it right here, against the glass, just above the smudge, which his hand has just left there, on the other side.

I bet he can tell, by the glint in my eyes, that this here is like, real special, because looking at it you must also imagine the beat, the heartbeat going blip, blip, blip across the screen, from left to right, which means the baby is doing fine, real fine.

For a second Lenny is drawn to me, to the smile on my lips— but then, just before he can take a good look at the picture or say nothing, the phone rings.

So with a long screech he slides open the door, and passes me by on his way to the hall, in a rush to answer the thing.

"Hello," he says. "Aunt Hadassa!"

And after a long pause, which means she's going at him real good, he slumps against the wall, saying, "What? What did you say? Is there something wrong, I mean, at your end of the line? No, I am fine. Really, I am. Thank you for asking. What? My hearing? It is just as fine, aunt Hadassa. It is just... Just, I am a bit surprised. I cannot believe what you have just said."

Then he says, "Let me see now, do I remember correctly? You used to hate her, didn't you? My God, how you cursed, how you laid out all the reasons why I shouldn't, under any circumstances, have married the girl—even if she is pregnant! And after the wedding, you would not even return my calls. I got a whole week of silence—thank God—after which it was back to the same old thing: there was no stopping you on the phone, lamenting what you called, the *sorry event*. Why, just yesterday you gave me an earful—didn't you?"

"What?" he cries. "Can you repeat that, now? Anita, *she* deserves better?"

His lips tighten. "Hell," he says, this time under his breath, so I can't barely guess the words, "what is the matter with everybody today?"

And back to his usual voice he tells her, "Yes, I *am* listening, aunt Hadassa, of course I am. Yes, I know I should be careful, much more careful with her. Really, I promise. Yes, I realize she is still dizzy. Of course, I will do that—"

And to himself Lenny mutters, like, "Everyone is telling me, lately, just what she deserves. Some even care so much about the two of us as to say it behind my back. I mean, my own son..."

Now he bends down, as if aunt Hadassa is weighing him down, somehow.

"Well, fine," he tells her. "I will talk to him, too—but really, I can assure you—"

By now, his hand is well on its way to put the phone down, but then he jerks it up, just to say, "No. No, you are quite wrong. Really. I find him to be a well adjusted young man. Well, as happy as can be expected, of course, under the circumstances."

"No, I am not at all worried about him. And no," he gasps, "there is none of that. As far as I can tell. No. Absolutely nothing. No trace of jealousy."

And then, at last, the old man drops the thing in its cradle.

When he finally comes to bed that night, Lenny lays there for a long time without even stirring, as if he can't bring himself to close the gap, or even to try to reach over it, somehow, and touch me. I bet that in his head it's like, a ceasefire, and so me and him, we must build what so far, we've managed to destroy— by which he means, our defenses.

And so he figures that we can, perhaps, be safe from injury, and safe from inflicting it—but only if we hide from each other. I swear, this isn't no way to end a battle.

Lenny's kinda silent, except for heaving a sigh from time to time, which means he's still tied up at trying to hide feeling guilty—but anyhow, he isn't quite ready to forgive, or to be forgiven.

Then, out of the blue he says, not exactly to me but to the dark ceiling over us, "You know, I have thought about aunt Hadassa, what she said."

And me, I say, "Oh Lenny, just forget it," real soft.

And I roll away from my edge, a little closer to his side of the bed, like, half the distance to him, hoping he'll come halfway too and just, just hold me.

Instead, he's holding his grudge.

In a dry, guarded tone Lenny says, "I've left you an envelope on the kitchen table. First thing tomorrow morning I want you to take it, count the money, and then," he don't even say, *Anita*, "then go open a bank account in your name."

And I go, "What's that for, all of a sudden?"

And he goes, "Let it not be said that I am not giving you that which you deserve."

And in my aching heart I'm telling him, like, What I deserve is not to be made to feel like some fucking bitch. I'm your wife now. Before the wedding we used to have something, like, some good moments, some places where we was happy together. Can't you fight, Lenny, to get us back there?

Which is when he turns over, in a big hurry, to the other side, like there's something real exciting to be found over there. Then

—before I have a chance to say nothing to him—his breathing gets awful deep, so I reckon he's fallen asleep.

Meanwhile, a distant rumble can be heard from outside.

It comes in fits, and from time to time reaches closer, rattling the window pane. I lay there wide awake, listening to the thunder, dreading what I know is sure to come next. I count the seconds in my head till finally, here it is: a fork of lightning comes tearing through in the night sky, zig zagging across the half-turned blinds.

And in a blinding flash my wedding dress, which is hung right there, opposite me, in the corner of the bedroom, comes alive. The heavy satin rustles like it's just about to breathe. The lace trembles in the cold air. And for a moment the beading glitters. It blinks, like it's trying to bring back some memory. So bright, so dazzling!

Then the dress sinks back into the dark.

So I slip off the bed, and feel my way, somehow, to the window to bolt it, and to turn them blinds, so Lenny won't wake up to the sound of the storm, 'cause clearly, you can tell that he needs his rest.

Now I touch something. It feels kinda round. Must be the oval frame, the frame of the standalone mirror, which used to belong to his ex-wife, Natasha.

I turn my head away, so as not to catch sight of the face—the pale, wide-eyed face, which I try to tell myself, is mine—but already, it's too late to believe that. Piercing me, out of the black void of the glass, is her sad, heart-rending look.

Which brings a thought into my head: Natasha, she isn't my enemy no more, because at this point it's over, I ain't a threat to her. Like, now I ain't the *other woman* no more.

Instead, I've grown to become what she used to be.

So it shouldn't scare me so, I mean, the fact that we look so much alike, because at last I've come full circle, just to learn— like she did, at the time—how bitter it feels, to see the moment coming, and be too weak to stop it, or even to avert your eyes, when you find yourself betrayed.

I can't change none of the things I've done to get here, and none of what it takes to be here, in her place—but I this I swear: never before did I feel this sorrow, this dark, crushing sorrow for what happened, and for how she ended up.

Like ma used to say, The only hope you have, Anita, is to look at yourself in the mirror—and find regret.

I cross to the window, which is the moment I begin hearing the sound. On the surface it seems to blend with the howling of the wind, and the scraping of bare branches across the edge of the roof—except it isn't coming from outside, and it's just a whimper at first.

Even so, it takes me by surprise, 'cause Lenny don't dream— or so he says. And for sure, he don't never talk in his sleep, 'cause no matter if it's day or night, his jaw is set firm, and them muscles, they're always tight around his lips, which looks funny with his eyes closed, but also a bit stern.

Anyhow you can see, just by looking, that at this moment he isn't hardly his usual self. So I rush to his side—but can't get nothing, not a word of what he mumbles, because now that he's in the grip of some fear, he don't barely make sense.

It takes my breath away to look at Lenny, 'cause he feels awful helpless, like a baby, almost. After a while he starts whining—not from his throat but from an inner place, deep down in his guts. From there he wails, wrapped up in his nightmare, as if he's about to be cut away, like, lose the one dear to him.

Me, I reckon it's something you might expect, like, when you're expecting: my heart pounds with great worry inside me, so much so that it hurts, even, like I'm already a mama—and not only to my little one.

So the fact that Lenny, he's like, twice my age, flies clear out of my head. I cuddle him, real gentle, and feel his big body trembling here, in my arms. And I rock him back and forth, back and forth, like he's a child, and I try to calm him down, whispering, "Sh... Sh..." And I hug him, even tighter now, 'cause he's shaking like a leaf. "What is it, Lenny?"

By now his voice is so intense. It's rising, rising to a shriek, "Taaah! Taaah—"

Which is when I figure, like, he's trying to call someone, call her back, real urgent, to make her stop just there—just before she reaches the rift, the edge of what he sees in his dream—so he don't end up losing her.

So I murmur, close to his ear, "Here I am... All's fine, I promise. I'm here, by your side, my dear, dear Lenny. Don't you worry."

And again he calls, only softer this time, "Taaah..."

I let his head lean on me, on my bare shoulder, and at once the chill's gone, both inside and out, because I kiss him—so long and so tender—right here, in the middle of his forehead. And I hope I can take on his burden, that burden of guilt, and of pain too, because in the end I don't really mind, I don't care no more if the name he's calling is mine—or else, if it is Natasha.

A Price Would Be Paid

Chapter 27

As Told by Ben

And on the other hand, something must be done to take care of me, because my stomach is growling. This morning there is no breakfast waiting there, on the kitchen table —not even a morsel of food. Instead, tucked in a wrinkle of the white tablecloth are a few peculiar specks.

Wiping the sleep from my eyes I get closer, and discover a pair of pearl earrings and a matching pearl necklace, with a silver fishhook clasp. There are also a few bunches of hundred dollar bills, which must have poured out of that large manila envelope. They are tied with rubber bands, and scattered in plain view.

I lament my misfortune, realizing I should have risen from bed much earlier, because there she is, already counting some of them, holding them close to her chest, as if trying to rearrange a deck of cards without being too obvious about her game plan.

At my age, having to ask my father for pocket money is an embarrassment. As for Anita, I suppose it is no fun for her, either. At stake here is independence, at least for a time—for one of us. Oh, money! Sweet freedom! I figure it is not only on my mind, but on hers too, so naturally, it is the *one* thing neither one of us is quick to mention.

I stare at Anita. She stares at me. I have no idea how much cash we are *not* talking about—except to know it is a whole lot. It could pay the rent for a whole year, maybe.

Somehow this big heap of money—the likes of which I have never seen in my life—changes things between us. At this moment I am watching her with the eye of a rival, realizing that I must stop wasting time blowing hot and cold. This is war!

I must fight, must make a move—if only I knew what it could be—or else, she will soon plunder what I believe to be rightfully mine. And yet, I find myself wavering.

I wonder how it came about that she got her hands on those pieces of jewelry, which in a flash, look terribly familiar. One thing seems clear: I have been looking for mom's pearl earrings in all the wrong places during the last few days.

Maybe Anita can see all that—the doubts, the suspicions—in my face. Her cheeks turn, all of a sudden, as red as apples. I should have ducked, because out of the blue, here comes a rubber band, vibrating, singing in the air, missing me by a breath.

She tightens the oversized cotton shirt, which used to belong to my father, around her waist, trying to tidy it up by smoothing the crinkles. And something wild seems to flicker in her eye when she looks up at me, while plucking at another rubber band.

"As usual," she says, "you're acting like a child."

And I say, "What did *I* do?"

And she says, "You want others to make decisions for you."

And I say, "Why, what did *I* say?"

And quite sharply, she counters, "Exactly."

And I say, "Exactly what?"

And she says, "You didn't say nothing exactly—so you think I don't get it?"

For lack of an answer, I shrug.

Anita fixes me with a bright gaze. This time it is all but sultry, which immediately makes her seem so effortlessly irresistible. "I bet I can tell what you're thinking, like, right now," she says.

And then, in a tone that mimics mine, she acts *me* out, as if she could tell, somehow, every thought that has crossed my mind just now, as if it were etched on my forehead.

"*The jewelry,*" she says in that lowered tone, a tone that is just like mine, "*it belongs to my mom; the money—to my father. So I guess, if I wait long enough, I should get it. I mean: All of it!*"

I shrug again, so on she goes, mocking me uninterrupted, speaking from deep down in her throat, as if in my voice.

"*Yes, it is entirely mine, well, almost—even though I am not at all greedy, no, not at all! So like, despite not having a penny to my name, I am in no hurry to grab it already. And anyway, what is it doing here, just like that, out in the open, instead of in a safe or something? That woman, she should keep her hands off it, because really, it don't belong to her, and never will! It belongs to my family! And she, she comes from outside. She should not even come close enough to breathe on it—much less, touch it! Her being married to my father? That's nothing, really. Nothing more than a sad mistake!*"

I make up my mind not to show her how embarrassed she has made me feel, and when that fails me, there is always Plan B, which is this: to avert my eyes.

So I keep lowering them till they fall right there, on the manila envelope—only to discover her name writ large on it, in his handwriting.

"It is just that I wonder, I mean, about my father," I mutter. "What on earth made him give you all this? Not that you don't deserve it—but why—why now?"

"You mean, he must have gone nuts," she says. "I swear, he's out of his mind, that's for damn sure."

"I mean, something must have happened to him, all of a sudden."

"Something did happen," says Anita, "but I ain't exactly sure what to make of it. Lenny cried in his sleep last night."

"Really? *My* father? I cannot believe it. Are you sure? Maybe he just snored, or sighed, or whistled from his nose?"

In place of an answer, she goes on to say, "Then, way before dawn, he got up, and trust me: He looked plenty strange. Frantic! Searched every drawer in his desk. Said he's gonna be late coming home tonight, and I said, What, again? And like, what's your excuse this time? And he said not to worry, 'cause like, he needs to look at some docs and some papers and stuff with his lawyer."

"Mr. Bliss?"

"You know him?"

"Yes," I say. "When I was away in Europe, my father wrote to me once or twice about consulting him. You see, Mr. Bliss always pops up at times of misery."

"Misery? Like what?" asks Anita.

"Ten years ago," I say, "He put together the divorce papers for my parents."

She says nothing, but at the mere mention of the word *divorce*, her skin turns papery white. She seems to be weighing some odds in her mind, as if to compare her version of the past against mine—or else, to project it onto the present.

According to my recollection, Mr. Bliss provided legal advice one more time, five years later, after the divorce had already taken place. He helped my father transfer some assets into his name, assets which up to then, had belonged to mom.

My parents had been leading separate lives at that point, so to me, this whole transfer business seemed more than a bit odd: It seemed utterly confusing, to the point that I did not know if to laugh or cry—but now, with the secrecy about mom's condition lifted, at long last, I think I have gained some clarity, with which I can try to reconstruct the timeline of events.

So this, I guess, is what must have happened: about five years ago, mom was diagnosed with a form of Alzheimer's. By transferring her assets dad wanted, perhaps, to shield her estate from the costs, the treatment costs which she was likely to face, as her disease would go on, making its progress.

I try to think of a short version of what happened, which I can tell Anita.

At last I say, "My father wrote a letter to me, in which his tone was unusually gloomy. I could see that he was pondering the mistakes he had made in his life—"

"Me being one of them, I bet."

"It was, I think, the first time he wrote to me about having a sense of his own mortality."

"Like, what does that mean?"

"He lost his appetite, which used to be immense, and began saying vague things, thing such as, *Life hangs by a hair*, which made my own hair stand on edge with worry. I imagined him doing something rash, something unusually reckless, such as putting a blade to his throat. And a fear fell on me from my own thoughts."

Anita looks puzzled.

"I don't recall him saying nothing like that," she insists. "I must have gone back to my mama, just then."

"At the same time," I tell her, "my father mentioned that he had gotten some assets, which had not been in his name before, so now he was trying to figure out what to do with them, in case, God forbid... If, you know... I mean, should he die. So his long-time lawyer, Mr. Bliss, put together a will for him."

"Have you seen it?"

I pace around the kitchen, feeling uneasy. "No," I say, noting an unsteady tone in my voice, and hating it. "I have never even asked my father about the details, never wanted to be bothered with some convoluted legal clauses, because, I mean, being an only child, I trusted him to be fair, to take care of me."

"I wish I had a pa like yours," says Anita. "Someone who's gonna care for you, like, always."

Which brings me to a halt. I recall, all of a sudden, how I found myself wondering about him. I remember thinking that he had not only been disloyal to mom, but was perhaps unfair as well. He told me he would be managing her assets for her, but that hardly explained why they were transferred in his name.

It might have been just a coincidence, I told myself—but once the deed was done, the tone in his letters changed back to normal, by which I mean, annoying. Lots of useless fatherly advice. I guess that meant that he went back to normal, and so, thankfully, did his appetite.

In his letters from then on, there was rarely a mention of mom—except to suggest, in a vague way, that she was away, perhaps on some tour, giving piano performances here and there, in distant places around the world. Only now do I recognize that what I was given was a sketch of reality, which was as faint as it was misleading. And yet, being away, I rarely asked any questions of my dad, because I wanted to trust him. I was so desperate for this sketch to be true.

Meanwhile, Anita avoids breaking my silence. Holding her breath, she traces that wrinkle across the white tablecloth, till her finger is only a touch away from the two pearl earrings. I can see their twin glint mirrored there, in her eye, the luster floating over the green shadow, which seems so intense at this moment, now that she is tempted. Her tongue passes, with great thirst, slowly over her red lips.

By the end of that lick, she seems to have come to a conclusion. She says, first to herself, "Lenny has something up his sleeve, but it isn't divorce papers. Things ain't *that* bad, I don't think. I bet it's a new will, then."

And to me she says, "Yes, it must be that. And you're wrong, totally wrong about one thing: your father has two sons to consider, 'cause like, you ain't an only child no more."

And with that, Anita pushes away from the table, and takes a step back to the kitchen window, and stands there in profile, bathed in sunlight, as if to give me a chance to take her in, to discover the change taking place in her.

At first I cannot see it, I wouldn't, because look, her arms and legs are just as scrawny as ever—but then she starts turning away, and the light is so dazzling as to play tricks on me. It is erasing and redrawing the creases of his shirt around her curves, which suggests to me, at that second, crumpled tissue paper encasing a pear.

I watch the earring dangling there, from her fingers, as she flicks a wisp of her auburn hair, and brings the thing to her earlobe. A matching earring is dangling opposite her, glistening out of the pane of glass.

"Anyhow," says Anita. "This morning Lenny got out of bed with a pretty foul mood, telling me not to wait up for him. And me, I tried to make light of how things had turned up between us, so I didn't tell him nothing about how he'd cried last night, 'cause anyway, he won't even believe me. And instead I kissed him, leaving him no choice but to kiss me right back, which in spite of himself, he did."

"And I shouldn't even tell you, and even if I did, I shouldn't, really, blush over it like this—but what started with a tiny tickle, and an innocent little smooch on the lips ended up, to my surprise, with a big flair—like old times, almost! So I made the mistake of not paying close attention to nothing he said after that, 'cause like, I didn't want to trouble myself with no more questions—till I got up from bed, and came here to find this envelope, see here? With them bundles, big bundles of cash, inside."

I cannot help asking, "What is that for?"

"Whatever it is, I don't deserve *this*."

"Well, *he* thinks you do."

"No, you don't understand," she says, shaking her head. "I ain't the *other woman* no more. A wife, that's what I've become, and not just because of a wedding, or a mistake in the way things came about—but because, you see, here I am. Ten years!

I deserve better than an afterthought, I mean, better than someone swaggering out of the bedroom and like, making a big display of throwing his cash at me after having sex—no matter the damn amount! And I bet it's small change for him, anyhow."

Then Anita rises up from the table. Her motion is abrupt, as if she has come, in a blink, to a point of decision. "Here," she says, pushing the entire heap across the table, to the very edge. "Want it?"

I hesitate, "If he did leave it for you, then..."

Anita cuts in, "You can have it, Ben. All of it."

I step back from her. "No," I say. "I cannot take it from you."

Which brings a smile to her lips, which is playful and at the same time, full of spite. Impatient, she lays her hand on one of the bundles, and snaps lightly at its rubber band. "I don't want none of this money, Ben, you can take it or else, return it to him, or whatever. Don't make me decide things for you. I ain't your mama."

And in a snap, she tosses the bundle up in the air with all her might. The thing rises up, bending and flipping in the glow of morning light, till I make up my mind to reach up and catch it.

At which time, with a pop, dozens of bills separate out of the pack, as if a bird has just shot through the place, shaking out her tail feathers. There is a big, vigorous flurry of green. Hundred dollar bills go flying, drifting to and fro in the crisp, golden air as if to tease me, falling out of my grasp in a grand swirl all over the floor.

"Money don't come cheap," says Anita. "There's something I want in return."

And before I can ask, What is it, she takes my hand in hers and places it right there, on the coarse fabric of that shirt, on her belly. Instantly I feel warm—not just on the palm of my hand, but all over, inside.

"All I want is a fair deal," she says. "And it's not even for me that I'm asking this. It's for my baby. You can't judge me for that —so just, don't. Now I ain't stupid, Ben. I reckon Lenny has big expenses, like, taking care of your mom living there, at that Sunrise home, and all. Anyhow," she gives me a look, "he's gonna do right by *you*, all right. Just remind him he has two sons, will you?"

Is that all she wants, I ask myself, and as if to confirm, she nods at me, saying, "He should do right by both of them. Just promise me that, Ben. To you he'll listen."

Then, without even waiting for an answer Anita stuffs the bundles back into the envelope. With a swift motion—as if she denies herself the space of even a single second to think, to regret her decision—she drops in the pair of earrings, and the pearl necklace as well.

"Wait! Why don't you keep that, at least?" I ask her.

"I wish I could," she says. "Just a few years ago I would be dying, just dying for the chance to touch, let alone wear something so expensive, so stylish. I swear, I would have killed for that chance! For a girl like me, it's awful tempting. But I can't do it now. Believe me, Ben: I've tried. When I bring that earring near me it's like, I feel Natasha rushing in, like she's coming to breathe something right here, right in my ear. And her whisper —oh God!—it's so freaking faint that I can't even tell no more what it is that she wants from me."

"You are so superstitious, it is cute," I say. "I suppose you never dare play her piano."

In place of an answer, Anita slips back to the window, and fumbles in the breast pocket of the shirt, and digs out a red lipstick. On her back I can, for an instant, spot a light impression of the clasp of her bra. I can tell—by reading the motion of fabric around her shoulder blade—that she is applying a fresh rim around her lips.

Perhaps to her, she does not look like herself today, because there she is, leaning into the glass, twirling a red wisp of hair around her finger, as if to make sure it is really her.

The glass gives a glimpse of what lies beyond, a gray street view, over which flows a faint line, the line of his stiff collar, peeling away from what looks to be her neck. From this angle I think I can spot also the hollow, the reflected hollow between her breasts, and a vague impression of something plump and fruity. Perhaps a mouth.

So I say, "I suppose you never dare look in her mirror, either."

And she turns over her shoulder and gives me a look, as if to say, No! It ain't true, and I so hate you for guessing that! Like, I don't need none of your stupid comments—so don't you start, now!

Which of course, I ignore.

"The way I see it," I go on to tell her, "you must choose, and soon. Either you get rid of everything here, I mean, empty this place, no matter what my father says, and make it yours, I mean, truly yours—or else, for your own good, move out of here and go, make your home someplace else."

"I've thought about that," she has to admit.

A moment later she says, "Yes, you're so right! I'm gonna totally empty this place!" And her mind leaps ahead of mine, because now Anita comes up with, "Of all them old pieces of furniture, the first thing to go is this: the white piano."

The piano? It is so dear to me, and carries so many memories of mom, her piano lessons and her rehearsals and concerts, that at once I change my position, and say, "What? Why? And how, how dare you? I mean, how can you even think of getting rid of *that*?"

She lays her arms around my neck, as if to calm me down, and she says to me, in a softer voice this time, "The piano, it don't belong here, and it don't really belong to me—or even to you. It belongs to your mama, right? So let's do the right thing, and bring it to her."

I hesitate to ask, "What, to Sunrise?"

And she smiles, "Yes, Ben, to Sunrise!"

And then, then her arms find a way to wrap around my shoulders, and in turn—before I realize what it is I am doing— my hand slips around her waist, first over that shirt, then under it, so now my fingers are in the small of her back, clasping her tightly against me. I can feel every curve, every dimple on her, which makes my body come towards hers and cling, much too stiffly, to her.

I feel the flow, the blood swelling wildly in my veins, and my flesh melting here, under her touch, and at the same time hardening there, under the crotch of my jeans, making me rise, rise from a newly formed core down there, in a truly immense way.

Her face is close, so close that the freckles on her nose turn suddenly into a milky blur, below which I can sense a smell, the strawberry smell of the lipstick on her mouth. And yet, in spite of nearly bursting out of my skin with this enormous erection, I make no advance, for fear she may guess that I do not know what I am doing.

She may bid me withdraw, or laugh at me, or even reject me outright.

I try to control myself, making absolutely no move—except for one thing, which is stronger than me: trembling. Oh, and another thing: sweating. I suppose I should remove my palms from her breast, because by now they are so wet, wet to the point of being sticky.

But before I can bring myself to do that, Anita takes pity on me, for which I shall forever be grateful. She brings me in, and rubs her cheek against mine, so now her hair flames all around me.

I fall to my knees before her, pressing my head below the mound of her belly, nosing around, down the slope to the red fuzz right there, between her legs. Which makes her hips roll this way and that around me, and her knees part slightly as she comes down, and she holds me, with great softness, and kisses my hair, my eyes.

And her lips—

I should not tell you anything about her lips, how sweet and moist they are. I should not tell you anything, period. Not sure right now if that is what I have just done. If so, I should edit it out. Erase it.

Wait; let me just do that.

Rewind. Record.

And Anita smiles, "Yes, Ben, to Sunrise!"

After which she bustles about, and with a new burst of energy she runs to the living room and wraps the piano in a few layers of blankets, which she ties around the legs, so its surface would not be scuffed or gouged. She calls some piano moving experts, and negotiates a price, and tells them to be extra careful and strap the thing securely to a dolly, or else.

She orchestrates the arrival time with the administration at Sunrise home. She calls each one of my three aunts, just to give them a chance to give their blessings for the move, or not.

Finally, Anita calls my father once, twice, three times in his office, and cannot leave a message, because the answering machine must be full.

So she dials Mr. Bliss's number, which she has managed, somehow, to find in a notebook in some drawer, and talks with his secretary, who seems quite surprised to be asked about Lenny.

By now everyone is on board regarding the piano—everyone, that is, except my father, who for the moment, cannot be reached anywhere.

Meanwhile I get a large frying pan, and turn the heat up, and start pouring batter till it hisses in there. I do it because I must. I must get myself busy, to delay thinking about what has happened here between us, to avoid realizing that a price would be paid for it. Sooner or later he would know what we have done.

No doubt I would be severely punished, and so would she.

I manage to burn the batter into pancakes, lifting one after another with a spatula into an attempted flip in the air. It turns out that despite years of trial and error, and above all, of unreasonable hope, still, to this day I am just as I used to be: an incredibly lousy cook.

By the time I am done, the scene is a mess. It brings to mind a charred battlefield. Some of the batter has ended up drizzling on the cooktop, and spattering onto the floor, mostly on my left foot, and on a limp rubber band, and a previously crisp one-hundred dollar bill, both of which are lying down there, in the dust. But I do not mind—and neither does Anita.

She plops down in the corner, and seems tired now, which I can tell, because she is even shivering a bit. I heap the pancakes onto a paper plate, and splash a chipped coffee mug with orange juice, and tear open a bag of salted peanuts which I got yesterday out of some vending machine, all of which I set in front of her—right there on the table—as if they were a truce offering.

I do it because on one hand, something must be done to take care of Anita.

Rewind. Play.

And on the other hand something must be done to take care of me, because my stomach is growling.

Bei Mir Bistu Shein

Chapter 28

As Told by Ben

The last thing I want to see is his face, when he comes home to realize that—poof!—the grand piano is gone. Vanished! My father is known to have an eccentric attachment to things, especially to that old, massive, ornately decorated, polished white beast. Why, you may ask? I have wondered about it, too, and can offer only this: it brings back to him a certain presence, the presence of mom, playing. So perhaps for him, it is a remnant of love: namely, guilt.

By the time I turned sixteen, mom had developed an unexplained fear, a fear of getting lost, which was quite pronounced, even as she headed out for a short walk, such as to the grocery store on Wilshire Boulevard, not more than a couple of blocks away. She seemed to rely, with an increasing sense of anxiety, on the familiar, and would become ferociously shaken if a chair was accidentally moved out of position. We all knew that the instrument—which was only hers, because I had stopped playing by then—was sacred. It was not to be touched.

And so, too, was she.

Which explained, of course, his restlessness. And later, his affairs. Yet in spite of them, my father had a lingering sense of obligation to her. To this day, he would never dream of letting go of that piano of hers.

But—holy cow—it's already too late! I suspect that tonight, he would be not only surprised—but enraged, too, because the place looks so vacant, so foreign without it, as if it were not ours, but the next door neighbor's apartment.

There is, suddenly, so much air.

I imagine him coming back home, later this evening, and taking a step back—away from the mat—to make certain he has unlocked the right door.

He would call, "Anyone home?" and an echo, a crisp echo would rattle the air, as if to announce an unusual depth, an emptiness.

He would then raise the key to his eyes, staring incredulously at it. It must be the right one, or else the lock would have jammed—but even so, the old man would check it again carefully, as if some bend, some scuff on the metal might, perhaps, explain the wrong turn of things.

He would rub his eyes, amazed to discover Beethoven's bust planted down there, in the dust, on the floor, its eyes frozen in dumb confusion. Discarded. No longer perched on top, it seems to have shrunk—or else the space has, somehow, ballooned around it.

The marble head seems cropped by a beam of light on one side, and a pile of music notebooks on the other. The sculpted shoulders lean against streaks of peeling wallpaper, blackened streaks that have previously gone unnoticed, crumbling away in the shadows, behind the bulk of the piano, which is now missing.

I cannot begin to guess what my father would say, if he would say anything at all, I mean, before he starts shouting.

I suppose he would blame this on his new wife, and—by association—on me as well. So I make up my mind to avoid trouble, or more precisely, to avoid him, which is something I have been getting better at doing over the last few days.

Chased by the sound of the dolly rumbling heavily across the floor, then down the stairs, and by the shouts of the movers yelling occasional warnings to Anita and me and to each other, I am relieved, finally, to see the moving van, loaded with piano and bench, lurching into the street.

Which is when I figure I should go somewhere, anywhere but here, perhaps to that hell hole called Sunrise, which is also where the van is headed.

I recall the pale, gaunt faces, the bent figures I have seen there, some attached by tubes to life-support machines, developing bed sores, others staggering around in slippers, slit open to accommodate bunions.

I would have to take in the odor, the unmistakable odor of decay and antiseptic, which is so nasty, so repugnant that the best hope you have is to be driven quickly out of your senses. But then, this I know: while there, I would be with mom.

And what is even better, I would not have to talk if I do not feel like it, because as far as I know, she is silent now. Utterly silent.

Soon, her piano will arrive. Watching it, her heart would skip a beat. Imagine that, I tell myself, because imagine I must. There must be some trick—perhaps as simple as reciting a few notes—some trick by which I can stir something, some memory in her mind. Mom cannot possibly be lost to me. She is merely asleep, waiting for a nudge. Her fingers can still tap, I think I have seen it on my last visit. They must remember various patterns of stroking the keys. They must remember music.

I doubt mom belongs here, or in any other such place, so I keep telling myself, This must be just a nightmare. I imagine she can still wake up, and open herself to a new day. I just need to believe it bad enough.

Assuming my father is still at work, Sunrise Assisted Living is the last place I would have expected to find him; which, as luck would have it, turns out to be a complete miscalculation on my part.

There he is, in the large dining hall, pacing impatiently to and fro, then around the long Formica table, some distance away from the elderly figures hunched there, some over their walking frames, others in wheelchairs. He has me caught in his sight as I get in, and a minute later I feel his grip on my arm.

"What—what are you doing here? Oh," he mutters, "never mind. I don't want to hear you now. No! Don't say a word."

Which leaves me no choice but to rebel against him, and so I ask, "And why not?"

"Oh, stop—just stop it," he says, looking over his shoulder, clearly in anticipation of my mother. "It is always too many questions with you."

And I stress, "Why?"

And he says, in a hushed tone of voice, "Just go. Go away, before she gets here."

So I cry, "What?"

"Your mom," he says, "she used to tell me repeatedly that she will not want any visits from you."

"Now that," I say, "is a lie! It just has to be!"

But my father insists, "Ben, you do not understand. Natasha would never have wanted you to see her like that."

And to my question, "So then, why are *you* here?" he replies, briskly at first, "Just because."

But then he goes on to explain, "With me, she had little choice. I have been the one watching over her, the one who has seen the change. But you, son—you are still blind to it. Go away! Trust me: she would tell you so herself, if she could, because see, you are the one she cherished."

And I say, "Huh!" to which I add, bitterly, "What an odd way to show love."

"Yes," he says. "I grant you that. But consider this, Ben: she wants you to remember her the old way, the way she was. Bright. Talented. Most of all, healthy."

For a while, neither one of us speaks. The old man looks remarkably tired, his jaw less defined than usual, perhaps because of the gray stubble on it, which takes the edge off the features of his face. He must have skipped his morning ritual, by which I mean, his shave.

So I soften a bit, just enough to ask him, "And you, dad? You miss her? I mean, the way she used to be?"

For a minute he holds his breath, and I see him glancing at a dark silhouette passing across the far windows of the dining hall.

Then he says, "She still walks on both feet, still looks the same, more or less. To a stranger, Natasha still looks as if nothing at all is wrong with her. The shell, so to speak, is intact. You are young, son, and may laugh at what I say, but to me she is beautiful. Pure. As if only a few days have passed since I first laid eyes on her. But on each visit I see changes. Each time, her mind disappears a little bit more."

"Dad, you still didn't give me an answer."

"Do I miss her? No, son," he says, and takes a long, painful pause. "Not all the time."

"Was it difficult for you, bringing her here?"

"For several weeks, I had dreaded what she would say. That morning I got up from bed, and found her talking to the mirror. I said, This is a special day, Natasha! Let's go out for breakfast. And pointing straight ahead, at the glass, she said, OK, and what about *her*, is she coming, too? And I said, No, not today. Just you and me. Oh, she said, OK. And to her reflection she said, Goodbye. And so we came here."

"Again, dad: you still didn't give me an answer."

"Was it difficult to bring her? No," he says. "The difficult part was to leave her behind, and go home, and find myself lonely, lonely and empty and, at long last, free. I stood there, on the threshold, without her, not knowing what to do with my hands."

"And mom, what about her? Having clung, so hard and so long, to that which was still familiar around her, did she resist being left here, in a strange place, suddenly alone? I mean, was she furious? Did she cry?"

"All along," he says, "she was uneasy about making plans for herself. She insisted on going back home, staying there until, she said, The good Lord would show pity, and take her. But that morning, when at last we got here, to Sunrise home, I found a new way to respond, which I admit, I am not proud of. I told her that the apartment was about to be fumigated for termites."

"You *what*—"

"So she agreed to stay here, temporarily. I knew she was unable to keep track of time. In fact, I counted on it. I told her the work would take one more day, and the next day I said, one more, and the day after that, one more, and so on, and on, which seemed to convince her, somehow—until, to my relief, she stopped asking."

"Listen to me," I say angrily, finding myself forced, yet again, to repeat. "Was she furious? Did she cry?"

"No," he says, and his voice turns stubborn. "If she did, I did not see it."

"And she stopped asking? Stopped talking, even?"

"Yes," he says. "That is correct."

"No wonder," I say, resisting a sudden urge to spit in his face. "You lied to her!"

My father glances at me, contempt flashing from his eyes.

"Who the hell are *you* to judge me. Much do you care! You were not even here, goddam it! To this day, you have no idea what happened, what I had to go through, over the years, with her," he grumbles. "So just spare me the—"

This is when his eyes widen, and a few things happen at such a fast pace, that the details threaten to escape me. So at the risk of confusion, here goes:

There is a distant sound of rumbling, it draws closer, grinds to a stop, the figures, the misshapen figures at the table, they turn around, highly agitated, some of them scream, at high pitch, at the movers, who have just arrived, talking to someone, some woman in a nurse uniform, no, it's the care giver, forgot her name, Martha. Some papers change hands, mark *Donation* here, please, and a signature there, now hold the door, wider. The dolly is rolled in, first here, then there. It's too far, careful now, stop! Now it's too close to the windows, and the table, someone says, might be in the way, that's a safety hazard. So on go the wheels, turning, squeaking until the thing is lined, properly now, against the wall, and the blankets, a few layers of them, are being untied, unwrapped already from one leg, then another. They look OK, no scratches, and the dark figure, the silhouette out there, she raises a hand, as if moved around by some invisible strings, and it claps to her mouth.

My father cuts off mid-sentence, shocked at the sight, at the white piano, his face turns red, dark red with blood, just as I thought, as I was afraid it would, he rushes ahead, hugs her, walks her over, step by step, to the far corner, tells her to breathe.

"Breathe deeply," he says, which is when I come to attention, because this is the instant when I recognize, of course, who she is. Mom.

"My God," he glares at me, eyes narrowed with suspicion. "What—what have you done, you and Anita?"

At that moment, with barely a thud, my mother slips out of his hold and, in a snap, collapses to the floor. By the time she comes to, moments later, the movers have already gone, and Martha has gotten everything and everybody firmly under control. Now she guides mom into a comfortable, upholstered chair, and slides it next to a window, which dad, now deathly pale, throws open.

Then she adjusts the resealable tape of a diaper over the hip of one of the seniors, wipes the dribble from the chin of another. Martha brings in an assortment of simple musical implements, such as bongos, tambourines, toy bells, egg shakers and xylophones. She hands one of them—a metallic triangle— to mom, and the rest to the other seniors to play, as if they were children, eager children about to put together an impromptu live show.

One of them, a decrepit, toothless hag cruises up to the front in her wheelchair to get a better look at the piano. Frail, much like a wooden puppet, she drags her bony, crooked body over to the bench, slides open the cover, and bangs at the keys.

The melody is familiar, but played haltingly, and with an awkward touch, which makes me wish mom would stand up, walk over there right now and show them, show all of them just how it is done, and what fine music ought to sound like, performed with inspired virtuosity by the hand of a renowned pianist, trained from early in life in a variety of memorization techniques.

But no: there she sits, her long fingers idle, her eyes nearly shut, as if trying to block out all distractions, perhaps to divine a particular sequence of music, or to recall the fierce, blind stare emanating from an imaginary bust, the bust of Beethoven, or else just to drift off.

The other seniors gather around the toothless amateur, and they start shaking their wrinkled fingers in the air, in pantomime of her gestures, and humming, *La-la, la-la-la! La-la, la-la-la!* One of them is so swept by the rhythm, as to warble in a thin, cracked voice, somewhat out of tune,

> *Bei mir bist du shein,*
> *Bei mir host du chein,*
> *Bei mir bist du alles oif di velt.*

For some reason the singing grates, quite harshly, on my nerves. I am surprised to find myself so upset. For a time I do not even realize I have water in my eyes. The entire space starts swimming in front of me, and I am glad that my father does not seem to notice it, or else he may think I am weeping.

Weeping—can you imagine that?—out of some weakness or something.

The reason I am so lucky as to be ignored is that his face hangs there, away from me, over his chest, and is held in that position, nearly masked by the palms of his hands. I get the feeling that under that cover, his mind has been carried away elsewhere. Perhaps he is thinking about the first time he saw mom.

From reading his stories I know it happened quite by chance, when he accompanied a friend to some concert, and sat there, raising his eyes from the second row, and there she was, up on stage, aglow in a sphere of light.

His heart started fluttering inside. It pounded so hard that he thought he would pass out, which was fine by him, because he considered himself, at that moment, kissed by luck.

One could not wish any better than to die a happy man.

In his eyes, she was the most beautiful girl in the world—not only because of the hazy glare of the spotlight, through which he saw her rosy blush, the long, slender arms, and the glitzy black dress, but because of the heavenly, harmonious music, which she made reverberate in the air, all around her.

To me you are beautiful,
To me you have grace,
To me you are everything in the world.

For the longest time, my old man sits there, utterly motionless, in the midst of bells being shaken and bongos being beaten by unsteady hands. Only the top of his head, gripped tightly in his fingers, is visible to me between this sagged shoulder and that, in the back of the crowd.

And it is not until the end of the song—when everyone sitting in the divide between him and me has joined in an intoxicated, disorderly chorus, singing loudly, *I've tried to explain, bei mir bist du schoen*—that the next line makes his hands fall, suddenly, into his lap.

I've tried to explain, bei mir bist du schoen,
So kiss me, and say that you will understand.

It is at that phrase, *and say that you will understand,* that I see him wincing. Having sensed, somehow, the weight of my gaze, his jaw clenches. My father turns his head abruptly, to pull himself back from view—but not before I realize, to my complete shock, that he is awash in tears.

There are claps and numerous shouts—Bravo, bravo!—and after a while, as if guided away by an invisible hand, they scatter around. The show is over.

Looking at the door on the other side of the space I see it turning on its hinges, and squealing to a close behind my father. I think he is fortunate, so fortunate to have left just before having to witness the rest of it.

Stirring out of the chair, my mother opens her eyes. At first I want to cheer her on, to cry, Come on, bring them to their knees, now! Show them who you are, what you are made of! Play, mom, play for me!

And it is then that she drops her chin, as if she were a broken marionette, into an unbearably silly, open-mouthed grin. It is babyish at best, and lacks any hint of comprehension.

Then she lifts a tremulous hand—on which a steel triangle is hooked—and jerking a little metal wand, strikes it once. The thing gives a high pitched, flat tone. It is a dead sound, meaningless, perhaps because it occurs entirely out of context, chiming noisily when no one even expects it, when no one but me is left there to listen—let alone imagine how she could play.

I dream, as I must, of her fingers darting, soaring in a dazzling blur, long after the cover has been pulled over the keys of her white piano.

The Long Wait

Chapter 29

As Told by Anita

Then he says to his son, You should go, because this place can't hold the two of us for much longer, and because a young fellow like you must be hungry for adventure, and eager to see the world, and the last thing you want is to remain here, stuck in this stuffy place, with a grumpy old man, so here's some money, it should be more than enough—if spent modestly—for travel expenses, and stay in touch, and good luck with everything.

And Ben tries to say No, quite to the contrary, there's much more space now than there ever was, with the grand piano cleared out of the way, just look at Anita over there, stretching her arms and doing quick twirls, all across the room.

At hearing all that, Lenny just clenches his jaw—but he don't even grumble or nothing, and I bet he's holding his tongue just to drive home the point, like, how calm he manages to be, and how there isn't no sign of anger in him, or nothing.

All the same Ben seems to know that he's being punished. So without even glancing at me—like I'm the one to be blamed for all this—he bites his lip and goes into his room, where he can't help kicking the wall once or twice, after which he comes out to the kitchen, and kicks the refrigerator and then opens it, to look for an ice pack.

Then Ben spends some time wandering in and out of the living room, and making noise, long enough for his father to change his mind if he wanted to, or even to forgive him outright, for whatever it is that needs to be forgiven—but Lenny has already gone out to the balcony, where he can't hear nothing, not even me pleading with him, asking what happened, what the hell happened between them.

His silence is new to me. It's like, shouting from the walls. And what I read into it is like, if I didn't show so much leg back then, when he first laid eyes on me, ten years ago in that ice cream shoppe, and if I didn't wear them hot pink, high heel shoes, which forced him, somehow, to lose his head over me— which could never have happened otherwise—then things would be totally different now:

Nothing would end up tearing this family apart, and instead, the piano would still be crouching in place, and Natasha, his first wife, would still be here to play it—or at least, to pass her hand fondly over its back, and twiddle her fingers when she's done checking for dust, and smiling to herself, because like, all's well. All would be just fine.

Lenny acts like I'm some stray kitten that's wandered in here, and he's taking his distance. He isn't nowhere near me, and like, he's deaf to his son, on account of the noise, 'cause of punching them keys, the keys of his typewriter, pretty damn hard.

So at last Ben says to him, he says, "Fuck you, and your fucking money!" and turns to his room, and packs his stuff, like his old family Album, and that manila envelope with them bunches of hundred dollar bills, which I thrust, on impulse, into his hands, 'cause at that moment there's some immense force in my heart, which is stronger than me, and it makes me care for him awful deep, which is totally a surprise to me, and even more than that, a mistake.

It's against everything I've planned in my head, and I know it —but still, I don't even care at this point if Lenny happens to see it.

Then Ben buckles his rumpled suitcase. His long lashes cast a shade over his eyes, hiding how confused he must feel right now, and his slender body is strained, not so much because of the suitcase, but because of something that only the two of us can share: the burden of being young.

Then, without saying goodbye—not even to me—he's out the door.

In the first couples of months or so after his son left, Lenny's been very quiet. In some ways, things ain't all that bad between us. He comes home every night, even asks—when he cares to look at me—if the baby's started kicking already. His question is kinda polite, and it don't really break the silence, just marks a place from where we can restart it.

Anyhow we're together, so I don't have to worry no more about where he is, and I don't have to call aunt Hadassa, who has her sources, and I don't have to listen to her squirming, trying to spare me from knowing what this entire town already knows, which is, that Lenny's been sleeping around.

It's always the same thing now. Me and him sit down at the kitchen table and eat dinner together, like a normal family, except that we do it in silence. Then we settle into that old, sagging couch—him in one corner, me in the other—and wait. What it is we're waiting for isn't exactly clear. At first I could swear it was, like, a word from Ben—but now I figure it's a good thing the day's getting shorter.

Tonight—the first moonless night of this winter—I can sense a change in Lenny, which starts, for me, with the scent of his aftershave.

It's Aqua Velva. It's been a long time since I've caught it on him, and I can get a bit tipsy just by tipping over, like, to take it in. He grips the faded armrest and gets up, with some effort, from his corner, and puts on his fingerless leather gloves, with which he can type, especially on cold nights. Then he goes out to the balcony, and I can see him fumbling for something there, in the drawers of his desk. Finally he brings back a handful of tapes—I hope none of them is mine—and the tape recorder, which he sets up across from me, on the floor next to Beethoven's bust.

From down there Lenny turns to me, and I see the question in his eyes, like, Is it too late already, for the two of us?

And aloud he says, "Anita? Want to dance?"

Over the last couple of months he hasn't given voice to no anger, and neither have I, which I figure can't hardly be bad, 'cause without words any feeling—even rage—can peter out, so that one of these days, it's gonna be left there, dull and limp, somewhere behind us. It can happen, 'cause his son isn't here between us, and time passes.

Like ma used to say, Time heals all wounds. Which sounds pretty stale, but it must be true, 'cause I've stopped thinking by now about my youth going to waste. Instead I'm thinking about the fact that I've stopped thinking about that.

So in the end, we're back where we started, almost. Lenny's my man. He's mine. Me, I'm his. All's clear. Nothing gets confused.

"Well?" he murmurs. "Do you?"

I reckon the reason he's talking to me, like, under his breath, isn't only because he's unsure of me, of what I'll say after the long, icy silence—but also because he can't stand the echo, which seems to have moved in here with us lately.

So I whisper, as soft as I can, "I do."

He inserts one of them tapes, and sets the tape recorder to *Rewind*, then *Play*. At first I almost expect *my* voice to come on, but then, by the spring in his step as he's coming over, I figure it's gonna be music. He reaches out to me, so I peel off his glove, and his touch feels nice, it's warm and strong, the way I remember it.

Lenny helps me out of the sofa, which is good, 'cause I feel pretty heavy lately, and if I stand up by myself I tend to stop, just to look down to check if I my feet can still be spotted there, under the round mound of my belly.

I rise into his arms, and note that his forehead comes down more heavily than ever, right over his eyebrows, and the crease in the middle—which as always, remind me of my pa—is deeper now. He must have shrunk a little, too. Maybe not, maybe it's just something I imagine.

Now Lenny lays his hands on my hips, careful at first, like we're strangers. If we was strangers for real, things would get wilder, faster. I draw a bit closer, and put my hand on his shoulder, and rise to the tips of my toes to reach up, to comb his thinning hair, awful gentle, with my fingers. I slick it back, 'cause in my eyes it's always made him look so handsome, like one of them old movie stars.

In turn, his hand brushes my hair, gathering it up, for a second, into a pony tail, and I close my eyelids, feeling how at first he hesitates. The old man waits there for a long while, before leaning over and kissing them.

I bet that like me, he remembers that night, the first time we danced, 'cause now that the tape recorder has finished giving out the long, rustling hush, and the music comes on, it's the old song, doubled by a ghost of its sound: something slow from the sixties, which years ago used to bring tears to ma's eyes, 'cause like, it awakened her to being lonely, and now it brings them to mine.

Lenny cups my face in his hand and pecks me lightly on the cheek. Then he starts showering me with the littlest kisses, all along the trail of tears, his mouth slipping down the skin of my neck. And I laugh—not only on account of being ticklish, but because suddenly I'm aroused, and even a touch nervous. And I say, "Let's just dance," which is echoed, like, by the laughter of the walls.

So Lenny backs away and I come, and then in reverse, he comes as I back away, and we go and come, come and go this way for a long while—but we don't hardly move from the same spot, here by the sofa, even though there's so much space now around us, for dancing and what not.

It's not only me wondering about it—it's Beethoven as well, his blank eyes following every one of our moves from down there, on the floor, like he's annoyed at his bad luck, having to witness all this—and in slow motion, too!—and his neck, despite being solid, must be terribly cramped, and like, he hopes to be relieved of that pain pretty soon, and stretch his neck, and could we please stop idling there like some tired old couple, and come stomping off in his direction, and break it already.

By now Lenny has undone the buttons of my blouse, and he loosens it this way and that, and then, in one firm pull it's already down, which allows him to take one breast in his mouth, and lick the skin all around it.

At once, my nipple grows big. He gives it up in favor of the other one, which he starts sucking. Now I'm divided between my two halves, 'cause the first breast, which is wet, starts cooling off as it dries, and the second is like, burning. I twist my body side to side, to offer him first the one, then the other, and again.

Pretty soon we go out of order, and in a heated haste we find ourselves tossing the pillows of the sofa to the floor, first the pillow out of what is usually his corner, then the one out of mine, and we stumble rolling down, till we land on top of them, more or less. So he cocks his head, looking up at me, waiting, 'cause like, now it's me on top. And it's at that second, just as I start groping for the zipper of his crutch, that—out of the blue —the doorbell rings.

But like, there's nobody there.

By the time Lenny returns from the door, I've crossed the floor on all four, all the way to Beethoven, and turned him around so he don't face us no more, and instead he points his nose at the corner, and I've come right back to lay, in a foxy pose, on them pillows.

But somehow, I know that Lenny knows that we ain't exactly in the mood no more.

"Who—who was that?" I ask.

And he says, "No one."

And I point at what he carries behind him, in his hand, "And what's this?"

And shrugging, he says, "Don't know."

And I say, "So, open it."

And real stubborn, he says, "Don't want to."

So half nude I rush to the kitchen, and bring a kitchen knife and cut through the flap of the box, and there—to my surprise —lays a bottle of Rosé Champagne, flanked by two stemmed glasses, the kind you can stack in layers to build them champagne towers, like the one we had at our wedding.

At first, my bet is that this is a gift from my husband—who else—which takes my breath away, it's so cool, so awesome, especially because I haven't gotten nothing from him lately.

So I twist my hips walking up to him, and snatch one of them glasses and put it in place, right over my left breast. Before I got pregnant, and become so full of curves, it would have been a perfect fit—but now, not so much.

Then, just before opening my mouth to ask him to uncork the bottle, I realize my mistake.

"Take it off, take that thing off right now, right this minute," he stammers, and his forehead curves down over him even heavier and more wrinkled than before. I can't even blame him, or no one, 'cause really, I reckon it's too late for us.

So without saying a word I obey him, and remove the glass from my heart, and watch him, again in silence, as he rummages through the box in search of a note, or something. Which he finds, finally, down there at the bottom. In square, printed letters the note reads simply, "To Anita."

No return address, no signature, no date, nothing.

The old man looks long and hard into my eyes, like he's searching for answers, not exactly sure if to punish me, like I was a naughty school girl, or to send me back home to my ma. After a while he figures he can't do neither, so he just turns his back on me, and punches the box so it can collapse on itself, and stuffs it in the garbage can, along with the uncorked bottle and them two glasses. Then he goes to the bathroom, and the water starts running for his shower.

I try not to be angry, or hurt. I sit there in the dark, and wait. I can't tell exactly what it is I'm waiting for.

So, *Rewind. Record.*

What is there to say? I reckon it's stupid, it don't make no sense to hunger so bad for a change. Still... It's a strange feeling, knowing that someone out there is playing with a thought about me, daring me to risk everything I've got, like, this marriage, this shelter for my baby and me—all for nothing. For a bottle of champagne.

The water's still running in the shower, wisps of vapor escaping as far as here in the living room. By now the glass door is all steamed out, so the balcony out there, which is facing ours, is pretty much washed out, and you can't see the wintery sky no more, and you can't even tell that it's moonless. And like, everything is suddenly nothing but a guess—except for one thing:

I swear, I must be crazy. I know I am, 'cause the only path to see clear out of this place is through what I write here, into the steam, on the cold, hard surface, with my finger.

Ben.

The Source of Trouble

Chapter 30

As Told by Ben

Of one thing I am certain this time: The source of trouble between my father and me is nothing else but that book, or whatever he is calling that thing which he is trying so hard to put together. I can understand why you laugh. If someone said this to me I would laugh, too. Still, it is the one explanation that fits the string of events, and it makes increasingly more sense to me, the more I reflect on it. Which is what I have been doing ever since he threw me out. Yes, for once I am certain, and it took me four months of following him, and of being invisible.

For all his faults, I have never found reason to doubt how deeply my father loves me, which makes his anger so devastating now, and also, so puzzling to me—not just the anger itself, but the constancy of it, the fact that it would not relent, not even to let him answer my letters, which by now, I have stopped sending.

So every evening I find myself drawn back to that place. I pass through the back alley, wrapped in a knitted, black scarf all the way up to my ears. It is tied in a thick knot around my neck, cloaking me as if to ward off the cold.

I slip into the bushes at the side of the apartment building, behind the large garbage cans. This is where I take my time, to let my eyes grow used to the dusk. If the light comes on in his balcony—as it often does, around this hour—or, if the glass door suddenly squeals along its rail, I sink back into the darkest dark. Here I cast a quick glance around, to make certain no one is there to see me, or to sense the surge of my heart, and I wait, till I see him coming out.

Then, when at last my heartbeat grows calm, I draw near—but not too near, so there is no way for the old man to suspect that I am here, at such a close range, looking up at him. And even if he did, I trust that he is blinded by the light of the desk lamp, and cannot find me out here, in the shadows. So I stand below his balcony for a long time, not a muscle stirring, and watch him.

I see the desk lamp flickering across his glasses. From time to time he pushes them, with one finger, up his nose. I see the reflection of his hands, large hands wearing fingerless leather gloves, going at the keyboard in spurts of punched sequences. His eyes shine then with inspiration. Other times—when he is betrayed by his muse—he stops typing altogether, and even curses himself out loud.

Then he scratches some corrections into the sheet of paper, and the creaking of his chair gets more frequent, more pronounced. After a while, a faint voice comes on. The first time I heard it—it was late December, I think—I found myself strangely moved. It compelled me to risk revealing myself.

So without taking a second to think, I clung to a drain pipe going up the next building, fumbled about, climbed onto a crack, or a nick, or maybe it was some missing brick in the wall. I nearly faltered, and then—in one leap—flung myself up into a balcony, the one opposite his, which was, as luck would have it, empty.

From here I glanced back at him, afraid he might have detected the rattle of the railing, which was, unfortunately, still going on, vibrating in the air, even though I tried to make it stop already, by gripping the metal bars, bringing them to a freeze in my hands—but no: there he was, crossing something out, then crumpling his papers furiously and starting over, as if nothing else in the whole world mattered.

Next to me, in the corner of the balcony, I spotted a large clay pot, where dry geranium had withered, scenting the air. So I perched on its lip, expecting the neighbor to come out any minute and raise hell—but no: they must have fallen asleep, or something. And so, I was feeling unusually bold, as if I dared steal someone's seat in a theater.

This, I thought, was the best place to watch the scene, and to gain some clarity. At this height, I would enjoy an uninterrupted view of him. At this distance, I would examine my father's actions in a cold, analytical manner, free, so I thought, of emotion. I would be able to pay closer attention to what I thought I heard, so I might remove from my mind any doubt about it.

You must be careful, said a voice.

There was a raspy quality to it, which startled me, because it sounded so close, so vivid. It came not from inside his apartment —but rather from the top of his desk, from the tape recorder. It was a voice to which the old man seemed to be listening obsessively.

Rewind, Play, Rewind, Play, he slapped one key, then another, alternating between them numerous times, leaning over them closely, as if to register in his mind every nuance of the way Anita talks.

You must be careful, Ben, said her voice. And then again, a thousand times over, *The words you leave behind you, they ain't yours no more.*

What surprised me was not merely the fact that my father had the nerve to listen in, to study her most intimate, secret moments. Simple curiosity would have explained that, and could, perhaps, have been forgiven. No! This was something completely different, something I could not put in words right away.

So I slipped off my perch, over the railing, down the pipe, around the bushes, and back into the alley, chased by confusion, before it hit me, all of a sudden, with sharp clarity: her voice is his. So is mine. In the process of writing, he has crossed a line, crossed it into an altogether different reality, which is all made up. He has come to consider us his characters, characters with no claim to privacy. In his mind, our thoughts are his for the taking.

That, I believe, is the only explanation to his tape collection, the voices he owns. As an author, he wishes to capture us—as genuinely as language can—in the most touching, most vulnerable of moments. He cannot help but invade our mind, our heart, our guts, because he needs to feel us inside, refine our voices, perhaps even guide us from one scene to the next. He aims to determine how our story would end. In his madness, he puts faith only in himself. He is God.

From time to time, in spite of himself, he welcomes our rebellious nature, because it offers him a new, unforeseen twist in his tale. Which is not to say he enjoys his power. Quite the opposite. I come there often to watch him, and I can tell you that as this long winter bores on, he seems to plunge deeper and deeper into despair—especially when hearing me, I mean, my voice ranting on tape.

Lately, his wrist seems to be painfully tired, because of the incessant typing. But somehow he presses on. *Play*. He listens to me—breath fluttering in his throat, as if to hold himself back from a fit of crying—then he takes a short pause, and *Rewind*, he listens again.

Meanwhile, immobile in the shadows, I cannot ask him to stop. I feel exhausted slouching here, motionless, against the bars. I cannot even bring myself to clap my hands over my ears. A thousand times over, here it comes, here it is, trembling with a rising inflection. I try not to hear it, but carried over to me by a light breeze is *my* voice, betraying my secret. It says:

And through the wall, the space, the wall, can Anita hear the pounding, the loud pounding of my heart? Can she feel me, breathing her name? Does she whisper back to me, Stop it, stop it right now?

For the author in him, this, I figure, should be considered pure gold. He must be terribly pleased at the opportunity to take what I said and mold it anew, reducing here, embellishing there, channeling every turn, every twist in the flow of my passion. But then, for the lover in him, trying to place his trust in the hands of those he holds dear—his wife, his son—every word must be driving a dagger into his heart.

And yet, despite the pain, I see him pressing on, forcing himself to listen, then to write. His new character—a paper version of me—starts taking shape. It is given a voice, which is drawn out of my throat. Every word makes me a touch weaker. Soon I will be completely drained of breath.

I look at my father across the divide, and for the first time in my life, I *wish* for uncertainty. I wish I would have a doubt left in me. If I did, I could still wonder if he might, one day, want me back.

I could still hope.

It does not even matter that he cannot see me at this moment, because now, after so many *Play, Play, Play* repetitions, we both know—we cannot avoid knowing—that we are on opposite sides. We are rivals, regarding each other with deep suspicion, because we can no longer look into each other's eyes. I am waiting here, longing for my dad. He is waiting over there, writing my voice.

Around Me Around Him

Chapter 31

As Told by Anita

Aunt Hadassa calls me to say that he's called her, this time from New York, just to say hi and to let her know all's well, he's traveling around the country, having the time of his life. So I tell her, like, Good for him, and I mean it—but I'm careful not to mention no doubts, 'cause like, why should I make her worry. So the only one I ask is myself, Why do I still have that funny feeling, like he's never left town?

Like, a week ago I went shopping with her, and we stopped on Montana street, outside the window of a baby furniture store, 'cause that cradle—the one with the arched canopy, with them cute ruffles over it—caught my eye, it was so adorable! And then, then I could swear I spotted them eyes glinting there, in the glass. That look, it was terribly familiar. So without having to turn around I already knew that someone, someone I used to know was standing there, directly behind us, on the other side of the street.

I won't have noticed that man at all, if not for the odd way the chin was wrapped with a scarf, over the nose and ears, which wasn't even necessary, 'cause there wasn't no wind, and it was such a warm, sunny March day.

But it turned out that it wasn't Ben, after all. I mean, the shoes wasn't exactly right, and way he walked away was kinda different. And the hair was all wrong, it was much too long. And, he wasn't even looking at me, the way I thought he was. Like, there wasn't even a glance. I really don't get it. I thought I had a sharp eye, but somehow I must have misread the reflection.

Enough, I told myself then, what's the matter with you?

You think someone—anyone—would bother taking another look at you now, waddling around with your belly coming forward like that, like a beach ball?

Then we went into the store, aunt Hadassa and me, and I think she could tell—in spite of me trying to smile—how tense I was. So she bought a little something for me—well, for the baby, really: a mobile, with plush toy animals dancing around it. For now, I mean, until I get a cradle for my baby, it's hung up in the bedroom window, right in the center, where the blinds meet.

So at night, when I feel sad, or tired, or just sleepy, I pull out the little string to wind the thing up, which makes the animals go fly—fly like a dream—so slowly around your head.

And at the same time, it brings out a sweet lullaby, chiming, *Twinkle, twinkle, little star... How I wonder what you are...*

I stand here, by the window under the mobile. I touch the glass between one blind and another, and watch them animals, mirrored. They come in like ghosts, one after another, right up to the surface, swing around, and fly back out, into the dark. Then I gaze at them stars up there, so far beyond, and ask myself if they're real—or am I, again, misreading some reflection.

But after a while, all of that don't matter no more.

What matters is only what's here. I touch my skin right under my breasts, which is where the little one's curled, and where he kicks, 'cause he has to. Like, he don't feel so cosy no more. Here, can you feel it? I reckon he wants me to talk to him. He can hear me inside, for sure. He can hear every note of this silvery music.

It ripples all around him, wave after wave. I can tell that it's starting to sooth him. It's so full of joy, of delight, even if to him, it's coming across somewhat muffled. Like a dream in a dream, it's floating inside, into his soft, tender ear.

I close my eyes and hold myself, wrapping my arms real soft —around me around him—and I rock ever so gently, back and forth, back and forth, with every note of this silvery marvel. You can barely hear me—but here I am, singing along. I'm whispering words into myself, into him.

And this is the moment when, like one, we're happy.

No Second Look

Chapter 32

As Told by Ben

H ere is my latest revelation: I have been in hiding for so long that at this point, by some strange twist, my mind starts rebelling against me. I know it, because—in spite of my efforts to disguise myself, to alter my looks and behavior—I find myself wishing to be found out.

To this day I do not exactly know why, why I attempted this transformation in the first place, except to say it was something I felt compelled to try. It was the only way to stay in town, and to remain close, physically at least, to my father, he who had cast me away.

So I put a black rinse on my hair, which at first—until I got used to it—looked somewhat artificial to me: not just the color, but the shine, too. I let it grow longer, so that in a matter of a few weeks it hung just short of my shoulders. And unless I swept my bangs sideways, there would be no way for you to spot my eyes.

Next I bought a suit, a secondhand suit made of charcoal blue pinstripe wool, the kind I would never be caught dead wearing, I mean, in my previous, normal life. It made me look a lot wider, I thought, because of its double breasted cut, and the heavy shoulder pads. An overcoat, a pair of new dress shoes and my old, black scarf put the finishing touches on my costume.

I glanced down at myself thinking, what sort of a man was I trying to turn into? A yesterday's hippie, who had evolved, somehow, into a white-collar character? Would I not be drawing more attention than I usually do, and becoming easier to recognize, dressed in way which to me, was peculiar?

The answer, to my surprise, was No. People—even those who used to be my neighbors—would not give me a second look when I passed them on the street.

I suppose they mistook me for someone who spent most of his time counting money, such as a clerk in a bank or something. I looked formal, which helped me land a job, my first job, not only since my return to Santa Monica, but ever. It happened quite by chance.

Back at the beginning of January I was walking aimlessly up and down Wilshire Boulevard, and happened to spot a *Teacher Wanted* sign in the front window of this place, which turned out to be a local music academy. On a whim, I went in, and gave my real name—Benjamin Kaminsky—because it is quite common, and because I had no time to think, and because I wanted, in my heart of hearts, to leave some trace of myself, so if someone went looking, they could, eventually, find me.

I presented myself as a pianist, whose academic credentials had been lost back in Bulgaria, or some such place. I said I was eager to start working immediately, and for low wages, and completed this introduction by dashing over to one of the pianos and playing my old version of *The Entertainer*, which—to my astonishment—got me the job on the spot.

The very next day, as I approached the entrance to the music academy to start my afternoon schedule, my heart took a leap: I thought I caught sight of a familiar outline coming around the opposite street corner. A broad-shouldered man could be spotted advancing toward me with long, steady strides. Turning there—no longer with a limp—and walking down the other side of the street, was my father.

Gazing at the pavement, the old man seemed lonely and withdrawn. Over a month had passed since our quarrel. The memory of it swung there, in the space between us, like a double-edged sword: ready to cut in both directions.

I needed to believe dad was thinking about me, imagining me someplace else, perhaps traveling abroad, this time on my own dime, having refused his offer of support. Was he worried about me? Did he go back to regarding me as a son, instead of a rival? I wanted to be on his mind, now that I was out of his way.

Cloaked in my black scarf I felt close to invisible, secure in my new identity—but at the same time an urge came upon me, a strong, undeniable urge to be discovered. There was no fighting it.

I hurried over, and—quite abruptly—stepped into his path, and crossed him.

Coming against me he raised his face, and was looking far out there, perhaps at the stormy sky over my shoulder. For just an instant I dared look directly into his eyes. In my heart, anger clashed with something I had trouble naming: maybe love, maybe not. If he were to touch me right then, I had no idea if I would break his arms or fall into them, sobbing.

The moment came and went. Not once did he show any sign of recognition. Absent-minded, my father passed me by as if going around some thing, some inanimate object. An empty suit, for all he cared. An obstacle.

Even so, I was hopeful. With every step my father had taken along the way, I could not wait for him to take a second look at me—but then remembered he had neglected to take even the first one.

I stood there, hidden from him in plain view. Being unnoticed should not have shocked me so—but somehow, it did. As if planted in the pavement I froze, looking at his back, which was growing smaller and smaller, obscured by one passerby, then another, until at last it faded out into the distance.

His gait never slowed down, nor did he turn around.

Since that day I followed in his footsteps—I mean, literally—even in broad daylight. I trailed him, usually at a safe distance, about half a block behind him, and could feel the sweat welling up in my armpits, and running down my spine, even in cold weather. When necessary I took cover behind parked cars. If it became evident that he was distracted I moved a little closer, and so, learned everything there was to know about him, every habit that had escaped me before:

What time my father would leave for work. How he would raise his head to see Anita up there, leaning her elbows on the windowsill or combing her red hair. Where he would spend his lunch hour. How he would run his finger across the laminated menu, straining his eyes under his ill-fitting bifocals. His manner of nodding to the waitress to ask for his bill. Her manner of flirting with him. The slant of his pen, the way it rested on his fingers as he scribbled something, hastily, on his napkin.

Perhaps it was some expression that came upon him, some words that were just right, and could be put on the lips of this or that character in his book—or else, it was her name and phone number.

I was envious of him, and had no doubt he could get any woman he wanted, because my father was a strikingly handsome man, still, and the pomade in his sleeked-back hair could detract nothing from that, nor could the gray. Besides having Anita, he could get any other woman, which from time to time, he did— except, of course, for one woman. The one I had blamed him for losing.

Which brings me to what I see, having followed him just now into Sunrise home. He has just entered the dining hall through the heavy double doors.

I am holding them slightly apart, as if they were two parts of a fractured shield, and with one open eye I am trying to watch, as best I can, through the chink.

Seated at the head of the long Formica table, there he is, gazing at her. I mean, at my mother. Here is my family, the way it used to be, almost.

If I were to focus strictly on my parents, ignore the entire background of this place, and let the clutter and the smell of it just fall away, this could take me back to a different time, a time in my childhood, when our kitchen table was set for the Passover meal. What comes back to me first is the tinkle, as my father finished blessing the wine, and clinked his glass against hers, against mine.

I remember: the table was draped, all the way down to the floor, with mom's best, rarely used tablecloth, made of the smoothest ivory satin you ever touched. Dad sat at the head of the table, mom to his right, I opposite her.

All day long she had been cooking, which infused the air with a wonderful aroma. In it you could detect a sharp whiff of horseradish and of gefilte fish and sweet brisket and red cabbage and roasted potatoes, all of which made my stomach growl. It went on growling until he finished reading the long, archaic text in the Hagadda, which meant little to me, except a vague notion of the utter futility of patience.

I remember: my mother ladled the clear, golden chicken soup and set it here, steaming before my eyes, with three matzo balls floating inside, which was her way of giving. "It's hot," she said. "Make sure to blow on it first." Yes, the smell of her cooking was good, but then, the taste! Just wait till you took the first bite —

At this point I must snap out of my thoughts, because I can sense—even from this distance, through the interval I hold open between the doors—a subtle movement inside. I put my eye to the crack: yes, it is him. My father dips a tablespoon in a bowl, which is set directly in front of her, and raises it. Some kind of thick soup can be seen rolling in it, dripping over its rim. From here, I can see his lips moving, and guess at the words.

"Here, Natasha," he leans over to her. "You must be hungry."

She stares at it, not saying a thing.

Then he brings the tablespoon ever so carefully under her nose, so she may first smell the food, while he is keeping a napkin ready right there, under her chin.

I have not seen them together for ten years, so what he does in these circumstances surprises me. Even more so, what he says.

"Here," says the old man, holding out the tablespoon. "Open up, dear."

And he touches it gently to her lips. Which is when she parts them, and you can see her licking, tasting, head coming forward, hungrily now, for more.

"Now, now! Wasn't that yummy," he says, as if to cheer up a child.

And he smiles at her, a painful smile that tells me one thing: he knows that—unlike a child—she is bound to forget this moment, and unlearn the little that is left in her, I mean, the little that is left of her skills.

He knows—how can he not?—the futility of his efforts, of his care. Still he goes on, wiping the dribble from the corner of her mouth. Which suddenly brings back to me a memory of how she would do this for me, once upon a time.

"Wait," he tells her. "Not so fast."

One spoonful after another he feeds her, with boundless patience. I cannot imagine where he finds the strength in himself to go on.

Every time she swallows, he tilts a bit closer, looking up at her face as if, hoping against hope, he is still trying to find a glint, maybe of some recognition, some awareness—finding none.

"There, there," he says when at last, the bowl has been scraped clean.

It becomes clear to me that in spite of their divorce, in spite of his remarriage, things here stay the same. In sickness and in health, my mother is—and will remain—his responsibility. Here is my family, the way it is.

And yet, where she is going, he cannot allow himself to follow. Nobody can.

My father pushes the bowl away and gets up, looking tense, and older than usual. His expression makes me forget, in one instant, all his flaws, and the reasons for the quarrel between us. It must be incredibly hard for him. Is there any point in him being here? How would he know if she can still receive what he gives? Has the last line been crossed?

I recall what I learned in medical school about Alzheimer's. By a strange twist, it makes me imagine the disease spreading, over time, from the neocortex part of her brain all the way down to the reptilian one, which inevitably forces her to go back, way back in time from who she used to be. Her mind is receding, step by step, on its rocky journey, a journey to a different place, where she is no longer a middle aged woman, no longer a girl, or even a toddler, and who knows at this point if she is a baby, still.

Then, on a sudden impulse, my dad bends over her, so his cheek is suddenly right there, next to her face, only a breath away from her lips, and I know, I just know what he wants, what it is he is waiting for.

And this, this is the moment when the truth comes to me, clear and naked in its full ugliness, and I cannot deny it, cannot ignore the horrific meaning of what she who used to be my mother does next:

Sensing a presence next to her, she stirs back, as if by instinct, and for a split second smacks her lips. He may think this is a sign, perhaps of gratitude. I can see the sudden relief, the surprise in his smile. His eyes start closing, as if in anticipation of a kiss.

And then, then she opens her mouth, like some animal—a lizard comes to mind—hungry for its prey. She stays there, seemingly lazy, utterly motionless, jaws dropped, chin hanging, waiting for her feed. Waiting, waiting, waiting for more. Waiting without a word. Waiting with a need that can no longer find its satisfaction, the need of a body, an empty shell of a body whose mind has finally left it. Waiting, because mom will never be able to give.

At once I let go of the double doors so they swing, and come to a close. And I turn, and I run, run out of that place as fast as I can, so as not feel her eyes, looking at me without taking me in.

I am still running. I have to, because I find myself held still in that moment, when the truth has come to me, damn it. Who can be so brazen as to deny it, and who wants to take a second look.

Not The End

Chapter 33

As Told by Anita

He's been so busy, punching away at the machine and crumpling page after page into the trash bin, that lately I can't get a word through to him no more. Oh, he's replacing this tape with another and like, listening to my voice all the time—but not to me.

Which makes me wish sometimes that I was some written piece, some character in his book, 'cause I would be more real to him that way. I see myself as *her*, a thing of fiction springing to life, like, right out of them letters—which are so dense, so crammed on that sheet of paper, that there isn't no space to breathe—and smoothing all them creases in me with a slight, crispy rustle, which for sure, would win his attention right away.

I bet he would let himself stretch the truth about me to create her, 'cause like, the paper can take it. His story would draw the longest legs and the sexiest ass and the most perfect pair of boobs you could ever dream up. What's more, she would become a mouth, like, for things that go on in his head, things so fucking raw and intense that they frighten him.

Them words he writes, they would all come out of her lips, stained with ink and scratched out here and there, to say the things that in real life Lenny wishes he could blurt out, yet holds himself back, as best he can, from doing so. But then, that Anita won't be *me*.

By now I've learned my lesson, I learned it good: I won't leave no more pieces of me laying around. When I'm done with the tape recorder I pop my tape out, and stash it away at once, like, behind Beethoven's bust or under it or some other such place, and I cover it with papers and stuff.

This way Lenny don't get it in his hands, to listen to my voice, to study the way I *enunciate* things, so he don't have no excuse to ignore the *real* me. And what's more, he can't get hurt by what he don't hear, by what wasn't meant for his ears in the first place, so he don't feel so jealous no more, and like, he don't try to forget it, to blank out how hurt he is.

Which is good, 'cause then there isn't no need to argue between us, like, if he's the one betraying my trust by listening to my tape—or I'm the one betraying his, by what I say.

Anyhow, this evening he's different. I hear him pacing around the balcony, between his desk and the wall behind his chair, which is a small feat all by itself, 'cause like, there isn't barely room to move out there. Then, after two hours of this Lenny throws his hands in the air, and comes in to tell me he's stuck.

Which makes me raise one of my eyebrows, like, "You sure don't look stuck to me, 'cause here you are, running around." And what I mean by *running around* is clear to both of us.

What can he say to that? Nothing, that's what.

Anyhow, I don't want to sound bitter at him, 'cause I care for Lenny, really, I do. So I ask, "Now, how d'you mean, stuck?"

And he says, "Oh, stop it. You are never going to understand me."

And I say, "Just try me, Lenny."

And he goes, "I am stuck, stuck, stuck! Stuck in a rut! I will never succeed in getting anything done. I am wasting time here, exhausted, not being able to think, and why? Because unwittingly, I am too busy complaining to myself over my wasted time."

And before I can tell him to stop talking nonsense, or else put it in writing, he goes on to say, "Damn it. I cannot write a single line."

"But like, why?"

"Because," he groans, "every word gets me closer to *The End*."

So I try this, I say, "Maybe there is no end, really, and all you can do is just cut off at any point, because life just goes on, like, even if you leave me right here, right in the middle of a sentence. That," I say, "could be *The End*, too."

"No, no, no! It is not that simple."

"I bet it's simpler than you think."

"No," he says, "I am not *that* tired, not yet. Cannot abandon it, cannot leave off just like that, in the middle, because the story needs something, it needs to be completed—but then, I do not know where it goes from here, and for the life of me, I cannot find *The End*, even though I know—I know it's closing in on me."

"If you can't add no words, don't you think you're already done?"

"No," he says. "At this point, no. I cannot stop writing—and I cannot write. I am left in midair, hanging from a cliff."

"So? Just let go."

And he stares at me strange, "Wouldn't you like that."

I ain't exactly sure I get what he means by that, but instead of explaining Lenny runs back to the balcony and leans over his desk, scribbling something real fast in the margin of a page, like he is chasing some idea with his pen. Then he waves his hand, pretty wild, calling me to come out there and listen.

He pushes his bifocals up his nose, which is totally useless, 'cause they just slip down again. And this is what he reads to me:

She knew not to expect hearing the end of the sentence, because the old man had already slammed the door behind him. She could guess where Leonard was heading, probably to that fake old blond, who lived on the southern fringe of town.

The next morning she woke up to the sound, the insistent sound of knocks at the door, and a sudden fear squeezed her heart as she opened it, to find two grim-faced cops.

When they hesitated to say what they came in to say, she screamed. She did not want to learn that the old man had been found lifeless, nor did she want to see the snapshots they had taken, right there at the scene, snapshots that revealed all the tedious details of how he had ended up lying there, with a half crooked smile, in the other woman's arms.

"Awesome!" I tell Lenny. "I'm so glad to hear this."

His eyes pop, "You are?"

"Sure!" I say. "Me, I was kinda afraid you're writing something real, like, something about us. Now—with what you've come up with, right there—I can see awful clear that it ain't nothing but fiction."

By way of an answer Lenny crumples the page, and sinks back in his chair, muttering something about how I don't understand him, him and his creative ideas and this particular blueprint he is drafting, for a new kind of a novel, and what a damn fool he is, like, every time he repeats the mistake of using me for a listener.

"Then," I say, "find yourself someone else to listen. Me, I don't much like the sound of how you wrote it."

"The sound?" his eyes widen once more. "What sound? And, what is wrong with it?"

"Noise," I say. "Just too much of it! That's what you get when you try to end things, like, with a bang. Me, I don't even want to imagine all that slamming, and them knocks at the door and what not. Come here, I want you to hear something."

I take him by the hand, and somehow Lenny lets me. He's curious, I bet, so I lead him straight to the bedroom. I come to a stop right there, under the musical mobile, which I hung just last night in the window, between one blind and another.

Then, I pull the little string, so the thing starts turning around, and playing its tender notes. "There... Hear this? Now here's a sound I do like."

He closes his eyes to listen, so I ain't exactly sure what he sees in his head. After a while Lenny says, "You know, I like it too. Just a delicate little whisper of a lullaby. Maybe you are right, Anita. Maybe that is what I need. Maybe that is what is called for, I mean, not just to heal both of us—but also, to complete the story. Listen! Here is a note—I could just detect it, just now —a note that could mark the end."

"But then," I say, "it could mark a beginning, just as well."

And for the first time this evening he looks straight into my eyes. At that moment I can tell that he sees me, like, for what I am. I mean, he sees beyond what he's put on paper, with them longest legs and that sexiest ass and them boobs and what not. Yes, now he sees in me something more than all that, something else: a woman, expecting.

At that instant a sudden pain makes itself known in me, right down my back. It starts turning there, deep in my belly. Which is when I figure that I've felt it before. It's come and gone several times this evening—only it seemed awful dull up to now, which like, lets me ignore it.

This time it's sharper, and it lasts quite a while, which makes me wince. "Aw," I say.

But anyhow, Lenny don't even hear me, 'cause he's back to scratching his head, on account of being confused about his story, and about what this music could tell you, and how he could use it in his story, like, to mark the end.

"Yes," he whispers. "Just a sound of bells, chiming, chiming, chiming. And behind that, the breath of a baby asleep in the cradle, rocked to sleep by a mother's hand. Maybe that is what is needed."

"Aw," I say again.

And he says, "Such a gentle sound. No doubt, Ben would like it."

I stare at him in surprise, 'cause for several months Lenny's been so mad, so angry at his son, that he didn't hardly mention his name—nor did he allow me to mention it.

"So now," I say, like, with caution, "all's fine? Like, you've forgiven him?"

"I do not know about that," he says, sounding pretty touchy.

A minute later his voice seems to soften. "What I *do* know—I can feel it in my bones—is this: any day now, my son will be coming here, to my door, and—"

"You have two sons, not one," I cut in.

"He will be coming back," says Lenny, right over my words. "Looking for the thing, the one thing only I can give him: a story."

Me, I can tell he don't pay no attention to anything I say, so all I can do is at this point is just breathe hard for a few seconds, and then repeat, "Aw," a third time.

Meanwhile Lenny's busy arguing with himself.

"Whenever I read what I've written, it seems so sketchy to me, so goddam fragmented! Just a jumble of moments, and some voices here and there, lost in the clutter. What am I missing? How come I find myself falling short, so terribly short of where I thought I was going? What the story needs is a meaning—or else all my work, and all my sleepless nights have come to nothing, nothing, nothing in the end."

His eyes seem to beg me for some hint, some meaning, like I could give it to him. What can I say to that? Nothing, and he knows it.

So Lenny starts pacing around the bed, and he reaches the mirror, the oval mirror standing there, slightly tilted, in the corner. Here he stops, and glances at the scribbled page over there, in his reflected hand.

From where I stand, them letters look pretty odd, them words scrambled—right turned left, in turned out—right there, on that patch of white, clutched by the ghost of his hand, deep in the glass. Lenny leans in, so his nose nearly touches that other nose, the one in the mirror, like he's trying to go in, to read what's in there. And his shadow inside, it's trying to read, just as hard, what's out here.

It's like, a riddle, waiting to be solved.

His bifocals, they've come loose from his face and dropped off, so he searches for them here and there across the floor. No matter, he'll find them later. Then, like, by mistake, Lenny gets too close to the mirror and—bang!—hits his forehead against it. I ain't exactly sure how it's happened. Anyhow, you can tell he's growing restless, 'cause the paper in his hand starts rustling, till the writing becomes just a blur, on both sides of the glass.

"There must be *some* significance to all this," he mutters. "And it must be extracted. It must be put in words—or else, my son would open the door, and I—I would not be ready for him."

"So?" I say. "What is it you're afraid of?"

"Ben would come in, and there would be no one to see but an old man, an old man standing there, his mouth open as if to start singing, and just cold breath coming out."

And with that Lenny pushes the frame of the mirror, so now it's tilted awful sharp, and it's like, sticking clear out of the corner, right here between me and him. He lifts a hand, like, to correct it, to straighten the thing, which is when we start hearing the knocks.

Them knocks, they come rapping, rapping real timid at first, there at the entrance door. Then comes a squeal, like that of a key which—having been inserted—starts turning, real slow, in the lock.

The old man turns his back to the mirror, which is still pretty crooked.

"My God," he mumbles. "Not now! I am not ready for him."

And then, then he takes a shaky step back, stumbling—

Am I Covered

Chapter 34

As Told by Ben

And I rush to his side, hearing glass splitting from the mirror, then crunching underfoot, shards spreading across the floor and plinking as they hit the far corners and the walls. His head has sunk over his breast: at first glance, no blood. No pomade, either, which makes him look odd. His scalp is pale, nearly bald, with wisps of dull, disheveled gray hair hanging from it.

Then my father stirs, takes an agonized breath and staggers to his feet, trying to push himself, somehow, away from the oval frame. Perhaps because he is in shock, his knees give way under him.

He stumbles again, so I catch him in my arms, noting how frail the old man has grown over recent months. He even seems to have shrunk a bit. I carry him to their bed as if he were a baby, and lower him into it. Still curled in my arms, he grips the scarf around my neck with his shriveled fingers, plays with its fringes, and suddenly pulls at it with such force that for a moment I find myself choked.

But somehow I manage to lay him down, which he lets me do without further quibble. With great care I remove his socks, because there are slivers of glass pinned to them. Next I pull off his trousers, because some of the fragments fell into the bottom cuffs.

From the corner of his eye my father looks up, first at Anita, who has risen from the corner and come forward to help me strip him, then at me. I can hear him mumbling something, so I bend over him, putting my ear to his lips. "Cover me up," he whispers.

So I unfurl the blue sheet over him, and tuck it under the mattress, and layer a wool blanket on top of that, and arrange it carefully around him.

Meanwhile Anita raises the setting of the thermostat, because without having to say things out loud, we figure that—in spite of the spring weather—he must somehow be cold.

The old man looks into my eyes and shivers. He mutters, "Am I covered?"

"Yes," I say. "You are."

"Are you sure?" he asks, sharply now.

"Yes," I say. "Do not worry. You are covered, completely covered."

"No!" he cries, tearing the blanket off and thrusting it madly to the floor, uncovering his thin, bare legs. "No, I am not covered—not yet! You'll have to wait longer, quite a while longer, until I am laid to rest!"

"Stop, Lenny," says Anita. "Your son's come back, like, to be close to you, to be forgiven."

The old man scrambles up to his shaky feet, and stands there, on top of the bed, hands twitching, eyes flaring with some strange glare, perhaps on the verge of craziness.

"Stop it," she repeats, taking a step toward him, spreading her arms to catch him if he falls.

I wonder if I should let him know that for the last four months I have been following him, and her too.

I have been delivering little things—such as a note or a bottle of champaign to their doorstep—entering the apartment from time to time when no one was around, reading the papers on his desk, taking a pen or leaving one of my own, even using his tape recorder to record my voice, wishing to be found out in any one of these ways. Wishing to come back home. By April, the desire has reached such a level, as to push me in the door just now, in spite of knowing they are inside—or maybe because of it.

Instead I just say, "Calm down, dad, will you? If you want me to leave, just say so." If he has longed to see me, he gives no sign of it. So again, I stress, "If you want me to leave, I will."

The fall he took, and the shock of seeing me must have brought out the hurt, the resentment in him. His eyes narrow, darting between the two of us.

"You," he turns them on me, "you want to bury me right now. I know, I just know you do. Goddamn it! I can feel it in my bones!"

And she says, "Ben don't want nothing bad to happen here, and for sure, he don't—he don't want you dead."

"And you!" he points his finger, this time at her. "It is all because of you, and you know it, dear!"

Which makes her bite her lips, even cringe. She moves back into the corner, and leans into her wedding dress, which for some reason she dyed, wild orange and purple. The colors are aflame around her.

"Please, dad, stop shouting at her," I say. "What did *she* do?"

He hops to the edge of the bed, screaming.

"What? What did she do? What did she do? How, how can you ask, even, What the fuck did she do?" He grabs the sheet, and ties it crudely around his underwear, and sways his hips mockingly, wobbling widely this way and that, like a drunken fashion model on impossibly high heels, trying to stay, somehow, on the catwalk.

"Stop it," I say.

In turn he twirls the fabric, flapping it around his waist, "Did she lift her little black dress for you, like this? Did she bend over, like that?"

At this point he has come dangerously close to falling off the bed, leaving me no choice but to grab him around his thighs, and bring him forcibly to his knees.

"Is this where she had her way with you?" he cries. "Here, in your mother's presence—I mean, in her bed?"

"No," I say. "Not here." Which makes Anita cringe again.

I catch sight of my watch. Thirteen minutes past one.

After a while Anita raises her wet eyes to him and says, "Me, I don't expect to be forgiven. But here's your son! Your son, Lenny! Look at him! He needs you. You need him. Let him off the hook already. Do it, do it now!"

My father lays there, on the bare part of the mattress, utterly spent, staring blankly at the cracked mirror.

She pleads, "He's your flesh and blood, for God's sake—not one of them characters you write about, not one of them voices there, inside your tape recorder! You're so alone, spending all your time with them things, blocking out everything else. You've gone back too far already, to places in your head that ain't even concrete, places where you can't touch no one, and like, you can't be touched in return!"

"You are wrong, so wrong," he says, bursting with arrogance. "The characters I write, they can touch you—even if I cannot."

Anita bites her lips. Thirty three minutes past one.

He turns away from her. "They can touch you—even when I am gone."

She cries, "Enough! I—I—you're tearing me, inside!"

"Maybe one day, you are going to look back and listen to what I wrote. Maybe then you will remember me—"

"No more *Rewind, Rewind, Rewind*," says Anita. "Just, stop it, right now! *Stop*! You're tearing me!"

I doubt that he has heard her.

"Look around you, find what's real," she begs. "Look at your son. Don't tear him away no more! Let him in, Lenny!"

He shows no sign of hearing her. But after a while, a breath comes out of his lips, as if a balloon has released its air—not in a single pop, but haltingly, little by little, till the fume has been spent, and the rage gone, so that now he is left there, empty. Then my father lifts his hand and unties the knot of the sheet, letting it unwrap and slip off, down to the floor. I pick it up, and with caution I move closer, and cover him.

Then I sit there, by his side, not knowing what to say, not knowing what *can* be said at this point. I shake my head, wishing I could shake out the words, I am Sorry, dad. Forgive me.

Which is when I notice, all of a sudden, what he sees there, in my mother's standalone mirror. The thing is leaning haphazardly on one leg, tilted out of position, broken. And there —between the cracks shooting out from the center, where it has shattered—there, if you focus, hands can be spotted. Pale woman's hands. They come rising, rising slowly towards him, as if to take hold of him and pull him in.

My father shuts his eyes. On his lips I can see the word, *Natasha*.

I wipe my eyes and glance at the mirror again.

By now the hands have clenched tightly into white-knuckled fists. Above them, a cloud of red hair comes into view, and under it, a face. The features are contorted, because she is cringing with intense pain. This time, Anita nearly folds over herself.

Forty seven minutes past one. Which is when I know, all of a sudden, that I have arrived just in time.

She is in labor.

During our cab drive to the hospital, I cast a glance over my shoulder to see Anita in the back seat, arms crossed over the mound of her belly, clutching each other till the flesh turns white. Her face is flushed, her breath labored, and her lips—when I can see them—are bearing the bite marks of her teeth.

I tell her that she will be in the best of hands, because from what I heard back in medical school, a durable artificial hip was developed five years ago at UCLA, and the first total shoulder replacement was performed there, also around the same time. She says nothing to that, perhaps because at the moment she is taking time to cringe, and to filter an occasional, "Aw" between her teeth.

Meanwhile my father takes this opportunity to snap out of his daze, and he leans forward to tell me that it is not a hip or a shoulder we are talking about, but the birth of his son.

When the cab arrives at the hospital, my three aunts are already there, waiting for us by the curb. I have no idea how they have managed to get here so fast, or from where they have already fetched a fancy hospital wheelchair, into which Anita, breathing hard, is now being transferred.

Aunt Hadassa grips both handles, readying herself for taking charge of pushing the thing. In her haste to be here on time she must have neglected, somehow, to paint in her eyebrows. Also, she must have forgotten to nudge her puffy, white hair into place, so now it is piled up on top of her, lopsided. Dangling from her padded shoulder is her purse, in which you can spot, among other things, her knitting needles and a large ball of yarn. She is prepared for the wait.

"My, my," says aunt Fruma, and aunt Frida follows that with, "What took you so long?"

As for aunt Hadassa, she taps her foot with a mixture of impatience and glee, and says, "Nu? It's time already!"

And with that, the three of them whiz by me, wheeling Anita with great gusto into the open doors of the hospital.

I turn to my father, thinking he may need help to get out of the cab, but he refuses me. He leans back into the seat, shuts the car door and rolls up the window.

"I am not coming in," he says, his voice weak, but insistent.

"But dad, she is in labor," I say. "I thought you would want to be there, by her side, to hold her hand, or something, during the —"

"No, Ben," he says. "I cannot help her with her pain—and she cannot help me with mine. No one can. Let's not pretend about it."

"Are you not feeing well?" I say. "You really need to see a doctor yourself, you know. You may have a concussion, the way you slipped and fell into that glass—"

"Enough! I feel fine," he says.

"Here," I try to reopen his door, "let me help you—"

"No," he closes it again. "No need for that."

"You cannot just ignore such an injury," I say. "It makes no sense, dad. Let me, let me take you in, to Emergency—"

"No," he says, in his most stubborn tone.

"At least, let me take a look at your head."

His jaw is firmly set. "No," he repeats.

Then, perhaps noting the frustrated expression on my face, he relents—but just a little.

"If you really want to help me, son," he says, "get back in."

There is no arguing with him when he gets that way, so I get back into the cab, this time next to him, and before I finish closing the door on my side, dad has already given his directions to the driver.

"So," he says, "Let's go! To Sunrise Assisted Living."

Lay Me Down

Chapter 35

As Told by Ben

At the end of the cab ride to Sunrise home, the silence is finally broken when my father glances at me, and his face softens, and he says, "Anita is right. I have been tearing her, inside. I need to separate between what is real and what is not."

And I say, "This here between us, this is real. And the loneliness, too."

In return he says, "I am so sorry, Ben. I do not know what came over me tonight. I guess I was not prepared for you. Forgive me."

I turn to him, utterly in surprise, and notice that he is bringing his eyebrows together, the way he does when he has a severe headache. He looks in my direction through clouded eyes, as if his vision has suddenly blurred.

This, I think, is the first, the only time he has asked me to forgive him, for anything. Usually all I get from him is excuses, excuses and blame. My father is right, forever, always. But not now. Which is why the idea comes to me that perhaps, he feels as if he is not going to make it through the night. At once, I push it out of my mind.

Still, his lips are moving. "Now that you are back," he lets out, "things will go back the way they ought to go. I want you to know it."

I see him forming words, but his voice is too weak to carry them. So I bend over, putting my ear to his mouth.

He breathes, "Here—now—I could not have written it any better."

And a moment later, "This is the most important day, the most important hour of my entire life. I can see things clearly, more than ever before, as if from a distance. You," he takes a pause, "you have made your share of mistakes—but the whole thing started with mine."

"Sorry, dad," I say.

And he says, "It is my fault, and we both know it. Both of us have been paying the price. Don't—don't worry, son. I am going to fix it."

These few words between us do me good, and my lungs expand and suddenly I can breathe so much easier than before —even though I am left wondering what he means by *the whole thing* and how exactly can it be fixed.

The cab comes to a stop in front of Sunrise Assisted Living at ten minutes past five, early in the morning.

I have expected to see the doors locked for the night—but to my surprise they are thrown open, and someone is being carried out on a stretcher, soon to be loaded into an ambulance, which is parked slightly ahead of us. As the medics pass by my side I glance at the stretcher, and recognize the head lolling to one side, peaking out of the white sheet. I recognize it because of the black, utterly toothless mouth, which is open in a long *O*, as if in the middle of singing.

I help my father out of the cab. He is having some trouble balancing on his feet, so I practically carry him past the medics, past the young, unfamiliar woman dressed in a nurse uniform, who is darting this way and that around them in great confusion. She must be in charge of the night shift crew. We are inside, barely noticed by her.

Martha, the care giver, has not arrived here yet. Outside, outlines of the medics can be seen, shadows rushing to and fro. The flashing of emergency lights comes in through the windows, and starts strobing around us in the empty dining hall as the ambulance moves away.

Without saying a word, my old man points his finger at the third door in the row of doors along a long corridor. It is the only door that is open, perhaps because the old, toothless patient has just been lifted out of bed from there.

I bring him in, knowing in my heart that this is where he has been heading all night long. I wonder if he can find the words, if he can even explain—to himself most of all—what possesses him to come to this place. There are two twin beds in the room, one of them unoccupied, just as I expected. In the other, lays my mother. In her deep slumber, she looks as if she is smiling.

"Now," says my father. "Lay me down."

My old man seems dizzy as I lower him into her bed. From time to time he is given to uncontrolled shaking, so I pull the blanket over both of them.

Then I go back and close the door to the corridor, which at once darkens the room. It is a vacuous black, a nothingness that is falling in upon us. I have to feel my way around, as if my eyes have suddenly grown blind. Finally I reach the corner of the room and crouch down there, on the floor, and I hear him panting, panting in distress. The one thing that seems to help him relax is listening to the sounds around him, especially to the sound of my mother breathing, and to my voice saying, I am here, dad. I am right here if you need me.

After a long while the room starts to take shape. You can slowly discern the folds, the faint folds of the curtains, and the light seeping in under the wavy edge. And there, in the bed, you can see his outline, combined with hers.

By now my father must have forgotten, somehow, that this is not his place. His eyes wander in confusion, trying to decipher the shadows of the room, and his hand jerks searchingly around him. The more I watch him, the more I become convinced that he is trying hard to control it, to reach out and press some key, which only he can see. But he cannot guide his hand quite where he wants it to go—nor can he stop it from trembling.

At last, he lifts his head to me and whispers, *Record*.

By which I think he means, Remember. Or maybe he means, Talk to me, Ben.

So I start describing this room to him, especially the light poking a hesitant finger through the slit between the curtains, and stripping the darkness away from the empty bed next to them, a bed which is bare, because the sheets have already been taken away, to be cleaned and sterilized for the next person to lie here.

I go on to tell him that I knew the old woman who used to occupy this bed. He seems to be listening, so I start drawing from memory how, on my first visit here, she would hunch her shoulders over her empty hands, and lift her head to gape at me, and how her mouth would breathe slowly into the air:

Then the traveller in the dark... Thanks you for your tiny spark...
He could not see... Which way to go... If you did not twinkle so...

I sing these words for him, with a voice that is thin and barely audible, just like hers used to be. And I hope that it brings to his mind the musical mobile I have seen, in the window back home, hung between one blind and another. I hope he can fall asleep now, dreaming of reaching up, of pulling that string, to make the plush animals turn around, and go flying overhead faster and faster till all is a blur, to the sound of that silvery note, which is chiming, chiming, chiming, as if to announce a moment of birth.

Afterwards, I cannot figure out for certain at what point my voice has trailed off, leaving me lost in a jumble of memories, fearful to open my eyes, fearful to glance at my watch, to figure out the moment, the exact moment when I have realized that I am alone.

All I know is that somewhere along its arc, the light has crawled across the wall and leapt onto their pillow, and it is resting there now, on his open eyelids.

It is a fairly strong light now, a glare that can blind you if you look directly into it, which strangely he seems to be doing. So I rise to my feet to pull the curtain shut, and then, in spite of myself, I glance at him. His chest barely rises.

He lays there, having wrapped himself in my mother's arms, his eyelashes still somewhat aflutter, his hands still shivering slightly over his heart, his face pale, nearly blue, and I know that if I would leave him at this moment to go look for Martha, the care giver, it would be over. Dad would be gone by the time I rush back.

So I draw closer and stand there, behind the head of the bed, over my sleeping mother. From this angle, his ribs seem to move —but I think it is because of her body clinging to him, and because of her breathing, which is so deep and so peaceful. I lean over her arms to take his hands in mine, absorbing his shiver, taking it into my flesh, until finally it dies down.

And the light, growing even brighter, washes his face, till all that is left is a smile, frozen.

Play. Stop. Eject

Chapter 36

As Told by Anita

Next morning I'm sent home empty-handed, while my baby must stay at the hospital a few more days, to get something called colored light therapy, 'cause like, he's been diagnosed with jaundice. But does anyone care? Hello there? I try to call home, for Lenny to come pick me up—but as usual I end up just managing, somehow, to get back on my own.

I open the bedroom window, and feel warm spring air coming in, blowing gently into my face, which feels like a promise. Like, it's gonna be good. It's gonna be a beautiful day.

I rewind the musical mobile, and listen to it chiming, chiming, chiming over my head for a long while. And there I stand listening, not knowing what to do, not wanting to admit to myself how I feel. Anyhow I'm glad you can't see me sniffling, and blotting the corner of my eye, 'cause like, there isn't no one here I can hug, and no one to hug me right back.

Lenny isn't back yet, and neither is Ben. The place seems kinda empty to me—more so than usual—like a spirit has left it, on account of the piano, which is gone, and the shattered mirror. And it's messy, because of the glass, which is strewn all around me, crushing underfoot as I move around the floor, until finally I stomp off to the corridor.

Then I'm empty. Exhausted. Can't bring myself to hold a broom straight, like, to sweep away all them broken pieces. In a daze I wander into Ben's bedroom, and within moments I'm asleep in his bed.

When I open my eyes again, it's already the next morning.

I wake up to a sound, an annoying sound of knocks at the door, and a sudden fear squeezes my heart as I open it, to find two grim-faced cops. It almost feels like I've read this story before.

When they hesitate to say, like, what they've come in to say, I make up my mind I ain't gonna scream. Instead I stick my thumbs in my ears, 'cause I don't want to hear, don't want to learn that my husband's been found lifeless. And for sure I don't want to be asked no questions, 'cause like, I don't hardly have answers.

I cup the palms of my hands over my eyes, 'cause I don't want to see the snapshots they're trying to show me, which was taken right there at the scene, snapshots that show him lying there, curled, in Natasha's arms. How he got there, no one seems to know—not even them cops. They want *me* to tell them, like, how it happened.

So in spite of myself I can't help peeking, between one finger and another, only to find that in some of them pictures, his face muscles seem awful relaxed. I bet it's just a trick of the camera, some flash, which makes him look like he's laughing, almost— even though the crease on his forehead hasn't barely smoothed up.

Which reminds me of my pa, who left me such a long time ago, that I can't remember nothing of his face no more, I mean, nothing but a crease just like this, in the middle of his forehead. And even that's turning into a blur now. I swear, it's because of them tears. Damn, I miss him. I miss him so.

No, Lenny. I ain't gonna cry.

A week after the funeral, which I couldn't attend because of a sudden fever, I get a call from Lenny's attorney, Mr. Bliss. Which is a sure sign—if you didn't know it already—that this is a time of misery.

He coughs up something like, "Mrs. Kaminsky, I hope you shall know no more sorrow." And I go, "Really? That makes two of us."

Then Mr. Bliss goes on to say he's stunned, simply stunned to hear what's happened, and congratulations are in order, Mazel Tov for the baby, what's his name? And he can't find Ben, do I happen to know his address? A phone number, at least? No? And to come to his office just as soon as I can, because of the will, which Lenny has changed again only three days before his passing, and because of a key to some secret drawer in his desk, both of which must be handed over to me.

I don't exactly bother to tell him that I've known about that drawer for quite some time now, and that I've managed to pry it open—right after them cops finally left—with a kitchen knife.

It's like, I had to stab something, someone. If Lenny was gonna pop in right then, I was gonna kill him right on the spot.

What I found in the drawer was like, confusing. There was no way for me to read the whole thing clear through to the end, 'cause it was way too long, and anyhow, from the beginning, them letters was too small, and the writing too dense or something, which made me start yawning right away.

Even so, I know one thing: for Lenny, this must have been a labor of love, something he did for his son, for Ben to remember him by. I must find him, and let him know that.

Several times over the last few months, Ben would come in here—but only when I wasn't home. Like, he was invisible. He hated this place, but couldn't do without it. Them memories in his head, they would play tricks on him, pulling him back here. Also, I figure he wanted to stay close to his father. And to me too, I bet.

I could always tell, later, that I'd just missed him, because there was a trace of his smell, like, still hanging in the air, and because he'd moved things around: a pillow had been squeezed into the corner of his bed, or there was a new footprint in the dust. I swear, he must have wanted to be found out.

But not anymore—or else he'd be here, to talk to them cops. So I find myself saying what needs to be said—not directly to him, but to the tape recorder. I'm careful to sound as dry and cool as my voice would let me, 'cause you don't never know who's out there, listening.

When I'm done, I place the tape in its plastic case, and tuck it down there, behind Beethoven's bust, which I turn around to face the balcony, so the tip of its nose kinda shines in the daylight, which can draw your attention. I hope that sooner or later, Ben's gonna notice it. My voice sounds pretty formal—but it's too much, now, to do it over.

Your father left you a stack of pages here, in a secret drawer in his desk. It's his story, which he finished—or at least, was close to finishing it. I bet he wanted you to read the thing.

Where shall I mail it to? Let me know.

For two days I wait, and there isn't no answer.

Then, on the third day, I come in from my daily visit to my baby at the hospital, and the moment I unlock the door, I see that Beethoven has turned around, somehow, so its face is totally in the shade, but like, them marble eyes seem to glare pretty hard—this time at the entrance, at me. Tucked behind it, I spot the same tape I've used—except it isn't in the plastic case no more.

So my heart starts to hammer, inside. I put the tape in the tape recorder, and *Play*. My voice isn't there. It's been erased. Overwritten. His voice sounds drier, and even cooler than mine. It says:

Burn it.

Which sets me back on my heels. At once, I go ahead to *Record*:

It don't belong to me. You do it.

This time, a whole week passes by until Beethoven swings around. Ben's voice says:

I can't. This story has our voices in it.

So I say:

I bet he tried to write 'us'—but them characters ain't who we are. Now, the thing I'm worried about is not his story—but the tapes, which I'm about to destroy. Unless you tell me not to.

It's just, I don't want them to be found, 'cause the cops were here twice already. It's like, they ain't exactly sure what to look for. They don't seem to get how Lenny hit his head on the mirror and still managed to get to Sunrise home, with no one seeing him coming in. They don't really believe that's what happened.

I bet they suspect I might have killed him—but like, why would I stash his body in someone's bed, let alone Natasha's? Then, there's Mr. Bliss: he tells me now he wants to visit, to give me his condolences or something.

So by tomorrow, our voices is like, history. Gonna be erased. Or, if you wish to keep them, I can mail them tapes to you. Just tell me where to.

A week drags by—seven sleepless nights—during which I find myself missing my ma so much that it hurts, because now that the little one is finally here, I don't even get how she did it, like, how she managed to take care of me all these years, all on her own. No wonder she ended up being grumpy, which is one thing I'd rather forget.

Between feedings I go through the process, erasing one tape after another. I do it by recording stuff over them. What kind of stuff? Just anything.

Like, my baby crying at night. The way his whining turns into a giggle as I touch my nipple to his lips, just before he settles into his rhythm, like, suck, suck, swallow, breathe; suck, suck, swallow, breathe. The way I lay him over my shoulder and pat his back, to ease the hiccups. The distant sound of a door sliding along its track, as the neighbor comes out to her balcony—the one opposite us—to water her pot of geraniums. Some kid out there, practicing his piano. Stuff.

Then, late one evening, I notice the tape's changed place. This time, it's out in the open, right under Beethoven's nose. It's like, a hint that there isn't no need to hide what we say to each other.

Ben's voice says:

I happened to be out of town for a few days, so did not get your warning in time, about the tapes I mean, nor could I stop you.

As to my father's story, I still do not know what to do with it. I glanced at it, lying there in that secret drawer, and even read a few passages, some of which were too painful for me—and others which I cared nothing for, as they seemed overly fictional.

At one point the whole stack fell out of my hands, and the papers spread out. I picked them up and stuffed them back in the drawer, as best I could—but they are totally scrambled now. I doubt I can rearrange them so they will be in the right order, I mean, his order, the way he wrote it. Can you?

I wish I had the tapes, but what's gone is gone.

I say to myself, Oh shoot, and let a week go by before responding:

I did give you time to stop me.

Ben's silent, no sign from him for more than a week. I ain't even sure if the tape's been touched, like, if he's got my message. I don't want to wait no more, so this morning, before going out for my walk down to Santa Monica beach, which I do every day with my baby, I record over my previous message:

Where are you? Me, I know you can't be too far.
You angry with me?

Later, like, twenty minutes into my walk, I figure I need a sweater for me, and a blanket or something for the little one, 'cause I reckon it's turning kinda windy. So I go back, and I think I see someone, some passerby running the other way, into the back alley.

I climb up the stairs, turning over my shoulder once or twice, to see if I can tell who it is, 'cause like, something about him looks awful familiar. But like, he's already gone.

Then, as the door opens, I see that the tape recorder's been moved, and I tell myself, Look! It's still recording! So I hurry in, *Stop, Rewind, Play,* and then I close my eyes, and like, I take him in, because I so enjoy the sound, the deep sound of his voice.

No, not angry.

How can I be? I will never forget what you did for me.

And later, I could not believe it when you pushed the yellow manila envelope into my hands, with all that money in it, the day dad threw me out. I only used a small portion of it, that first week. By now I've nearly replenished what was spent. I am working now, and plan to give you back the amount in full.

Oh, and another thing.

I'm so glad that in addition to that envelope, you put the photo album in my suitcase. I barely noticed when you did it, nor did I realize what it was that I carried out with me, as I left this place.

Since then, I cannot tell you, Anita, how many times I have taken the album out, and opened it to that one page, on which a picture used to be missing.

You must have noticed it: at the top, there is a picture of my mom, from the time she was very young—perhaps your age—and pregnant. At the bottom, there is a picture of a little boy fascinated by that single candle in front of him, on his birthday cake. In between these two pictures, there used to be another one, which—try as I may—I cannot remember. Strangely, it has gone missing.

In its place I find, to my surprise, a small, black-and-white ultrasound image. It shows a profile of a baby, curled in the womb. I know, of course, that it could not have been me. The photo paper is much too fresh, and hasn't even begun to yellow. Even so, that picture —which you must have inserted there—has filled a hole.

Somehow it makes me feel as if the first stages of my life have been fully recorded.

What can I say to that, except:

Don't look back, Ben.
Like, don't Rewind.
Play.

To which he answers, later that night:

Stop.

It is your turn now to find me.

Eject—

Editorial Notes
As Written by Mr. Bliss, Attorney

In writing this Introduction I shall make every effort to avoid making it read like a legal brief. As an attorney at law, I claim neither knowledge nor any kind of experience in the task of literary editing. However, the body of work that my longtime client, Mr. Leonard Kaminsky (hereby named The Author) left behind him, which was found, rather unfortunately, in a fragmented and highly unfinished state, made it necessary for me, for professional as well as personal reasons, to rise to the task.

I served the author for nearly thirty years. Smart and tightlipped, he gave me the impression of someone who is likely to conceal some secret affairs, someone with a healthy appetite for the ladies, an appetite matched only by his experience.

Which at the time, I considered enviable.

Quite often, when I would attend a concert, I could recognize him down there in the front row, accompanied from time to time by an extremely blond girlfriend, whose name as I recall was Lana. He would listen intently to the music, his face glowing with joy, which was as remarkable as her boredom.

Such were the circumstances when, according to the newspapers of the time, he fell madly in love with his first wife, the renowned pianist Mrs. Natasha Horowitz (later, Kaminsky). The spark happened instantly, while he was watching her performing on stage. Soon afterwards they married, over the bitter objections of her family.

Then, less than six years ago, the author mentioned to me (quite abruptly and out of context) that having suffered through the misfortune of watching her deteriorate, he was determined to assemble a 'collection of voices', with the goal being the 'preservation of time.'

However, until unearthing the pile of notebooks, which contained various fragments, various blurbs of his writing, and until coming upon the three audiotapes, which were labeled in his handwriting, I had absolutely no inkling what he had meant.

Once these fragments came into my possession (as no one else would claim them) I found myself obligated to review and arrange them, as best I could, into a coherent whole.

I aimed to do it in such a way as would benefit his survivors, or more precisely, those he had named in his latest will: his older son, Mr. Benjamin Kaminsky, twenty-eight years of age, born to him by his first wife; and his younger son, Nathan Kaminsky Junior, one month old, born to him by his second wife in April of this year.

My conversations with the author were infrequent at best. The last time I saw him was three days prior to his being found lifeless.

We talked strictly about routine matters of law, as they related to his investments and his will. Thus I must admit that he never shared with me his ideas about the art of writing, nor did he mention that his attention (aside from work) was focused on recording certain sounds, capturing certain objects (such as *The White Piano*) in words, and furthermore, preserving certain events (or as he would say, certain 'moments in time') on paper. Which in later days, would prove crucial in piecing together what led, eventually, to his untimely death.

Therefore, I have no way of knowing what final form (if any) the author envisioned for these fragments, and in which order he would have presented them, had he lived to finish the task. Perhaps he knew, somehow, that his days were numbered, which would explain certain morbid phrases (such as *Dead Man's Fingers*) which he had incorporated into his latest fiction.

In trying to fill his place, I regarded myself as more than merely the editor of that which he had left behind. I regarded myself, truly, as its *custodian*. Thus I found myself engaged in an editorial guesswork, which to me, was as thrilling as it was confusing.

My dedication to the task was unusual. It surprised even me. I must have been studying these fragments far too long (perhaps to the verge of obsession) and thus, being utterly exhausted, I can no longer see the whole. Which (I confess) leaves me puzzled.

In spite of this, the text (such as it stands, at this point) must see the light of day, so that you, the reader, with your power of observation and your unbiased judgement, may assist me at some point in the future, and contribute much needed, fresh insight.

On the morning just preceding his last day, the author called me with instructions to set up a special fund, under my care, for the purpose of paying the rent for his place of residence for the next couple of months. Regretfully, his family (such as it was) dispersed soon after, and the key was entrusted to my keeping.

Therefore I decided to use this opportunity, sad as it was, to examine the various compartments of his desk (its drawers and file cabinet, and elsewhere). For no apparent reason, the notion that something was amiss happened to cross my mind. Thus I managed to convince myself that my curiosity was purely professional.

After a few hours of sifting through an incredible mess, which by no means could have been typical of him, I finally gave up. Old bills, out of date address books and crumpled shopping lists were all scrambled together in front of me. One of the drawers, the so-called secret drawer, showed marks of a knife cutting into its locking mechanism. I closed the drawers, utterly in disgust, and got up from the desk, thinking the search was futile. It was over with, done. That was when the pile of notebooks on the floor suddenly caught my eye.

I still go back there from time to time, unlock the door and sit at the kitchen table, and reflect on what I have learned. I ponder what seems so suggestive in his fiction, and ask myself if this is what really happened. I still entertain some hope (which is waning, gradually) to find additional notes, which might have been concealed by the author (or perhaps, his survivors), and which might provide me with more clues on how to join the fragments.

If I talk to myself, an echo answers from the walls.

I like to believe that the author would have approved of my editorial decisions, or at the very least, that he would not have been entirely skeptical of some of them. Also I hope he would find my publishing the text here, in this book, beneficial for his survivors. God willing, it may become a source of income for them (for I would take no part of the reward). In addition, the book is a memoir of sorts, or more precisely, it will become that, in time. In a long time.

As far as I can tell, this 'preservation of time' (as he would say) was recorded, originally, on a number of audiotapes (most of which have not been recovered, so far).

Without giving away the story I can say only this: for the most part there were two distinct voices (a male and a female) each of whom was about to reveal certain facts about the author, and about each other. With startling honesty, they relayed their memories, and their most intimate desires, right there on audiotape. They did it without shame. And rarely, if ever, did they take into account that he, the author, would (at some point) listen in on their discourse.

Which eventually, he did.

Thus, by his handwriting, these voices were conveyed (for lack of a better word) to paper. At what cost to his sanity the author carried on this task, I have no way of guessing. The disclosure of intimacy between the two characters, or even the suggestion of it, must have caused him immeasurable pain.

For the first time in his life he, the so-called *Keeper of Secrets*, unravelled the secrets of others—and found himself betrayed.

At times I wonder: did he really have the guts to listen to the entirety of their confession? Or did he stop mid-stream, finding himself unable to go on?

How could he possibly reconcile his role as an author, all-knowing and remote, with his direct role in their lives? It seems that he was determined to hover from above, to observe events as they unfold, and to steer himself away, clear out of intimacy, out of danger—and yet, he could not help but wade straight into it.

The only way this could be done is if the characters stole the story from the author and then ran away with it, uninterrupted. Which, of course, is just a fantasy of mine. It could never happen.

However, I digress. I tried various methods of arranging the fragments, so that out of discrete, yet disconnected moments described in them, I could, perhaps, recreate the continuity of time; that is, tell a story. A complete story.

In doing so I held myself back, as best I could, from the temptation of stepping into the role of the author. The task, I told myself repeatedly, was strictly one of editing. At first I attempted joining all the fragments corresponding to the male voice into one story; and likewise, all the fragments corresponding to the female voice into another. However it quickly became clear to me that (try as I may) each of the two disjointed stories seemed to be lacking, in chronological specificity, in background detail and above all, in objectivity.

Therefore I came up, at last, with a more complex, yet cleverer method: one of combining the two voices by alternating them (at a certain rhythm) so the story can become more mutually supported by them; and indeed, more orchestrated. Thus, it is fuller, and can be perceived as a sort of a dialogue, or better yet: a musical duet.

This book also serves as the highest form of complement I could pay the author, posthumously of course. When I unearthed the pile of his notebooks, and began sifting through them, I was surprised, even deeply moved by certain passages. I am not a man given to reading prose, much less poetry. However, decoding these fragments felt (to my astonishment) as if the voices came alive. Over the rustle of paper in my hands, they spoke directly, and at times almost lyrically, to me.

I find it necessary to write this introduction because no one else would. By the time I was prepared to ask for his assistance, the older son had already left, presumably for Europe. I am uncertain if he did so, in part, to express an objection to some of my editorial decisions—or indeed, to the task as a whole.

I can appreciate (but politely disagree with) his point of view. He may well be concerned with an alleged violation of his privacy (as first hinted in A Wall, A Space, A Wall). Indeed, some sensitive, even explosive family matters concerning the author, the older son, the first wife and the second wife were indadvertedly exposed here.

However, let me argue that in my opinion, the author regarded these matters purely as input material for his fiction.

Therefore, so do I.

Presently, the second wife, Mrs. Anita Kaminsky, is no longer residing in the Author's place of residence, which has been partially emptied. The four poster bed has been removed, as was the piano. The oval, standalone mirror in the bedroom lies on the floor, in pieces. Glass shards are still strewn all the way back to the other corner. The tape recorder seems to move around the place. Sometimes it can be found under the desk, in the balcony.

Other times, it appears next to Beethoven's bust.

To my knowledge, the second wife is still in town. So far (possibly because of her grief) she has refused to talk, much less write anything in his honor. I suppose that having given birth only a month or so ago, the task of commenting on the author's life (and on this story) is somehow not the first on her list.

To her credit, I must report that the title was inspired by her words. When I asked her, "Any suggestions? What shall I name the book?" she shrugged at first, saying simply, "Call it anything.

I don't fucking care." However, on her way out of my office, she stopped by the door, and just before going out of sight, threw a smile back at me, and said, "Anything. *Apart from Love.*"

Now, to say that Love appears sparingly in the text would be an understatement. The characters seem to avoid saying this word, quite deliberately at times, even when being consumed by its fire.

There are, however, three notable cases, where the phrase Apart from Love appears in the text. It takes on one meaning in the first two cases, and another meaning in the third one. This ambiguity explains, perhaps, why that phrase struck me in such a remarkable way, and why I settled, finally, on this title and no other.

After a while I whispered, like, "Just say something to me. Anything." And I thought, Any other word apart from Love, 'cause that word is diluted, and no one knows what it really means, anyway.

Anita to Lenny, in *Apart from Love*

Why, why can't you say nothing? Say any word—but that one, 'cause you don't really mean it. Nobody does. Say anything, apart from Love.

Anita to Ben, in *The Entertainer*

For my own sake I should have been much more careful. Now— even in her absence—I find myself in her hands, which feels strange to me. I am surrounded—and at the same time, isolated. I am alone. I am apart from Love.

Ben, in *Nothing Surrendered*

Before his passing, the author came up with temporary working titles for some of the fragments. His titles had a poetic slant to them (such as *A Woman, Forgotten,* and *A Place Called Sunrise*). They were adopted here as chapter headings, for lack of a better, more comprehensive naming scheme, for which I am still searching.

Other fragments he left nameless. In such cases I tried to invent appropriate titles. The ones I came up with can be easily recognized, as they have a down-to-earth slant to them (such as *Go Back to Your Mama,* and *No Omelette For You.*) Simply numbering the fragments was deemed unsatisfactory, as I constantly shuffled and reshuffled them, in an attempt to identify a correct logical and chronological order.

Of the thirty-six fragments collected here, only one was published during the author's lifetime. More precisely, a fragment titled *Leonard and Lana* was published as a short story some thirty-five years earlier, in a periodical that has since gone out of business. However, after its publication, it has undergone considerable changes by the author.

At first I considered omitting it altogether. I debated with myself, thinking I should do so not only because it had been published previously, but because its events were clearly outside the principal scope of time.

It is worth noting that in this fragment, the character (apparently representing the author as a young man) acted as if he were utterly inexperienced with women, which was starkly different from the way he would have presented himself these days.

In all, seven notebooks were discovered, one in a secret desk drawer, the rest in one pile, under a heap of sheet music that laid on the floor, in the corner of the living room, under a marble bust of Beethoven.

The notebooks were of different bindings, shapes and sizes, and contained written or typed blurbs of text, which appeared so tight and so dense as to make reading practically impossible.

To decode their meaning I had to look at them through a magnifying glass, and then, with a fine brush, mark tiny white dots between the letters, in places where I figured that spaces should have occurred.

In several cases, the pages were clearly out of order. It took me the better part of a month to set them in place; more precisely, in what I assumed to be the right place. As the author would say: it seemed as if someone had cast the notebook up in the air, and let the pages fall as they may, descending like parachutes behind enemy lines.

- One notebook, which (by its paper quality) appeared to be the oldest among them, was hand written in blue ink on brittle, yellow papers, which were originally stitched together to form a notebook. Most of them seem to have fallen out of place. They were found in the so-called *secret drawer*, crumpled and stuffed into it completely out of order.

- Three other notebooks were in fact legal pads (with my office logo on top) which I must have given the author, I suppose, some time ago, in one meeting or another.

- Another notebook consisted of a fake leather binding, clasped together to hold a few Xerox copies of the same fragment. The original, however, was never recovered.

- Another notebook held loose notes, which the author made to himself, containing various (seemingly unrelated) flowery phrases. There is no mention of any of these phrases in any fragment of this book. Perhaps he considered making use of them in some future story. Some of the notes were written on the back of a checkbook. Others were printed on the back an old music sheet. One, with a simple drawing of a heart, was scribbled inside a paper napkin.

- A bunch of papers were simply stapled together in one corner, and preserved under the green-tinted glass, which laid, a bit askew, on top of the desk.

The author made corrections by hand in the margins of these papers. He did so in pens and pencils of different colors, some of which have already faded. Thus, to my disappointment, some phrases have grown entirely illegible by now.

However, in a number of cases I detected what I thought was a rather feminine handwriting, which seemed suspiciously different from that of the author (in slant, size and shape).

Whoever it was, she attempted making various corrections, most of which were utterly crude. Words were badly misspelled, and there were glaring grammatical errors. Therefore, acting as the editor and custodian of the text, I decided to ignore such corrections.

In addition to the notebooks, two audiotapes were found, only a week ago, neatly wrapped behind the bottom drawer of the author's desk, which explained, incidentally, why it had never closed properly.

- One audiotape was labeled "Beethoven's Fifth" and dated eleven years ago.

- The other was labeled "Benjamin, Age 12" and dated sixteen years ago.

The voice on the second audiotape was clearly a child's voice. However, halfway through the audiotape it was overwritten (accidentally, I assume) by a soft, slightly raspy voice, closely resembling that of the second wife. Then, towards the end of her discourse, some commotion can be heard in the background: a voice, presumably the author's, shouting loudly, "No! Not that one—" and then, nothing. Nothing but crickets.

The discovery of the second audiotape shed some light on his writing method. By no means can it be regarded as a simple case of transcribing. I took great care to study it in detail.

First I compared the recorded child's voice to its corresponding fragment (titled *Only An Empty Dress*). Then I compared the recorded voice of the second wife to its corresponding fragment (titled *In My Defense*). Only then did it become apparent to me that the author had invested considerable effort, in both thought and time, to shape the raw input and flesh it out into moments.

Perhaps that was what he had meant by the 'preservation of time.' Indeed, the author strove hard to bring out what he considered the essence of each moment. Thus, in conveying the first half of this audiotape to paper, he downplayed certain passages, making them much shorter than originally recorded, especially where the child's voice became excessively verbose, or was lost in repetition (of the same emotion or idea).

In conveying the second half, he corrected some of the most atrocious grammatical errors (in places where he deemed them overbearing). However, he left enough of them in place, perhaps to keep the voice of his second wife vibrant and thus, authentic.

According to her, these two audiotapes were the only ones left out of an immensely large 'collection of voices'.

However, a third audiotape was found only a day ago, in the corner behind the marble bust of Beethoven. How I missed it on my previous searches is quite beyond me. Its audio quality is poor, to the point of sounding scratchy, probably because it had been recorded over previous (now lost) content, several times over.

In spite of this I managed to hear some of the passages, which I have been transcribing all night long, the author's pen trembling in my hand, and which you can read in the last two fragments: *Lay Me Down* and *Play. Stop. Eject.*

There is no telling where the rest of the audiotapes might be found.

Until the very last moment before submitting this text for publication, I plan on reading and rereading it, looking for gaps in chronology, logical misalignments between fragments, even outright errors, which might have escaped me. I am still tormented by my own doubts as to this editorial guesswork.

Therefore I would not put it past you, the reader, to sense some dissatisfaction, as I do, in the current state of this book. It was unfinished, and still is.

I wish I could be more confident of its veracity and completeness. I wish I could do more. This, I suppose, is the nature of the quest for truth—even if it is truth in fiction.

Uvi Poznansky

~ The End ~

To be continued with

STILL LIFE WITH MEMORIES BUNDLE II:

The Music of Us
Dancing with Air
Marriage before Death

About The Story

Apart from Love is not your typical love story. All-consuming, heart-wrenching, and dark, it is an epic that starts when Ben returns to meet his father, Lenny, and his new wife, Anita. It is then that he discovers a family secret. How will they find a path out of conflicts, out of isolation, from guilt to forgiveness?

My Own Voice ("As told by Anita"):

Ten years ago, Anita started an affair with Lenny, in spite of knowing that he was a married man. Now married to him and carrying his child, how can she compete with Natasha's shadow, and with her brilliance in the past? Lenny tries to transform Anita, despite her rough slang, regardless of what happened to her in the past. He wants her to become Natasha. Can she survive his kind of love?

Faced with his compelling wish, and the way he writes her as a character in his book, how can Anita find a voice of her own? And when his estranged son, Ben, comes back and lives in the same small apartment, can she keep the balance between the two men, whose desire for her is marred by guilt and blame?

The White Piano ("As told by Ben"):

Coming back to his childhood home after years of absence, Ben is unprepared for the secret, which is now revealed to him: his mother, Natasha, who used to be a brilliant pianist, is losing herself to early-onset Alzheimer's, which turns the way her mind works into a riddle. His father has remarried, and his new wife, Anita, looks remarkably similar to Natasha, only much younger. In this state of being isolated, being apart from love, how will Ben react when it is so tempting to resort to blame and guilt? "In our family, forgiveness is something you pray for, something you yearn to receive, but so seldom do you give it to others."

Behind his father's back, Ben and Anita find themselves increasingly drawn to each other. They take turns using an old tape recorder to express their most intimate thoughts, not realizing at first that their voices are being captured by him. These tapes, with his eloquent speech and her slang, reveal the story from two opposite viewpoints.

Do you like historical fiction about the 20th century, especially when it is tinged with romance and wrapped in a family saga? Then this series is for you.

What's in a Name

The title *Apart from Love* comes from a phrase used in the story:

After a while I whispered, like, "Just say something to me. Anything." And I thought, Any other word apart from Love, 'cause that word is diluted, and no one knows what it really means, anyway.

Anita to Lenny, in *Apart from Love*

Why, why can't you say nothing? Say any word—but that one, 'cause you don't really mean it. Nobody does. Say anything, apart from Love.

Anita to Ben, in *The Entertainer*

For my own sake I should have been much more careful. Now— even in her absence—I find myself in her hands, which feels strange to me. I am surrounded—and at the same time, isolated. I am alone. I am apart from Love.

Ben, in *Nothing Surrendered*

3

About The Author

U vi Poznansky is a *USA TODAY* bestselling, award-winning author, poet and artist. "I paint with my pen," she says, "and write with my paintbrush."

Uvi earned her B. A. in Architecture and Town Planning from the Technion in Haifa, Israel. During her studies and in the years immediately following her graduation, she practiced with an innovative Architectural firm, taking part in the design of a large-scale project, *Home for the Soldier*.

Having moved to Troy, N.Y. with her husband and two children, Uvi received a Fellowship grant and a Teaching Assistantship from the Architecture department at Rensselaer Polytechnic Institute. There, she guided teams in a variety of design projects and earned her M.A. in Architecture. Then, taking a sharp turn in her education, she earned her M.S. degree in Computer Science from the University of Michigan.

During the years she spent in advancing her career—first as an architect, and later as a software engineer, software team leader, software manager and a software consultant (with an emphasis on user interface for medical instruments devices)—she wrote and painted constantly. In addition, she taught art appreciation classes.

Her versatile body of work can be seen in two websites: her blog includes thoughts about the creative process, reader reviews, author interviews, excerpts from her novels, voice clips from her audiobooks, poems and short stories. Her art site includes bronze and ceramic sculptures, paper engineering projects, oil and watercolor paintings, charcoal, pen and pencil drawings, and mixed media.

Coma Confidential, Overkill, Overdose, and Overdue are novels in the *Ash Suspense Thrillers with a Dash of Romance* series. With each new case, Ash uses grit and intuition to solve the crime.

Virtually Lace is the first volume in a multi-author thriller series, *High-Tech Crime Solvers*, where the authors bring each other's characters into their books.

My Own Voice, The White Piano, The Music of Us, Dancing with Air, and *Marriage before Death* are novels in the *Still Life with Memories* series, a family saga with a love story that develops in the face of hardship and illness over two generations, starting at the 1980's, then harkening back to WWII when Lenny, a soldier, and Natasha, a rising star, first met. These books are also offered in two bundles: *Apart from Love* and *Apart from War.*

Rise to Power, A Peek at Bathsheba, and *The Edge of Revolt* are novels in *The David Chronicles*, telling the story of David as you have never heard it before: from the king himself, telling the unofficial version, the one he never allowed his court scribes to recount. In his mind, history is written to praise the victorious— but at the last stretch of his illustrious life, he feels an irresistible urge to tell the truth. These books are also offered in a trilogy.

In addition, *The David Chronicles* includes six art collections: *Inspired by Art: Fighting Goliath, Inspired by Art: Fall of a Giant, Inspired by Art: Rise to Power, Inspired by Art: A Peek at*

Bathsheba, Inspired by Art: The Edge of Revolt, and *Inspired by Art: The Last Concubine.*

A Favorite Son, a new-age twist on an old yarn, is inspired by the biblical story of Jacob and his mother Rebecca, plotting together against the elderly father Isaac, who is lying on his deathbed.

Twisted is a unique collection, laden with shades of mystery. Here, you will come into a dark, strange world, a hyper-reality where nearly everything is firmly rooted in the familiar— except for some quirky detail that twists the yarn.

Home and *Can We Still Love,* Uvi's deeply moving poetry books in tribute of her father, include her poetry and prose as well as translated poems from the pen of her father, the poet, author and artist Zeev Kachel.

Uvi wrote and illustrated two children's books, *Jess and Wiggle* and *Now I Am Paper.* Watch the beautiful animations she created for these books on YouTube.

A Note to the Reader

Thank you for reading this book! I hope you enjoyed it. I invite you to check out more books from the same pen. There is always a new project on my drawing board, so come back to check it out.

I would love to hear what you thought of this book. You have the power of bringing it to the attention of more readers, by posting your own review. It would mean so much to me.

And another thing you can do to help me spread the word is this: please tell your friends about my work. How else will they hear about the story? How else will the characters, who sprang from my mind onto these pages, leap from there into new minds?

Bonus Excerpts
Excerpt: The Music of Us

My son, Ben, has been gone for a month now, staying in some youth hostel in Rome. If I call him, if I stumble into revealing how scared I am that his mother is losing her mind, he may listen. He may heed my fears, grudgingly, and come back here, not even knowing how to offer his support to me. Should I ask for it?

The last thing I wish to do is lean on him for help. He is not strong enough, and whatever the problem may be with her, I can grit my teeth and handle it, somehow, all by myself. Besides, I pray for a spontaneous change in her. I mean, her memory may take a turn for the better just as quickly as it has deteriorated.

Given this hope I decide that for now I will not schedule the head X-Ray that her doctor recommended for her. I figure she has been through so many checkups, so many exams to rule out depression, vitamin B deficiency, and a long list of other possible ailments, all of which has been in vain.

So far, the results have failed to produce a conclusive diagnosis, and this new X-Ray will be no different, because from what I have read, Alzheimer's disease can be determined only through autopsy, by linking clinical measures with an examination of brain tissue. So this new medical hypothesis is just that: a hypothesis. One that cannot be proven; one that cannot go away. An ever-present threat.

Perhaps all she needs is rest. Time, I tell myself. I must give her time. Meanwhile I resolve to keep her condition secret from everyone, especially from my son. Let him enjoy his time away from home, his independence.

Since his departure I called him only once, three weeks ago, and said little, except for blurting out the mundane, "How's Rome?"

"Great," he said vaguely, adding no particulars.

I could not help myself from asking. "So, what about your plans?"

"What about them?"

"D'you have any?"

"For now I have none," he admitted, and immediately changed the subject. "How's mom?"

"Fine."

"Is she?"

"She is," I lied, hoping that the sound of my voice would not betray the tensing of my muscles, the tightening of my jaws.

"Oh good," he said. "Really, really good."

There is only one thing more difficult than talking to Ben, and that is writing to him. Amazingly, having to conceal what his mother is going through makes every word—even on subjects unrelated to her—that much harder. I find myself oppressed by my own self-imposed discipline, the discipline of silence.

And what can I tell him, really? That I keep digging into the past, mining its moments, trying to piece them together this way and that, dusting off each memory of Natasha, of how we were, the highs and lows of the music of us, to find out where the problem may have started?

To him, that may seem like an exercise in futility. For me, it is a necessary process of discovery, one that is as tormenting as it is delightful. If the dissonance in our life would fade away, so will the harmony.

Sometimes I go as far back as the moment we first met, when I was a soldier and she—a star, brilliant yet illusive. Natasha was a riddle to me then, and to this day, with all the changes she has gone through, she still is.

I often wonder: can we ever understand, truly understand each other—soldier and musician, man and woman, one heart and another? Will we ever again dance together to the same beat? Is there a point where we may still touch?

Excerpt: Dancing with Air

O vercome, suddenly, by exhaustion, Natasha stepped out of my embrace and plopped onto her suitcase. "Ma came to say goodbye, " she said. "I saw her across from me, as we left the shore. She was offering a prayer, tears running down her cheeks. Then, once out to sea, the Germans fired at us."

"Really? What happened?"

"The ships, they took up their positions in the convoy and plodded ahead. Straightaway, two of them were lost. One ran aground. The other, suffering from engine trouble, turned back to the harbor. And as for us I thought that was the end."

I shuddered at the thought.

"This journey," said Natasha, "it was more challenging than anything I've gone through in the past. Even watching Papa during his last months was easier, in a way, because back then I was on the outside, observing his pain."

I waited for her to continue.

After a slight reflection, she added, "I could only guess what was happening to him, I mean, the ways his illness drained his mind, the ways he suffered. But now, I wasn't an observer. I lived it, Lenny! Everyone on board—including me—was going through the same fear, the same hardship."

I could not help but ask her, "What were you thinking, putting yourself at risk?"

In reply, she rose to her feet. "For this very moment," she said, clinging to me, "I would go through it all over again."

I took a step back, to stress, "Your Mama, she's beside herself with worry, and as for me—"

"You talked to her?" asked Natasha, her eyes twinkling. "Of course you did, how else would you know to wait here for me? She doesn't get it—"

"And neither do I!"

"But Lenny, it's so simple! I missed you—"

"That's no reason, Natasha, for what you've done. Why leave home, especially now, when we're at war? If you love me, keep yourself safe, if only for my sake! Why, why put your life at risk —"

"Perhaps," she said, "I'm not looking for safety! Have you ever thought of that? Perhaps something else is more important to me."

"Like what?"

"I can't continue to depend on others, Lenny, the way I've done all my life. This is my time to change, to demand new things of myself, even if they happen to frighten me, even if I'm scared out of my mind."

"Not sure I understand—"

"Please try, Lenny."

"What is it you want?"

"Just this: to stop leaning on those closest to me."

"You could've done that back home, couldn't you?"

"That's the place where I'm being taken care of, to the point of feeling stuck. Worse than that: suffocated. Someone, usually Mama, drives me to where I need to be. Someone points me to the dressing room, calls me to the stage. I'm nothing more than a mechanical doll. All I do is respond."

"You do much more than that! You excite audiences, Natasha! And to me, you're an inspiration—"

"Yes, you admire the way I play, but in truth music is the only thing for which Papa trained me."

"You're too critical of yourself," I said.

To which she said, "No, Lenny. I've seen him decline, seen him lose his mind, and if—if, like him, I'll ever lose mine—how in the world will I recover? How will I find my way, when I've never developed the skill to do so?"

I lowered my head before her.

"Never," I said, "until now."

"Exactly," said Natasha. "Until now."

And a moment later, blotting the corner of her eye, where a tear was forming, she whispered to me, "Come closer, Lenny, snuggle up, but never, ever let me lean on you."

Excerpt: Rise to Power

To show respect I fall to my knees before him. The floor is cold, having absorbed the damp of a long winter. The surface is porous, even crumbly here and there, cut of rocks from the Judea mountains. So is the surface of the stage, right in front of my eyes.

I cannot help noting the marks drawn by his spear in the film of dirt up there, around his boots. Scratch, twist, scratch again... No wonder he seems to be in such a royal pain: with all these attendants here to serve him, not a single one has managed to come up with the bright idea of sweeping the floor. They all carry weapons, but not one has a broom.

Sitting nearly immobile, Saul seems as chalky as the walls around him. He sits crumpled—in an odd way—upon the throne. His nails keep digging into the little velvety cushions that are stretched over the carved armrests. Not once does he give a nod in my direction, nor does he acknowledge my presence in any other way.

Which agitates me. It awakens my doubt, doubt in my skill. Much the same as I feel in my father's presence. Repressed. On the verge of acting out.

So, rising to my feet I blurt out, "Your majesty—"

"Don't talk," whispers one of the attendants. "Play."

I am pushed a step or two backwards, so as to maintain proper distance from the presence of the king. My name is called out in a clunky manner of introduction, after which I am instructed to choose from an array of musical instruments. I figure they must be the loot of war. So when I play them, the music of enemy tribes shall resound here, around the hall.

I pluck the strings of a sitar, then put it back down and pick up a lyre, which I make quiver, quiver with notes of fire! Then I rap, clap, tap, snap my fingers, and just to be cute, play a tune on my flute, after which I do a skip, skip, skip and a back flip.

It is a long performance, and towards the end of it I find myself trying to catch my breath. Alas, my time is up. Even so I would not stop.

Entranced I go on to recite several of my poems, which I have never done before, for fear of exposing my most intimate, raw emotions, which is a risky thing for a man, and even riskier for a boy my age. Allowing your vulnerability to show takes one thing above all: a special kind of courage. Trust me, it takes balls.

So, having read the last verse I cast a look at the attendants, especially the ones closest to me. Their faces seem to have softened. I can sense them beginning to adore me. One of them comes over and taps my shoulder, which nearly knocks me off my feet. Another one laughs. Others wipe their eyes.

Then I glance at Saul, hoping for a tear, a smile, a word of encouragement. Instead I note an odd, vacant look on his face. Utter indifference. It stings me. Am I too short, too young, too curly for the role he has in mind for me?

Wiping the sweat off my brow I bow down before him and turn to leave the court, which is the moment he leans forward on his spear.

"Stop right there," says Saul. "Tell me: what can you do best?"

To which I say, "Recover."

He glowers at me as if to ask, Recover? From what?

"From this," I point out, daring to be honest. "Rejection."

Excerpt: A Peek at Bathsheba

Wrapped in a long, flowing fabric that creates countless folds around her curves, she loosens just the top of it and lets it slide off her head—only to reveal a blush, and mischievous glint, shining in her eye. It is over that sparkle that I catch a sudden reflection, coming from the back window, of a full moon.

Looking left, right, and down the staircase, to make sure no one is lurking outside my chamber door, I let her in. Then I lock it behind her, so no one may intrude upon us.

In a manner of greeting I raise my goblet. It is a gift from my supplier, Hiram king of Tyre, and unlike the other goblets I have in my possession, this one is made of fine glass, with minute air bubbles floating in it. With a big splash I fill it up to the rim with red, aromatic wine. In it I dip a glistening, ruddy cherry, and offer it to her, with a flowery toast.

"For you," I say. "With my everlasting love!"

Bathsheba takes the goblet from my hand, and raises it to her lips. "Love, everlasting?" she says, raising an eyebrow. "What does that mean, in this place?"

I hesitate to ask, "What place is that?"

"This court," she says, with a slight curtsy, "where the signature feature is a harem, which is as big as the king is endowed with glory."

"Glory is a good thing," say I, lowering my voice. "But sometimes it is better to meet in the shadows."

"Especially," she says, matching her voice to mine, "when there are so many others."

"Here we are," say I. "It's just us."

"Really," says Bathsheba, sipping her wine and ever so delightfully, licking her lips. "It must be a special night, then! Just you and me, and no one else, no one else at all."

Yet I cannot avoid feeling the presence of someone other than me in her thoughts, perhaps her husband, Uriah, who is one of my mighty soldiers and the most trusty of them. Earlier today he must have received his transfer orders to join the cavalry in the eastern hills, where he would be stationed outside the city of Rabbah.

I have a catch in my throat as I tell her, "I'm so glad you came."

Bathsheba lifts her eyes and looks straight at me.

"Really," she says, in her most velvety tone. "You mean, I had a choice in this matter?"

Her question stumps me at first, because how can I admit that she is right, so right in asking it? Instead I just shrug.

"You do have a choice," I say at last. "And I hope you'll make it."

"I'm so glad to hear that," says Bathsheba. "With that ape, I mean, that bodyguard of yours knocking so loudly, so rudely, and for such a long time at my door, I had my doubts about it."

"You can go, if you wish," I stress, with a reluctant tone. "But I wish you wouldn't. Stay with me, tonight."

Bathsheba picks the stem of the red cherry, and takes little bites out of it. In her pleasure she hums, and smacks her lips. Then she raises the goblet to my lips, letting me take in the aroma. I do, and then I take a long gulp.

With a slight sway of her hips Bathsheba walks past me, knowing I cannot take my eyes off of her. She wanders about my chamber as if she were the one owning it.

"You've been brought here by my order," I whisper to her, across the space. "But I am the one held captive."

Excerpt: The Edge of Revolt

A t last, "Decisive action may be easy for a king," I tell her. "But as a father I must weigh every word I speak, because in the future it may leave a scar upon the hearts of my children."

Somewhat reluctantly she says, "I understand."

"I hope you do," say I. "They are, all of them, my flesh and blood."

"Then, act as a king," she says. "Not as a father. Name the one who will succeed you, the one who—in your judgement—may become a better ruler than the others."

I have to admit, "I have yet to make up my mind," which fills her eyes with worry. She knows all too well that Solomon, being the younger son, has less of a change to win my favor.

"Decide," she says. "And make your wishes known. That in itself may bring about a change, a peaceful transition of power. Otherwise, I'm afraid there will be mayhem. It will start at sunrise."

I let go of her hand, because to say my next sentence I must not lean on anyone.

But before I can muster my pride, and take air in my lungs, and clear my throat to state, in my most regal tones, "I am still the king, am I not," I find myself staggering. In the next instant, there I am, a heap of arms and legs spilled on the floor, twisting in agony from the sudden chill overtaking me.

I reach up, trying to breathe her name. And I wonder what this suffering may look like, to her and to a heavenly city watching over me, floating silent and forlorn on the hill.

Overhead, a cloud breaks off from the others and moves in a new direction. Its wooly, dim grays are drifting across. I squint, rub my eyes. Now, in a separate layer, another image starts floating past: the way she looked, right here on this roof, when we came out of these doors the very first time.

I remember: scattered petals flew off, swirling in the glow around her long, silky hair that started cascading under her, onto the tile floor. In the background, a vine of roses twisted over the wooden lattice and into it. Between its diagonal slats I saw a diamond here, a diamond there of the heavens. I wondered then about the black void that was gaping upon us, dotted by a magical glint of starlight.

Separated from her by the thought of a kiss I sensed her heat, and the gust of air, which was sweetly scented by roses and by her flesh—but I could not tell if the breath between us was hers or mine. Which is when I knew, for the first time in my life, that she would always be part of my essence. I would be part of hers.

Accidentally the goblet, which she had set down next to her, tipped over and some of the wine spilled over her hip. The crisp sound of breaking glass rang in my ear. It marked the moment, from which I could not turn back. Never would I be able to put it out of my mind.

Yes, this was my fault: taking a woman that belonged to another. Soon after came the blunder: bringing her husband, Uriah, back from the front, that he may sleep with her, which would have explained her pregnancy ever so conveniently.

And when that did not go as planned, then came another mistake, the worst of all: sending him back to the battlefield, with my sealed letter in hand, arranging for his death.

All the while, my boys were learning their own lessons—not from my psalms but from my deeds. One error begets another, each one bringing a new calamity over me, over my family, and over this entire land. Sin followed by execution, followed by revolt, escape, execution, revolt...

Had I known back then the results of the results of my mistake, the curse looming over my life ever since that time, would I still choose to do it?

Bathsheba tries to raise me to my feet. Her fragrance brings back to me the sunny, warm hues of spring. The fears, the doubts flee away when we are that close. I adore the way she calls my name, the way she sighs. With every sweet word I fall deeper into her eyes.

How can love be a mistake? In my passion for her—then as now—what choice do I have?

I want to tell her, "Let me close my eyes. Let me remember."

Books by Uviart
Coma Confidential

(Volume I of *Ash Suspense Thrillers with a Dash of Romance*)

Kindle: B07L92YHST Paperback: 978-1791691592

Overkill

(Volume II of *Ash Suspense Thrillers with a Dash of Romance*)

Kindle: B084GDK156 Paperback: 979-8644328192

Overdose

(Volume III of *Ash Suspense Thrillers with a Dash of Romance*)

Kindle: B07VP4S6PK Paperback: 978-1086703665

Overdue

(Volume IV of *Ash Suspense Thrillers with a Dash of Romance*)

Kindle: B08S724T4G Paperback: 979-8599499671

Ash Suspense Thrillers: Trilogy

(Volume I-III of *Ash Suspense Thrillers with a Dash of Romance*)

Kindle: B0893MJNSY Paperback: 979-8648269644

Virtually Lace

(Volume I of *High-Tech Crime Solvers*)

Kindle: B07L968RXD Paperback: 978-1790407187

My Own Voice

(Volume I of *Still Life with Memories*)

Kindle: B013TA3FBS Paperback: 978-0984993215

The White Piano

(Volume II of *Still Life with Memories*)

Kindle: B013TAU7L4 Paperback: 978-1517049447

The Music of Us

(Volume III of *Still Life with Memories*)

Kindle: B013TCYWHC Paperback: 978-0-9849932-9-1

Dancing with Air

(Volume IV of *Still Life with Memories*)

Kindle: B01I4ENROY Paperback: 978-1536896534

Marriage before Death

(Volume V of *Still Life with Memories*)

Kindle: B0746NW5CD Paperback: 978-1974001736

Apart from Love

(*Still Life with Memories Bundle I*)

Kindle: B006WPITP0 Paperback: 978-0-9849932-0-8

Apart from War

(*Still Life with Memories Bundle II*)

Kindle: B07MMZLD7Z Paperback: 978-1792131592

Rise to Power

(Volume I of *The David Chronicles*)

Kindle: B00H6PMZ0U Paperback: 978-0-9849932-4-6

A Peek at Bathsheba

(Volume II of *The David Chronicles*)

Kindle: B00LEPPDV6 Paperback: 978-0-9849932-7-7

The Edge of Revolt

(Volume III of *The David Chronicles*)

Kindle: B00Q5WVKA6 Paperback: 978-0984993284

The David Chronicles: Trilogy

(Volume I-III of *The David Chronicles*)

Kindle: B00QYGF6WG Paperback: 978-1797440699

The David Chronicles: Art

(Volume IV-XI of *The David Chronicles*)

Kindle: B08YWSH7HC Paperback: 979-8721612886

Inspired by Art: Fighting Goliath

(Art book. Volume IV of *The David Chronicles*)

Kindle: B01MSBNSE4   Paperback 978-1797726212

Inspired by Art: Fall of a Giant

(Art book. Volume V of *The David Chronicles*)

Kindle: B01MSBS82Q   Paperback: 978-1092307765

Inspired by Art: Rise to Power

(Art book. Volume VI of *The David Chronicles*)

Kindle: B01N2786VX   Paperback: 978-1092263207

Inspired by Art: A Peek at Bathsheba

(Art book. Volume VII of *The David Chronicles*)

Kindle: B01MUFS9OA   Paperback: 978-1092306225

Inspired by Art: The Edge of Revolt

(Art book. Volume VIII of *The David Chronicles*)

Kindle: B01N6ZG0W8   Paperback: 978-1091306158

Inspired by Art: The Last Concubine

(Art book. Volume IX of *The David Chronicles*)

Kindle: B01N2AXQP2   Paperback: 978-1092302715

A Favorite Son

Kindle: B00AUZ3LGU Paperback: 978-0-9849932-5-3

Twisted

(Dark Fantasy Short Stories)

Kindle: B00D7Q3IY4

Paperback: 978-0984993260 Nook: 2940151689588

Home

(Poetry)

Kindle: B00960TE3Y

Paperback: 978-09849932-3-9 Nook: 2940151729468

Can We Still Love

(Poetry)

Kindle: B0GV3G23V4 Paperback: B0GY8Q1Y9Z

Virtually Yummy: Recipes that Inspire

(Cookbook)

Kindle: B085BDNDM5 Nook: 2940163988655

Apple: id1501182051 Kobo: 9781393589853

בית

(Poetry in Hebrew)
Paperback: 978-1494920968 Nook: 1127367962
Apple: id1302908918 Kobo: 9781540199966

Jess and Wiggle

Kindle: B013D1W0SM Paperback: 978-1494920968

Now I Am Paper
Kindle: B00YQS4O72 Paperback: 978-1494919429